SILVER RAVENS

What Reviewers Say
About Jane Fletcher's Work

Isle of Broken Years

"Fun, fast, and deeply entertaining, *Isle of Broken Years* is one of the better uses of the Atlantis myth I've yet seen in fiction. I enjoyed it a lot, and I feel confident in recommending it."—Tor.com

"*Isle of Broken Years* is an amazingly inventive story that started off being the tale of a noblewoman being captured by pirates and veered off into something way more interesting and fantastic."—*Kitty Kat's Book Review Blog*

The Walls of Westernfort

"Award-winning author Jane Fletcher explores serious themes in the Celaeno series and creates a world that loosely parallels the one we inhabit. In *The Walls of Westernfort*, Fletcher weaves a plausible action-packed plot, set on a credible world, and with appealing multi-dimensional characters. The result is a fantasy by one of the best speculative fiction writers in the business."—*Just About Write*

"…captivating, well-written stories in the fantasy genre that are built around women's struggles against themselves, one another, society, and nature."—*WomanSpace Magazine*

"*The Walls of Westernfort* is not only a highly engaging and fast-paced adventure novel, it provides the reader with an interesting framework for examining the same questions of loyalty, faith, family and love."
—*Midwest Book Review*

"*The Walls of Westernfort* is...a true delight. Bold, well-developed characters hold your interest from the beginning and keep you turning the pages. The main plot twists and turns until the very end. The subplot involves likeable women who seem destined not to be together."—*MegaScene*

"In *The Walls of the Westernfort*, Jane Fletcher spins a captivating story about youthful idealism, honor, and courage. The action is fast paced and the characters are compelling in this gripping sci-fi adventure." —*Sapphic Reader*

"Jane Fletcher has a great talent for spinning yarns, especially stories of lesbians with swords. *The Walls of Westernfort* is a well written and suspenseful tale...Fletcher effectively intertwines the intrigues of the assassination plot with a young woman's inward exploration...and yes, there is romance. ...This book is a page-turner; you will have a hard time finding a stopping place."—*Lesbian Connection Magazine*

Rangers at Roadsend

"In *Rangers at Roadsend* Fletcher not only gives us powerful characters, but she surprises us with an unexpected ending to the murder conspiracy plot, pushing the story in one direction only to have that direction reversed more than once. This is one thrill ride the reader will not want to get off."—*Independent Gay Writer*

"*Rangers at Roadsend*, a murder mystery reminiscent of Agatha Christie, has crossed many genres including speculative fiction, fantasy, romance, and adventure. The story is an incredible whodunit that has something for everyone. Jane Fletcher, winner of the Golden Crown Literary Award 2005 for Walls at Westernfort, has created an intelligent and compelling story where the reader easily gets drawn into the fascinating world of Celaeno, becomes totally absorbed in the well-designed plot, and finds herself completely enamored with the multi-faceted characters.

"Jane Fletcher, an amazing talent, gifted storyteller, and extraordinary plot developer, is one of the best authors of contemporary fiction today—in all genres. *Rangers at Roadsend* will convince you of that."—*Just About Write*

Temple at Landfall—*Lambda Literary Award Finalist*

"*The Temple at Landfall* is absorbing and engrossing tale-telling of the highest order, and the really exciting thing is that although this novel is complete and 'finished,' the door is left open to explore more of this world, which the author has done in subsequent books. I can't wait to read the next Celaeno Series volumes, and this book is a keeper that I will re-read again and again. I highly recommend it."—*Just About Write*

"Jane Fletcher is the consummate storyteller and plot wizard. Getting caught up in the action happens as if by magic and the fantasy elements are long forgotten. The world Fletcher creates, the characters she brings to life, and the rich detail described in eloquent prose, all serve to keep the reader enchanted, satisfied, yet wanting more. A Lammy finalist, *The Temple at Landfall* is surely a winner in this reader's book. Don't miss it."—*Midwest Book Review*

Dynasty of Rogues

"Jane Fletcher has another triumph with *Dynasty of Rogues*, the continuing story in the Celaeno series. This reviewer found the book clever and compelling and difficult to put down once I started reading and easily could be devoured in one sitting. Some of the characters in *Dynasty of Rogues* have visited us in other Celaeno novels, but this is a non-linear series, so it can be understood without having read the other stories. ...*Dynasty of Rogues* has it all. Mystery, intrigue, crime, and romance, with lots of angst thrown in too, make this fascinating novel thoroughly enjoyable and fun."—*Just About Write*

"When you pick up a novel by Jane Fletcher, you will always get a riveting plot, strong, interesting characters, and a beautifully written story complete with three-dimensional villains, believable conflicts, and the twin spices of adventure and romance. Ethical and moral dilemmas abound. Fletcher writes real characters, the type that William Faulkner once said 'stand up and cast a shadow.' The reader can't help but root for these characters, many of whom are classic underdogs. I give the highest recommendation for *Dynasty of Rogues* and to the entire Celaeno Series."—*Midwest Book Review*

Exile and the Sorcerer

"Jane Fletcher once again has written an exciting fantasy story for everyone. Though she sets her stories in foreign worlds where the traditional roles of women are reversed, her characters (are) all too familiar in their inner lives and thoughts. Unlike the Celaeno series (which I highly recommend) where there are no men, this series incorporates male characters that help round out the story nicely. …Fletcher has a way of balancing the fantasy with the human drama in a precise way. She never gets caught up in the minor details of the environment and forgets to tell the story, which happens too often in fantasy fiction. …With Fletcher writing such strong work, readers of fantasy will continue to grow."—*Lambda Book Report*

"*The Exile and the Sorcerer* is a mesmerizing read, a tour-de-force packed with adventure, ordeals, complex twists and turns, and the internal introspection of appealing characters. The author writes effortlessly, handling the size and scope of the book with ease. Not since the fantasy works of Elizabeth Moon and Lynn Flewelling have I been so thoroughly engrossed in a tale. This is knockout fiction, tantalizingly told, and beautifully packaged."—*Midwest Book Review*

Wolfsbane Winter—*Lambda Literary Award Finalist*

"Jane Fletcher is known for her fantasy stories that take place in a world that could almost be real, but not quite. Her books seem like an alternative version of history and contain rich atmospheres of magic, legends, sorcerers, and other worldly characters mixed in with ordinary people. The way she writes is so realistic that it is easy to believe that these places and people really exist. *Wolfsbane Winter* fits that mold perfectly. It draws the reader in and leads her through the story. Very enjoyable."—*Just About Write*

The Shewstone

"I was hooked on the plot and the characters are absolutely delightful."
—*The Romantic Reader Blog*

Visit us at www.boldstrokesbooks.com

By the Author

Celaeno Series

The Temple at Landfall

The Walls of Westernfort

Rangers at Roadsend

Dynasty of Rogues

Shadow of the Knife

Lyremouth Chronicles

The Exile and the Sorcerer

The Chalice and the Traitor

The Empress and the Acolyte

The High Priest and the Idol

Wolfsbane Winter

The Shewstone

Isle of Broken Years

Silver Ravens

SILVER RAVENS

by

Jane Fletcher

2020

SILVER RAVENS

© 2020 By Jane Fletcher. All Rights Reserved.

ISBN 13: 978-1-63555-631-5

This Trade Paperback Original Is Published By
Bold Strokes Books, Inc.
P.O. Box 249
Valley Falls, NY 12185

First Edition: July 2020

CREDITS
Editor: Cindy Cresap
Production Design: Susan Ramundo
Cover Design By Tammy Seidick

Note to Readers

The story makes reference to Playfair, Caesar, and Vigenère ciphers. I have not tried to describe the encoding processes in detail, judging that, in my hands, the cryptographic intricacies would not make for exciting reading (Dorothy L. Sayers could do it, I can't). For anyone interested in learning more, information about all three is readily available online.

I have also taken huge liberties with the Mabinogion.

With a host of furious fancies
Whereof I am commander,
With a burning spear and a horse of air,
To the wilderness I wander.

By a knight of ghosts and shadows
I summoned am to tourney,
Ten leagues beyond the wide world's end,
Methinks it is no journey.

from Tom O'Bedlam's Song
Anonymous—first recorded early 17th century

Prologue

Dorstanley, Dorset
The first May Day following the restoration of King Charles II
to the throne.

"I dare you."

"Why should I? What do I get?"

"I'll think of something." Eleanor spoke with her head tilted coyly to one side. Her eyes glinted, taunting, teasing, under heavy lids. The sway of her hips promised a reward that would not be forthcoming. She was playing games again. Tamsin knew it, but was unable to say no. She tore her gaze from the strand of blond hair fluttering across Eleanor's cheek.

For the sake of her pride, she should tell Eleanor to find herself another toy. Yet, as much as Tamsin wanted an end to the games, even more she wanted Eleanor to smile at her again, although this did not mean she had to roll over like a puppy. First, she would make Eleanor work a little harder.

"You're being childish." Tamsin crossed her arms and looked away in a show of indifference.

A solemn peace surrounded St. Benedict's parish church. The service was over, and the rest of the congregation had gone to join the revelry on the village green. She and Eleanor were alone in the graveyard, except for the pair of ravens that nested in the bell tower. There was some comfort, knowing the birds would be the only witnesses when she submitted to Eleanor's silly dare.

"You're frightened. You're frightened the devil will snatch you away."

"No, I'm not." The denial was out before Tamsin had time to think. Eleanor smirked, seeing her barb hit home. Tamsin stepped away, angry at herself for being an easy target. "But I'm not missing out on the fun. Listen. The music's starting."

Distant laughter mingled with the sound of fiddle and drum. The maypole was back on the green after sixteen long years of banishment by Parliament and the joyless Puritans. Now Lord Protector Cromwell was gone, and all the talk was of the new King Charles's return. There would be dancing around the maypole for the first time since the year Tamsin was born.

"It won't take long. Then we can go to the maypole." Eleanor caught Tamsin's hand and swung their arms to and fro like a skipping rope. As ever, her touch melted Tamsin's resolve.

"RHARR. RHARR. RHARR." The old cock raven launched himself from the bell tower, cawing as he swooped overhead.

Eleanor jumped at the sound, jerking her hand free and raising her arm as if to ward off attack. The alarmed reaction was both unexpected and telling, bringing a sudden understanding. Eleanor was on edge but had been hiding it.

Now who's frightened?

Eleanor had picked the dare not because it was childish and she wanted to make Tamsin play the fool, but because the idea scared her. She dared not do it herself. Tamsin squared her shoulders and turned to face the ancient stone, sheltering by the yews. The game had changed, and the challenge had become irresistible.

Hobs Geat had stood in the corner of the graveyard for as long as anyone could remember. Legend said it was even older than the church. Village children grew up with the stories: the devil had turned a sinner into stone; witches danced around it naked under a full moon; folk who slept in its shadow were never seen again. Children would squeal and shudder, pretending to be frightened, but deep down inside everyone knew it was safe—or so Tamsin had assumed. Maybe some were more gullible than others. Tamsin smiled as she wove between the gravestones, aware of Eleanor trailing behind. The hems of their skirts brushed through the long grass.

Despite the midday sun, this corner of the churchyard was cold. Hobs Geat was a finger of granite more than twice Tamsin's height, pointing to the sky. The grass around it was clear, as if even the gravestones were unwilling to approach. Only the yew trees seemed drawn to Hobs Geat.

Their branches twitched in the breeze, reaching out to caress it. Their weaving shadows flitted over the weathered stone.

Tamsin stopped, close enough to touch the raw, rough rock, pockmarked by weather. How well had she studied it before? Orange lichen mottled the northern side, creating fantastic shapes, like demons or faces contorted in pain. The pagan stone did not belong here, tethered to a Christian church, but it did not frighten her.

"You don't have to do it."

Tamsin glanced over her shoulder, amused. For once, she had won. "Why not? You want me to go round it widdershins, right?"

"Tamsin?"

She ignored the plea in Eleanor's voice. Three times, widdershins. That was the dare, the one detail all the children's tales agreed on. But she was no longer a child.

Tamsin began walking.

Eleanor cowered in the relative safety of the second to last row of gravestones. Self scrutiny played no part in her nature, but she was aware of being pulled between two emotions. Teasing Tamsin was so much fun—far more so than with the village boys who trailed after Eleanor, making doe eyes. They were boring. Like fairground puppets, anyone could tug their strings. Whereas she could never be quite sure if Tamsin would come to heel when she snapped her fingers.

But now, Eleanor was feeling nervous, and she did not like it. The stupid stone made her skin prickle. It was Tamsin's fault, agreeing so easily. The dare was not meant seriously—of course not. Tamsin should have known it and insisted on going to the maypole.

The music was getting louder. Eleanor turned her head and looked in the direction of the green, although it was hidden from sight behind the houses. A burst of cheering must mean the dancing was about to start. Several lads had asked her to partner them. She had said yes to some—not that she really wanted to. Who would Tamsin dance with? She was taller than most boys. Eleanor's mood brightened. Could two girls dance together? That would make a better dare. They should forget the nonsense with Hobs Geat.

She turned back as Tamsin began another circle. To Eleanor's surprise, bands of mist were rising from the grass, swirling around

Tamsin's knees. Eleanor looked up. How had the weather changed so quickly? Yet the sky overhead was unbroken blue.

A sudden clamour of church bells pealed out, splitting the air, and driving both ravens from their roost. Eleanor jumped so hard she had to grip a gravestone for balance. Her heart hammered in her chest. But it was just the midday chimes, the same as every day, although seeming somehow duller than normal, as if muffled by fog.

The ravens circled the bell tower. A feather drifted down and landed at Eleanor's feet—a black feather, dark as Tamsin's hair. The prickling returned, sharper than before. Eleanor would not stay in the churchyard a second longer. They must leave at once and forget the horrible stone. She turned to Hobs Geat.

The mist was gone, and so was Tamsin. Eleanor was alone in the churchyard. "Tamsin. Where are you?"

Only the breeze in the yews answered.

Tamsin must be hiding behind a gravestone or a tree, ready to leap out. A mean, childish trick, as if Eleanor was not already frightened enough.

"Tamsin. Stop playing games."

Eleanor took a step forward, then another. Despite the warm sunlight, the air around the stone was chill and damp. A raven cawed loudly, sounding like laughter.

"Tamsin. Come out. Please."

She looked up. Hobs Geat hung over her, an evil presence, reaching for her, sucking her in. Soft voices whispered words in a strange language. They were calling to her, seeking her out, coming for her. She could tell.

Eleanor hoisted up the hem of her skirt and ran. The lychgate swung shut behind her with a wooden thud. The ravens returned to their roost. Around Hobs Geat, a final wisp of mist soaked into the ground, and faintly, from a long way away, the last echo of Tamsin's voice faded to nothing.

Once again, St. Benedict's church was at peace in the May sunlight.

CHAPTER ONE

Islington, London
The last Friday in April. Present day.

The high-pitched whine picked its way along Lori's nerves and set up home in her jaw. The surgery door was useless at muffling the sound. It only meant she had to strain to hear the drill—she did not want to, but her obstinate ears insisted on tuning in. The torment was worse than a mosquito in the bedroom when trying to sleep. She shifted on the chair in the vain hope a change in angle might help. The motion sent another throbbing wave up the side of her face, sharp enough to make her nose sting.

Relax.

She closed her eyes and took a deep breath to clear her thoughts. Where had her family been when she lost that milk tooth? Whichever part of the globe, the people did not subscribe to tooth fairy myths. Lori's playmates insisted she drop the tooth in a rat hole as a gift, and for weeks after she had lain awake at night, worried the rats might like it so much they would come for the rest.

Lori jolted back to the here and now. This was not going to work. There must be something to take her mind off both toothache and dentist's drill. The poster on the reception wall, a bubble-shaped blue elephant holding a toothbrush—*Nelly says, "Don't forget to brush"*— might have worked better had she been three rather than thirty.

The room held two other people, the receptionist and a middle-aged Sikh man in a smartly tailored suit. Neither looked as if they were eager to strike up conversation. The businessman was hidden behind a copy of the *Financial Times*, while the receptionist was engaged in an ongoing battle with her computer. Judging by her expression, she was losing badly.

Her shoulder length, wavy blond hair was a match for Lori's although in the receptionist's case, it was clearly due to bleach and a perm, rather than genes. They had little else in common. The receptionist's shape and posture suggested she had not seen the inside of a gym recently, if ever. Her face was a kaleidoscope of makeup. Deep purple varnish coated her half-inch long nails. Leaving anything the colour nature intended was apparently not her thing—and nor were computers. Would she welcome an offer of help?

It might provide a distraction, but before Lori could decide, another burst of pain erupted. Her tooth was trying to tunnel its way out through her ear. Helping the receptionist was a non-starter. Lori had little enough patience with the computer illiterate at the best of times, and this was most definitely not the best of times. Her life had been on a fast track to hell even before the molar started its comedy routine. Thankfully, her dentist had squeezed in an emergency appointment, else she would have been forced to survive on ibuprofen and sympathy until Monday.

In the middle of the room, a mound of magazines was threatening to slide off a low table. The glossy covers suggested all were devoted to food, or gossip about celebrities, or decorating ideas for people with a kitchen large enough to hold a five-a-side football match in. The semi-pornographic photos of cakes and desserts seemed particularly inappropriate in the circumstances. Arranging the magazines neatly would undoubtedly be more fun than reading them.

Lori riffled through the pile in the hope something more interesting had snuck in. She was nearing the bottom when the title *Zettabyte* caught her eye. She shunted the rest back, hoping they would stay put. However, a few escaped and landed on the foot of the Sikh businessman. Lori smiled an apology as she scooped the magazines up before returning to her chair.

As hoped, *Zettabyte* was devoted to computing, with headlines and artwork suggesting it was aimed at the crossover between IT professionals and gamers. The news section led with rumours of the imminent collapse of Ganymede Games and regrets that the upcoming project, *Rank and File*, would never be released. Old news. Ganymede Games had gone into liquidation four weeks ago, putting her out of a job. Had she known it, unemployment was just the start of her problems.

According to the magazine cover it was the March edition, and had presumably come out at the beginning of the month. The deadline for job applications would surely have passed. Even so, Lori flipped to the back, in search of adverts. Why not round off the day by tormenting herself over missed opportunities?

Instead, she found a two-page spread of puzzles, including a crossword. Someone who was clearly unfamiliar with the concept of arithmetic had attempted to complete several of the number grids. Presumably this someone was not the original purchaser. Nobody capable of switching on a computer could be so inept. Lori glanced up at the receptionist—or maybe they could.

Lori took a pen from her bag and started on one of the unspoiled grids. She was running sums through her head when the sound of the door broke her concentration. The previous patient had returned. The elderly woman stood by the desk, rummaging through a bulky purse while muttering under her breath.

"The dentist will see you now, Mr. Singh." The receptionist peered through the gap between her monitor and the woman. The businessman folded his newspaper, flipped it smartly under his arm, and marched through the door. "You'll be next, Ms. Cooper."

Hardly a surprise announcement, given that it was 4:35 p.m. on a Friday and Lori was the only person waiting. After a copious amount of additional muttering, the elderly woman finally left, allowing Lori to return to the puzzles in silence, interrupted only by occasional sighs from the receptionist.

Lori finished another number grid, balancing the rows and columns. Unfortunately, the remaining puzzles were so badly scrawled over, there was nothing she could do with them. This left only the crossword and a multiple-choice section. Lori briefly considered the crossword, since the mathematically challenged bungler had left it untouched, but instead went to the multiple-choice section. The bungler's ticks would not stop Lori from circling her own answers.

Question 1. Which comes next? 43, 41, 37, 31,
a) 17
b) 25
c) 20
d) 29
e) 16

That was easy. The sequence was counting down prime numbers. Lori circled d, and then spent a full minute wondering what possible arithmetic the bungler could have been using when he or she picked b as an answer.

"Ahem—Ms. Lauren Cooper."

Lori looked up. The Sikh businessman was back and both he and the receptionist were staring at her. This time, she had not heard the door.

"You can go in now, Ms. Cooper."

"Yes. Thank you."

Lori returned the magazine to the pile on the table. *Zettabyte* had proved a very successful distraction.

Half an hour later, Lori was back in reception. Pins and needles tingled around the numb section of her face. Her nose itched and she could tell her lips were sagging to the side. But it was more than worth it to be rid of the toothache.

The receptionist's handbag was in the middle of her desk. Her smile was tight and false, leaving no doubt that she held Lori responsible for delaying the start to her weekend. "Everything all right?"

"I hope so, once the anaesthetic wears off. How much do I owe?"

The receptionist peered at her screen, treating it to a dumbfounded expression that might have been justified were it displaying in Linear B. "It's not on the system yet." She slid out from the desk, said, "Excuse me a moment," and trotted through the door leading to the restroom.

While awaiting the receptionist's return, Lori investigated the new filling with her tongue. It felt strange, and the tingling was getting worse. How long would the receptionist be? Was it worth sitting down again? She moved to the table. *Zettabyte* was where she had left it, tempting her. Most of the multiple choice remained, and there were the puzzles that had been ruined by previous bungling. She could draw out new grids and even attempt the crossword. What else did she have to do that weekend?

There was still no sign of the receptionist. Quickly, Lori flipped *Zettabyte* open. She would not stoop to stealing the entire magazine, but nobody would miss the puzzles. Apart from the crossword, all were either complete or spoiled, and the backs of the pages were covered entirely in adverts. Squashing any feelings of guilt, Lori carefully tore out the two sheets. They were folded and safely in her pocket by the time the restroom door reopened.

The receptionist had evidently been using the time to adjust her makeup. The purple lips were questionable, and the blue blusher was wrong in so many ways. Skin should not be that colour.

"Here we are." She tapped the keyboard with the air of a woman prodding a sleeping tiger. "That'll be a hundred and seventy five pounds. Is that all right?"

What would happen if she said no? They could hardly take the filling back. Lori pulled out her credit card. Her savings would cover that month's bills and the next, but soon money would become an issue. How long would finding a new job take? All the papers said there was a shortage of computer programmers.

Light rain was falling when Lori emerged into a typical grey spring evening in London. She turned up the collar of her jacket and joined the flow of people making their way home. The door of the Red Lion pub opened as she passed, allowing warmth and the hubbub of voices to escape. Groups celebrating the end of the working week surrounded the fashionably dilapidated tables.

A glass of wine would be welcome. Lori paused for a moment, but she no longer had workmates and did not want to start drinking alone. Going into the pub would be a mistake. Quite apart from anything else, until the anaesthetic wore off, half of what she tried to drink was going to end up running down her chin.

Lori continued along the street, shoulders hunched, matching her thoughts to the rhythm of her footsteps. How had everything gone so wrong, so quickly? Just one month ago, she had a job, a home, and a girlfriend. First, she had lost her job. The girlfriend and the home had followed in quick succession. Lori rubbed the side of her face in a pointless attempt to massage away the tingling. Concentrate on the positives. The toothache was gone.

Numbness was giving way to pins and needles. Lori pressed experimentally at the side of her mouth. Her lips seemed fully under her control again. Carefully, she took a sip. The tea stayed in her mouth.

Adam flopped onto the settee beside her and took a noisy slurp before setting his own mug on the coffee table. "How's your tooth, hun? Still there?"

"I think so."

"You think so? Do you need a second opinion?"

"Can I trust your opinion?"

"Bite me."

Lori laughed and flexed her jaw. "The anaesthetic hasn't fully gone. But I'm sure it'll be fine, the dentist knows his stuff."

"That fossil you go to? Maybe he does, but I wouldn't let him play around in my mouth."

"Why not? He's good."

"If a man's going to put his face close to mine and tell me to open wide, I want him young and gorgeous." Adam flipped around on the settee, imitating the pose of someone in a dentist's chair. "Like this, looking up into his eyes. I tell you, nice scenery makes everything more bearable."

"My vote goes with experience."

He returned to a normal position. "I don't mind a man learning on the job."

"You'd let a car mechanic loose on your mouth?"

"Been there. Done that. Got the photos."

"We're talking about dentists."

"They're still men." Adam struck his forehead dramatically. "Of course, hun. That's your problem. Look, we'll find you a nice, young, female dentist."

"The receptionist was young and female."

"And?"

"And nothing. Maybe she once had a brain cell, but it must have died of loneliness."

"What did she look like?"

"As if she'd been caught up in an explosion at a paint factory. Way too much makeup."

"Has anyone ever told you you've become middle-aged far too young?"

"Yes. You have."

"And I'm right."

"I want someone I can have a sensible conversation with."

"You've been trying sensible ever since we met, and where has it got you? I think what you need is someone who can shag you senseless."

Adam grabbed her hand and shook it to punctuate his words. "Let Nathan and me find you someone. We can be your vetting agency. We'll take you out tomorrow night."

"I have—"

"No. I know what you're going to say. You have a broken heart and aren't in the mood. It's like falling off a bike. You have to get straight back in the saddle." Adam paused, frowning. "Is that the right phrase?"

"It should be falling off a horse."

He made a show of thinking. "In your case, bike works better."

"I—" Lori's phone rang. She fished it from her pocket and checked the caller ID.

"Jessica?" Adam must have seen her face fall.

Lori nodded as she thumbed to answer. "Hi, Jess. What's up?"

"Hi. Am I interrupting anything?"

Adam held his nose. Lori ignored him and focused on the wall. "No. We were just chatting."

"Right, well, I was wondering if you could call round and pick up your things."

"What things?"

"Stuff you left behind. I've got it packed ready for you."

"Can't you hang on to it a while longer?" Adam's spare room had been overflowing, even before she moved in.

"I'm sorry. We really need the space."

More than I do? "Not just for a week or so?"

"Oh, come on, Lori. Be fair. You can't expect to use my house as a storage facility forever." Jess's voice dropped. "It will be better to have all your belongings with you. You need to make a complete break."

Of course. She should have guessed. It was all for her benefit. Jess was just being thoughtful. Meanwhile, Adam was lying on his back on the floor, imitating a dying fly.

Lori closed her eyes. "When would you like me to come over?"

"Is tomorrow okay?"

"Yeah. Sure. Fine. What time?"

"I'm getting my hair done in the morning and Zoe's having friends round later. We'll need to get the house ready." *Heaven forbid I might interrupt them vacuum cleaning.* "Shall we say between two and three? And if you get caught by Mrs. Jameson, I'd rather you didn't say anything about moving out. You know how nosy she gets."

Anything particular you'd like me to wear? "Right. See you then." Lori ended the call and carefully positioned her phone on the table beside the tea mug. The urge to throw something at the wall was overwhelming, and neither object was a good idea. Anger, misery, or a combination of the two, threatened to fill her eyes with tears.

In an instant, Adam had slipped onto the settee and wrapped an arm around her shoulders. "Hey. Come on, hun. You're better off without her."

"It's just that…" Lori's throat tightened painfully.

"It's just that you've got lousy taste in girlfriends."

As if he was anyone to talk. "I thought we were doing so well together."

"With Jessica? To be honest, I never knew what you saw in her."

"She's…" *What?* Lori slipped out of Adam's arm and took a sip of tea to ease her throat. After four years together, what was her main impression of Jess?

Adam had his own ideas. "She's as much fun as a wet dishcloth. She's every cliché about a chartered accountant brought to life—no, half-life. I'm surprised she managed to have an affair. I didn't think she had it in her." He held a hand to his mouth. "Oops, sorry. That's not tactful, is it? But you know what I mean. She's dull. Always has been."

"She's not that bad."

"What's the most exciting thing she's ever done?"

"I don't want excitement."

"Everyone needs excitement in their life, a bit of adventure."

"It's overrated."

"Your parents are still going strong."

"Precisely. I'd had enough adventure by the time I was fourteen to last the rest of my life." Lori drained the tea. Adam was not so far off the truth. A large part of Jess's attraction had lain in her being, not dull, but safe and normal. There were so many loonies around. Lori patted his leg. "Thanks. I need you to keep me sane."

"That's asking a bit much, hun." He scooted back to the other end of the settee. "Anyway, what did the wet dishcloth want?"

"She wants me to go round tomorrow and pick up some more of my stuff."

"When?"

"Between two and three."

"Can't you make it later? I'd go with you for moral support, but Nathan wants me to watch him play football. We'll be back by four."

Adam scrunched his face in thought. "Oh…I'll come with you. I'm sure Nathan won't mind."

And Lori was absolutely certain he would. "It's all right. I'll go on my own. There'll be more space in the car."

"How much is there?"

"I've no idea." And where was she going to put it?

The same question clearly occurred to Adam. "Maybe if we pull the settee forward we can stack stuff behind."

Which was another thing Nathan would mind. He and Lori had never warmed to each other. The antipathy might not plumb the depths reached by some of Adam's previous boyfriends, but Nathan definitely had his place in the string of lovers who resented their friendship.

She and Adam had met in the GLBT group at university during freshers' week, and had hit it off. Over the years, they had nursed each other through a series of train-wreck relationships. Jokes about using each other as a vetting agency were old. It would put them both in line for long-term celibacy. Lori was yet to date a woman Adam liked.

She shook her head. "No. I'll take whatever Jess has found down to my parents' house with the rest of my stuff. They've got plenty of space."

"Are they back?"

"No. Still trekking down the Andes. But I've got a key. I can air the place out for them."

"Do you know how they're doing?"

"Mum's talking about opening a sanctuary for retired llamas."

"Llamas retire?"

"Presumably. I think they're like donkeys."

A key sounded in the lock. "I'm home."

"We're in the lounge," Adam called back.

Nathan appeared in the doorway. He smiled at Adam and gave a curt nod in Lori's general direction. "What's for dinner? I'm starving."

"Spag bol. The sauce is done. I just need to cook the pasta." Adam wrapped his boyfriend in a hug and planted a kiss on his lips before heading into the kitchen.

Nathan dropped into the vacated spot on the settee. "How's the job search going?"

You want me gone. I get it. "I sent off another two applications this morning. But I've heard nothing back from the others."

"Games companies?" Nathan's tone made it clear he did not think video games were a proper job for an adult. Lori's parents would agree, although their opinion of a motorbike courier would not come much higher. Like all Adam's boyfriends, Nathan was pretty, but unlikely to feature on anyone's list of inspirational thinkers. However, she had to concede he looked good in motorcycle leathers.

"No. One was telecoms and the other security systems."

"How do you rate your chances?"

"Hard to say."

"Do you think you'll stay in London?"

How far away would you like me to go? "In the long term, who can say? But I'll be heading down to my parents' place sometime next week."

"How long for?" Nathan made no effort to hide his eagerness.

Lori slid down in the seat. Part of the reason she and Adam stayed such good friends was knowing when to back off. She did not want Adam and Nathan arguing over her, and anyone could see it looming on the horizon. "I'd been thinking just a few days. But once I'm there, I might as well stay awhile."

Adam stuck his head around the door. "Don't you need to be in London for jobs? Not stuck in Devon. Have they got electricity down there?"

"Dartmouth is hardly the back of beyond. It'll be handy for Exeter and Bristol. If I get an interview in London I'll come stay with you."

"What about your parents?"

"They won't mind. And they're not due home for a month. With luck, I'll have found a job by then."

Nathan smiled. "Devon's nice. You should treat yourself to a holiday."

Chapter Two

Lori sat on her bed with the laptop balanced on her knees. There was nowhere else to work. Less than a quarter of the stuff stacked around the walls was hers. Adam and Nathan had been using the small bedroom for hoarding junk before she arrived. The only clear horizontal surface was the bed. Even the improvised side table was made from piles of books. Whatever Jess wanted her to take would have to stay in the car boot until she reached Devon. Fortunately, Mum and Dad believed in storing memories, not possessions, so there was no shortage of space in their house.

They had built careers from travel writing and environmental activism. Hitchhiking the length of the Andes was their latest adventure. Even though they looked down on her career choice, Lori could not fault them on embracing new technology. Their podcasts got millions of hits. But after a childhood living out of a backpack, Lori needed to know where she was going to sleep that night. Grandma had been right, a tree without roots could not bear fruit.

She ought to let Mum and Dad know she was moving in for a while. Not only was it polite, it was also possible they had installed new security systems. However, it meant telling them she had lost her job. Their response would be predictable. They would tell her to seize the chance, go wild and hit the road—live off grid for a while. They made no secret that her degree in computing and the resulting desk job left them bewildered. How had they produced such humdrum offspring? Video games were for people who did not lead interesting lives.

Lori chewed her lip. She had to get a new job before they returned home, or run the risk of being kidnapped and dragged off to Kathmandu, or wherever they were headed next. Attached to their last email was a photo of Dad lying flat on his back on a pebble beach with two penguins standing on his chest. The signature line was definitely a dig at her. "Virtual reality is an oxymoron."

She typed:

Hi Mum and Dad
Hope you're having a great time. Just to let you know, I'm planning on driving down to Dartmouth sometime next week. Is it OK if I stay for a while? Anything you'd like me to do while I'm there?
Love Lori
XXXXX

She hit send before she had a chance to change her mind. She now had however long it took them to reply to work out how to field the inevitable questions.

Next stop was a job website and the daily trawl for new vacancies, but summoning the enthusiasm was harder than normal. She stared again at Dad's photo. Penguins—loud, smelly, chaotic, but also strangely endearing, as long as you were taller than them. She batted the memory away. There was no need to revisit the Antarctic as an adult. She was staying put.

A roar came from the TV downstairs. Presumably someone had kicked a ball into a net. The choice of viewing was Nathan's, and Adam was happy to go along with it—for now. Lori gave the relationship another six months at most, but there was no point saying anything to Adam.

She could go downstairs and join them, but it would take more than a pert, leather-clad bottom to get her watching football. However, staying in the bedroom was not an attractive option either—eight o'clock was far too early for sleep. Lori rested back on the bed and stared at the ceiling. Where did she go from here? How had her life gone tits up so quickly?

She shut the laptop, and pulled out the magazine pages. Forget the brooding. At least the puzzles were fun. She was about to continue with the multiple-choice questions, but then decided to try the crossword instead. The format was slightly unusual, with answers to clues sometimes split between separate locations, as with the first clue:

1 across & 29 down: Setting for a monochrome lament (7, 10)

Lori tapped the pen against her knees. The trouble was, you had to get into the puzzle setter's way of thinking, and people could be so perverse and hard to understand—even the ones you were not in a relationship with.

Monochrome? Black and white? Or maybe grey? Or even Gray? Lori punched the air. Of course, that was it. The lament was an elegy, and the answer was obvious. Gray's "Elegy Written in a Country Churchyard" had been Grandma's favourite poem. The crossword was not the classic cryptic sort—which was not a bad thing in her mind—but cryptic clues to general knowledge questions.

The words *COUNTRY* and *CHURCHYARD* went into the empty spaces.

Lori switched between puzzles until only one final crossword clue remained. After a sudden burst of inspiration, she filled in *ATTILA THE HUN*, and put her pen down. Everything was complete.

A yawn surprised her, as did the silence. When had the drone of the TV stopped? Adam and Nathan must have gone to bed some time ago. She had not heard them climb the stairs, or anything else. The house could have been burgled and she would not have noticed.

Too late now to shower; it would have to wait till morning. Lori stripped off her clothes and changed into pyjamas. The pages, including the sheets of substitute grids, lay across the bed. She considered them one last time. Maybe she should buy a book of puzzles. It would keep her occupied during the empty days.

She was about to collect the papers, ready for the rubbish bin, but stopped. Something was niggling her. Something half noticed, but pushed to the back of her mind while pursuing other problems. She riffled through her memory, going from puzzle to puzzle. What had pinged her attention?

There it was—number sequences that repeated across the different puzzles far more often than could be accounted for by coincidence. Lori flipped her notebook to a fresh page.

2, 19, 1
5, 12, 6
7, 9, 14
11, 4, 7

No other sequences were repeated anywhere, yet each of these four lines appeared multiple times.

Lori frowned at the numbers, searching for some logic or pattern, but came up with nothing. It had to be no more than an odd coincidence. But then, just as she was about to give up and go to sleep, another curiosity struck her. When she compared the second column to the answers in the multiple-choice section, the answer was always the "a" option, whereas the answers in the third column were always the "d." Was it too big a leap to think of across and down?

She picked up her pen again. The answer to multiple-choice question 19 was a-11, and question 1 was d-29. When applied to the crossword, 11 across was *THE*, and 29 down was *CHURCHYARD*. It was the work of seconds to produce:

2: THE CHURCHYARD
5: AT MIDDAY
7: WALK THREE
11: ENTER THE

She stared at the lines. They looked like a partial set of instructions. Could it be mere chance? Was she reading too much into it? Everyone had heard the folklore about MI5 using the *Times* crossword to recruit spies during World War II, but even if the stories were true, they would not still be doing it. Nobody these days played games with national security. Yet, now that she thought about it, the pages from *Zettabyte* did not have a link to the solutions. Normally in magazines these were printed upside down on another page, but not here. The puzzles really were a test.

Lori ran a hand through her hair. She did not want to be the next Jane Bond, but might an IT company have hit on an imaginative way to recruit software engineers? She could not help laughing at herself. *Fat chance of that.* About as likely as her fairy godmother appearing in a puff of glitter, ready to set her up with Princess Charming and a happy ever after, complete with talking mice.

She slid the sheets between the pages of a book, turned out the light, and shuffled into bed.

❖

The front of the building was the same as eleven days before, when it had still been her home and everything she wanted in life. An unremarkable, well-built house in a safe, respectable street. The biggest danger was becoming the subject of gossip. The curtains of Mrs. Jameson's front room twitched even before the car had stopped.

A cold, dull weight settled in the pit of Lori's stomach. One difference stood out. Zoe's motorbike was parked diagonally across the driveway, taking the space that had once been hers. Lori sidestepped around its front tyre to ring the doorbell, trying not to get dirt on her jeans.

The lock taunted her. Eleven days ago, the key had been in her pocket. Eleven days ago, she had returned from the job centre and let herself in. Eleven days ago, she had found Jess and Zoe, sitting together at the kitchen table.

In itself, this was no great surprise. Jess had been working from home more frequently, and Zoe was a regular visitor. Her bike was often parked on the road when Lori got home from work. Why had she not been more suspicious? With hindsight, the signs were clear enough. The story that Zoe had called in for a coffee on her way to DJ at the local gay bar was ludicrously weak. The disco did not start until nine o'clock.

Eleven days ago, the charade was over.

Even before a word was said, Lori had known what was coming. Zoe's posture wavered between cautious and combative. Jess's lips were squeezed in the familiar pout at the beginning of a passive-aggressive sulk. Normally, what followed was several hours of sniping, trying to make Lori agree she was being either unreasonable or a bully, and possibly both.

That day, it was all over much quicker. Just long enough for Jess to explain how, once again, it was all Lori's fault. If she had not lost her job, then she would not have been hanging around the house all day, so Jess and Zoe could have carried on their affair without upsetting her. But now that everything was out in the open, Lori would be able to move on—as a euphemism for move out—and take her life in new directions. In fact, Lori would be quite childish to see it as anything other than Jess giving her a range of exciting possibilities to explore.

The lump in Lori's stomach started to crawl up her throat. She clenched her teeth, determined to get through this meeting without another scene. *Nice, slow breaths.* Rerunning the conversation through her head was unhelpful.

The door opened, and for the briefest moment she thought Zoe was standing there. Jess was wearing an unironed, shapeless T-shirt proclaiming, "I've got zero fucks left to give." Her jeans were ripped at the knees. Her hair was pink and shaved on both sides. Was this the result of that morning's hairdresser appointment? It might not be a full Mohican, but how would it go down at corporate meetings on Monday? What had happened to the sober, senior finance executive? But if Jess was suffering from some sort of midlife crisis, it was no longer Lori's concern.

"Hi." Jess's face was fixed in a false smile.

"Hi."

"You made it all right."

As if there was a risk she might have already forgotten the way. Lori did not even bother nodding in reply.

After a moment of indecision, Jess stepped back, inviting her in. "I'll get your things. They're upstairs."

"Thanks."

Jess's fashion sense was not the only change. Mismatched shoes were scattered along the hallway. A discarded coat lay on the stairs, turning it into an obstacle course. Opened junk mail was piled on the hall table, needlessly delaying its date with the rubbish bin. It was doubtful if the vacuum cleaner had been out of the cupboard since she left. Clearly, Zoe was making her mark in all sorts of ways.

Through the open door to the lounge, the lower half of Zoe's legs were visible, stretched towards the TV, an open beer can by her feet. A soap opera was playing—one that involved people shouting at each other while wearing hospital scrubs. Zoe made no attempt to acknowledge Lori's arrival, which was just fine.

"Do you want help carrying the stuff down?" Lori offered.

"No. It's all right. Stay here." Jess raised her voice. "Zoe. Lori's here for her things."

Zoe grunted in reply.

"There's quite a few boxes."

This time Zoe did not even grunt. Clearly, she did not respond to hints.

"A hand with them would be nice."

"In a minute."

Jess's tight smile grew tighter. She looked as if she was thinking about saying more, but then scuttled up the stairs, avoiding the coat. After a minute of thumping about, she reappeared, peering around the stack of four printer paper boxes. She edged her way down, feeling with her feet. "It's okay. I'm fine. It's…yes. Okay. Nearly there."

The implied criticism finally provoked a response from Zoe—she turned up the volume on the TV. Was the honeymoon over so soon?

Jess glared into the lounge as she handed over the boxes. "Here you go. I'll get the rest of your stuff."

"Right."

Lori carried the boxes to her car, and arranged them in the boot. By the time she returned, Jess was on the doorstep, her arms stretched around three bulging rubbish sacks. A four-foot-high yucca stood on the ground. Where had the plant come from? Jess obviously considered it hers.

She eased two bags from Jess's grip. Judging by the feel and weight, they contained her winter coat and warm sweaters, which would not be required for months. Did Jess really need to clear everything out so urgently?

"I'll take these, if you can bring the other one," Lori said

"What about the yucca?"

"Keep it, or throw it out." Adam's spare room did not have space and the plant would not survive a week in the car.

Lori dumped the two sacks in the boot and waited for Jess. "That's it?"

"Yes. That's everything. Um…I don't know if…" From the way Jess stood, blocking the path, she did not want Lori back in the house, but neither was she ready for her to go.

"If what?"

"You're doing okay." Jess's tone made it more a hopeful statement than a question.

Lori shrugged in reply.

"Still at Adam's?"

"For a few more days. I'm going down to Dartmouth next week."

"Oh, that's nice. Say hi to your parents from me."

"Will do." Mum and Dad had met Jess twice, and had not been impressed on either occasion.

"You ought to join them, next time they travel. See more of the world."

Thanks for the advice.

"Anyway, I'm pleased you and Adam are getting a chance to catch up."

Was Jess angling for gratitude at helping to cement their friendship?

"You and me. Well…our relationship hadn't been going anywhere for a while. We'd got into a rut, hadn't we?"

We had?

Jess's monologue continued. "You need to grow, and I was holding you back."

You had an affair and kicked me out purely for my benefit?

"We must be true to our real selves."

That's why you dyed your hair pink.

"And Zoe needed somewhere to live."

But I didn't?

"Her flatmates were always getting at her. She can be…" Jess swallowed

She can be a lazy pain in the arse, and you're wondering whether you really want her as a permanent household fixture? Lori was in no mood to offer sympathy. "I'll be off then."

Jess looked startled, then confused, and then came the familiar pout, as if she still had the right to claim Lori's attention.

"Take care." Lori opened the car door.

"Wait. Before you go, I was going to ask about the TV."

"What about the TV?"

"And the fridge. You paid for half. What do you want to do about them?"

Who got custody of the TV set was not at the forefront of Lori's mind. The house was Jess's, although she had paid half the mortgage while living there. What percentage of the contents did she have a claim to? "What do you suggest?"

"I'll pay you for your share. How much do you want?"

"I'll leave it to you. You're the accountant. Send a cheque to me at my parents' when you've worked it out." Whatever her faults, Jess could be trusted to play fair with money.

"Will do. Bye. Safe travels." Jess retreated up the driveway. "I hope you find someone nice. You need to meet new people. Spread your wings."

Jess vanished into the house before a suitable reply came to mind. Had she always been so unbearably insensitive? Adam would, no doubt, answer with a very firm yes.

Lori rammed the car into gear and pulled away from the curb. Without warning, the street blurred. A teardrop ran down her nose. *Damn.* She was not upset. She was angry. *Spread your wings.* What did Jess think she was? A bloody caged budgie? Lori dashed a hand across her eyes, but the tears continued.

Two streets away, she pulled to the side of the road and parked. This was stupid. She could not see where she was going. Crashing the car really would put the finishing touch on the month from hell. Lori fumbled through her pockets for a tissue, without success. The shop at the petrol station sold them. It also had a coffee machine of dubious quality and a row of wobbly high stools. Lori got out of the car and locked it.

"Hi, luv. What do you want?" The woman at the counter greeted her.

"Coffee, please."

"Black? White? Cappuccino?"

"White. No sugar. And a pack of tissues."

"There's a lot of these colds about." The cashier smiled sympathetically and pressed a few buttons on the drinks machine, which started making hissing sounds. "Be with you in a minute, luv."

Lori nodded and looked down. Her eyes were threatening to fill again. Two shelves of magazines lined the underside of the counter. Despite her wobbling vision, the name *Zettabyte* stood out.

Lori pulled the last copy from the rack. "I'll have this as well."

"That's the old April edition, luv. The new one will here on Monday. It always arrives a few days early."

"That's okay. I haven't read this one yet."

The cashier put a polystyrene cup filled with steaming brown liquid on the counter. Theoretically, it might be coffee. "That'll be eight thirty-four, luv."

Something else to go on the credit card. Lori took the coffee, tissues, and magazine to the rickety stools in the window.

A row of women sat under dryers in the salon opposite. Cars passed up and down the road. A mother dragged a crying child along, avoiding two young lads coming in the opposite direction, jostling in a game of who could push the other into the gutter. It was Saturday afternoon in north London, and her life was going nowhere.

Hastily, Lori blew her nose and flipped *Zettabyte* open on the puzzle page. She was not going to give in to self-pity. The styles of puzzles were not identical to the previous month, although the multiple choice and crossword remained. She dug a pen from her pocket.

CHAPTER THREE

The sound of the TV was an undulating mumble from downstairs, punctuated by screams and dramatic bursts of violins. That night was Adam's turn to pick the TV channel, and he had a liking for old black-and-white horror movies—another trait Lori and he shared. She was tempted to go down and join them. Nathan had been much more sociable since learning she was moving out. However, she wanted to tweak her CV for a new job application.

She balanced the laptop on her knees and scrolled to the proficiency section. The skill set specified in the advert was not a perfect match for her. Glossing over the gaps required a degree of creativity and took longer than expected. Eventually, she was happy she had not stretched the truth beyond her comfort level. She added a brief cover note and clicked send, then checked her inbox.

The usual amount of spam had got past the filter and was quickly deleted. Mum and Dad had not replied, which must mean they had no internet access—something that never seemed to bother them. A few ex-Ganymede Games employees had sent updates. So far, five had found new jobs and one had decided to pack his bags and spend the year travelling. This was Danny Harris, who used to sit at the desk beside her. He was currently in Moldova. Mum and Dad would approve.

She selected a suitable emoji, then scrolled through the other emails. Pete Frasier suggested that after working on *Rank and File* they could all enrol in the armed forces. Developing the war simulation game had ruined the company. More resources had been poured in than could ever be recouped. Lori replied with a link to the French Foreign Legion recruitment page and closed her laptop.

The TV was silent. Had Adam and Nathan gone to bed so early? Her watch still gave a while until ten o'clock, so it was not hard to guess what they were doing. She pulled out *Zettabyte* magazine. This month's puzzles centred more on codebreaking than pure arithmetic. Luckily, she had gone through a phase in her teens of playing around with ciphers—Playfair and the rest. Her knowledge was in need of brushing up, but that's what the internet was for.

She completed one number puzzle and thought about starting another, but instead switched to the crossword. The first clue read: *1 across & 5 across: Looks like an afternoon for three kings (7, 7)*.

Looks like an afternoon? P.M.? Prime Minister? After completing the previous crossword, Lori had a feel for the way the puzzle setter's mind worked. She opened the laptop and typed in a search. Three minutes later, after several rephrasings, she had the answer. Stanley Baldwin, the only Prime Minister to serve under three different kings—George V, Edward VIII, and George VI.

Smiling, Lori filled in the bygone politician's name and moved to the next question.

Lori sat at the kitchen table. Adam and Nathan had gone to the Sunday afternoon cinema, so she was alone in the house. She had passed on the offer to go with them. Supposedly, the film was a comedy, but the reviews were decidedly lukewarm. She suspected Adam's only reason for going was to ogle the leading man. Apparently, there were a couple of completely gratuitous nude scenes.

She took a sip of tea and returned to the puzzles. All the mathematical and geometry ones were finished, and she had a strong hunch about how the links to the crossword would drop out. The mechanism was not the same as before, but the diagonal lines on a large number grid were looking suspiciously non-random. She would know for certain once the multiple-choice section was complete.

A short while later, she had four more lines of instructions. The hunch about the diagonals had been correct.

1: GO TO
2: THE CHURCHYARD
4: PLUS STANLEY

5: *AT MIDDAY*
7: *WALK THREE*
9: *ROUND THE*
11: *ENTER THE*
12: *HALFWAY HOUSE*

This was no coincidence. Somebody was hiding a set of directions in the puzzle pages of a magazine. Surely it was too elaborate to be an inside joke by the staff at *Zettabyte*. So what was going on?

Might a TV producer be looking for program contestants? The few clips Lori had seen of reality TV shows were enough to put her off. Was it likely anyone would use complex maths puzzles to select people willing to engage in naked mud fights on live TV? But maybe not all such shows were quite so inane. She could ask Nathan. He would know.

Of course, what she wanted was a job in computing. GCHQ would suit her down to the ground. It was in an attractive part of the country and the work should be interesting. However, she was not getting her hopes up over something so blatantly in the realm of "too good to be true."

There was another possibility. *ENTER THE HALFWAY HOUSE.* Could it be a secret message from an underworld gang? Drug cartels had the money to bribe *Zettabyte* over the puzzle pages. Except, solving the puzzles was hard enough when sober. Spaced out on cocaine? Lori shook her head. A mobile phone would be a quicker, easier, and far more reliable way for smugglers to make contact with each other.

The missing lines were intriguing, but trying to guess them was a waste of time. The May edition of *Zettabyte* would be on sale tomorrow. Then what? Would she carry out the instructions—whatever they turned out to be? That was the big question. The list of things that might go wrong started with being made a fool of on national TV and went downhill from there. Regardless, her curiosity was fired up, and she had to know what the full set of directions said.

The street door opened. Adam and Nathan were back. Lori slipped her notes inside the cover of the magazine and called out. "Hi. How was it?"

"Fun."

"Stupid." Adam shared her low tolerance for weak plot lines.

"You were laughing all the time."

"At it. Not with it." They entered the kitchen. Adam grabbed the kettle. "Who wants tea?"

"Not for me." Nathan pulled a lager from the fridge.

"I'll have one, thanks." Lori held out her empty mug. "Was the film as bad as the reviews?"

"Better."

Adam groaned dramatically. "Worse. It passed the time. But only if you turned your brain off first."

She would give the film a miss.

"How was your afternoon?" Nathan took a seat opposite. He was becoming noticeably friendlier the closer her departure came. Lori had a vision of him sobbing and hanging around her neck when it was finally time to go. No. Scrub that image—there was no need to get carried away.

"It was productive." She adjusted the edge of *Zettabyte* so it aligned with the table. "I might even be on to a job."

"Really? That's fantastic." Adam patted her shoulder. "What is it? Where? Do you have an interview?"

She should have kept quiet. "It's all very tentative. I don't want to say too much in case it falls through."

"Who's it with?"

Lori shrugged.

"It's in computing, right?"

This was getting silly. "I can't say anything, yet."

Nathan frowned at her. "You're making it sound very mysterious. Are you applying to the secret service, or something?"

"Just call me Q." Lori could tell her laugh sounded forced. The kettle boiled. She used the temporary distraction to switch subject. "So what was the best bit of the film?"

Adam poured water into the mugs. "Apart from the end credits?"

"Oh, come on. It wasn't that bad."

She leaned back in her chair. In all honesty, there was precious little chance of the puzzles leading to a job. No matter. First thing tomorrow morning, she would be at the newsagent.

Lori did not wait to get back to Adam's house before starting on the crossword clues. She had *Zettabyte* open on the puzzle page as soon as she left the shop. One answer jumped out. *7 down: Against the clock,*

the restored red dish wins. (11). This had to be a traditional anagram, and she did not need to unscramble "red dish wins." How many eleven-letter words containing a w could be thought of as meaning "against the clock"? Widdershins, the old-fashioned word for anticlockwise.

By the time she was home, several more ideas had struck her. She threw the magazine on the kitchen table beside her laptop and put the kettle on. Adam and Nathan were both at work, so she had the house to herself and the whole day free. The job search could wait till tomorrow.

Time rolled by. Some of the knowledge required was definitely on the obscure side of general. She would never have found the archaeological site of Tel Dor without the internet. The mathematics went from modular arithmetic to probability theory. But finally, it was done, just as the wall clock showed a quarter to four. Adam would not be home for another two hours.

With her fingers wrapped around the umpteenth cup of tea, Lori studied the completed puzzles. Somewhere in the double spread had to be clues to the remaining lines. Yet, an hour later, she was still scowling at the pages. The links were more deeply buried than before, if they were there at all. Was that it? Someone's idea of a joke? Were the *Zettabyte* staff giggling as they imagined the upset customers? Alternately, March and April might be the second and third sets of instructions. The missing clues could be in the February edition. How hard would it be to track it down?

WIDDERSHINS.

Her eyes caught on the word, sparking a sudden flash of inspiration. She could work backwards from the four missing lines: 3, 6, 8, and 10. Find these numbers, and maybe it would reveal how the links were embedded.

Lori took one look at the pages and laughed as everything fell into place. Each missing number appeared exactly four times on either side of the double spread. Using a ruler and soft pencil, she joined the threes to make two crosses, took the numbers where the lines intersected, then linked them via the multiple choice to the crossword.

Within minutes she was looking at:

1: GO TO
2: THE CHURCHYARD
3: IN DOR
4: PLUS STANLEY

IN DOR PLUS STANLEY was the confusing part. A churchyard indoors? Plus Stanley—did it mean Greater Stanley? Was there such a place?

Lori went back to her laptop and tried variations on the search, until hitting on Dorstanley, a tiny village in north Dorset she had never heard of before.

The only webpage devoted purely to the village was an amateurish effort from the parish council. Nothing worth the effort of updating the server had happened since a cake competition the previous July. But a parish council meant the village had a church, and so presumably a churchyard. Yet it must hold dozens of gravestones, maybe hundreds. How to know which was the right one?

The second link was a list of Neolithic monuments in the British Isles. The entry for Dorstanley read:

A twelve-foot-high menhir, known locally as Hobs Geat, stands in the churchyard of St. Benedict's parish church in Dorstanley, Dorset. Dated circa 2800 BC. Visiting possible at all reasonable times. Free parking by the War Memorial.

That must be the stone in question. Rather than take the motorway to Dartmouth, she could cut across country on the A303 and go via Yeovil. It would be slower, but more scenic, and the route passed with five miles of Dorstanley. She could stop off for lunch, since the instructions said midday. However, they also specified the old Celtic festival of Beltane, which was now called something else. Halloween? Lori typed in, *Beltane, date.*

So no, not Halloween but May Day—Wednesday. The puzzle setters were not giving her much time, but it was no problem. There was all of Tuesday to gather her things and inform everyone who needed to know about the change in address. She could leave after the morning rush hour had died down on Wednesday and be at Dorstanley easily by midday.

Lori took a deep breath. Somewhere along the way, she had made a decision. The old adage, *It's the things you don't do you regret the most.* She did not want to spend the rest of her life wondering.

It might turn out to be someone's idea of a joke, but she was going to do it.

Dorstanley was more of an ornamental hamlet than a village, thirty or so houses, huddled around the junction of two minor roads. The triangle of grass at the intersection was dominated by a couple of medium sized trees. A weathered bench in their shade had been used by birds for target practice. At one side of the green, the road was just wide enough to park a car without causing an obstruction. No one else was currently there, but Lori made sure to leave room, should another driver want to stop. She turned off the engine and got out.

The village was quaint, in the chocolate box fashion typical of Dorset. Most of the houses still had straw thatched roofs. Flower baskets hung from the black, antique lampposts. In one corner of the grass, the War Memorial took the form of a Celtic cross. Its polygon plinth held two dozen names, mostly from the First World War, with a few tacked on from the Second.

Nobody was in sight. Dorstanley was clearly the sort of place where not much happened. There was no pub and no shop. Lunch would have to wait until Yeovil. Hardly surprising the cake competition was still on the parish webpage. It must have been the highlight of the decade. The locals were probably still arguing about the result.

The weather was on the cold side for early May. Low hanging cloud turned the sky dull grey and carried the threat of rain. With the benefit of hindsight, the thin polycotton shirt and trousers were too lightweight for wandering around outdoors. Her interview suit with its wool jacket would have been warmer, but she could not take the situation seriously enough to wear it. Equally, faded jeans and T-shirt were out if she wanted to make a good impression. With one eye on the clouds, Lori pulled her raincoat from the back seat and slipped it on, then glanced at her watch—only eight minutes until midday. She was later than anticipated due to roadwork outside Andover.

Fortunately, she did not have far to go. A hillside rose on the north side of the village. Set against the green backdrop, the steeple was visible over the nearest row of thatched roofs. A footpath between two houses clearly led to the church and would be quicker than the road.

A ripple of nerves fluttered through her stomach. She was about to make a complete fool of herself. For a moment, Lori was on the point of getting back in the car and leaving. Then a door opened and an elderly man emerged with an equally elderly basset hound on a lead, the first sign of life in Dorstanley. It would look odd if she drove away now. Anyway, having got this far, she might as well go through with it.

She exchanged a cursory good morning with the dog walker, checked that notepad and pen were in her shoulder bag, just in case things turned out better than expected, and headed off on the short walk.

The footpath ended at a traditional style lychgate, complete with roof. The churchyard beyond was like thousands of others, with gravel paths and uneven rows of graves set amid neatly clipped grass. Yew trees lined the edges. The headstones came from the last two centuries, with some illegible ones that might be older. Most graves were small and plain, though the Victorians had left some over-extravagant tombs, complete with weeping cherubs. Several of the newer graves were decorated with fresh flowers.

St. Benedict's church and its square bell tower looked authentically medieval, with a few later additions. Gargoyles in the form of dragons and goblins projected from the roofline. As far as could be judged from the outside, the stained glass in the gothic windows dated to the nineteenth century. There was no sign of TV crews, secret service agents, or anyone else. The dog walker had gone in a different direction.

Lori paused by the porch. The interior had a bench on either side and a notice board carrying details of a mother and baby morning group, the times of services, and another cake competition—or was the poster left over from the previous year? The church door was shut. A minor TV personality might be hiding inside, along with camera crews and sound guys. It would take her a moment to check, but just three minutes remained till noon, and she was yet to find the menhir.

Luckily, it did not take much finding. Lori saw it as soon as she rounded the end of the church. The finger of granite stood alone in a corner. The grass around it was clear of gravestones.

As she drew closer, a feeling of strangeness grew. A chill breeze carried a wisp of mist past her face. The stone was old, very old. The weight of centuries hung heavily on it. The rustle of the yew trees sounded like murmurs of a long forgotten language, and she could not shake the idea that the menhir knew she was there. Lori reached out, brushing her hand over the stone. Nothing other than time and the elements had sculpted the rough faces.

Another wisp of mist coiled around her fingers. Was it a TV effect with dry ice or her imagination? Either way, the hair rose on her neck. She would have backed away, but a peal of bells rung out, harsh and loud, jerking her back to reality. It was midday. Lori straightened her shoulders. Time to forget the whimsical nonsense about sentient stones and talking trees. She would do what she came for, and when nothing happened, she would walk away, thankful nobody was around to laugh at her.

The mist thickened and the temperature dropped a few degrees as she completed the first circuit. The abruptness of its onset was startling. One more thing to chalk up to climate change. The weather forecast had made no mention of it that morning. The hems of her trousers flapped wet around her ankles, picking up moisture from the grass.

Another anticlockwise circuit, while still the church bell chimed. The mist turned to dense fog. Now she could no longer see the church. The freak weather would make driving to Devon a nightmare. Lori pulled her raincoat tight at her neck and hurried to finish the final circle. The echoes of the last chime faded away as she returned to her starting point.

She had done it. So what now?

Lori peered into the fog, hoping for a figure to emerge. Was anyone there? The conditions made it impossible for an observer to have seen her complete the circuits, but surely whoever it was would take the weather into account. Meanwhile, the fog was lifting, although not as quickly as it had arrived. St. Benedict's church was a dim shape, seeming smaller and more distant than before.

Still nobody came. It was all a joke after all, unless, rather than blunder around in the fog, the puzzle setters were waiting for her by the lychgate. Either way, hanging around was a waste of time. She should head back to her car and go in search of lunch.

However, no one was under the small wooden roof when she reached it. Lori had not really expected otherwise. She clenched her teeth to bite back a selection of obscenities. The pranksters should have picked the first of April for the hoax. She looked back one last time, then pushed the gate open.

Directly opposite the churchyard, no more than a dozen steps from where she stood, a pub sign hung outside a rustic building. Lori stared at it. Why had she not spotted the pub before? She was normally more observant, though admittedly, on her arrival, she had been too busy looking for TV cameras atop the bell tower, or MI5 agents hiding behind trees.

Hopefully, the pub would do food. If the sudden change in weather had caused an accident, getting to Yeovil might take hours. Even an orange juice and packet of cheese and onion crisps would hold her over and give the fog the chance to lift.

A breeze sprung up, tearing holes in the mist. Seen more clearly, the outside of the pub did not inspire confidence. *Forget the rustic bit, decrepit is a better word.* On second thoughts, did she really want to go in? But the smell of wood smoke cast the deciding vote. An open fire was unusual in May, but the weather definitely warranted it. The chill had etched through to her bones.

As Lori approached the door, creaks from the swaying sign made her look up. The picture was weathered away, but the words were just legible, *The Halfway House*. Of course. The last part of the instructions. Maybe it was not a joke after all. Whoever set the puzzles might be inside. Her stomach tightened. The moment had come to discover whether she had been played as a fool.

Lori pushed open the door.

Chapter Four

The gloom was the first thing to strike Lori. The windows were tiny and glazed with thick green glass. Only a watery haze filtered through to supplement the red glow of the fire. The area behind the service counter was without lights. No concealed spots sparkling on rows of multicoloured liqueurs and spirits, no illuminated handles, no glass-fronted fridge filled with bottles of fruit juice and foreign beer. Was the power out?

Her eyes began to adjust. The Halfway House in Dorstanley had gone overboard on "ye olde worlde charm." Blackened timbers supported the ceiling. The plaster between them was stained and pockmarked. Worn slate flagstones paved the floor. The furniture was made from dark wood, with no two chairs the same. There were no beer pumps at all, just three barrels on a shelf behind the bar and a wine rack to one side. The landlord was taking retro to a new level.

Lori finally spotted the barman, lurking in a doorway to one side. He was easily six feet tall and two feet wide, with a build that spoke of muscle rather than fat. Taken with his squashed nose and cauliflower ears, he was either an ex-boxer or rugby player. Lank dark hair lay over his head like a pancake. His clothes were old, shapeless, and covered in grime. Had he just come from inspecting the fuse box in the cellar? That would explain the absence of lights.

If the pub was experiencing electrical problems, a cooked lunch was unlikely. Then again, from the state of the barman, it might be wiser not to eat anything prepared on site. Fruit juice and a packet of crisps would have to do.

She approached the bar, but before she could speak, the man pointed to the corner by the fire and growled, "Thems who you wanna be a-talking with."

How did he know why she was there? Although, given the pub's ambience, what else would bring new customers in? "Right...thanks."

Lori took a deep breath to gather herself. *Hold back on the crazy dreams. Be sensible.* No matter how this went, she did not want to be caught off-balance and come over as a gullible fool. She turned around.

Three figures sat at a table with their backs against the wall. The set-up certainly made them look like an interviewing panel, which was a hopeful sign. They were the only other customers in the pub. Lori's eyes had adjusted to the dim light, but shadows and the flickering firelight obscured the details until she reached the table.

Not MI5 then.

So much for trying to prepare herself for all scenarios. The two men and a woman were dressed like refugees from a Renaissance fair. All three sported oversized white shirts with billowing sleeves, constrained by form hugging, laced up, black leather waistcoats. Possibly, in the woman's case, it functioned as an external bra. As far as could be seen with the table in the way, they wore identical black leather trousers. Around their throats were twisted metal hoops with Celtic knotwork on the open ends—torcs they were called, if Lori remembered correctly.

The men glanced at their companion, who sat nearest the fire. The hint of a question was mirrored on their faces, while the woman's eyes stayed fixed on Lori in calm appraisal. It left little doubt as to which of the three would be taking the lead.

The woman was in her mid-thirties. Her hair was dark, almost black, and cropped short. A decision about eye colour would have to wait until the electricity was back on. Her firm jaw set the tone for the rest of her features. She had the sort of face that would be perfect for an army recruiting campaign. She would not even need to change her hairstyle.

The large silver buckle on her black belt was in the form of a bird, possibly a crow or a raven. The metal glinted in the firelight. Her left leg was visible at the side of the table, encased in leather trousers and a laced-up boot reaching nearly to her knee. The style was more combat than kinky, and the colour was—surprise, surprise—black.

The woman kicked a stool Lori's way. "You decoded the clues. Congratulations. Take a seat."

"Thank you." The fire was putting out enough heat for Lori to remove and fold her raincoat. She placed it with her shoulder bag on a spare seat and sat facing the trio. "I'm Lauren Cooper."

She leaned over the table, holding out her hand. After five long seconds, when nobody showed any intention of shaking it, she put it back in her lap. Not the most sociable group. Already Lori's thoughts were shifting towards making a quick exit.

"You can call me Tamsin."

So was this not her real name? Lori gave what she hoped was a polite smile. "Good to meet you at last."

"For sure. I was beginning to think nobody would ever decode the clues. This was our sixth attempt." Tamsin's smile revealed even white teeth, but nothing of her mood or intention. The trace of a West Country burr modulated her accent, though it was competing with something else. American? She jerked her thumb to indicate the man sitting beside her. "This is Finn, my lieutenant."

The unexpected paramilitary title was disconcerting. Lori worked at maintaining a bland smile. "Nice to meet you, Finn."

He gave a curt nod.

Finn was older than Tamsin by a decade or so. His hair was thinning on top and just long enough to show the grey at his temples. The loose shirt did not disguise his wiry arms—the sort that looked as though they might snap in a gust of wind, but possessing as much strength as a bodybuilder's bulging muscles. His narrow face emphasized his high cheek bones. Several days had passed since he last shaved. His skin was weathered and lined by scowl marks.

He was scowling now. His lips opened in what was more sneer than smile. His teeth were small, shark-like. *Finn.* Lori had the image of a shark's fin slicing through water, with a whole lot of danger hidden beneath.

"And that's Widget at the end," Tamsin said. "He's our techie. You can thank him for putting the puzzles together."

Did none of them use a last name—or a real one for that matter? Maybe she was not the only person put in mind of a shark when it came to Finn.

Widget was the youngest, probably a few years short of Lori's age. His hair was blond and close cropped around the sides, though it stood up an inch on top, trimmed flat like a cartoon character. He had well-balanced features, set in a youthful, square-cut face. In fact, all three were well above average in the looks department. Even Finn exuded the raw masculinity of an aging TV detective. Were they actors?

Widget gave the first genuine smile she had seen so far. "Congrats. There was me thinking I'd have to make the clues easier, which would kind of defeat the point, you know." His accent was easy to place. Welsh.

"They were fun. And I'm pleased I made the grade."

The barman lumbered over and dumped four tankards on the table. "Here's beer f'yer."

Lori looked up. "I'm driving. Do you have a fruit juice?"

Ignoring her, the barman slumped back to his counter. Quite apart from her not ordering the drink, his customer service routine needed work.

"Don't worry. You won't be driving anywhere else today," Tamsin said.

"Pardon?"

"We've got an urgent task for you."

"A job?"

"You could look at it that way."

"Um...." How did you interpret that?

"You'll be starting today." Tamsin made it a statement of fact.

I think I get a say in it. Lori put her hands in her lap, while doing her best to keep up a front of calm professionalism. Whatever they wanted her for, the certainty was growing that she had no interest in doing it. "Don't you want to know my employment background?"

"Do you want to tell us?"

"You don't think it might be relevant?"

"You made it here. That's all we need to know. Unless you want to confess to having someone help you with the puzzles."

"No. I did it all by myself." Lori's irritation level surged. Who did these people think they were?

From their get-up, they could be a rock group—some sort of gothic/electric-folk crossover. Maybe they wanted their website updated. In which case they had gone down a ridiculous path to find a designer. Not only was puzzle solving no proof of HTML knowledge, but a simple job advert would have been far easier.

Lori glanced at her watch. Would it be possible to escape before the pubs in Yeovil stopped serving lunch? She should act as though she was taking them seriously, nod and make suitable noises, then get out. She pulled the notebook from her bag. "What exactly does this job involve?"

She held her pen hovering over the page, in the hope of nudging the interview along

"You'll find out."

"Pardon?"

"It can wait." Tamsin took a sip of beer and settled back in her chair. "The main thing now is to sort out the story. What have you told your friends and family?"

"About what?"

"The reason why you're here. What did you say to them?"

"Obviously, not a lot. I don't know much, and you're still not telling me anything." Lori's patience was at the point of giving out. "What is this all about?"

"Did you mention Dorstanley?"

"I doubt anyone would have recognised the name. But—"

"You're looking for work? You're unemployed at the moment?"

"Yes, but..." Wasn't that the whole purpose of this charade?

"Are you married?"

"No."

"Living with someone?"

"Is that any of your business?" That was it. She definitely did not want the job.

Widget laughed. "Ooooh. Bit of bitterness there, I'd say. Just broke up, have we?"

What the...? After a moment to compose herself, Lori put her notebook back in her bag and picked up her coat. "I'm sorry. I think we're all wasting our time here." She began to stand.

"Sit down." Tamsin snapped out the order.

Lori obeyed, mainly out of surprise. "Look. I don't know who you think—"

"I'm just trying to work out how long it'll be before you're missed."

A fist of ice grabbed Lori's stomach. Tamsin was not joking. *Stay calm. Act normally.* Showing alarm would be a mistake. "Actually, my parents were expecting me an hour ago. The traffic getting here was appalling." Lori fished her phone from her coat pocket. "I should call them."

"It won't work. There's no reception here."

Tamsin was right. Zero bars showed. "If you don't mind, I'll just pop outside. I don't want them worrying."

"It won't work out there either." Tamsin smiled. "And you're a bad liar. At midday you were due to be at Hobs Geat, not meeting your parents." She tilted her head towards Widget. "Are you okay to lay a trail?"

"Should be." He reached over and plucked the phone from Lori's fingers.

"Hey!"

Widget ignored her protest and batted her hand away. "Yep. It's all here. Contacts. Mum and Dad."

"What do you think you're—"

"Your car's parked by the memorial?" Widget glanced up, both his smile and his tone casually cheerful. "Keys in your bag?" He snatched it from the chair and peered inside. "Anything you want me to grab from the boot?"

"You can't just…" Lori's throat tightened. Kidnap. She was being kidnapped by three leather clad goons—four, since the barman was clearly in on the conspiracy. "What do you want with me?"

They ignored her.

"The car will be there," Tamsin said. "There's nowhere else to park in Dorstanley."

"Right you are." Widget stood and downed his beer. "See you back at Caersiddi, then." He swung her bag over his shoulder and sauntered from the pub.

Lori's mouth was dry and her hands were shaking too much to risk picking up the tankard. "What do you want with me? We can't pay you. We're not rich. My parents might—"

"We aren't after money."

Every other option was worse. *Keep calm. Keep calm.* There might be only one chance to escape. She must think clearly. "So what do you want?"

"As I said. We have a task for you."

Lori forced her hand to steady enough to pick up the tankard. The beer was cool in her mouth. "What sort of task?" Tamsin and her gang clearly had no regard for the law. "I'm not a hacker."

"Hacker?" Tamsin looked thoughtful. "You're in computing?"

"Yes." What did they think she did? "You want me to write code?"

"It involves code. But not in the way you're thinking. Do you have much experience in encryption?"

She took another mouthful of beer while gathering her thoughts. "Umm...I'm familiar with the relevant IEEE standards, and I've implemented routines for SHA-2."

Finn muttered under his breath, "That'll be a fat lot of bloody use." The first thing he had said so far. He had a strong Irish brogue. Maybe Finn really was his name.

Tamsin grinned at him. "He means it's a little less high-tech than you're used to. As a child, did you play with secret codes?"

"Doesn't everyone?"

"You'd be surprised."

"You want me to encrypt something?"

"Other way round. Our queen has a document written in code. She needs you to unravel what it says."

Queen? The loony index was creeping up. They might be a cult—one rich enough to place the puzzles in *Zettabyte*. However, money did not rule out drug fuelled orgies and human sacrifice. Lori glanced at the door, but the barman was lurking in the darkness. She abandoned any thought of making a run for it.

"What sort of document is it?"

"Queen Rianna will tell you everything you need to know when we get to Caersiddi. And don't worry about being paid. She's very generous. I think you'll be happy with your reward, if you succeed."

"And if I don't?"

"Let's worry about that if it comes to it." Tamsin's smile carried little comfort.

"Supposing I say I don't want this job?"

"That's not an option."

Their eyes met and held. Even in the circumstances, Tamsin was an extremely attractive woman, but Lori did not need Adam to tell her that a deranged kidnapper would mark a new low in poor girlfriend selection. Was there any chance this was all part of some TV show? Was a B-grade celebrity about to leap out of the shadows shouting, "Surprise!" Some of Lori's previous lovers had turned out to be acting a part, presenting a facade of being sane and normal. Pretending to be crazy would be a first—and weighing up Tamsin as if she could be a potential girlfriend was crazy as well.

"Where are you taking me?" And would there be a chance to escape on route?

"If I tell you, you'll think I'm mad."

As if I don't already.

Tamsin drained her tankard and grimaced. "Dammed rat's piss. Come on." She sidled from behind the table and stood.

The ice in Lori's gut erupted in ripples up her spine. From the dimensions of the sheath on Tamsin's belt, the knife it held would classify as an illegal combat weapon in the eyes of any policeman who saw it, although possibly it could be passed off as a costume accessory, if she was on her way to a historic re-enactment. However, the same would not apply to the modern pistol on her other hip. The sight of the grip protruding from the black leather holster transfixed Lori. Things had just got even more serious.

A jog to Lori's shoulder broke her out of the horrified daze. Finn was also on his feet and standing beside her. "Shift yourself, or I'll shift you."

Lori hastily downed half of her beer, partly to bolster her courage, and partly because her mouth felt like she had been chewing sawdust.

Rather than take the front door, Tamsin disappeared into a dark opening at the rear of the bar. Lori's legs were rubbery and she had to steady herself with one hand on the table before following. The short passage was unlit, but daylight glimmered at the end. Finn positioned himself at the back, blocking any hope of escape. They passed through a storeroom stacked with sacks and barrels before emerging behind the pub.

While she had been inside, the clouds had cleared and the sun had come out. The glare was dazzling after the gloomy bar. Through half closed eyes, Lori squinted at the small cobblestone courtyard, lined with low buildings. Most old pubs had either knocked down their stable blocks to make a car park or turned them into B&B accommodation. These were still in use for their original purpose. An open wagon and two shaggy carthorses awaited them. This was not going to be a high-speed getaway.

Three more cult members were seated on the open tailboard of the wagon, dressed in the same white shirts and black leather as the others. All were armed. They had been chatting in the sunlight while they passed around a bottle. One immediately jumped down and stood in front of Lori. He was tall, well over six foot. She had to tilt her head back to look up at him. He had a long, rugged face and an untidy mat of red hair that stuck out at angles. He studied her as if she were a piece of equipment, or a racehorse, then spouted something in a flowing musical language.

"I don't understand what you're saying."

"I said, so you're the wonderful code wizard, we've been waiting for all this fucking time." He spoke English with a rolling Scandinavian accent. "Do you think you're up to the job?"

"That's what we'll have to find out," Tamsin answered for her. "Everyone, this is...Laura?"

"Lauren."

"Lauren. Right." Tamsin placed a firm hand on Lori's back and propelled her toward the wagon. "Widget's laying a trail. Shorty, you and BH wait for him while the rest of us head back."

"Sure thing, Captain." The tall man snagged the bottle from the tailboard and sauntered into the pub, ducking to get under the doorway. Shorty? Maybe the gang wanted to avoid using their real names, but could they not manage a little originality?

Another cult member, a woman who presumably went by the initials BH, hopped down from the wagon and followed him in. The letters undoubtedly stood for something equally witty. Her skin was dark, almost blue-black in the shadows around her eyes. The set of her cheekbones and the hint of natural gold in her hair suggested her ancestry lay in Australia rather than Africa. Her age was hard to guess. She possibly had a few years on Finn, though she moved with the grace of a dancer.

The last of the group remained seated. Smiling broadly, he extended a hand to help Lori onto the tailboard. "Hiya. I'm Hippo. Good to have you along."

Another stupid nickname. Hippo could not be older than thirty. His features were Arabic, although his accent was far harder to place. He had square shoulders, a barrel chest, and bull neck. His heavy build might be the origin of the name, although his weight was all solid muscle rather than flab. He was the only one wearing a sleeveless shirt, revealing biceps that could have featured on the cover of a weightlifters' magazine.

The cult was doing well on multicultural credits. It was also scoring highly in the eye candy department. All the leather clad cultists could have found work as fashion models. Were they actors? Was the wagon a prop? Lori rapped her knuckles on a panel. It felt like solid timber rather than painted plywood.

A bench ran along either side of the wagon. However there was little space to sit, due to the piles of crates and sacks. Assuming the kidnap was for real, Tamsin was obviously planning on a long siege. Up at the front, Finn hopped into the driver's seat and loosened the reins.

Tamsin climbed in and raised the tailboard. She gestured to Hippo. "Go ride shotgun with Finn. I'll keep an eye on our new recruit."

"Right, Captain."

Hippo clambered over the cargo, stopping briefly to reach behind a sack and pull out a double-barrelled shotgun. *Not just a turn of phrase then.* Lori closed her eyes. How far would they get before they were surrounded by a police armed response team? And what was the chance she might be hit in the crossfire?

Tamsin settled on the bench opposite, then turned her head and gave a sharp whistle. Four huge mastiffs emerged from the stables. The dogs had spiked collars, brindled coats, wide, slobbering mouths, and red eyes. Lori looked again to be sure. Red eyes? Could it be genetic? Given their size, she did not fancy anyone's chance of getting them to wear coloured contact lenses.

With a jolt, the wagon started forward.

"Where are you taking me?" Maybe not the most important question, but the one most likely to get a sensible, honest answer.

Tamsin leaned back, stretching her arms out along the side of the wagon. "There are many names for it—Alfheim, Elysium, Kalapa. Take your pick. The locals prefer Annwyn. I just don't advise calling it fairyland."

So much for sense and honesty. Lori buried her face in her hands.

CHAPTER FIVE

After a couple of minutes, Lori raised her head and looked around. Already the houses of Dorstanley were out of sight. She could not even see the smoke rising from the chimney of the Halfway House. In fact, she could not see much of anything.

The weather continued acting strangely. The sun shone brightly overhead in a clear blue sky. However, thick fog blanketed the horizon. Visibility was good for fifty yards or so, and then there was a billowing wall, as if the wagon was in the middle of its own private clear patch. Obviously, this could not last long. When they re-entered the fog, she could jump from the wagon. Except guns were not the only problem. The vicious looking dogs went a long way to explain why the gang had not bothered tying her hands and feet.

Lori peered into the fog, hoping for sight of something comforting—something like a nice blue and yellow police car.

The small region she could see was unexpectedly barren and windswept, open heath rather than farmland. The pastures, wheat fields, and hedgerows she had passed on the way to Dorstanley were gone. The road was a rutted dirt track. The route had obviously been chosen for stealth, but Dorset was too well populated to stay out of sight for long. Soon they would have to reach a village or main road.

"Here. You'll need to wear this." Tamsin was holding out one of the torcs.

The style was similar to artefacts seen in museums. However, the metal was dull grey rather than gold. It was also heavy and cold in her hands, and most definitely not something Lori wanted to wear. Was it a cult symbol, like the silver birds on the gang's belt buckles?

"Why?"

"Believe me. You need to wear it, and never take it off while you're in Annwyn," Tamsin's tone was absurdly insistent.

"You think wearing cheap reproduction jewellery is a matter of life and death?"

"It's more than that. It's made of iron, so it will block magic. A chunk like this, close to your head, will protect you."

"Oh, of course." *Silly me not to have known.*

However, giving free rein to sarcasm was not a good move. Tamsin had a gun, and challenging her version of reality was unwise. *Bloody typical.* Tamsin was an incredibly attractive woman and completely off her rocker. Although her obvious insanity was maybe a good thing. If Tamsin were just a little less deranged it would be very easy to give in to a hormone-driven interest in her. This would be dangerous for two reasons. Not only was she an armed criminal, she was also most likely straight. Who knew how she might react? *But supposing she isn't straight?*

Lori stamped on the thought and concentrated on the iron torc. The band was a half-inch thick, but the braiding made it flexible enough to twist open and slip around her throat. The ornate ends lay heavy on her collarbone. Despite what Tamsin said, there was no way she was going to sleep wearing it.

Tamsin was watching her in a way that was unsettling, for some of the right, and an awful lot of the wrong reasons. When Jess said about meeting new people she should have specified sane ones—or at least ones who would at least give their real name.

"You said I could call you Tamsin. Is that short for something?"

Tamsin's face hardened. It seemed as if she would not reply, but then she said, "If you must know, it stands for Thomasina. It's a name I hate. The only person who could get away with calling me it was my mother, and she's long gone. Tamsin is fine. If we get to know each other better, and become friends, I might let you call me Tazer."

Don't hold your breath. "Do you have a last name?"

"I did once."

"And now?"

"I've got six passports. If you're really interested, I'll let you see them and you can take your pick." Which was the sort of line that could sound intriguing, even sexy, in a spy movie, but not in real life, when spoken by a crazed kidnapper. *Why couldn't she be a sensible, law-abiding, chartered accountant?* Although Jess had not turned out too well.

The wheels hit a series of bone-jarring ruts and there was no padding on the seats. Lori's teeth cracked together. The vehicle was quaint, but neither comfortable nor quick. "Why the horse drawn wagon?"

"We get stuff delivered to the Halfway House. Might as well pick it up while getting you, and it's too much to carry on horseback."

"Wouldn't a transit van or large SUV be better?"

"It would. Except there're no petrol pumps where we're going."

"And where is that exactly?"

"I told you already. Annwyn."

The name was not anywhere she recognised…or did she? Hearing it a second time, pinged a memory. "Isn't that from the Mabinogion?" It was not a real place, but why should it be? Tamsin was off with the fairies.

"It's mentioned there. Have you read the book?"

"No. But a guy I worked with had. He wanted to insert references into a fantasy game we were developing."

Tamsin's easy smile returned in full. "Probably just as well if you aren't familiar with it. Most of the stories are unreliable."

"Most?" *Really?* "And which bits are reliable?"

"Some names. For instance, Powel was one of my predecessors."

"Your predecessor?"

"Captain of the Silver Ravens. The first branch of Mabinogion is a garbled account of one of his missions."

"You're captain of the Silver Ravens."

Tamsin nodded.

"Who are?"

"The elite squad in the army of Rianna, Queen of the Fay."

There was no answer to that. *Fairyland special forces.* She should have guessed. The belt buckle now made sense, but things were not getting any better.

Tamsin continued. "I'll understand if you're having trouble taking what I say seriously. Once we get to Caersiddi you'll find it easier."

"Caersiddi?"

"Queen Rianna's castle. It lies in the middle of Annwyn."

"Right." Talking was pointless. She needed to concentrate on watching for a chance to escape.

However, Tamsin had not finished. "You think I'm crazy."

You've got that much right.

"But I might as well run through some things you ought to know. It'll save time later, when you've seen that I'm just as sane as you."

Which might be quite some way off.

"Earth and Annwyn are linked worlds. Once, there were dozens of portals between them. Now there's just the standing stone in Dorstanley. The easiest way to cross over is by going round it three times widdershins at noon on one of the quarterdays."

"Quarterdays?" Why was she even bothering to ask?

"Beltane, Samhain, and the rest. The four big Celtic festivals are when the barrier between the worlds is weakest. But if you know what you're doing, you can step through anytime. The quarterdays are when people stumble across by accident. Normally, Jimmo takes care of them."

"Which one is Jimmo?" She ought to keep the names clear, in case she ever got to make a statement to the police.

"The barman at the Halfway House. He was the first person I met when I was young and foolish enough to walk around the stone for a stupid dare."

At the front of the wagon, Hippo twisted round and gave Tamsin a huge grin. "Good job you've grown up, Captain. Can't imagine you taking a stupid dare now. I mean, it must be my memory playing tricks—that fuss last month over the bet between you and Captain Cheng."

"I wasn't going to cave in to an Iron Raven. It was a point of honour."

"It was a dragon."

Lori glanced between them. "Dragon?" *Seriously?*

Tamsin shrugged. "Just a small one."

Hippo laughed and turned back to the road.

Dragons. The cultists had to be on drugs. Lori stared into the fog. It was not lifting, and nor were they any closer to leaving the clear patch. If it were not a ridiculous idea she might have thought it was travelling with them. The effect had to be a coincidence.

"You don't need to worry about dragons." Tamsin spoke like someone giving well-meant reassurance.

I'm not. Just the crazy people who believe in them.

"You won't be seeing any at Caersiddi. They stick around the borders."

"That's good to know." Might as well humour her.

"There's plenty of other dangers in Annwyn, but as long as you wear the torc, and follow Queen Rianna's orders, you'll be safe."

"That would be Rianna, queen of the fairies?"

Tamsin drew a sharp breath. "You don't believe a word I'm saying. To be honest, I don't blame you. You're welcome to be as cynical as you like for now, but keep Queen Rianna out it. None of us will find your attempts at humour funny. She deserves nothing but respect."

So that was how to push Tamsin's buttons. Useful knowledge, if only for knowing what to avoid. Provoking armed lunatics was not a safe hobby. "Okay."

"You'll understand when you meet her. Queen Rianna is..." Tamsin's expression softened. "Without her, Annwyn would be in chaos. Fay can be disloyal, cruel, destructive. They'd turn their world into a bloodbath in their petty wars. They'd make all humans slaves...worse than slaves, and believe me, that option exists in Annwyn. The fay are masters of magic, but Queen Rianna is strongest of all and protects us. If not for her, I might not be dead, but I'd be wishing I was. I owe her everything. My life is hers, to do with as she wishes. Every one of the Silver Ravens would willingly die for her. She is everything a queen should be—noble, kind, wise, and fair."

And as an encore she dances the cancan on water.

"You'll understand when you meet her. Working for her is a privilege. But don't worry. She's also very generous. If you decode the document for her, you can expect to be well rewarded."

In dollar bills stamped Bank of Fairyland, no doubt.

"There are mountains of gold in Annwyn. It's as common as sand is on Earth."

In which case a sackful or two is hardly a noteworthy act of generosity. However, it was clear that Tamsin was besotted with her fairy queen. Was it an indication she might not be totally straight? *No. Don't go there. I want safe—okay, Adam, maybe dull and boring, but safe.* Tamsin was not safe. How long before the cultists' absurd fantasy ran out of steam?

"Why does Queen Rianna need human soldiers? Can't she magically turn ants into an army?"

"Iron. It's deadly to all Annwyn life. The slightest scratch can kill. Rulers of Annwyn have recruited human soldiers for generations. We maintain the rule of law and stop criminals from seizing power. When the queen's older sister went insane, we helped Queen Rianna restore peace to Annwyn."

So who's protecting whom? To take Tamsin's story at face value, the Silver Ravens were mercenaries employed by a usurper who had overthrown her own sister. "The six of you keep the peace for the entire kingdom? Or are there more of you back in Annwyn?"

"There's just six Silver Ravens. The Iron Ravens form the majority of Queen Rianna's army."

Hence you're the elite special forces.

"We're approaching the border, Captain," Hippo called out.

"Thanks." Tamsin stood, bracing one hand against a crate for balance, and drew her pistol.

"What are you doing?" Lori's voice came out as a squeak.

"Just a precaution. Slua have been active lately, and they've taken to hanging around the border. Nine times out of ten you don't get a whiff of them, but it pays to be ready." Tamsin held her pistol up as she scanned the encircling fog.

She's crazy. Utterly, stark raving, wear underpants on your head, crazy. Lori slid onto the floor of the wagon and pressed herself into a corner, trying to present as small a target as possible. It would be no protection if Tamsin aimed at her, but it reduced the risk of being shot by accident.

"Shit," Tamsin swore under her breath. "This ain't one of those times." She raised her voice. "D'you see them, Hippo?"

"Yes, Captain."

The blast of the shotgun split the air like thunder, so loud it hurt. Too late, Lori pressed her hands over her ears. Who the fuck was Hippo shooting at? Tamsin also took aim at something. Whatever her target, it gave no reaction to being shot at. No shouts or screams, and blessedly, no return fire. Was there anything out there, or were they battling drug-inspired hallucinations? And did she want the answer badly enough to risk peeking over the side? The wagon came to a halt and a second pistol began firing. Finn had joined in.

Tamsin towered over her, feet planted square on the deck, an image clad in black and white. Her pose was that of a hero in an action movie, making no attempt to take cover. Was it still possible she was an actress? That this was a stunt? Could they go for a coffee afterwards?

A dark shape flitted overhead, gone before Lori got a clear look. That was it? Were they shooting at birds? She scrambled to her knees for a better view.

They were not birds.

Lori had no idea what the flying creatures were, but they most certainly were not birds.

A flock swooped around the wagon. She had misjudged the size on her fleeting glimpse, assuming the black shape nearer than it was. The creatures were as large as a human, with batlike wings fanning out in place of arms. They were skeletally thin, shaped like the outline of shrouded, black, flying corpses.

One plunged straight at the wagon. Caught between horror and shock, Lori was riveted to the spot. The creature was devoid of detail. It was a hole in the sky, rushing in to swallow her. She had to duck out of its way, but could not move.

The blast of a pistol. The hole twisted around on itself and vanished. In a daze, Lori watched Tamsin focus on her next target and fire again. Her shots were punctuated by the roar of the shotgun. Suddenly, the shapes clustered in a tight group and vanished into the fog.

Tamsin lowered her gun. "That's it. They're going."

"Nasty little buggers," Finn spat.

"You can say that again." Tamsin returned her pistol to its holster. "They're breeding again. I'll sort out a hunting party once we get to Caersiddi."

"Oh, goody," Hippo said cheerfully.

Lori remained frozen on her knees. What had just happened? She was hallucinating. She had to be. They had slipped something in her beer at the pub, or maybe was she having a nightmare.

Tamsin put a hand under her armpit and urged her back onto the bench. "Are you all right?"

"What were they?"

"Slua."

"And what the hell are slua?"

"What Finn said—nasty little buggers." Tamsin was grinning. "They exist in the space between the worlds. In ones and twos, they keep out of the way. But when their numbers go up, they start making trouble. As for what they are..." She shrugged. "Who knows? But they vanish when you shoot them, and that's good enough for me."

"But..." Lori buried her face in her hands. Somebody was crazy, and she had to accept the possibility that the somebody might be herself.

Tamsin patted her shoulder. "It's okay. You'll get used to it."

The wagon lurched forward. Lori raised her head. After travelling in their private pocket of sunlight for so long, they were finally about to enter the fog. Rolling mist flowed into the wagon, and then the cloud wall engulfed them, deadening the sound of wheels and the clop of horses' hooves. Tamsin became a dim shadow on the seat opposite.

Lori had read that, despite the way they seem, dreams only lasted a short while—ninety seconds or so. The time for this one to end was long past. Yet, stubbornly, the dream kept going. *Now. I need to wake up now.*

Sounds sharpened as the light returned. A few more yards and the grey wall parted.

The wagon trundled down a gentle, grassy slope, between two rows of standing stones. Overhead, white puffy clouds drifted across the bluest sky Lori had ever seen. A range of snow-capped mountains lined the horizon on either side. Directly ahead, the grassland rolled on until it met silver waters, sparkling in the sunlight. Was it a lake, or the sea? She could not see the opposite shore.

A knot of guards stood nearby. They were dressed in a similar fashion to Tamsin and the others, with the addition of a silver breastplate, chain mail sporran, and Roman style helmet. The armour was bizarrely incongruous with the automatic rifles they all carried. One had an ornate crest on his helmet, which presumably made him an officer. He hailed Tamsin with an informal salute, then waved the wagon by. The dogs padded on behind.

Lori looked back. Billowing fog was still framed between the two standing stones at the top of the avenue. Beyond them, the grassland gave way to a wood. Nowhere was there a hint of houses, farms, hedgerows, or roads.

Tamsin tapped her knee and pointed. "There. See on the promontory overlooking the sea, about two miles away. That's Caersiddi."

The castle looked as if it had grown, rather than been built. The collection of towers and battlements was constructed from the same white rock it stood on, carrying an unbroken upwards sweep from the waves. She was certain it had never appeared in any tourist guide to the historic sights of England.

Lori swallowed. "I guess we're not in Dorset any more."

❖

The wagon continued its approach along the shoreline. On closer viewing, the castle had to be real. If Caersiddi was a product of her imagination, then Lori disowned her subconscious—being drugged or dreaming was no excuse. Even Ludwig II of Bavaria would have dismissed the plans as preposterous. Had the builder never heard of gravity? A child might fall for such a storybook fantasy, but one hit from a trebuchet and the elegant towers would be a heap of rubble.

The castle stood atop a promontory, overlooking the sea. At its highest point, the cliff easily soared two hundred feet above the waves. Battlements and buildings formed tiers like a wedding cake, with an ethereal, fairytale keep cresting the peak. Brightly coloured banners fluttered from too many turrets to count.

On the landward approach, the lowest ring of fortifications formed a curtain around the base of the headland. At either end, graceful buttresses emerged from the water. Everything was built from polished marble, all the more startling in contrast with the blood-red tiles on the pointed roofs. The white stone sparkled in the light of the setting sun.

Lori did a mental double take. Setting? "Is it evening already?" Surely they had not been on the road that long.

Tamsin smiled. "It is here. And back in Dorstanley, it'll be the second nightfall after you did your trot around Hobs Geat."

"What?"

"Time doesn't flow at the same rate between the two worlds. A month passes on Earth in the space of a day on Annwyn. You can leave Caersiddi after breakfast, spend a week on Earth, and still be home in time for dinner. Widget can take as long as he needs sending emails, arranging postcards from abroad, moving your car, stuff like that, and still only be half a day behind us getting back."

"That's…" Impossible? She might be drugged and hallucinating—it would be the easiest explanation—but she could no longer ignore the possibility that everything Tamsin told her was true.

"The flipside is you can't spend much time in Annwyn if you want to go back to the Earth you knew. Like in my own case. I was born during the Civil War—"

"The American Civil War?"

"No. The English one."

"That was over three hundred and fifty years ago."

"Yup." Tamsin's grin broadened. "Are you going to tell me I'm aging well?"

"I, umm…" Far and away, the best looking tri-centenarian Lori had ever seen. There were not many thirty-five-year-olds who came close either. Lori looked away. Maybe Tamsin was not utterly bat-shit crazy, but she was still a kidnapper, and she was still dangerous. The Stockholm Syndrome was a trap—armed, baited, and ready for her.

"I'd look even younger if I hadn't been splitting time between here and Earth, setting up investments."

"Investments?"

"For when I retire. I can't be a soldier forever. Queen Rianna has let me spend enough time on Earth to arrange things. The crackdown on money laundering makes gold a little tricky to dispose of. But I've got front companies in my name, and a couple of California gold mines that had supposedly run dry. I bought them and suddenly they're churning out gold by the barrelful. It works as far as the IRS and FBI are concerned. We can help you sort out what to do with your reward from the queen when you return to Earth."

Tamsin had said when, not if, which was encouraging, but how long would it be? In six fairy-months, fifteen years would elapse on Earth, and the task might easily take her that much time. Even if she got home with a wagonload of gold, how could she explain her absence? *Welcome to Fairyland.*

"This is the source of those folktales, isn't it? Thomas the Rhymer, Rip Van Winkle. It's based on people who've been to Annwyn and returned."

"In part. Some is just people making stuff up. I mean, there's dragons, hellhounds, boggarts, things like that. But no unicorns."

A shame. As a child, Lori had wanted a pet unicorn. Her first real disillusionment with travel had come from learning there was nowhere she could go to find one.

Her childhood had been a sequence of huge, snowy mountains, more miles of dry desert, ever denser forests full of insects she was not allowed to touch, different piles of falling down walls that were even older than Grandma. What was the point? No matter how far you went, you were still limited to what was already there. The very first video game Lori worked on, she had insisted on unicorns.

Mum and Dad could not understand why she did not want to travel. They had shown her the world and she was not interested. At first, Dad called it teenage rebelliousness—which he would have approved of, had it taken any other outlet. Mum felt it more personally, as rejection and criticism. It was not, of course. It was all far more complicated. Would she get another chance to explain it to them?

"Are you okay?" Tamsin must have seen her expression waver.

"I was thinking about my parents. We haven't met up for nearly a year. They've been abroad. I'm wondering if I'll ever see them again."

"Ah, yes. That. Sorry." Tamsin sounded genuinely apologetic. "Are your parents old?"

"Mid fifties."

"Hopefully, the decoding won't take you long. You should be back before they're claiming their pensions."

And on the other hand, she might not.

The shadow of the gatehouse fell over them as the wagon reached the castle. The silver teeth of a portcullis hung overhead. The ornate metalwork was clearly designed for show rather than defence. As in every other architectural detail, Caersiddi was too pretty to be taken seriously.

Guards with silver breastplates and helmets stood on either side, looking suitably medieval, apart from their machine guns. They saluted as the wagon rolled past. Lori looked back over the route they had come. The sun was dropping, stretching the shadows. A first thickening of dusk gathered under the distant trees. The framed patch of fog where they had arrived was now just a blur on the hillside, but still in comfortable walking distance.

If she got the chance to escape, should she take it? The grassland offered little in the way of cover, so getting by the guards unseen would not be easy. Maybe she could sneak past at night. But then there were the slua. Lori closed her eyes, trying to block out the memory. No—the journey was far too dangerous to attempt without an armed escort.

She was a captive in fairyland. Mum and Dad would be so jealous.

CHAPTER SIX

Finn brought the wagon to a halt just inside the gates. The large outer bailey of the castle was markedly less pretty and more practical than might be expected from the ethereal fantasy of the exterior. This was evidently where the unromantic, day to day army life took place. The walls were lined with stores, stables, and workshops. One corner had rows of low buildings that were possibly barracks.

Soldiers on the drill ground looked to be winding down their exercises for the day and the nearby target ranges stood empty. However, the clang of metal and rush of bellows still resounded from an open fronted smithy, and the chimney of a large, double-barrel roofed building was venting a thick column of smoke.

Several people nearby were without breastplate and helmet. Lori saw that, like the Silver Ravens, all wore iron torcs, but not the distinctive belt buckles at their waist. Evidently, these were Iron Ravens, ordinary grunts not up to hazardous covert missions such as kidnapping unarmed computer programmers.

As yet, the terrain was mainly flat, rising slightly toward the next ring of battlements. A well-worn path cut a straight line through the military encampment to another gatehouse, even more ornate than the first. The ground was hard packed dirt, scored with ruts and hoof prints. A few trampled blades of grass were the only greenery.

Lori's gaze travelled on. The castle rose above her tier upon tier, wall behind wall, with the impossible fairytale keep hanging over it all, a silhouette against the sunset. The last rays of daylight hit the tops of the turrets, burnishing the red tiles. Lanterns appeared in the deepening shadows.

Tamsin swung herself over the side of the wagon. "I'll be back in a minute. Wait here with Hippo." She disappeared through a doorway on the inside of the gatehouse, with Finn following close on her heels.

Hippo came around to the back and slipped a bolt, letting the tailboard drop. "Do you want a hand down?" He offered his arm.

"I can manage." She was not a delicate maiden, at risk of fainting.

In some strange way, having her feet on the ground, made it all seem more real. Now that she no longer had the protective sides of the wagon around her, some part of her mind finally gave up on the pretence that she was on a ride at a theme park. She put her hands in the pockets of her raincoat and tried to act calm. Whistling would be overdoing it.

A woman wearing huge leather gauntlets led away the red-eyed mastiffs.

"Why did you have the dogs along?" Lori asked.

"To scare off the grey reivers." Hippo sounded cheerfully unconcerned.

"Are they like the slua?"

"Nope."

"Do I want to know about them?"

"Nope."

"But it'll be safe for Widget and the others without them?"

"They'll be on horseback, without the wagon. They can outrun the reivers easily."

So all she had to do was steal a fast horse and get it past the guards without being seen. Thoughts of returning to Earth on her own took a further step back.

Three small figures came out of nowhere and rushed towards her. Children? Here? Instantly, surprise switched to shock. She was mistaken. They were not children. They were not human. Lori stumbled out of their way, almost falling. However, the creatures ignored her and leapt into the wagon.

They were short, four feet tall at most, and scrawny, all arms, legs, knees, and elbows. Their skin was dull, mottled green. Sparse ringlets of dull brown hair were plastered to their heads. Ragged clothes flapped around their limbs. One leered down at her from the wagon and gibbered something. Its face was too wide and too flat. Its eyes were slits, and its nose a blob. Its mouth was filled with teeth, pointed like needles.

Each creature grabbed a sack then scuttled away in the direction of the stores.

"Are they fay?" If so, they were nothing like Lori had imagined.

Hippo laughed. "No. Of course not. They're boggarts."

"Boggarts?"

"They're mostly harmless, if you're wearing a torc. Don't worry, you'll get used to them. They do the donkey work round here, as long as somebody keeps a watch on them. Otherwise they'd just loaf around, scratching their arses." He beckoned for her to stand back. "Come on. We'll leave them to it."

The boggarts returned for a second round of sacks, chattering among themselves. Hippo ignored them and, with a sweep of his arm, indicated the whole castle. "So, Lauren. What do you think of Caersiddi?"

"It's umm…" *Not where I expected to end up when I left Adam's this morning—or whenever it was.* "Impressive. And you can call me Lori."

"I'm Hippo."

Yes. I know. "That can't be your real name."

He laughed. "Of course not. We all get nicknames. You'll get one too, if you stay here long enough."

Something to look forward to. "Why Hippo?"

"The guys saw me dancing."

"And the other Silver Ravens? They all have nicknames too."

"Well, Shorty stands for itself. Same as Widget—that's a slang term for a bit of equipment."

Or a GUI control. She nodded. Hippo might not be the brightest bulb on the Christmas tree, but, if nothing else, he was friendly. "What about Finn? Is that his real name?"

"Nah. The story goes, when he first came to Annwyn he was a bit overweight. He told someone he'd like to be thin, but he couldn't pronounce his tee-haitches.

"Finn? Overweight?" He was not now.

"It was a long time ago. Anyway, he got his wish. All it took was exercise and healthy living."

"The other woman in your group? BH, wasn't it? Are those her initials?"

"She's our tracker. BH stands for bloodhound. She grew up hunting kangaroos across the desert."

So it was sparkling wit and sophisticated humour all round. "Australian."

"Yup. Except her people had another name for it back when she came through. She's been in Annwyn longer than anyone else. She looked after me when I was a baby."

"You were born here?"

He shook his head. "Nobody is. Annwyn mucks up women's cycles, if you know what I mean." He blushed faintly. "You should ask the other women about it."

"How did you get here as a baby? Did you crawl around a standing stone?"

"There's a cave with an underground river that used to be a portal. I was put in a basket and left to float through."

"Why?"

"Probably an offering to the djinn. That's what the desert folk called the fay." He shrugged. "Or maybe they had something personal against me or my parents. I can't go and ask. They'd all have snuffed it eons ago."

The boggarts finished unloading. Lori took a seat on the tailboard of the empty wagon. The door in the gatehouse remained closed. What was going to happen now?

"So Tamsin's the only one who doesn't have a made up nickname. It's just a cut down version of her real—"

Hippo stopped her with a hand on her arm. "She's Captain when we're on duty, and Tazer when we're not. You should stick with Tamsin." He lowered his voice. "I overheard you ask what it was short for. You were taking a risk there. She's flattened people before over the other name. Still, she must like you if she owned up to it."

The ridiculous uptick to her pulse rate was followed by a flash of irritation. "She hasn't seen enough of me to like."

"The captain's quick to size folk up, and spot the wrong 'uns. It's one of the things that makes her good at the job. Take it from me, you're doing okay with her."

Well, she's not doing okay with me. I don't like being kidnapped. Tamsin was the leader of an armed mercenary gang. Only a gullible fool could imagine there was a chance of any sort of friendship between them. She had to keep a grip on the facts. She was being held against her will, and her first goal was to escape.

"The avenue of stones we came through, that's the only way to get to Earth?"

"Is now. There used to be portals dotted all over. Like I said, I came through on an underground river. For BH, there's a big rock in the desert that used to have a portal in it. But they've all been closed. Now there's just Hobs Geat left."

"Why?"

"Don't know. Queen Rianna must have a reason, and that's good enough for me." Hippo was also clearly infatuated with the queen.

The door in the gatehouse opened and Tamsin reappeared. "Sorry about the wait. I had things to sort out. I'll take you to Queen Rianna, now."

"Now? Isn't it a bit late?" An anxious flutter unsettled Lori's stomach.

"Don't worry She won't expect you to start work tonight. But she'll want to see you. She's keen to get the decoding done as quickly as possible."

"Right." *No pressure then.*

The guards on duty saluted as Tamsin led the way through the second gateway, Lori paused to take in her new surroundings. The change was startling. The outer bailey had been an army camp. This was a baroque fantasy garden.

The terrain rose in a series of terraces, interlinked by broad, winding stairways. Each tier was laid out with lawns, flower beds, ornamental trees, and statues of fantastic beasts. The scent of roses and honeysuckle carried on the breeze. Dozens of fountains cascaded between levels. The surrounding buildings were domestic in style rather than military, with large windows and open balconies.

Several groups of off-duty soldiers were relaxing in the garden. The sound of good-natured banter mingled with the splash of fountains and the twitter of birds. Two people lay under a tree, in a lovers' embrace, kissing passionately. Their gender was hard to state with one hundred percent certainty, but both appeared male. Of course, Tamsin and BH were hardly examples of fragile femininity. Regardless, nobody seemed at all bothered.

A few boggarts scuttled back and forth, heads down, knuckles almost dragging on the ground. They were cleaner and better dressed than those in the outer bailey. Each one wore a small black poncho, emblazoned with the symbol of a white raven. A memory dropped out of nowhere. Tabards—that's what the garments were called. The experience with fantasy role-playing games might prove more practical than ever expected. Although she could be excused for not anticipating her current situation.

"This is the middle bailey. Where we humans live." Tamsin pointed out a building with a large entrance porch. "That's the mess hall. And over there is the Silver Ravens' quarters. I expect you'll be given a room with us."

Better than a dungeon. One less thing to worry about.

"You don't need me any more, do you, Captain?" Hippo asked.

"No. Have a good night."

Hippo waved an informal salute and headed for the Silver Ravens' quarters, while Tamsin, Lori, and Finn zigzagged a route up through the garden, switching between flights of stairs. The steepness of the land increased as they climbed higher. At the top of the middle bailey stood another gatehouse.

The light was fading fast, and burning torches were set in brackets on either side of the arched entrance. This gate was also guarded by its complement of human soldiers. However, rather than salute and allow them through, one of the sentries called out. It sounded like a challenge, although the words were hard to make out.

A door set in the arch of the gatehouse opened, and somebody stepped out—somebody who could only be one of the fay. He was male, an assumption based more on clothing than looks. Surely fay women did not sport padded codpieces—at least, Lori assumed it was padded, and preferred not to take the thought further. His silken hose and loose shirt shimmered iridescent blue and green in the torchlight. His short cloak would make a peacock envious. It rippled dramatically in the breeze, but was unlikely to provide much in the way of warmth.

The fay's skin was pale blue. His hair was long and white. It was too dark to see his eyes, but Lori made a bet with herself they would turn out to be either silver or violet. He was the same height as Tamsin, five foot nine or so. His build was so light-boned that a description of "willowy" was inadequate. And, of course, he had pointed ears.

He held up his hand, showing off long, delicate fingers. "Alith da sei?" His musical voice was pitched higher than normal for humans. Lori did not need to understand what he said to pick up on the disdain in his tone.

Tamsin replied in the same language.

I'm going to need a translator while I'm here. Of course she would. Stupid to have not given it a moment's thought before. Universal English was one of the more unrealistic conventions of sci-fi films and TV.

The fay inclined his head to examine Lori. Judging by his expression, he was unimpressed, although possibly fay always looked as if they had just found something smelly on the sole of their shoe.

After a few seconds of silence, he said, "Ae esi calida," then stalked away. The door closed behind him.

Presumably, this was permission to proceed. Tamsin continued through the gatehouse. A push from Finn prompted Lori to follow.

Tamsin glanced back over her shoulder. "This is the inner bailey, where the fay live. As you saw, access is more tightly controlled. Humans aren't allowed to just wander around in here, but we're on the queen's business, and besides, we're her Silver Ravens."

The ground was now rising steeply, almost sheer in parts. The inner bailey took the form of a three-dimensional maze of stairways, verandas, patios, and ethereal towers linked by archways. Fountains of liquid light flowed from the mouths of stone dragons. Thornless roses climbed the walls. Banners hung from every window.

Lori tilted her head back. Turrets and balconies hung over her, lit by a myriad of candles, lanterns, and torches. Caersiddi was both exquisite and disquieting. The beauty came with too much sugar. She could not shake the feeling it was candy-coating, and that something quite different lay beneath the facade.

Boggart servants scurried around, ignored by haughty fay, who posed ornamentally at strategic points along the route. As expected, fay women did not wear padded codpieces. Instead they favoured flowing dresses in the distressed damsel style, made from same the shimmering rainbow material as the official at the gate. They watched the trio of humans pass, their faces masks of bored indifference. The fay were not endearing themselves. Was it valid to assign human emotions to their features? Fair or not, Lori preferred the boggarts.

Would Queen Rianna be any better? Tamsin had claimed so, but Tamsin was hardly a neutral observer. She was in love with her queen— that much was obvious. Still, this did not necessarily mean Tamsin was wrong, but something jarred. Red flags were fluttering.

They climbed yet one more flight of stairs, avoiding a pair of boggarts sweeping up rose petals. From her position a few steps behind, she had a good view of Tamsin's rear end. A very good view. Lori restrained a groan. *I need a slap.* Was it that simple? Jealousy? Welcome to the Stockholm Syndrome with added dyke drama—just possibly the very last thing she needed.

After a final assent, they reached a drawbridge spanning a chasm in the rock. On the other side lay the keep. The guards here were fay, armed with silver halberds. They eyed the humans with the same disdain as their fellows, but issued no challenge.

The keep's interior matched the outside. The first room was a large open lobby under a domed roof. A branching staircase swept up through two stories, joining ring galleries that marked the upper levels. In daytime, windows in the dome would let in light, but now crystal chandeliers provided illumination in shimmering rainbow colours. The arches, columns, and balconies were all beautifully proportioned. The marble floor tiles were polished to a sheen. Gold thread glinted in the wall hangings. The whole scene below just cried out for a troop of multicoloured miniature ponies to come prancing through, leaving behind multicoloured poop for an overworked boggart to shovel onto the roses outside.

Tamsin led them up the staircase to the top floor and then through a wide double doorway. This section of the keep rose higher than the lobby. They entered what was obviously the royal audience chamber. At the far end, a silver throne stood on a raised dais, lit by yet more chandeliers hanging from the high vaulted ceiling. Behind the throne was a huge stained glass window, decorated with floral patterns, although now the colours were lost to the night. On either side, a high gallery ran the length of the hall, presumably to provide spectators with a grandstand view, though at the moment, both floor and balconies were deserted.

Tamsin stopped a few yards from the empty throne.

Lori stopped beside her. "Do we need to let someone know we're here?"

"Don't worry. Her Majesty will have been told."

"Right."

For a while, nothing happened, except for Lori's hands getting sticky and her stomach developing a lump.

A sudden bustle of activity sounded from an open archway. Tamsin and Finn dropped to one knee, heads bowed. Lori did not need Tamsin's sharp gesture to work out she was supposed to do the same. Her heart hammered in her chest. Supposing Queen Rianna decided she was not up to the job. Would she be sent back to Earth or simply disposed of as a waste of time?

"Tal cello a da." How could such a high, tinkling voice be so authoritative? Presumably, it was permission to stand, since Tamsin and Finn both got to their feet.

Queen Rianna was seated on her throne. An elderly male attendant stood on either side, and a gaggle of fay clustered in the background.

I don't like her. An instant gut reaction. *Nobody with pointed ears and blue skin should be that attractive.* Maybe it was the cheekbones so sharp you could use them to slice fruit, or the perfect bow of her lips. Her skin was flawless, as long as you were not put off by the colour. Had Rianna been human, Lori would have guessed her age on the low side of forty.

Tamsin gave a bow and spouted something lengthy.

The queen's eyes fixed on Lori. Her smile might not count as a sneer, but neither was it warm or reassuring—more the smile a biologist bestowed on her favourite lab rat. "Ealon na talina seila de."

If the queen expected a reply, she was out of luck.

Queen Rianna slithered from her throne and circled the group of humans. Her hips swayed with each slow step, setting off a kaleidoscope of swirling colour in her dress. Lori forced herself to stand still, battling the overwhelming urge to turn, keeping the queen in sight. Rianna's gaze was an itch between her shoulder blades.

The queen completed her circuit and stepped close. "Dion ae palloni, de sei? A cali."

If a woman in a bar had used the same tone, Lori would have taken it as blatant flirting. Did the same rules work with the fay? If so, she was not interested. However, she had won her private bet—the fay's eyes were a brilliant violet.

"Her Majesty wishes to know if you're willing to accept this task for her." Tamsin gave the translation.

"Tell her I'll do my best." Like there was a choice.

"Ae esi." The queen returned to her throne, although she remained standing. She rattled off another stream in whatever the fay language was called.

"Her Majesty says, if you succeed, you'll be given you your weight in gold as a reward."

And if I don't? Probably wiser not to ask.

"You're to be at the gates of the inner bailey tomorrow morning, after breakfast. Somebody will meet you and show you where you'll be working."

"I'll be there."

Queen Rianna turned to leave, but then looked back, fixing Lori with her eyes. "Kallio na chivas da calido. Dioletia dano annwyna falisi lo talina."

"Her Majesty says, do not underestimate the importance of this task. The fate of her kingdom hangs on your success."

So you'll be royally pissed off if I fail. That part did not need a translation.

Queen Rianna and her entourage left the hall.

Nothing else was said until they were back in the middle bailey. By now, true dark had fallen. The only light came from a few wavering torches. No moon had risen, and the sky was ablaze with a glittering array of stars, brighter than anything seen on Earth.

Finn nodded in Lori's direction. "Are you wanting me to sort out her room?"

I do have a name.

"I'll do it," Tamsin said. "You can take yourself off. I'll see you tomorrow on the target range."

"Right you are then, Tazer." Finn strolled away.

Tamsin showed Lori to a room on the second floor of the Silver Ravens' quarters decorated like a set from a low-budget Robin Hood film. The dark oak and white plaster walls were smoke blackened over the stone fireplace. The floorboards were old and warped, with stains partly concealed by a large rush mat. The four-poster bed and iron bound chest both looked suitably medieval. The only other furniture was a wooden chair and small table. After Adam's spare room, the absence of clutter was a relief.

The bay window would overlook the garden in daylight, but was now a dark mirror, reflecting back light from the wagon-wheel candelabra hanging in the middle of the room. Decoration consisted of three animal heads—a boar, a deer, and something Lori could not put a name to, despite her work on fantasy games. While a TV set would have ruined the Robin Hood ambience, there was not as much as a bookshelf by way of entertainment. Nor was there an adjoining room. It prompted a question that had been growing steadily more urgent.

"Where's the ladies'?" she asked.

"Which ladies?"

"The toilet? W.C? Restrooms?"

The confusion cleared from Tamsin's face. "Oh. That. There'll be a chamber pot under your bed."

"A chamber pot!" Something else that got overlooked in Robin bloody Hood movies.

"The boggarts who clean your room will empty it."

"I'm not…" It was pointless—what choice did she have?

"There's a flagon of water and washbowl." Tamsin pointed to plain white porcelain sitting on the table. "And a bar of soap should be around somewhere."

"Rather than software engineers, maybe you could kidnap a couple of plumbers next time."

"You're not the first to suggest that. Some way back, a team of Roman engineers built a bathhouse in the outer bailey. There's an adjoining lavatory block with running water. But you might not want to go wandering around in the dark. We still don't have street lighting."

Suddenly, everything was more than Lori could take. She fixed her eyes on the ceiling, fighting to maintain self-control. Was it too much to hope that she had unknowingly eaten a plate of dodgy mushrooms and was suffering from hallucinations? Maybe she would wake up in A&E.

Tamsin placed a hand gently on her shoulder, claiming her attention. "If you want, I'll take you to the latrine. Show you the way." Her voice was softer than before.

Lori pinched the bridge of her nose, hoping to furtively dislodge any tears. "Thanks. It's all right. I'm sure I'll cope." As a child, she had spent enough time camping and living in places without modern facilities. Back then, it had all seemed one big adventure. She just needed to recapture that spirit.

"You're going to find it tough at first. I know. It wasn't so hard for me. Day to day life isn't that different from how it was on Earth when I was born. It was everything else I had to deal with. I had to let go of a lot of certainties, especially after growing up with the Puritans in charge. But I soon saw that in a lot of ways it's better here. I can forget the priests pounding the pulpits with all their 'thou shalt nots.' I wear clothes I can run in. And nobody wants to set some poor sod on fire for being a witch—something I really appreciate, what with being a woman."

Which Lori did not need reminding of. The touch of Tamsin's hand on her shoulder was sending ripples down her spine. She battled to keep her tone light. "I think I'm going to struggle. I'm already getting separation anxiety about email."

"Widget will sympathize with you there. I wouldn't be surprised if he hangs around on Earth for an extra day or two, just to get his fix of the internet."

"Is he a recent arrival here?"

"No, just a nerd born ahead of his time. If I remember correctly, he was a friend of Charles Babbage when they were students at Cambridge together, except Widget ended up in Annwyn and never completed his studies."

"Babbage!" Lori covered her eyes with one hand. It was all too weird.

"Give yourself time. It'll get easier, and I'm here, if ever you need someone to talk to." Tamsin's voice was soft and sincere, a marked change from the self-assured captain of fairyland special forces. This conversation had the potential to take a dangerous turn.

The ripples down Lori's spine flared out, down her arms and legs. Her knees buckled. She stumbled forward and somehow managed to stay upright as far as the window. She braced a shoulder against the wall for support and stood with her back to the room, but her eyes were fixed on the reflection in the glass. Tamsin was far too attractive, and not at all the sort of woman Lori wanted to get involved with. The last thing she needed was to add one more entry on her sorry list of lousy, fucked-up relationships.

"I don't want time. I want to get back to earth ASAP. I've got family and friends waiting for me."

"You're fortunate. I didn't have any close family. My father ran off right after I was born. I never knew him. And Ma had died the previous winter."

"That's tough."

"They were tough times. The Silver Ravens are my family now." Tamsin's voice strengthened. "But I promise. I brought you here. Once you've finished the decoding, I'll take you back. If you want to go."

"You think there's any doubt?"

"You might find yourself falling in love."

"With who?" Lori managed to keep her voice steady, though her stomach did a bounce. Was Tamsin offering herself?

"With Annwyn. And maybe a little with Queen Rianna. It happens to everyone after a while."

Right. Her stomach returned to normal. No guesses as to who Tamsin had fallen in love with. "Maybe." *But don't hold your breath.*

"You'd make a welcome addition to the population of Caersiddi."

"Nice of you to say so. But you'll have to abduct other recruits if you want someone to stay." Lori pushed away from the window. "For now, I'll need to make use of the chamber pot."

"Of course." Tamsin turned to the door. "I'll see you get to the inner bailey gate tomorrow."

"Wait. One more thing before you go. What about food?"

"Hot meals are served in the mess hall. You'll hear the bell chime when they're ready. Any other time, you can have the boggarts bring you a tray. I'll have one sent to you now." The door closed behind Tamsin.

Once alone, Lori peered under the bed. The chamber pot was—thankfully—empty, though it did not remain this way for long. Balancing on your toes was the tricky part, just like when she was a child, using the squat toilets in various regions around the world. Of all the things she did not understand about her parents, their indifference to modern plumbing came high on the list. She slid the pot back under the bed. So much for promising herself to never again stay anywhere without hot and cold running water.

The door opened and a boggart tottered in carrying a wooden tray laid out with bread and cheese, along with slices of meat, fruit, something gooey in a bowl, and something else looking like cake. There was also a carafe of red liquid, which Lori very much hoped was wine. A drink was definitely in order, and probably more than one.

The boggart put down the tray and burbled at her.

"I'm sorry. I don't understand."

It burbled some more.

"This is fine. You can go." She made a shooing gesture, hoping it would get the message.

Still, the boggart did not leave and was clearly waiting for something—a tip? A niggling anxiety woke in Lori's stomach. The boggart's pose was non-threatening, but that was no guarantee it would not attack her. Like being left alone with a strange dog, the important thing was to stay calm.

She spoke clearly and firmly. "Go away."

The boggart flinched, then sidestepped around the bed, pulled out the chamber pot, and scuttled away. Clearly, it was an all-purpose domestic servant.

Lori stared at the food tray. Did she want to risk eating it? She had the washbasin for herself, but there was no point going after the boggart to ask if it had cleaned its hands recently. Her options were to eat what was on offer or go hungry. The same situation would apply as long as she remained in Annwyn, which might be quite a while.

Lori sucked in a deep breath. *Stay optimistic.* Maybe the fay had magical cures for food poisoning. She had been promised her weight in gold. This was no time to go on a diet.

CHAPTER SEVEN

Roars from the mess hall sounded as if a football match was taking place inside. Only the snatches of laughter reassured Lori it was not a full-on fight. So much for a relaxing breakfast to clear her thoughts before tackling the decoding. However, her only other option was another meal of bread, cheese, and cold meat in her room. After offering up a prayer to the goddess of nutrition—*please let the food be worth it*—she pulled open the door.

The scene was every bit as chaotic as the sound suggested. Rows of tables were filled with animated diners. Ages ranged from late teens to early fifties. Everyone was shouting, presumably to be heard over the people around them, who were also shouting. All were clearly fit and healthy. Men outnumbered women two to one, and black leather clothing was universal. It could have passed for an international bikers' convention. Possibly half the people were of European origin, but every other region was represented as well. The only non-humans were boggarts, scampering up and down between the rows.

Forget it. This isn't worth it. Lori was about to turn and leave, but then spotted Hippo, beckoning her over to the corner where he was sitting with BH and Shorty. Clearly, the other soldiers did not mingle with the Silver Ravens. No one else was near their end of a table, although elsewhere the benches were crammed full.

"Hey. You made it to breakfast." Hippo greeted her with a wide smile.

No. I'm still asleep in my room. Lori settled for a smile in reply as she slid onto the bench opposite him. So what if he was stating the obvious? His welcome was genuinely friendly, whereas Shorty and

BH merely nodded at her and went back to their conversation, in what sounded like the fay language.

The only thing on the menu appeared to be the contents of a large ceramic stewpot that stood in the middle of the table next to a basket of hollowed out bread rolls. From watching the others, Lori learned the rolls were used in place of bowls. She took one and ladled in a helping from the pot. A passing boggart dropped a spoon beside her

"Ready to start work?" Hippo asked.

"I guess so." Lori took a cautious sip. The stew tasted more like spicy fish than anything else she could put a name to. Not the most conventional of breakfasts, but not too bad either.

"Good luck with that." BH spoke in clipped English.

"Thanks. I think I'll need it."

Shorty joined in. "Rather you than me. That's for sure."

BH and Shorty lacked Hippo's warmth, but neither were they hostile—unlike Finn. His absence was a definite plus for Lori.

"That was the fay language you were speaking just now?"

BH nodded. "Hyannish."

"We use English when we don't want the little fuckers to eavesdrop." Shorty indicated a passing boggart.

Or when talking to captured computer programmers.

"But people keep changing the language." Shorty sounded as if it was a personal insult. "Take 'wicked.' For fuck's sake. Why can't they leave the meaning alone?"

"You'll do fine as long as they don't change the meaning of the word 'fuck,'" Hippo said. Lori had already noted it was Shorty's favourite adjective.

BH smiled. "It could be worse. You could have started with, 'whan that Aprille with his shoures soote, the droghte of Marche hath perced to the roote.' I've been playing this game longer than you."

Another boggart slid a tankard onto the table beside Lori. She sniffed it cautiously. "Beer? For breakfast?"

"Safest thing to drink round here," Hippo said.

"I don't suppose there's tea, or coffee?"

"Correct. There isn't." Tamsin had arrived. She dropped onto the bench beside Hippo and smiled across the table.

Lori's stomach betrayed her with a mini-flip. *No. Not interested. Don't go there.* She concentrated on her food. The inside of the roll had soaked up liquid from the stew.

"You can eat the bread if you want." BH must have seen her looking.

"And what you leave the boggarts will have," Hippo added.

Saves on the washing up.

"Where's Widget?" Tamsin asked.

"Playing with some new toys he picked up," BH replied.

"And Finn?"

BH's mouth curved into a lopsided smile. "Guess."

Tamsin laughed. "Right."

Finn's whereabouts were clearly some sort of open secret.

Lori chewed a little from the rim of her bread bowl, but it was too hard baked to be worth the effort, even with the stew to soften it. What she had eaten would do. She downed half the beer, hoping it was not too alcoholic. "I'd better be making a move."

"I'll come with you." Tamsin also rose.

"It's okay. You have your breakfast."

"It can wait."

Lori caught the glances shared between the other Silver Ravens. BH muttered something in the fay language that raised a laugh from Hippo and Shorty, and an expression of hurt innocence from Tamsin. There were various ways to interpret this interplay, none of which Lori wanted to pursue.

Tamsin fell into step beside her as they walked in silence, climbing stairs through the garden. The way Lori's body reacted to their closeness was just one more thing on her list of things to worry about—as if she did not have enough. "Do you know what language the encoded text is written in?"

Tamsin shook her head. "I know nothing about it."

"Length?"

"No."

"Who wrote it?"

"No."

"Why the que—"

"No. Honestly. I don't know the first thing." Her tone made it clear the subject was finished. If Queen Rianna was keeping secrets from her special forces, Tamsin was not about to question it.

They reached the gateway to the inner bailey. The fay official who came out to challenge them might have been the same one as on the previous evening. The look of contempt on his face was identical. He had a brief conversation with Tamsin.

She turned to Lori. "It's all cleared for you to enter. Just follow the boggart."

The guide in question was shuffling around inside the gates. The creature scurried off, but then stopped after a few yards, looking back, waiting for her. In the other direction, Tamsin returned down the steps, towards the mess hall.

Wait! Can't you come with me? Lori bit back the words. The thought of being alone with the fay queen was deeply unsettling, but asking Tamsin to hold her hand was both childish and pointless. *Time to put your big-girl pants on.* Lori squared her shoulders.

As on the previous evening, her boggart guide took her over the drawbridge to the keep, However, rather than ascend the main staircase in the lobby, she was led through a small side door. The change in decor was immediately apparent. Ornate floor tiles were replaced by slate, and the walls were simple white plaster. While far from run down, this was clearly where the mundane side of castle life went on.

They passed a hive of boggart activity in the kitchens, before climbing a narrow spiral staircase, finally emerging on the left-hand balcony overlooking the deserted audience chamber. Daylight through the stained glass window now splashed red, yellow, and blue bands across walls and floor. Several doorways peppered the back wall of the gallery. The one they had just come through was the smallest, wedged onto a corner, and disguised to be as unobtrusive as possible.

I get it. I only qualify for the servants' entrance.

No obvious staircase led to the main floor of the hall. Possibly it lay behind the door at the far end of the gallery. However, this remained a conjecture since, rather than leading her down, the boggart stopped outside an intervening doorway and babbled at her.

"This is where I'm supposed to go?" A logical conclusion.

More babbling.

Okay. Take it as a yes. After a moment to compose herself, Lori knocked on the door.

No one replied.

What next? She looked down at the boggart, who looked up at her. After a long, awkward pause, the creature tugged at the handle and the door opened. This was clearly the extent of its job remit. The boggart scuttled away, leaving Lori alone on the deserted balcony.

Still no sound came from within. She must be the first to arrive. Lori took a deep breath and entered what appeared to be a study or small office. A table stood in the middle of the room, strewn with scrolls and loose papers. Bookcases, charts, and maps lined three sides. The other wall had French doors, giving access to a balcony overlooking the glittering sea. Beside the window stood a tall cabinet.

The room was unmistakably for work rather than entertainment— no comfy chairs or cushions. The stools pushed under the table were purely functional. The cabinet looked as if it was made from recycled castle gates and intended to withstand a siege. The solid timbers were studded with iron rivets. The table would have been more at home in a farmhouse kitchen. The floorboards were swept clean, but without carpets or matting.

Easily the most eye-catching feature of the room was the view. The right-hand side of the door was propped open, allowing a breeze to circulate. Lori stepped towards it, thinking to go onto the balcony, but stopped, realising she had been mistaken. She was not alone. A silent figure stood motionless in a corner.

He was human, in his fifties, and short for a man, no taller than Lori's own five foot five. His build and features were nondescript, apart from his large bulbous nose and shiny bald head. He was dressed in a style similar to the fay, except the material did not shimmer, and his codpiece was less well padded. The colours were subdued greens and greys. His expression was utterly blank. His brown eyes were transfixed on the wall behind Lori. She glanced over her shoulder but could spot nothing of note.

She turned back. "Good morning."

He gave the impression of not quite focusing on her. "Queen Rianna will be here shortly." His voice was a dull monotone.

Great. "I'm Lauren Cooper. You can call me Lori." She held out her hand.

The man did not respond.

She lowered her hand. "And you would be?"

Silence.

"Do you have a name?"

"Yes." More silence.

"What is your name?"

"I am called Gaius."

Gaius was either drugged or totally apathetic about life in general.

"Are you here to tell me about the document that needs decoding?" If so, unless he became more forthcoming, the task would be very tough going.

"Queen Rianna will be here shortly. She will provide all necessary instruction. I am here to assist."

"Right." This was going to be a bundle of laughs.

The study door opened and the queen swept in, minus retinue. Gaius bowed his head and stuck his clenched fist to his heart, making a solid thud. Was she supposed to kneel again or copy him? Gaius was not giving any hints. Hoping that going down on one knee was only required for public meetings, Lori settled for a less forceful version of his chest thump. She did not want to leave a bruise.

Without acknowledging either salute, Queen Rianna glided across the room. She pulled a key from a fine chain around her neck and unlocked the cabinet. The shelves inside held a diverse collection of objects, including a row of small stone statues, a fur hat, and what looked like a pair of rolled up rugs. Queen Rianna selected a scroll from a rack of diamond-shaped pigeonholes, then closed the cabinet door.

The queen placed the scroll on the table. "Keila tal lo ae yarile da calido."

"This is the text Her Majesty requires you to decode." Gaius gave the translation. Presumably, this was his sole reason for being there, since he was not doing anything else.

Lori nodded. "Yes, Your Majesty."

Queen Rianna spoke again.

"On no account may the scroll leave this room. Nor may you take notes or copies with you when you go. Her Majesty asks if you understand."

"Tell Her Majesty yes, I understand." *She trusts me just as much as I trust her.*

Gaius continued translating in his listless drone. "As soon as you discover the key to the code you must send word to Her Majesty. You do not need to decrypt the entire text."

You don't want me to read whatever it says. "Yes, Your Majesty."

"Her Majesty has assigned me to assist you. I will be with you at all times and will report to Her Majesty on your progress."

Or lack of it. Lori said nothing.

The queen handed the cabinet key to Gaius. Clearly, he was trusted, although from the way she acted, Gaius might have been a peg on the wall.

"Her Majesty hopes to hear from you shortly."

Queen Rianna turned to the door.

"Excuse me, Your Majesty."

Queen Rianna stared at Lori, her expression somewhere between surprise and offence. "Asita a palloni chi da calido."

Without understanding a word, Lori had no difficulty picking up on the reprimand. The queen was obviously unused to lesser folk addressing her without permission.

"Her Majesty says her instructions are clear. All that is required is for you to obey."

"Please apologise to Her Majesty for me, but I need some background information. The more I know about the contents of the scroll, the quicker I'll be able to decode it. I need to make informed guesses about likely words."

"Her Majesty says all your questions may be addressed to me."

This was not encouraging. It took three attempts to get Gaius to reveal his name.

Unexpectedly, the queen relented. "Her Majesty says the scroll was written by her great-great-great-grandmother, Morgaine, first High Queen of Annwyn. It contains information about a spell that is vital to the existence of Her Majesty's realm. Due to its importance, Queen Morgaine wrote the spell in code, and entrusted the secret to her son and heir. This knowledge has been passed down through the generations. Unfortunately, Her Majesty's noble father, King Orfran, died before he was able to instruct her in this matter." Gaius's voice was devoid of emotion. "This is all you need to know."

I'm pretty certain I need to know a damn sight more. However asking further questions was unwise. Lori's gut instinct told her the regal disdain was just a wafer thin veneer over a whole lot of malice, and she had no wish to find out if her gut was right. *And Tamsin thinks I might fall in love with her!* Yet Tamsin and the other Silver Ravens were obviously besotted. Grandma was right—when it came to matters of the heart, there really was no accounting for taste.

After the queen left, Lori pulled a stool from under the desk and unrolled the scroll. The parchment was covered in neat lines of runes. It was not the Roman alphabet, and there was not a chance in hell it was in English. Morgaine was Rianna's great-great-whatever-granny. By the time you applied the thirty to one time ratio between worlds, Morgaine would have lived while the ancestors of the Anglo-Saxons were still talking proto-Germanic.

"Gaius, do you know what language this is?"

"No." He did not glance at the scroll.

A surge of annoyance flared. She had a challenging job, a zombie for an assistant, and a nasty feeling her life depended on the outcome.

"Gaius, you're supposed to help me," she snapped. "That means putting a bit of effort into answering questions."

"I do not know for certain what language it is."

"Make a guess."

"Most likely, Queen Morgaine would have used Hyannish, the language of Annwyn."

Lori rested her forehead on her hand. "How can Queen Rianna expect me to decode the scroll when I don't understand the language it's written in?"

"I will translate for you. We must strive to fulfil Her Majesty's will. It is our duty."

Gaius's deadpan voice and expression did not disguise a rebuke. His prominent Adam's apple bobbed when he swallowed. Lori froze, suddenly spotting what was missing. Gaius was the first human she had met in Annwyn who was not wearing an iron torc.

Somebody was using magic to control him, and it required no guesswork to know who that somebody was. Was Rianna inside his head right now, spying on them? Or was Gaius like a robot on autopilot? She needed to find out more about fay magic, its limits and potential. But until she learned otherwise, it was safest to assume everything Gaius saw and heard would get back to the queen.

A quill and inkpot sat on the table. Lori slid them towards Gaius. "Right. Sit down. First thing. I want you to write out the fay alphabet. Let me know which letters are vowels and which are consonants. Then make a list of letters that often go together, like T and H in English."

Maybe because he had direct orders to work with, Gaius was quicker to respond, but his movements were still stilted. What was the right word? Sleepwalker? Puppet? Zombie? It confirmed everything she suspected about Rianna. The fay queen was not to be trusted.

Lori ran a hand through her hair. Maybe if she completed the decoding and got back to Earth she could arrange a rescue mission for Gaius and anyone else in his condition. *Yeah, right.* How would that work out, her walking into a police station, saying she needed troops to rescue magically controlled slaves from fairyland?

One step at a time. First, she had to decode the scroll, otherwise there was a distinct chance she would end up like Gaius. Lori walked to the window and stared out, racking her brains. Did she have any clues to work with? Anything in the scrap of information Rianna had passed on? Could she make a guess at any likely words?

Lori grinned. One word was obvious.

"Gaius. When you've finished the alphabet, I want you to write the name of the queen who wrote the scroll—Morgan was it?" *As in Morgan Le Fay?*

"Queen Morgaine."

"Okay. Put her name down."

If Queen Morgaine was anything like her descendant, her name was going to be on the scroll at least a dozen times.

One more good idea that did not work. Lori scrunched the sheet of paper into a ball and tossed it away. The previous fourteen hours had seen a lot of good ideas that did not work. Pages of notes littered the table. She rubbed her eyes. A headache grumbled at the top of her skull. The lighting did not help. Electricity was yet to reach Annwyn, and the twin oil lanterns hanging from the ceiling were completely inadequate, somehow managing to create more shadow than light.

At her side, Gaius sat bolt upright on his stool, with his hands folded in his lap and his eyes fixed on the wall. His face was the same blank mask it had been all day. What was going on inside his head? He spoke only when asked a direct question, except for offering a mild rebuke if anything Lori said could be construed as criticism of Queen Rianna. He was every bit as quick as Tamsin to take the role of queen's champion. He might be more pedantic and less emotional, but neither of them were able to accept any fault in Rianna. In Gaius's case it was understandable. What was Tamsin's excuse?

Lori adjusted the set of the iron torc around her neck. She only had Tamsin's word it was protecting her. Would she know if the queen was rifling through her thoughts at that moment? The headache had spread to Lori's temples. She rubbed circles with her thumbs, trying to massage it away. If Rianna was rooting around inside her head, was it too much to hope the queen was getting a fair share of the pain? Lori pushed back from the desk and walked onto the balcony. Fresh air might help.

The sun had set, though the last glow of sunset still lined the horizon. Overhead, stars pricked the midnight blue sky. No moon had yet risen. Was there one in Annwyn? She could ask.

Lori leaned against the balustrade and looked down. The study was not the only room to take advantage of the sea view. Other balconies girdled the walls of the keep, some in darkness, others lit with candles. Far, far below, white surf was luminous in the night as waves slapped against the rocks. The hiss and rumble of the sea had been a constant undercurrent while she worked.

A whole day had passed, a month on Earth. How convincing was Widget's false trail? It need not be that good, as far as Mum and Dad were concerned. They would be thrilled to think she had dropped everything and set off to see the world—as if she would willingly go a week without internet access! Adam knew her better, but Nathan would be there to downplay any doubts. How long before anyone contacted the police? Not that it would do the slightest bit of good.

Soft laughter rippled through the night. Lori moved to the other side of the balcony. One floor below was the largest terrace of all, lit by a dozen lanterns. More candles decorated a small round table. Their light reflected off a bottle and wine glasses. Queen Rianna lounged beside the table on a cushioned bench. Her head was turned, looking back into the room behind her. She laughed again and spoke to someone inside.

Lori had no wish to discover how a charge of spying on the queen would turn out. She could not understand a word said, but there was no guarantee it would work as a defence. She was about to return to the study, but before she could move away, Tamsin joined Rianna on the terrace.

Tamsin's loose white shirt rippled in the breeze off the sea as she uncorked the bottle, and poured a glass for Rianna. The relaxed body language made it clear they were not sticking to the strict roles of mistress and servant. Lori was unsurprised when Tamsin poured a second glass for herself, then strolled across the balcony with it and rested her elbow on the handrail, looking out over the dark sea. All the while, she and Rianna engaged in easy conversation.

What were they saying? Lori wanted to know, but at the same time could tell there was nothing worthwhile to be learned. The tone made it obvious Rianna and Tamsin were swapping idle gossip—who had said what about whom, or their shared opinion of someone's latest lover. Lori did not need to understand the words to be sure nothing more important was being discussed.

Rianna joined Tamsin at the railing, standing close. Very close. Her voice dropped low. Lori could not have overheard, regardless of the language. Rianna placed a forefinger on the back of Tamsin's hand—a small gesture, and one Lori had no trouble decoding. They were lovers. *Bloody typical.*

Lori spun away and went back into the study. No need to see more. Now she understood what prompted Tamsin's devotion. The rest of the Silver Ravens were equally smitten, but there was nothing to rule out the same underlying reason. Just how widely was Rianna putting herself about?

Gaius had not moved. Too late to worry about what he might report to the queen. She rested her hands on the table and stared at the strewn pages of notes. She needed new ideas, and they were not going to come that evening. Her headache had faded, but she could sense it ready to make a comeback. Everything could wait until tomorrow, after a decent night's sleep.

"I'm finished for today. I need to rest."

"Queen Rianna requires that you complete your task as quickly as possible. Idleness is not permitted." Another of Gaius's reprimands.

"I know. But I can't think when I'm tired. Staying here will only waste time. No matter how long I stare at the scroll I won't achieve anything more tonight. And if I don't get enough sleep, I'll be no better tomorrow."

"You will return tomorrow, after breakfast." His monotone could have been either a question or a command.

"Of course."

"I will arrange an escort to the middle bailey for you."

"Thank you." Lori suspected the guide was to stop her snooping around the keep rather than save her any distress from getting lost.

Gaius rang a silver handbell by the door, the same bell he had used to summon boggarts to bring food and drink during the day. He then returned the scroll to the cabinet, locked the door with the key Rianna had given him that morning, and waited in silence until a boggart arrived.

"Tali a deri lo venire es." He switched to English. "Accompany your guide."

"I'll see you here tomorrow then. Good night."

Gaius gave no response. Lori had not expected one.

As she retraced the route through the keep and inner bailey, Lori tried to picture Gaius laughing, relaxing with friends or a lover. All that was gone. Everything had been stripped from him—his mind, his humanity, his soul, all stolen. Rianna had turned a man into a brain-dead puppet. How could anyone willingly serve her? It meant that whatever integrity Tamsin possessed could be bought with a bit of bedroom action—which would set a new record for shameless harlotry in the sad line-up of Lori's previous girlfriends. Not as if there was much chance of Tamsin wanting to join the list.

Nope. No way. Isn't going to happen.

Anyway, two-timing the queen was not a clever move. Little imagination was needed to work out how that would end.

Chapter Eight

When Lori awoke the next morning, weak light was squeezing through gaps on the shutters and ghosting across the ceiling of her room. She stumbled out of bed and cracked open the wooden boards an inch to peek out. Bands of pink and purple clouds lined the horizon. The middle bailey was indistinct in the gloom.

Dawn represented quite a novelty. The time mismatch between Earth and Annwyn must be to blame, the fairyland equivalent of jet lag. Lori never had been a morning person—one more source of conflict between her and Jess, who could not understand why she refused to go for a jog before breakfast each day.

Breakfast. Lori shifted angle a little. The doors of the mess hall were closed and nobody was going in or out. How long before the boggarts started serving? The only food brought to the study the previous day had been bread and cheese, with an apple thrown in as a token gesture towards her five a day. Even a repeat of the fish stew would be welcome. Of course, tea was rapidly working its way towards the top of the list of things she could not live without, but she was out of luck there.

Her wristwatch lay on the table. Unexpectedly, the time said 8:25 a.m. Lori took it back to the light of the window to make sure. However, the seconds were advancing, so it was not a dead battery. Annwyn days must be longer than those on Earth.

Would the bathhouse be fired up and running this early? She was certainly in need of a wash. Her suitcase from the car and a couple of bags were stacked in a corner of her room. She had noticed them when she came in the night before, but had been too exhausted to investigate.

A note lay on top.

Hi Pet,

I picked out the stuff that looked most useful. Let me know if there's anything else you'd like, and I'll send word to Jimmo to put it in the next delivery from the Halfway House.

I hacked the password on your laptop, and reset it to StrawberryCrabcakes. Ditto your email. Sorry about the intrusion, but I had to set a false trail. Your parents think you're working on geo-imaging with the Antarctic Survey, and your friends think you're doing something very top secret with NASA in Area 51.

Cheers,
Widget

P.S. I saw you worked on games. That's dead awesome. We have to chat.

Fine. Just fine. Lori bit back a few other choice words. But she had to credit Widget with choosing stories that would be believed, mainly because they were what the respective audiences would like to think was true. Also both stories precluded any unexpected visitors dropping by.

She opened her suitcase. Her laptop was there, lying on top of her clothes. Had Widget left the battery fully charged? Not that it really mattered. There was no point asking the boggarts for the castle Wi-Fi code.

Lori picked out fresh clothes, going for comfy and familiar. The ancient ragged jeans and baggy T-shirt would not impress anyone, but she was no longer in job interview mode. The old clothes came with a set of reassuring memories, a link with Earth. She even had her lucky pound coin in the small pocket at the front—lucky in that it was there whenever she wanted a supermarket trolley. She rolled the clean clothes into a bundle around her toiletry bag and left her room.

She stopped at the gatehouse to the outer bailey for directions. "Which way is the bathhouse?"

The Iron Raven looked at her in confusion, then entered into a muttered debate with his comrade. "What you want?" English was evidently not his first language.

"The bathhouse." Would doing a mime help?

"There. Fire." He waved his hand in an upward gesture.

"Smoke?" Lori made a guess.

"Yes. Smoke."

"Thanks."

Lori set off happily. Not only was the trail of smoke an easy signpost, it carried the promise of hot water. Soon she reached the building with twin barrel roofs. Wisps of steam and the sound of voices drifted through the open doorway. She was not the only one taking an early bath.

A boggart shoved what was possibly a towel at her and burbled something.

"Um…I don't understand." Was it mime time now?

"Follow me. I'll show you where to go." A woman looking like an Asian Olympic champion shot-putter had entered the baths behind her—presumably one of the Iron Ravens.

"Thanks." Lori followed her to a large room. A bench ran around the outside.

"Leave your clothes there. Remember the number they're under. The hot pool's through there, and the cold plunge is on the right."

Hazy expectations of what the bathhouse might be like ran smack into memories of visiting the Roman remains at Bath—communal nude bathing. But her options were this or cold water and the washbasin in her room. Soap was probably out, but she could wash her hair later, and deodorant was in her bag. Regardless, she would end up cleaner and less smelly than she was at the moment, and, thankfully, it appeared the bathhouse was segregated into male and female sides.

Lori stripped off. On entering the next room, she was hit by a wall of hot, humid air. Clouds of steam rose from a large rectangular pool and the surrounding tiled floor was warm under her feet. A wide set of semi-circular steps entered the water at the midpoint. Diffuse light came from windows high in the roof.

Several women were already there, relaxing alone or chatting with friends. Lori descended the steps and drifted towards a corner. The water was hot and faintly scented.

"Didn't expect to see you here."

BH had her back resting against the wall about ten feet away. Tamsin was on her other side. Both were so low in the water that nothing was visible below shoulder height, but that did not make things any less awkward. However, she could hardly ignore them. Lori waded over to take up position beside BH—the advantage being she could keep her eyes on the far wall without it seeming obvious.

"I woke early and needed a wash."

"It's a good way to start the day."

Lori made a mental note to bathe in the evenings.

"How did things go yesterday?" Tamsin asked.

"No progress, I'm afraid."

"The queen needs the decoding done quickly."

"I know. But I've got very little to work with. Do you really know nothing about the scroll?"

"Didn't even know it was a scroll. Could have been carved on a stone."

"You didn't ask the queen about it?"

"Of course not. If we needed to know, we'd have been told."

Lori risked a quick glance sideways. BH was nodding in agreement. Asking them more was pointless. Besides, how much trust could she put in anything the queen might have told them?

So, what did you talk about in a Roman bath? "Any plans for today?"

"We're going to the border to cut down on the number of slua, and then—"

A boggart scurried into the room and knelt down by Tamsin's side. It whispered in her ear.

Tamsin pushed away from the wall. "I've got to go. The queen wants to see me." She levered herself out of the water and stood, wearing only the iron torc and a grin. "And I better not go like this."

Lori felt her face burning. What were the chances of passing it off as an effect of the heat? She ducked underwater, hoping to wash the image from her mind. Not that she wanted to, but it was safer. Tamsin was very nicely put together. The faint lines of a dozen scars did nothing to detract from her defined musculature and well balanced frame.

By the time Lori resurfaced, Tamsin was heading in the direction of the cold plunge pool. The rear view was every bit as good as the front. Maybe the queen would want her naked. The resulting wave of jealousy was the most stupid part of all, but the memory of Tamsin and Rianna on the balcony would not go away.

"Does Queen Rianna have a husband?"

BH laughed. "Hardly. Fay don't go for things like that."

"Husbands, or marriage?"

"The whole tied down monogamy bit."

"They have open relationships?" *Been there, done that.*

For two of Lori's exes, an open relationship translated as, "I sleep with who I like, and if you so much as look sideways at me, I'll guilt trip you with the full two-hour spiel on the evils of possessiveness and the history of the patriarchal oppression of women's sexuality. Whereas if you go with anyone else, although I wouldn't dream of being so hypocritical as to say a word about it, for weeks afterwards I'll pick arguments about your timekeeping, the laundry, TV channels, snoring, and a million other things." Lori had no trouble believing Rianna would fall into a similar pattern.

However, BH was shaking her head. "They don't do relationships at all. If a fay likes the look of somebody…" She smiled and shrugged one shoulder. "You know. Someone gets lucky for the night. No need to worry about husbands." Her smile broadened. "Are you fancying your luck?"

"No." Certainly not with Rianna.

"You wouldn't be the first human to fall for her." BH clearly did not believe her. "Or the first to get lucky."

How lucky had Tamsin been? "You're saying the queen—"

"No. I'm saying nothing. Our queen can be very generous. Leave it at that. But a queen's generosity…" her smile broadened, "…can be well worth having. Maybe you'll be lucky enough to find out for yourself."

Rather than try denying it, better to shift tack. "With no marriage, how do they work out who's next in line for the throne?"

"For the queens, it's easy. They know who their kiddies are. Kings have harems and name whichever child they like most as their heir. Or sometimes they'll pick a niece or nephew."

Rianna's father must have been strapped for choice if she was the best he could do.

BH was still smiling at her. "So how about you? Do you have a husband back on Earth?"

"No."

"A boyfriend?"

"No."

"A girlfriend then, or a wife? I hear that's the new big thing on Earth these days."

"No. But I split up with my last girlfriend a few weeks ago."

"Ah. So you like the ladies." BH sounded pleased. "You're not alone in that."

Several hundred thousand in the last Gay Pride march suggested as much. Lori did not bother saying anything.

"What was your girlfriend like?"

"Her name was Jess and she was a chartered accountant." Sad how that summed up everything of note about her.

"Why did you split up?"

"She ditched me for someone else." Which no longer hurt. How had she got over it so quickly?

"Had you been together long?"

"Best part of four years."

"Ohhh, that's tough. Still, you might find yourself a good woman here in Annwyn."

"I think I've got quite enough to handle without throwing more trouble into the mix."

BH laughed. "Don't be so hasty. You could be in with a chance—not that I'm speaking for myself. The only woman I've ever gone for had blue skin, if you get my drift. And I got lucky." *So Rianna has been putting herself about.* "But I can point you in the right direction for some women here, if you like."

"Thanks, but I'm really not looking at the moment." Lori was certainly not interested in the services of a volunteer matchmaker.

However, BH would not let it drop. "Tazer is the same way, you know. She prefers women."

Which, while not coming as a world shattering surprise, was still something Lori had not wanted confirmed. It only put additional strain on her self-control. "I don't plan on hanging around in Annwyn long enough to get involved with anyone."

"I wouldn't worry about plans. Just go with your heart."

Which was advice that could get you into all sorts of trouble. Lori gave a noncommittal "Hmmp."

"Ha, listen to you. But take me and Danny. He was one of the Iron Ravens. Lovely, lovely man. We were together years. And we had plans, oh yes. We had plans to retire together and spend our last years on Earth. But he came out second best in a fight with a basilisk. Now he's the most beautiful statue you'll ever see, and I've got no plans left."

"Oh. I'm sorry."

"It was six years ago. I'm coming to terms with him not being here." BH began wading in the direction of the steps. "But I've got to be going. If I stay in here any longer I'll turn into a stewed prune. See you at breakfast."

Lori leaned back, resting her head on the rim of the bath, and stared up at the ceiling. An unspecified number of humans had got lucky with the queen, and she had no doubt Tamsin was included in that tally. However, Tamsin did not just go for blue-skinned women. Lori ducked herself under the water in another futile attempt to blot out the world. As bad ideas went, a fling with Tamsin was a complete no-no, but the temptation was there.

❖

Lori's fingers were stiff. She had not written this much by hand since leaving school. The archaic equipment did not help. She copied the final entry onto the depressingly long list, then added multiple links on each of her cross-referencing sheets. At last, she put down the quill and sat, massaging her hand. Would she be allowed to bring a ballpoint pen with her next time?

"Okay. Going by the number of letters, this is every possible instance on the scroll that might be where Queen Morgaine wrote her own name. Right?"

"No."

"What?" She stared at Gaius in confusion.

"If Queen Morgaine wrote her own name it would be shorter."

If Lori had been holding something heavy, it would have taken all her self-control not to throw it at him. "Why did you tell me the wrong number of letters?"

"I did not."

"So how is it wrong? I told you what I was doing, didn't I?"

"You said you were picking out all the words of the same length as the queen's name." Gaius tapped Lori's notes. "This is the correct number of letters for her name with the addition of the submissive declension, which is the proper form you or I should use. Queen Morgaine would have used the possessive form of her name in writing."

"You've sat there all morning watching me. Why didn't you say something earlier?"

"You did not ask."

Lori shoved back from the table. "I need to talk to Queen Rianna."

Gaius's face showed no reaction. "You have news to give Her Majesty?"

"No. I have to explain something to her." Maybe it was unwise, but Lori was too angry to care.

"Her Majesty does not require explanations. She wants you to decode the scroll."

"That isn't going to happen unless we make some changes."

"It is not your place to make demands."

"It's not a demand. It's a statement of fact. This task is impossible as things stand at the moment."

Gaius froze for a few seconds then nodded. "I will inform the queen." He left the room.

Waiting his return, Lori stared out the window, stoking her anger as a defence against fear. She was in deep shit, with no clear way out. If only her tooth had behaved itself. If only she had ignored the bloody puzzles. If only she had not fallen into Tamsin's trap. It was too late for all that. Wishing was pointless.

The door opened. "Sien a cali ae talin da." Queen Rianna's voice could have bored holes in stone. She was not happy.

Gaius plodded in behind her. "Her Majesty wishes to know why you have requested her presence."

Lori took a deep breath. "Please. Thank the queen for granting my request so promptly. But I regret to say, it's impossible for me to decode the scroll with you as my only assistant." She waited for his translation before continuing. "It's not that you don't do everything I ask. It's that I have to explicitly ask for every scrap of information. I need help from someone who can play a proactive role. Someone who can use their intelligence and imagination."

"Her Majesty says you are supposed to be providing the intelligence and imagination."

"I'm sorry, but you…" She paused, uncomfortable at discussing Gaius as if he were absent, even though, in a very real sense, he was. There was no point pretending he was playing with a full deck. "Gaius is less use to me than a dictionary. I can't even flip though the pages of his memory in the hope a random word sparks an idea. I need more help. An unknown language is the hardest code to break. That's why, in World War II the Americans used Navajo code-talkers."

"Are you saying you cannot decode the scroll?"

"I'm saying that, unless I get more help with the language than Gaius can provide, it might take years, and I know Your Majesty needs an answer quicker than that."

Queen Rianna stalked across the study, until she stood in arm's reach. "Quelin torq da calidi."

"Her Majesty instructs you to remove your torc."

Lori's stomach turned to ice. "Tamsin told me never to do that while I'm in Annwyn."

"Captain Tamsin would not mean you to disobey Her Majesty's commands."

Which was undoubtedly true. The only options were to obey the order, or have the queen summon sufficient help to overpower her. Lori slipped the torc from her neck and laid it on the desk. What next? Would she know if she was standing like a slack faced zombie? Her mind felt as if it was working normally.

Rianna's icy expression did not change as she placed a hand on either side of Lori's head. This was it. This was where the queen sucked her brains out. Instinctively, Lori tried to step back, but was too slow. Fog flowed into her thoughts, blanketing her in a shroud of apathy. She could see the room, but it was like an old photograph, a lost scene watched from a distance.

The mind fog lifted as quickly as it had arrived. Lori's nose and ears itched, and she could see stars, but apart from this she felt exactly the same as before.

"You may put it on again." Queen Rianna had returned to her previous position.

Lori snatched up the torc. It was ridiculous how vulnerable she felt without it round her neck.

"I trust you can now perform your task."

"I..." She stopped. Rianna was not speaking English. "I..." Hyannish was sitting in her head alongside English, and she was equally fluent in both. "I guess so. But how—"

The door closed. Queen Rianna had left, and no more answers would be forthcoming.

Lori collapsed on the nearest stool, struggling with surprise. Whatever had been done seemed permanent, the effect lasting after the torc was replaced. She touched the spots where the queen's hands had been. She needed to know a lot more about magic, its capabilities and limits, but that would have to wait.

Although his translation services were no longer needed, Gaius remained. He was going to be keeping an eye on her, maybe closer than before, now that she could work independently of him. She glanced at the bookcases. What would he do if she pulled out a book at random? Rianna had not forbidden reading.

"You must make all speed to complete Queen Rianna's task. Idleness will not be permitted." Gaius ran on a limited command set.

Lori rolled open the scroll. The fay magic had given her knowledge of the writing as well as the language. The runes were no longer strange symbols, but phonetic components. Had they formed proper words she could have read the text aloud. Decoding was going to be so much easier now that she understood the sentence structure. Already she could guess the location of prepositions, and the likely verbs and nouns.

Morgaine's name would be there, she was sure of it, and probably the words "Annwyn," and "spell." Lori sighed. Much easier—but it still might take a while.

CHAPTER NINE

L ori hurried down the stairways of the middle bailey. Gaius had not approved of her leaving work early, but she had missed dinner the previous day, and was not about to do so again. There was only so much bread and cheese her digestive system could take. She had made vague noises about possibly returning after she had eaten, with no intention of doing so. Quite apart from food, she needed a break from the room and, if possible, an ordinary conversation with someone who was still in possession of their own brain.

She ducked into the porch of the mess hall and collided with a tall figure who was leaving.

"Hey. Watch where you're going."

"Sorry." Lori realised who the tall figure was. Her pulse rate spiked. "Oh. Tamsin. Hi. I was worried I'd missed dinner." Through the open doors she could see the emptying tables and boggarts clearing away the remains of food.

"You…" Tamsin was staring at her.

Had she got ink on her face? "What's up?"

"You're speaking Hyannish."

"Am I?" She had not noticed. It was all very confusing. "Oh, yes. Queen Rianna did it. I told her I couldn't decrypt a foreign language. She told me to take my torc off. I know you told me never to do it, but I guessed it didn't apply to the queen's orders."

"Of course not. You're totally safe with her."

Which brought to mind Arthur Dent's quote about unfamiliar usage of the word *safe*. "Anyway, she did something, and then I could speak Hyannish, even after I put the torc back on."

"She'd have used transformation, rather than illusion."

"That makes a difference?"

"Oh yes." Tamsin glanced over her shoulder. "You'd better be quickish if you want to eat. I'll come with you."

"All right."

The benches were three-quarters empty, with a corresponding decrease in noise level. Finn and Widget were the only two left at the table used by the Silver Ravens. They got up as Tamsin and Lori approached.

"Back already?" Widget grinned at Tamsin.

"I'm going to keep Lori company."

"Right. Well, you won't mind if I don't join you." Widget's tone was light-hearted. "Oh, and there's a card game in Shorty's room. See if you can't talk lover boy here into going. It's my turn to take some money off him."

Finn gave a snort. "Like you stand a chance of that." He patted Tamsin on the shoulder, said, "Night, Tazer. See you tomorrow," and walked from the hall. Lori felt suitably ignored.

Widget started to follow him, but stopped and turned back. "Say, Lori. You used to work on games, right?"

"Yes."

"I don't suppose you know anything about *Warlords of Acadia III?*"

"No. It's not one I've worked on."

"Shame that. There was me hoping you could drop hints about Easter eggs. Never mind." He switched his attention to Tamsin. "Maybe catch you later in Shorty's."

"Maybe."

Widget left.

Once again, there was bread to use as bowls. The thick stew contained vegetables, the first Lori had been offered in Annwyn, although their variety was unclear. A platter of sliced meat also was laid out, species similarly unknown. Regardless, she helped herself to a generous serving of both. Tamsin sat on the other side of the table, watching her in a way that might give rise to difficulty in swallowing.

Focus. This was her chance to get information. "So, tell me all about fay magic. What was it you said just now? Transformation?"

"It's one sphere of magic. It physically turns something into something else. The torc protects you from being transformed while you're wearing it, but the change persists even after you put it back on."

"It's permanent?"

"It can be undone." Tamsin pointed to the fork in Lori's hands. "For the next month, you should be careful when handling silver. If you cut yourself with it, the transformation will be reversed."

"This is silver?" There were no hallmarks on the fork.

"Yes."

"Bit posh for an army mess hall."

Tamsin laughed. "The fay get nervous around iron and steel. That's why only sentries on duty carry guns in the middle bailey, and nobody's allowed them in the keep, in case of an accident. Silver and gold weapons won't hurt the fay—at least, no worse than they'd hurt us—but gold is too soft to hold an edge. Silver's the only metal they can make any practical use of."

"You said I only need to be careful for a month. Does the transformation become fixed at some stage?"

"Only because of how memory works. At the moment, you've got what Queen Rianna has implanted. But you're already making your own memories with this knowledge. The longer it goes on, the more memories of using the language you'll have, and they're yours. They'll stay with you, even if an accident with silver takes away the original knowledge."

"Right."

"On the other hand, a physical change can always be completely undone. Which is why it's worth carrying a silver blade." Tamsin indicated the knife on her belt.

"You said the torc protects you."

"It does. But if a fay transforms a mouse into a lion, the lion can eat you."

Lori chewed thoughtfully on a slice of lukewarm meat—it might have been turkey, or something similarly avian. Tamsin was watching, a half smile on her face. It would be so easy to give in to the temptation and switch to a more personal topic. It would also be profoundly stupid. Lori forced her thoughts back on track.

"You called transformation a sphere of magic. Are there other spheres?"

"Yes. The two main ones are illusion and enthrallment. Illusion makes you see, hear, and feel things that aren't real. It doesn't mean they're harmless though. The illusion of a lion couldn't kill you, but you'd have the illusion of pain when it bit you."

"Is there a difference between real pain and imaginary?"

"Not enough to get excited about. And the lion might scare you to death. But the instant you put the torc on, the lion and the pain would vanish."

"Could you drive somebody mad with illusions?"

"Probably. But the fay mainly use it as a game, like telling stories. If you didn't have the torc on, you wouldn't be able to trust anything around you. Even boggarts can make illusions, and you don't want to know what comes out of their imagination."

"Boggarts can work magic?"

"Some can. Like I said, they're good at illusion. Some can even manage transformation, but enthrallment is beyond them."

"Okay. So tell me about enthrallment."

"Enthrallment enslaves someone's mind, so the thrall has no will of their own."

That sounded like Gaius. However, Tamsin's expression became strained. The easy smile had left her lips.

"Is something wrong?"

"I was enthralled when I first came to Annwyn. It happened to a lot of humans. I spent years as a mindless slave. I don't fully remember all the details, which is a blessing. Most of the time went by in a daze. Nothing really sticks out. You can't care about anything or anyone, including yourself. It's not one of my better memories."

"Queen Rianna did that to you?"

"No." The denial was immediate. "Of course not. She was the one who freed me, and the rest of the Silver Ravens."

But not everyone. "When somebody's enthralled, are they controlled directly, like a puppet, or are they given commands they work through as best they can?"

"I can't say for sure. It's all too hazy. But I don't think fay would have wanted to be in close mental contact with thralls. Plus they used to have dozens—too many to control each one separately."

"Can they listen to what's going on around their thralls? Use them as spies?"

"I don't know." Tamsin shrugged. "Anyway. It doesn't matter now. There're no human thralls left in Annwyn. Queen Rianna freed us all when she took over."

"Yes, there are."

"What?"

"There are still enthralled humans."

"Who told you that?"

"I don't need to be told. I'm working with one in the keep. Gaius. He's like a zombie."

"No." Tamsin's tone hardened.

"You think I'm lying?"

"I think you're confused. Queen Rianna freed everyone, no exceptions."

"If she's told you that, then she's the one who's—"

"Don't you dare say that." Tamsin's voice cracked like a whip.

Lori froze. *Time to engage brain.* No matter what she said, she was not going to persuade Tamsin. "I'm sorry. You're right. It's hard for me to be sure about anything here. There's so much I don't understand."

The anger on Tamsin's face eased. "Maybe. But you need to think before you speak."

Excellent advice. She should write it on a note and put it under her pillow. Lori got to her feet. "It's been a long day. I'm tired and should go to bed. I need to be thinking clearly tomorrow."

A succession of emotions chased across Tamsin's face, ending with something softly regretful. "I'm sorry if I snapped just now. But Queen Rianna is…" She sighed. "You don't know how much she's done for me."

Tamsin was sincere. Lori was sure of it. Which left one option. *She's fooled you. I don't know how, but she's completely suckered you in.* And there was no way Lori could think of to change things. *Not my circus. Not my monkeys.* For now, at least.

Lori put down the quill. "I'm going for a walk."

"Queen Rianna requires you to complete your task as quickly as possible."

"I know. But my thoughts are stuck in a rut. I need to shake them loose. Walking helps me put my ideas in order."

Gaius froze, presumably running through his list of pre-programmed commands. "I will arrange an escort for you. Do not be away for long."

"I promise to think as quickly as I can."

Lori arrived in the middle bailey to find a group of Iron Ravens playing a game. The rules were unclear, but involved a rugby ball, hectic running around, full body-slam tackles, and a lot of shouting. She watched for a minute before moving on to the outer bailey, which was far from peaceful, but still less distracting than the soldiers' game.

A spiral stairway in one of the outer towers took her onto the battlements. The parapet had bevelled slots to allow archers—or in Annwyn's case, machine gunners—to fire out while protected from incoming missiles. Lori dug around in her memory. The up and down wall design was called crenulations, the gaps were embrasures, and the high parts were merlons. Yet more useless information from working on fantasy games.

She rested her forearms on the waist-high wall of an embrasure and looked out. On the other side of the wall was an expanse of open grassland, finishing in a strip of sand beside the sea. The warm afternoon air was heavy with the scent of wildflowers. The sky was cloudless blue. How much more pleasant it would be out there, walking alone with her thoughts.

Her eyes fixed on the distant mountains. A whole world was out there and she knew nothing about it. Would she be allowed outside Caersiddi on her own? And how safe was it? Dragons might not be the only danger—her mental brakes engaged—which was why she was not going to even consider the idea. By the age of fourteen she had visited enough places to last anyone a lifetime. Her travelling days were over. She would finish the decoding and get back to Earth as quickly as possible, with no diversions for sightseeing.

Lori began pacing the battlements, marshalling her thoughts. Now that she could read Hyannish, she was being far more productive in coming up with ideas that did not work. Over the previous day she had discounted all the easiest options, which was progress of a sort. The code was not a simple substitution cipher. That much was certain, otherwise she would have been able to pick out the repetition of common words, the Hyannish equivalents of "and," "a," and, "the."

More background information on Morgaine would help, an insight into the dead queen, and what had been important to her and her times. All Gaius could say was Morgaine had become High Queen a little over a century before and was nearly as far beyond criticism as her current day descendant.

Applying the thirty to one time ratio, meant Morgaine's reign began just before 1000 BC on Earth, the start of the Iron Age. Lori paused mid-step. Was that purely coincidental, given how dangerous iron was to fay? Regardless, it was hard to see how the correlation could have any relevance from the point of view of decryption.

Lori leaned her shoulder against a merlon and stared at the distant mountains while her thoughts moved on. With no way to recharge the laptop, she had to be very careful about the battery. The computer also carried the risk of overcomplicating things. Morgaine could not have created anything as complex as an enigma machine. *Keep it simple.*

How simple did she need to be? Back in 1000 BC, writing was just getting going on Earth. So few people were literate that encryption was hardly necessary and never went beyond simple Caesar ciphers—which were already ruled out. Since Morgaine could not borrow a technique from Earth, it meant she must have invented her own encryption method here in Annwyn, using just ink and paper, with maybe a little magical help. She would have needed to be a mathematical genius to come up with hash functions, so something like a Playfair cipher was far more likely. What would Morgaine have used as a key?

The explosive cracks of gunshots made Lori jump. She spun round, ending up with her back pressed against the wall of the parapet. Two crows that had been perched atop a nearby merlon took to the air. But the shots were not followed by shouts or alarm bells. The castle was not under attack. She rested her hands on her knees while her pulse slowed.

Seen from above, the outer bailey was more orderly than her initial impression suggested. Distinct areas were laid out for stores, workshops, drill yards, and target ranges. The barrack blocks must be home to the horde of boggarts who serviced the castle. They had to be living somewhere, and the doors were too low for either humans or fay. Now that she could speak Hyannish, was it worth getting a boggart's take on life in Caersiddi? It was a safe bet they would not be so enamoured of Queen Rianna.

Another shot rang out, coming from a target range just below where she stood. The Silver Ravens were at rifle practice. Lori stared down on them. Time was passing, and really she should return to the keep. But would Tamsin know anything useful about Morgaine? Was the idea just an excuse to go talk to her? Did she need to start second-guessing herself every time she saw Tamsin?

The answer to the last question was probably a yes, but the sight of the rifles had given rise to a temptation that grew ever more irresistible by the second. Without giving herself a chance to think better of it, Lori trotted down the nearest staircase.

"Hi. Have you come to join in?" Tamsin grinned, her tone making it clear she was teasing.

"Yes. If you don't mind."

"You're serious?" The surprise in Tamsin's voice overwhelmed any last doubts.

"Why not?"

"A rifle isn't a toy," Finn snarled.

"I know that."

Three of the Silver Ravens were lying down, rifles braced on a line of sandbags. Hippo had been preparing to shoot. He got to his knees and gestured to Lori. "You can take my rifle."

"This isn't…" Finn gave up, and stood back, scowling.

Lori got in position beside Hippo. The others, BH and Shorty, scrambled out of the way, clearly sharing Finn's opinion of the potentially dangerous waste of time. Lori caught Shorty rolling his eyes.

Hippo handed over the gun. "Now, you must be very careful. There's a live round in the chamber. This is—"

"A bolt action rifle. Specifically, a Remington M24."

Admittedly, there were only three rifles she could name on sight, but Hippo was not to know that. She smiled at him, then laid her cheek against the stock and flipped off the safety. The target was short range, less than a hundred yards. Muscle memory took over as she lined up the sights and eased on the trigger. The kick against her shoulder was familiar, but without any protection, the volume of the retort was not. Her ears rang. Health and safety inspectors were yet to make their impact on fairyland.

Lori ejected the spent cartridge, then fired a second and third time before resetting the safety and putting the rifle down. She twisted around into a sitting position. The row of slack-jawed, stunned faces was everything she could have hoped for.

"Three fucking bullseyes." Shorty was the first to speak.

Tamsin nodded. "That wasn't your first time, was it?"

"My last employer sent me on a month-long army training course."

"I thought you were a computer programmer."

"I was." Lori got to her feet, brushing dust from her T-shirt and jeans. "We were working on what was going to be the most realistic war game ever, called *Rank and File*."

Tamsin indicated for the Silver Ravens to resume the target practice while she and Lori took a few steps back. "I didn't know computing got so physical."

"Doesn't normally. But our CEO got the idea all the lead programmers should have hands-on experience, rather than rely on advisors. We got shipped to the States for an immersion course. I'd ended up specialising as a sniper."

"What made you pick that?"

"Nobody else wanted the job."

Not after the first day on the target range, when she outscored everyone else by an embarrassing amount—she would certainly have been embarrassed in their shoes. How the others found it so difficult was beyond her. You lined up the sights, squeezed the trigger, and a hole appeared in the target where you were aiming. That was all there was to it. Maybe Dad teaching her to shoot when she was four had given her a head start.

"You should let me have the details of where you went. We can send this lot along. Your instructors must have been good."

"Maybe. Our trouble was we came away knowing too much."

"In what way?" Tamsin was standing a little too close, and Lori was annoyed at herself for not minding in the slightest.

"War isn't fun. The game ended up too realistic. What kids want is to run around shooting people. There's nothing exciting about spending an hour taking a rifle apart and cleaning it. We tried to hold back on the realism, but it was hard to ignore all we'd learned."

Feedback from the beta testers had been full of words like dull, tedious, repetitive, and pointless. The disaster that was *Rank and File* had finished Ganymede Games.

"What range do you shoot?"

"I'm fine up to five hundred yards, as long as the weather isn't troublesome. I don't have the experience to adjust for wind accurately. And I never got anywhere close to advanced stuff like taking the curvature of the Earth into account."

"That won't be an issue here. Annwyn is flat."

"That's impossible. Are you kidding me?"

"No."

"What happens at the edge of the world?"

"If you go off one side, you come back in at the other."

"You've done it?"

"Yes. Twice. But it's a trick for emergencies only. You spend the next few days feeling like you've been turned inside out, and that's not fun." Tamsin gave the target another long, hard look. "When you've finished decoding you might want to try out for the Silver Ravens." Her expression made it unclear whether she was joking.

"You'd want me?" Lori heard the playfulness in her own voice. *Stop it. Stop it.* She had to be sensible.

"I might." Tamsin's grin was slow and easy. "Finn's our best shot, and he's pretty good, but we've been looking to recruit a proper sniper ever since Pobble went. None of the Iron Ravens who've applied have been up to scratch. You can try out, if you're interested."

Tamsin's tone suggested that the word "interested" applied to more than just becoming a sniper, and yes, Lori was most definitely interested. That was the problem. She took a half step away. "Actually, I'm here to pick your brains. I was wondering what you could tell me about Queen Morgaine. Any insight you might have."

"Queen Morgaine?" Tamsin shook her head. "I don't know what you think I can tell you. She was gone long before I arrived in Annwyn."

"But you still know more than I do."

"Why are you interested in her?"

"She's the one who wrote the scroll I'm trying to decode."

"Oh." Tamsin looked unsettled. It was information Queen Rianna had not seen fit to share.

Lori pressed on before Tamsin had the chance to work out whether she was compromised. "It's possible Queen Morgaine used a Playfair encryption scheme—I can explain that, but you won't find it very interesting. I need to get inside her head. What was the most important thing to her? I'm looking for a word or phrase she might have used as a key."

"I don't think she was too concerned about anything other than herself."

It runs in the family then. "How about children?"

"Her son, Arawan, was king after her, but they didn't have a good relationship."

"Long-term lovers? I know the fay aren't into formal marriage, but was there anyone who was important to her? "

"None who stand out. Most of her lovers ended up dead or in a dungeon."

Which was less than promising. "She probably didn't immortalise their names in her code then."

"No, probably not."

"You don't know of anyone she was close to?"

"No. She made more enemies than friends."

"She sounds like bad news all round."

"She did what had to be done. There was a crisis and the Council of Elders were going nowhere fast. Morgaine had been on the council, but lost patience with the bickering and time-wasting. She formed the Raven Warriors and took charge."

"She used human mercenaries to seize power."

"That's one way of looking at it."

What other way was there? "You think she was justified?"

Tamsin shrugged. "Things worked out okay. Annwyn's been more stable, and she stopped fay buggering around with Earth. There used to be hundreds of portals between the worlds. The fay would visit and stir up a shit-storm, just for fun. The old legends—Odin, Zeus, Horus, and the rest—that was fay pretending to be gods. Queen Morgaine put a stop to it. She closed down most portals, and put guards on the rest. She protected Earth, and let us go our own way."

"Are you sure it wasn't just that she didn't want other fay raising their own human armies against her?"

Tamsin hesitated, a denial clearly on her lips, but then she sighed. "Perhaps. She certainly wasn't bothered by humans being enthralled. Like I told you, it happened to me when I arrived. I spent my first five years here as a thrall. Luckily, I was given to Rianna, who was a princess then." Her expression softened. "She didn't treat me the way other fay would have. She'd have freed me completely if she could, but King Orfran, her father, forbade it."

"Why? The Iron Ravens were here weren't they? Or were they thralls back then?"

"No. Thralls are hopeless at fighting. They need to be told when to duck."

"So what was special about you?"

"Who knows? But it wasn't just King Orfran. After he died, Bronwen took over, and she had something against me too. She…" Tamsin's face shifted through several expressions, most of them awkward and strained. "Anyway, Bronwen was going to be a disaster.

Queen Rianna didn't want to fight her sister, but had no choice. She freed her humans, and we helped her overthrow Bronwen."

"What happened to Bronwen?"

"She died in the fighting. It wasn't what Queen Rianna wanted, but Bronwen wouldn't surrender when given the chance."

So, Rianna usurped her sister's throne and killed her. *Why am I not surprised?* And Tamsin saw nothing wrong in it. *There's something I'm missing.* However, time was passing.

"I need to get back to the keep."

"Yes, of course."

At the gate to the middle bailey, Lori paused and looked back. The Silver Ravens were at their target practice. For the briefest moment, she played with the idea of joining them. But no. She had been kidnapped and was effectively a prisoner. She must not lose sight of the true situation—especially when Rianna was added to the equation. The only sensible goal was to get away, as quickly as possible. Anything else was madness.

Chapter Ten

The temperature was climbing, and Annwyn was yet to discover air-conditioning. Lori opened the windows as wide as they would go and returned to her seat. Pages of notes littered the table. She stared at them glumly. Talking to Tamsin had suggested some keys to try out, but so far permutations on "close the portals" and "overthrow the council" had been no more successful than "High Queen Morgaine." Was she on the wrong track?

The sound of angry voices came in through the open doorway, breaking her concentration.

"I saw you."

"Saw me do what?"

"You dealt the last card off the bottom of the pack."

"You dare accuse me of cheating!"

"You dare deny it! Do you think I'm blind, or stupid?"

"I've never thought you blind, but as for the other…" The words were followed by the sharp grating of chair legs.

A third bored voice joined in. "Brothers, please. Let us keep some sense of decorum."

"Didn't you see him cheating?"

"Frankly, no. You're both playing so drearily I was having trouble keeping my eyes open."

Lori went to investigate. On a balcony below, two fay men were seated at a table, while a third stood, fists on hips. Two of the huge, red-eyed dogs—hellhounds—lay panting in a patch of shade. The balcony was smaller and farther away than the one where Rianna and Tamsin had been, but close enough to see and hear easily.

"Come. Sit down."

"I'm not laying another card with that cheat."

"I've told you—" The fay shoved back his chair, just as a boggart arrived, carrying a tray of drinks.

The unfortunate boggart was knocked sideways and the tray slipped from its hands. The bottle shattered on the paving, splattering wine up the legs of the standing man. The boggart dropped to its knees, hastily brushing the wreckage back onto the tray, using its hand as a scoop.

Would this put an end to the argument, or would they carry on once the boggart had finished cleaning up? Lori did not want to close the door, but she could not work through the disruption. The trouble was, it was so hard to judge fays' intentions from their expressions. They always looked bored and offended.

Movement at the other end of the balcony caught her eye. The two huge dogs had risen to their feet. They shook themselves off, then fixed their gaze on the kneeling boggart. The hellhounds' red eyes glowed as they advanced, teeth bared. The boggart squealed and scrambled away, until it was pressed against the balustrade.

Lori waited for the command to call the dogs back. It never came. The fay watched impassively, making no attempt to intervene. One dog lunged forward, fastening onto the boggart's shoulder, and pulling it to the ground. The other caught a flailing leg. The boggart's squeals changed to shrill, agonised howls.

Lori wanted to look away, but her eyes would not obey her. Splatters of green blood mingled with the red wine. The hellhounds shook the body between them, like puppies playing with a rag toy. The boggart's efforts weakened, as did its screams. One dog clamped its jaws on the boggart's throat, and at last all sound and movement stopped, although the hellhounds continued to worry at its body. Blood formed rivulets on the tiles.

One of the seated fay finally raised his voice. "Leave it. You're just making a mess." One dog obeyed immediately. The other had a final sniff. "No. Don't eat it. You'll get your dinner later." The fay turned to his standing companion. "There. Has that made you feel better?"

"No." The angry fay stormed off. The door slammed with a crash.

They had not been watching powerlessly. One fay had been controlling the dogs, venting his anger on a defenceless victim. They were callous, evil bastards. Lori's hands formed fists so tight they hurt. Her stomach threatened to empty its contents. But there was nothing she could have done to help the boggart, and nothing she could do now to avenge it.

The two remaining fay stayed seated. "What's that stench? Did it shit itself?"

"Probably. Shall we go?"

"Why not?"

As they left the balcony, Lori caught one last exchange. "I wasn't cheating, you know."

"Really? I'd have sworn I saw you slipping cards off the bottom. I'd said nothing in the hope you'd get the wretched game over with quickly."

The hellhounds trotted after them, leaving the body on the balcony, looking like a pile of paint soaked rags. Had it been an animal, its death would have been an act of wanton cruelty. But the boggart had been more than that. It could speak and think. It had been murdered, and the fay were unconcerned. Would they have any qualms over treating humans the same way? Lori doubted it.

She stumbled back to the study and slumped on her stool. Had Tamsin been present to witness the killing, what would she have thought? Would she have begun questioning her loyalty to the queen? But Tamsin was not there. Not there to witness the casual brutality, not there to see Gaius's pathetic condition, not there with access to information the queen clearly did not want known. Were Tamsin and the Silver Ravens sheltered from scenes like the one she had just watched? Or could fay control human minds, even when they wore iron torcs?

Either way, Lori could reach one alarming conclusion. The queen was not concerned at her observing what went on in the keep. The best interpretation was that she would be leaving the instant the code was broken, so what she knew did not matter. The worst did not bear thinking about.

Lori buried her face in her hands. She had to get away.

❖

Sleep was impossible. Lori rolled onto her back and stared into the darkness. Images of the boggart's death would not fade. Even if she did sleep, she was sure to have nightmares. She slipped out of bed and pulled a blanket around her shoulders, mainly for the comfort value. The heat of the day was lingering, well after the sun had gone down.

The fire making material beside the hearth included a box of normal, Earth style matches. After fumbling around in the dark, Lori lit a candle then sat at the table, watching the flame waver in the draft whispering through the window shutters. Candlelight created shifting patterns on the textured lid of her laptop. Before leaving Annwyn she should check that Widget's new password worked, but this could wait until she had a reason to turn the laptop on.

Creating a program to analyse the scroll would be simple enough. The mathematics was trivial. As long as she had eight hours of battery life to write, test, and debug the code, Lori would have backed herself to do it. If Morgaine had used a Playfair cipher, the laptop could spit out the key in seconds. The "if" part was the problem. Supposing she flattened the battery, only to discover her Playfair assumption was wrong. Supposing she ran into a more desperate need for the laptop.

Rianna should have sent Widget to Earth with the scroll. He had hacked her password, so he clearly had serious computing resources at his disposal. He could have decoded the text in far less time, taking far less effort than needed to set the puzzles in *Zettabyte*. Even if Rianna would not let the scroll leave Caersiddi, he could have brought a computer and power supply from Earth and set up in the study.

Why not? One possibility was that Rianna would not allow complex Earth technology into her keep. The other, more worrying option, was that even though Rianna could not read the scroll, she had reason to think it contained information she dared not let any Silver Raven discover. The bottom line for Lori being that the queen had a need of Widget's continued services, but not hers.

Lori did not want to find out what would happen if she was unable to break the code. But would it be any worse than what would happen if she succeeded? When the decoding was finished, would Rianna really allow her to leave Annwyn?

Lori wandered back to her bed and sat hugging her knees. Was there any chance she was being unfair? Would the queen have protected the boggart that day, had she been present? Gaius was enthralled, but he might deserve it. He might have been a violent criminal. His current condition certainly counted as unusual punishment, but was it any crueller than whatever other options the Annwyn legal system employed? Except, if there was something approaching a good reason for his condition, why was his existence kept hidden from Tamsin?

Tamsin. Lori closed her eyes, trying to block out the memory from the bathhouse. *That woman is just too damned hot.* Lori did not need Adam to tell her that acting on the attraction would turn out badly—not as if she had ever paid attention to his advice about women, otherwise she would never have got involved with Jess. He had been bang on the mark about her. Although, one of his main complaints about her ex-girlfriends was accusing them of being dull and insipid—two adjectives that did not apply to Tamsin.

Lori groaned. She was in danger of falling, and trying to pretend otherwise was pointless. Admit it. Tamsin had her gooey inside, and gooey in the head as well. And, in this spirit of honest self-assessment, was there any chance her attitude towards Rianna was affected by jealousy? Tamsin had lived in Annwyn for years and was far more knowledgeable about everything that had gone on there. If Tamsin trusted Rianna unreservedly, might she be right? Did Rianna deserve the benefit of the doubt?

No.

Lori knew deep in her gut. Rianna was dangerous, deceitful, and totally self-centred. And, from what she had seen that day, all fay were exactly the same. So what did this imply about any code Morgaine might have invented? Like the card cheat on the balcony, would she overestimate her own sleight of hand abilities and underestimate her opponents? Would she react rather than plan ahead? Would boredom get the better of her? The chances were that the code was very straightforward.

Lori lay back down. Over-thinking the problem was a mistake. The laptop was not necessary and was more likely to complicate the task than help it. When she broke the code, Lori was sure the solution would turn out to be simple, verging on the blindingly obvious.

❖

Two days later, the blindingly obvious solution still eluded her. Lori put down the quill and cupped her chin in her hand. The afternoon sunlight turned floating dust motes into sparkling columns. Little in the way of breeze entered through the open balcony door to stir the hot air. Hair stuck to sweat on the nape of Lori's neck and her forehead. This was a day to be on the beach, not stuck inside.

At the other side of the table, Gaius was doing his normal impersonation of a tailor's manikin. What was his story? When and where had he come from? And was it worth the effort of wheedling the information out of him? His name was Roman. Had he really been in Annwyn while two thousand years passed on Earth?

It was a worrying reminder that time for her friends and family was rushing by. Lori pulled over a sheet of paper and jotted down notes to make sure of the calendar count—six days minus a few hours, plus a bit for the time in the Halfway House. She frowned. How accurate was the thirty to one time-flow ratio? A month passing in a day sounded a touch contrived.

Widget probably had the exact figure. She could ask him when they next met. Except trying to work out the date on Earth was pointless. She was stuck in Annwyn until she broke the code. Wasting time was the last thing she should be doing. Furthermore, she had placed the sheet on top of the scroll and risked leaving dents in it. Rianna would definitely not be pleased at the slightest damage.

Lori took the scroll to the open doorway. Faint imprints showed when the scroll was held obliquely in the shaft of sunlight, but the marks did not match what she had just written. Her notepaper was too thick and the quill was too brittle to press hard enough. Yet somebody had left an impression, though it did not look like writing. What had this unknown person been doing, and had it played any part in decoding the scroll? She was due a lucky break.

In detective shows, shading with a pencil held sideways made imprints crystal clear, but whether it worked in real life was immaterial. Not only would it be awkward to explain defacing the scroll, but she did not have a pencil. An electrostatic detector would do no damage, but she did not have one of them either, and there was, of course, no electric socket to plug it into.

Lori turned the scroll around, tilting it in the hope of revealing more detail. Somebody had drawn a grid, several rows deep and two dozen columns wide. The regular lines would have required the use of a straight edge, and possibly explained the pressure applied. Each cell would have been big enough to take a single letter.

The sight pinged a memory from way back in her teens. What was the name? Vini-something? Vinegar? No, Vigenère. Why had she not thought of it before? A method of encryption created with a rotating cycle of Caesar ciphers, working off a single word key. Simple enough to do with pen and paper. Complex enough to be a bugger to crack. Morgaine's biggest issue would have been doing the arithmetic using the fay counting system. Roman numerals were intuitive by comparison.

Why had she not thought of Vigenère before? Admittedly, the last time she had played around with it she had been thirteen, but this was still no excuse for becoming fixated on Playfair. Lori could have slapped herself—blame Dorothy L. Sayers, and reading *Have His Carcase* over the previous Easter weekend.

On a fresh sheet of paper, Lori marked out her own grid. Fortunately, there was no reason not to use Arabic numerals and base ten. She simply needed the key, and the first word to try was obvious—blindingly obvious. The only thing Morgaine cared about was herself. What else would she use other than her own name?

Before Lori had worked through the cycle the first time round, she knew the code was cracked. "Tal ollan." She spoke the fay words aloud. *To join the.*

Gaius stood. "You have discovered how to decode the scroll."

"Yes. Morgaine used her own name as—"

"Queen Rianna must be informed at once."

"I'd like to be—"

She was alone. Gaius had never moved so quickly.

By the time the door opened again, Lori had got no further then the third line, and was still on how to set everything up, rather than what the spell did, or why it was so important. The only clue lay in the title, *To join the worlds in harmony*, which did not sound like anything that would interest Rianna. The current line was more in keeping, "Take blood from—"

"Gaius tells me you have succeeded in your task."

Lori stood and bowed her head. "Yes, Your Majesty."

Rianna stalked to her side. "You've been reading the scroll." It was an accusation.

"Ah…" Too late, Lori remembered the instruction given on the first day, not to decode the entire text. "I wanted to be completely sure. When Gaius left, I was testing the idea. It still might have been a coincidence, a few letters coming together by chance and forming a word."

"But you have the solution?"

"Yes, Your Majesty."

Queen Rianna sat on Lori's vacated stool. The eagerness in her eyes was unmistakable. "Tell me how it is done."

This took considerably longer than anticipated. Rianna displayed a remarkable talent for grasping the wrong end of the stick, but eventually she got the hang of the cipher.

She touched her fingertip to the word Lori had been about to start. "From a traitor. Blood from a traitor. How fortunate that I have a traitor to hand." Rianna's smile was pure malice. "You've done well and will be suitably rewarded. But in future, you will obey my commands without deviation. You may go."

"Yes, Your Majesty." Lori retreated to the door. A boggart guide was waiting outside.

Rianna spoke again. "When you get to the middle bailey, send a message to Captain Tamsin. I have a task for my Silver Ravens and wish to see her in my private chamber in one hour."

"Yes, Your Majesty."

Lori escaped. The code was cracked. The only thing to worry about now was whether she would be allowed to leave. Rianna was up to something, and Lori was sure it was not something good.

The fay word for traitor was shorter than the one on the scroll. Furthermore, given Rianna's shaky grasp of Vigenère, she could not have decoded it so quickly. So either she was making a wild guess, or she already knew about the blood and was deliberately lying. Whose blood did Rianna want?

The sun was past its zenith and the shadow of the keep covered half the outer bailey. Soldiers were working through their drills in the late afternoon heat, but there was no sign of the Silver Ravens.

"Excuse me. Have you seen Captain Tamsin recently?" Lori interrupted a pair of Iron Raven officers who were discussing something that required a lot of hand gestures.

"She went into the stable." One pointed.

"Thanks."

They resumed their animated conversation.

Lori paused at the entrance to give her eyes a chance to adapt. The horses were no more than the impression of large shapes and movement in the dimness. The smell of dung and wet hay was overpowering. A wuffle of breath and the clomp of hooves shifting position were the only sounds. Had Tamsin gone already?

"Hello? Is anyone here?"

"What it is?" Tamsin appeared in the light of the doorway.

"I've got a message from Queen Rianna."

"She sent you? Aren't you better employed—"

"I've done it. I've broken the code."

Tamsin's smile broadened. "Congratulations. Her Majesty will be pleased. Is that what the message is about?"

"I'm guessing it's connected. She wants to see you in her private chamber in an hour, though it was about ten minutes ago when she said that." Lori's wristwatch was completely out of synch with the long Annwyn days.

"I'll make sure I'm on time." Tamsin tilted her head to one side. "It was good of you to bring the message yourself. You could have got a boggart to do it, you know."

"I had my reasons."

"Really?" Tamsin's tone was low and teasing. She leaned against a post and angled her body forward.

How easy it would be to reach out and place her hand on Tamsin's waist. The invitation was clearly there. Lori won that battle with temptation, but could not make herself step away.

"Now that I've decoded the scroll, I'm done here. I need someone to escort me back to Earth. You said you'd do it."

"You want to go." Was that genuine disappointment in Tamsin's voice?

"I don't belong here. I need to get back as soon as possible, before too many months pass on Earth. I'll have some explaining to do as it is."

"Of course." Tamsin pushed away from the post. "I'll collect you after breakfast tomorrow and take you home."

"You can't do it tonight?"

"You've got your reward to collect. Remember?"

Would it sound odd if she said she was not bothered about the gold? "All right. Tomorrow, as soon as it's ready to collect. Promise?"

"As long as it doesn't interfere with whatever the queen needs me for."

"Thanks."

Would she be allowed to go? Rianna no longer had any use for her, but a bad feeling in the pit of Lori's stomach would not ease. She had come straight to Tamsin, not just to make arrangements to leave as quickly as possible, but so Tamsin would know she had no wish to stay in Annwyn. If Rianna prevented her departure, surely Tamsin would require a plausible explanation for the change in plan.

While talking, Lori's eyes had adjusted to the low light. Yet what she could see of the horse in the nearest stall still looked strangely out of focus. Its rump was powerfully muscled, although not quite solid, as if it were made of smoke. Lori rubbed her eyes. The animal's sleek coat was jet black, but gave the impression of being opaque.

"They're not normal horses, are they?"

"No. They can fly."

Lori peered around the end of the partition. "They don't have wings."

"They don't need them."

"How do they fly?"

"Magic."

"But…How?"

"I wouldn't bother asking. They just do. It goes back to Mathanwy, who created Annwyn. That's if he really existed and isn't a myth." Tamsin shrugged. "Assuming he was real, his descendants are the most powerful of the fay. Their magic goes beyond transmutation to world-forging. They can make the laws of nature whatever they want them to be. Hence Mathanwy chose to make Annwyn flat."

"Why?"

"That's another question you'll never get an answer to. However…" Tamsin made a show of sniffing her own armpit. "I should bathe and put clean clothes on. I don't want to meet the queen smelling like a stable."

"Probably best not."

"I'll see you tomorrow morning."

"Yes. Tomorrow."

"And well done with the scroll. I knew you could do it." Tamsin put a hand on Lori's shoulder and gave the slightest of squeezes, then she was gone.

Lori leaned against the nearest wall to steady herself. Tamsin's parting gesture had sent waves down her chest, through her stomach, and ending at a very predictable part of her anatomy, although the aftershocks had got as far as her knees.

If everything went to plan tomorrow, she would leave Annwyn forever. Undoubtedly it was for the best, but an annoying little lust-demon was decidedly pissed off about it.

❖

Lori rested her elbows on the windowsill. Annwyn had no moon, nothing to challenge the dazzling array of stars, and this was the last night she had to appreciate their glory. They sparkled like jewels scattered on black velvet. The starlight was strong enough to see by. In the garden below, two lovers strolled hand in hand. She watched them share a passionate kiss.

Would a fling with Tamsin have been such a bad idea? The option had definitely been there. Lori sighed. It was undoubtedly safer that she had resisted the temptation. The fay might be into the most open of relationships, but Rianna was too reminiscent of several jealous ex-girlfriends and the risk of annoying her was not worth taking.

Lori's thoughts were interrupted by a knock. "Yes?"

A boggart shuffled around the door. "Please, madam. I've got a message for you, madam. Please."

"What is it?"

"Captain Tamsin, madam. She says she's sorry, but she has to go away from Caersiddi for a few days, so she won't be able to escort you, like she said. She says she's very sorry, madam." The boggart shrunk back, as if frightened she might take her disappointment out on the messenger.

"Thank you. You can go."

The boggart disappeared. "Yes, madam." The words squeaked around the edge of the closing door.

Lori closed her eyes, trying to keep a lid on rising dread. She was still trapped in Annwyn. That was bad enough, but Tamsin would be absent. Supposing, when the Silver Ravens returned, Rianna said she had sent Lori back to Earth with a guard of Iron Ravens. Would Tamsin even bother to check the story out?

Of course not. Lori knew it, and Rianna would know it as well. The only thing in doubt was, did the queen want another zombie?

CHAPTER ELEVEN

Lori stood on the outer battlements. Overnight rain had left puddles on the ground, but now the sky was brilliant blue, as it had been every day. The Silver Ravens were assembling below while boggart stable hands attended them. Seen in daylight, the horses' appearance was no less disconcerting. Their shape was conventional, lighter than a carthorse, although stockier than an Arabian. However, their bodies did not look entirely solid, as if they had been shaded by someone using pencil rather than crayon. No wings. So how did they fly?

This was the question that had brought her out early—nothing to do with Tamsin. Lori shook her head and sighed. Attempts at lying to herself were getting worse. But she was not going to say good-bye, or wish Tamsin a safe journey and speedy return. Definitely not. She gripped the wall to anchor herself in place, just in case her legs disobeyed her and walked down the steps of their own accord.

Tamsin was adjusting something on her saddle while throwing the occasional comment at Finn, who stood close by. Several Silver Ravens were already mounted, walking their horses in circles, while trading good-natured banter. The horse's gait was perfectly normal, with no sign of levitation.

Tamsin finished whatever she was doing. She and Finn swung into their saddles, leaving one horse riderless. Was Rianna going as well? Was the mission simply bodyguard duty? A surge of hope swept through Lori. She would feel so much safer if the queen were somewhere else. But no. Tamsin attached the horse's reins to her saddle and led the small troop through the gate. Was it a spare mount, in case another horse had an accident, or were they were going to collect someone—possibly the unfortunate whose blood was required for the spell?

As they passed below where she stood, Tamsin looked up and waved. Lori's insides melted. This was silly and dangerous. Just as well temptation would be out of reach for a while.

The Silver Ravens formed a loose file on the grass outside the gate. Tamsin led them forward at an easy canter. Lori watched intently, but even so, the long grass concealed the point where the hooves stopped making contact with the ground. The horses trotted into the air as if they were going up a hill. No wings, no magic wands, no fuss.

Lori watched until they were dots in the distance. Now what?

Lori stared at the underside of her four-poster's canopy. Only an hour had passed since the Silver Ravens' departure, and already she was decidedly bored. She sat up, swung her legs round, and sat on the edge of the bed. With any luck Rianna was too busy concocting evil plans to bother with her. Regardless, hiding away was not going to help, and if she spent days stuck in her room she would go completely stir-crazy.

The possible nature of the evil plans nagged at Lori with feelings of guilt and curiosity in equal measure. She had no choice about helping Rianna, but that was a weak excuse, which never turned out well in the movies.

However, another thing that never turned out well was the nosy heroine making ham-fisted attempts at playing detective. Of course, in movies, the heroine would be saved from death at the end by a highly improbable sequence of events. Lori was not stupid enough to risk her life on a million to one chance. But equally, she could not just sit in the room.

The target range. Maybe she could borrow a rifle and—

Her thoughts were interrupted by a knock. This was unlikely to be good news. "Yes?"

A boggart stuck his head in. "Madam, please. Queen Rianna wishes to see you. You must come at once, madam."

"Did she say why?"

A stupid question that the boggart made no attempt to answer. "Please, madam, come now."

Lori's first urge to hide under the bed was absurd and no better than her second thought of running away. The only escape route was the portal—all she had to do was dodge the guards, and then deal with any monsters lying in wait. She was out of options. Lori hurried after the boggart. No matter what was up, making Her Frigging Majesty wait was not a smart move. *Stay positive.* Maybe, just maybe, Rianna wanted to weigh her against a pile of gold.

Soon, Lori was back in the familiar study. Gaius stood impassively in the corner, but this time he was not alone. Rianna was on the balcony with another human, one Lori had not seen before. The queen lounged against the balustrade, staring out to sea. She must have heard the door, but did not move while the minutes dragged out.

At last, Rianna turned from her contemplation of the waves. "Good. You've arrived."

"You wished to see me, Your Majesty?"

"Yes." Rianna sashayed into the room and seated herself on a stool. She was clearly in a good mood. With any luck, this was due to the code being broken, and she was feeling appropriately generous.

The other human followed. He was torcless and clearly enthralled, like Gaius, although younger and far more attractive—blond and rugged, and with the sort of looks that would have Adam salivating. His sleeveless shirt was unbuttoned to the waist, revealing the sculptured set of muscles beneath.

He stood behind Rianna, so she could lean against him, using his six-pack as a backrest. She reached above her head, sliding her hand under the man's shirt. He showed no reaction, even when she pinched his nipple.

Rianna's eyes fixed on Lori. "What do you think of him? Handsome, isn't he?"

"I...er...yes. I guess so, Your Majesty."

"But not to your taste, I think. So what do you like? Younger? Older? Dark hair? A little less masculine?"

"Not masculine at all, for preference."

The answer amused Rianna. She gave a tinkling laugh. "So that's how you play things. How silly you humans are, limiting yourself in that way. I don't."

"Many humans would agree with you." Which Lori had not the slightest problem with, as long as they did not expect her to do likewise, and restricted their own lovers to consenting adults—something that clearly did not apply to either man in the room.

Rianna leaned forward. "So, what sort of women do you pine for? Tall and dark? Or might you like someone with silver hair and blue skin?"

Lori's skin prickled. Had she turned pale? Rianna was beautiful and as attractive as a rattlesnake. She was also not the sort to take rejection well. Lori had dealt with enough petty, self-centred players to be able to read all the signs. But if she was right—and Lori desperately hoped that she was—Rianna was merely playing games with her.

"Is that why you've asked me here, Your Majesty?"

"Would you be happy if it was?"

"I'd be surprised."

"Really? Why is that?"

"Because I'm not as pretty as the man behind you."

Rianna laughed again. "Don't be so hard on yourself."

"Then for another reason, I think you have better uses for me." *Please let it be true.*

"Indeed I do. Though one does not rule out the other." Rianna's smile was unsettling. "But maybe it would be wiser not to distract you from your new task. I should make the most of your talents while you're here."

Did the word "here" relate to physical or mental presence? "I'd be happy to help, Your Majesty."

"While Morgaine's is the most important scroll, it isn't the only one. Other encoded texts have been left here. I've a fancy to know what they say."

At the queen's gesture, Gaius unlocked the cabinet and removed a dozen scrolls, which he spread across the table. They ranged from what looked like a one-page note to a small novel. The scrolls would keep her busy until Tamsin returned, and probably far longer. Should she be relieved or dismayed? "Which would you like me to start with, Your Majesty?"

"No preference. As I said, it's no more than a fancy on my part. I've no idea what any say. Pick one at random."

"Is there anything you can tell me about the authors?"

"I believe they were written by my ancestors, kings and queens of Annwyn. But that's all I can say."

Not that Lori put any faith in a word Rianna said, but if true, this meant the scrolls could contain anything. Bygone rulers had thought it advisable to conceal the contents in code. Maybe some were no more than private diaries, but others might be far more significant. Yet Rianna was giving her a free hand, unconcerned about what she might learn. The implications were not good.

"It'll be an interesting challenge, Your Majesty."

"Then I'll leave you to it. Gaius will assist, as before." Rianna swept from the room, with her toy-boy trailing in her wake.

Lori slumped on the recently vacated stool and eyed the row of scrolls. *Pick one at random.* Start with the shortest. The novelette could wait. Gaius returned the others to the cabinet.

"Gaius. I want you to write out a list of the names of all the previous kings and queens. Spelling the names exactly the same way they would have done themselves." Best to make that part clear.

She watched him work.

Quite possibly, the Vigenère technique had been invented by someone before Morgaine, and she had merely adapted it, using her own name, or alternately, later rulers had copied her. Either way, the list of names was the first thing to try. She had to discount the possibility of a copycat cipher first, before moving on. The fay struck her as being lazy and unimaginative. If one had come up with a workable idea, others would surely have used it.

Lori crossed off the last entry on the list, and put down her quill. Testing the names had taken over a day and produced absolutely zilch. Just to be sure, she had tried adding the title king or queen, and even writing the names backwards. She stared despondently at her latest page of failures. What next?

The weather was not helping, ramping up the temperature to the hottest day so far. Sweat trickled down her back and through her scalp. If she could not come up with a new idea she was in deep shit. *Sod it.* She was about the scrunch the sheet into a ball and chuck it across the room.

No. There was a better use for it. She folded the page several times, and wedged it under the door to the gallery, holding it open. A through draft might help.

Gaius's list had contained over forty monarchs, stretching back to the legendary Mathanwy. It had not helped that, before Morgaine made herself High Queen, Annwyn had been divided into multiple kingdoms. Had these people really existed, or were they fay equivalents of King Arthur? Except, of course, if Queen Morgaine was the inspiration for Morgan le Fay, then Arthur might also be real, possibly the first captain of the Silver Ravens.

Lori walked onto the balcony and stared out over the sea. *Think, think, think.* Was it worth trying the same list against another of the scrolls? Maybe she had picked the one scroll written by a non-monarch— or maybe somebody who did not quite make it to becoming a monarch. An idea wriggled into life.

Knowledge of how to decode the cipher was clearly a closely guarded secret. Most likely, bygone kings and queens had told only their chosen heirs. Hence, Bronwen would have been the sister instructed in the matter. Who could blame her if she had been unwilling to share the secret with her murderer? All of which explained why Rianna needed help with the decoding.

Lori returned to the table. "Gaius?"

"Yes?"

"This list of kings and queens, did any have siblings who were expected to inherit the throne, but died early?"

"There have been a few."

"Okay. Give me their names." She pushed a fresh sheet of paper in his direction.

Minutes passed before he finished. Lori ran her eyes down the new list in surprise. Gaius had displayed an unexpected talent for understatement in using the word "few." Being in line for the throne was more risky than expected. The new list was longer than the last.

This was not going to be quick, and might still be a waste of time. However, deep in her gut, Lori was sure she was on the right track. Sighing, she picked up the quill.

Lori crossed off the eighth name and yawned. Her shoulder joints cracked as she stretched her arms. She needed to move her legs and get something to eat. The ideal option was a walk to the mess hall, but lunchtime was long past. She would have to settle for a quick trot around the balcony and yet more bread and cheese.

She wandered into the sunlight, rested her arms on the balustrade, and took in the view. The waves glittered below and fluffy white clouds drifted overhead without providing any shade, although the breeze off the sea freshened the air. The sun was still high, but sinking. Even so, its rays hit so hard it was as though they were pushing her into the ground.

She returned to the study, intending to ask Gaius to arrange food, when a commotion rumbled in through the open door to the audience hall gallery. Curious, Lori went to find a spot where she had a clear view of the area around the throne, while keeping herself concealed behind a column. What was going on?

The angry voices were getting louder, and then the Silver Ravens appeared, with Tamsin in the lead. Behind her, Shorty and Hippo frogmarched a bound prisoner between them—a young fay man, tall, thin, and blue skinned. BH, Widget, and Finn followed.

The condition of the prisoner was in marked contrast to any other fay Lori had seen. Instead of iridescent silk, he was wrapped in soiled rags that would have shamed a boggart. He was barefoot. His hair was so filthy it looked brown rather than silver. His hands were tied behind his back, and further coils of rope were wrapped around his arms and chest.

He was the one making the noise. "You upstart slime have no regard for your betters. Do you think to gloat, presenting me in this condition? Do you think mud and rags could disguise the gulf between us? You should pray I never get the chance to demonstrate how far I surpass your wretchedness."

The Silver Ravens, for their part, looked singularly unimpressed by the stream of complaint. Hippo yanked the prisoner forward, to within a few yards of Rianna's throne, and then Shorty kicked the back of his knees, forcing him to kneel.

A fresh disturbance marked the far more sedate arrival of the queen and her retinue. Lori retreated farther into the shadows. The prisoner ceased his rant when he saw Rianna. He squared his shoulders and raised his head, clearly aiming for a belated show of cool defiance.

Rianna settled on the throne. "Gilwyn. How nice to see you again."

"The pleasure is quite mutual, Aunt."

"My title is Queen."

"Your title is usurper and murderer. I'll give you no other name than that."

Shorty raised a fist to cuff the prisoner, but Rianna made a gesture to stop him. "No. It's all right. Gilwyn was always prone to boorishness, even as a child. I blame my sister for not teaching him better manners."

"You dare speak a word against her."

"I dare to do far more than that, as you well know. Bronwen had many failings. Being too soft-hearted was the least of them. Annwyn's preservation demanded her removal. But please believe me, I took no pleasure in it."

"Believe you? What sort of fool do you think me?"

Lori did not believe her either.

Rianna sighed theatrically. "Poor Gilwyn. You sound out of sorts. Have you not enjoyed my hospitality in Caerbonec?"

"Your prison fortress? Look at my current state to find your answer."

"I only wanted to ensure you were safe and at no risk of getting caught up in silly escapades. What would dear Bronwen have said, if I'd let anything happen to you? After all, you are the last of my blood kin."

"Only because you've murdered the rest."

Gilwyn's claim was easy to believe. Was the mention of blood significant? Lori was sure the next word in Morgaine's spell had not been traitor, and even if it were, Rianna would seem a better fit.

"Oh, Gilwyn. You really can be wearisome." Rianna turned to Tamsin. "Captain, thank you for escorting my nephew here. You and your Silver Ravens may go now. I'm sure you're tired after the journey. My guards will find suitable accommodation in the keep for Gilwyn… on one of the lower levels, I think."

Of course Caersiddi had a dungeon. No fairytale castle would be complete without one.

The Silver Ravens bowed and left the audience hall. With them gone, the atmosphere changed and the fragile veneer of humour vanished.

"My sister was a weak fool, and you've inherited all her worst traits."

"If I had a blade at your throat you'd see how weak I am."

"If, if, if." Malice burned in Rianna's eyes. "I have news for you, you don't, and never will have."

Two enthralled humans entered the hall. One was Rianna's toy-boy from the previous day. The other was less pretty, but equally muscular.

They only appeared after the Silver Ravens had left, supporting the notion that their existence was hidden from humans Rianna needed to keep on her side. But, while it was confronting to have evidence for

Tamsin's innocence in the matter, the thralls were not being hidden from Lori. Had Rianna forgotten she was in the study, or did she not care?

"Take him below."

The thralls hauled Gilwyn to his feet. He tried to shake loose, but their grip was firm. This did not stop him from calling out as he was dragged away. "One day, you'll regret not killing me sooner."

"I'll kill you when it suits my purpose and not before. But not to spoil the surprise, that time is close at hand." Rianna also left, followed by her retinue.

Lori returned to the study. Rianna clearly had a lot going on at the moment. Was it too hopeful to think the queen had limited time to devote to minor players, such as kidnapped computer programmers? Maybe, once all the scrolls were decoded, Tamsin could take her home while Rianna's thoughts were occupied with other matters. Lori took a deep breath, trying to calm her thoughts, then picked up the quill with renewed determination. The sooner she was done, the better.

The mess hall was its normal chaotic hubbub. Boggarts scampered between the tables, carrying tankards of beer and platters piled with meat, bread, and fruit. Iron Ravens catcalled, laughed, and sang. The amount of alcohol flowing no doubt played a part in the turmoil.

The Silver Ravens were at their usual half-empty table in the corner. Lori dropped onto the bench beside Tamsin.

Hippo grinned at her. "We're back." As ever, stating the obvious, but welcoming.

"I know. I saw you in the audience hall."

"You did?" Tamsin sounded surprised. "What were you doing there? I didn't see you."

"I was up in a gallery. I'm still working in the keep. The queen has more scrolls for me to decode. I heard the commotion and went to see what was happening."

"Gilwyn wasn't a happy bunny, was he?" Hippo said around a mouthful of food. Then he gave Tamsin a poorly disguised wink and shunted along the bench to join Widget and BH in conversation. As subtlety went, it was a non-starter. Lori tried to work out whether she minded.

"It's good you're able to be of more assistance to Queen Rianna. I'm sure she's grateful."

Lori was not at all sure. "It means I'll have to delay returning to Earth."

"Whenever you're free to go, just let me know. Not that I'm eager for us to part company."

"It's not that I…" Lori bit her tongue. Unsafe waters lay ahead. "The prisoner was the queen's nephew. Had he escaped from somewhere?"

"No. He was being held in Caerbonec. That's another royal castle, some way south. Queen Rianna wanted to talk with him, so we were sent to make sure he arrived safely."

"Why was he in prison? What had he done?"

"Been a general pain in the arse." Tamsin shrugged. "I suppose it's understandable he sided with his mother."

"Do you know why the queen wants to see him now?"

"It's not my business."

"You just follow orders."

"Queen Rianna knows what she's doing." Tamsin's voice acquired an edge.

But do you? "I didn't mean it as criticism. I'm hunting for words and phrases people might have used as keys. It was a long shot you could help."

Tamsin relaxed again. "I would if I could. What sort of help are you hoping for?"

"I can look up place names and genealogies, but I don't know what's important, or when. I don't know any history for Annwyn, or the politics, the gossip, the myths."

Now Tamsin laughed. "How much time have you got?"

"How much can you spare?"

Tamsin finished her meal and shifted around so she was half facing Lori. "I'm free all evening."

"Then give me a history lesson."

"If that's all you want."

"For now." She was skirting around trouble, but could not stop herself.

The glint in Tamsin's eye said she was more than ready to meet Lori halfway. "I'll try to be quick. For Annwyn, the important things are magic and family. Family, because that determines who gets dumped on. And magic, because that determines who does the dumping."

"Dog eat dog."

"Exactly. Mathanwy was the magician who created Annwyn, and judging by the number of children he sired, he must have been a dog."

"Who did he sire them on?"

"Monsters—if the stories are true. He wasn't fussy. As I said, a dog. Anyway, Mathanwy was the first of the fay. He created Annwyn with the help of Danu, who was either his sister, his daughter, or his lover, or maybe all three. Fay families can get very confusing. But they fell out and another fay called Lyrr got involved—I've no idea where he fits in, but things got even more confusing. The final upshot was that Danu ended up the winner on points and most rulers in Annwyn claim descent from her. Although Lyrr's descendants kept stirring things up."

Tamsin continued her potted history of Annwyn. Her face was mere inches away. The rising noise level could justify this closeness, but Lori was not kidding herself that this was the only reason.

The stories went a long way to explain Gaius's list of dead siblings. Life and death in the royal courts of Annwyn made the Borgias seem like a kid's birthday party, although with less ice cream and cake. Rianna had been following family tradition in bumping off her sister. The main question was why had she left her nephew alive, though it made sense if she had known she would eventually need his blood.

Tamsin came to the end of another gruesome string of events. "Are you sure you want to hear more? Wouldn't you like a break, or a change of subject?"

The mess hall had emptied. Even though the room was now quiet, Tamsin had not moved away. Lori's stomach flipped. So very little would be needed for their lips to meet. She felt herself drawn forward. Her eyes started to close. Her body was taking control, without waiting for her to make up her mind.

Two hands landed hard on the table, making it shake. Lori lurched back, jolted from her lust-driven stupor.

Finn loomed over them. "Are you ready to go? Shorty has a couple of decent bottles stashed in his room." While not completely ignoring Lori, his words were not directed her way.

"Sure." Tamsin's eyes met Lori's. "Do you want to come too? Or we could go somewhere else."

"I…" *I don't want to give Rianna a reason to be pissed off at me.* Not that Rianna was the type of person who needed reasons. "I have to get back to the keep."

"Queen Rianna is keeping you working so late?"

"I've been left to set my own schedule. But I know she wants the work done quickly."

"Then I won't keep you." Tamsin rose. "Another time."

"Okay."

While mulling over Tamsin's stories, Lori picked at the remains of her now cold meal. The path to power in Annwyn was a tale of death and betrayal. Family counted for little more than identifying who you needed to kill in order to advance. Given the number of strange accidents in suspicious circumstances, prudent monarchs would leave it to the last moment before naming a successor, in case it gave their chosen heir the idea of speeding things up.

If the scroll she was working on came from a sibling who died before getting the chance to take the throne, it made sense if the death occurred towards the end of the parent's reign. Lori sat up. Returning to work at the keep had been an excuse, but maybe she should go back. Gaius could reorder the names, putting those who most closely predeceased their parents at the top.

Lori left the mess hall and hurried through the middle bailey. Night had fallen while she and Tamsin had been talking, and shadows lay thick under the trees. However, no restrictions had been placed on the times she could be in the study, and Gaius seemed permanently available. She would spend an hour or so, testing out the first ten names on the revised list, and then call it a night.

CHAPTER TWELVE

As it turned out, Lori needed only four tries to hit on the right name. The note was from a sister of King Orfran called Ceirwen, who thought her brother was trying to poison her. The evidence was highly circumstantial, but given subsequent events, hard to dismiss. Orfran had been father to both Rianna and Bronwen. The words *apple* and *tree* came to mind.

"Do you want to tell the queen that I've decoded this one?" she asked Gaius.

"The queen is in her bedchamber and should not be disturbed. I will inform her in the morning."

Better not ask how he knew.

Lori wandered onto the balcony. With nightfall, the heat of the day had faded, but the air was still warm. The sounds of the sea rushing over the rocks was soothing. Starlight glittered on the waves. She was the only one still up. The other balconies were now silent and deserted. The inhabitants of Caersiddi had gone to their beds—or someone else's. She spared a thought for Rianna's toy-boy.

She ought to go back to her room, but she was not feeling at all tired. The success of her hunch had given her an adrenaline rush. Eight days had passed since she arrived in Annwyn. The month was December, back on Earth, and her parents would be celebrating Christmas without her. How long before they realised something was wrong? Surely they would try to send a card to her at the South Pole. What was the chance she could complete the decoding and get back before a full Earth year elapsed? She would press on.

The scrolls were held in an array of diamond shaped pigeonholes. Thankfully, the past rulers had not been compulsive writers, with the exception of whoever had produced the novelette. She took all the scrolls out and laid them on the table. Morgaine's original scroll was among them, but no sign of the translation. Rianna would be holding on to it. Lori was tempted to continue decoding and find out exactly whose blood was needed, but this was unwise, with Gaius watching.

So which one next?

A hundred years separated Morgaine and Ceirwen. Lori picked up their scrolls and held them under a lantern. Even in the weak light, Morgaine's scroll was noticeably darker, which might be a result of age. She put down the two scrolls and picked up a third, the darkest of all.

Despite the parchment's colour, the ink was unfaded and the text was clearly legible, or would have been, were it not for the tiny handwriting. When unrolled, the scroll was less than two feet long, but the writer had packed a lot in. The sensible course was to wait until tomorrow, when the light was better, but an idea nagged at her. Even though she would not finish it that night, she had to try one obvious name.

While Gaius returned the other scrolls to the cabinet, Lori took a new page from her notebook and wrote the name "Mathanwy" in a new grid. "Now, we'll see about myths and legends."

The first letters were discouraging and did not make any words. She squinted at the minuscule writing. "I don't suppose there's a magnifying glass in the study."

Gaius did not reply. She had not asked a direct question.

"Is there a magnifying glass in the study?"

"Yes."

"Can you get it for me, please." She tried not to snap at him. It was not his fault.

The glass made a huge improvement. Her guess at two letters had been wrong. She tried again.

By my wisdom and power, I, Mathanwy, have called forth a new world, for the glory of my name.

He certainly had not suffered from excessive modesty. Lori was about to continue when a click made her jump. She twisted around, almost falling off her seat. The scroll slipped from her hand and rolled under the table. One of the bookcases had swung out, revealing a dark opening in the wall. *A frigging secret passage. I don't believe it.* She eyed the new entrance nervously, waiting for Rianna to appear. What did the queen want, and why come to the study this way?

But she was wrong. Gilwyn was the one who emerged, looking less angry, but no cleaner than the last time she had seen him. He froze, clearly as surprised as she was, although he recovered quicker.

"Two of my aunt's pets." He snapped his fingers. Gaius immediately slumped forward over the table, unconscious.

"What have you…" Lori slipped off the stool and backed away.

Doubt flickered across Gilwyn's face, quickly hidden by a sneering smile. "Or one pet and one lackey." He sidled cautiously around the edge of the room, his eyes fixed on Lori's throat. The bookcase swung closed behind him. "I don't suppose there's any point me asking you to take that thing off your neck?"

"None whatsoever."

"I thought as much."

Gilwyn had not expected to find an unenthralled human in the study, that much was clear. He was trying to act nonchalant, but there was no missing the way he maintained his distance from her and the iron torc. For Lori's part, she was more than happy to keep the table between them.

"Aren't you going to ask what I'm doing here?" Gilwyn asked.

"I assume you're trying to escape."

"Ooooh. I see my darling aunt picked you for your brains as well as your beauty." He tugged on the cabinet door. "Unlocked. That speeds things up." He smiled at her. "Do you want to know how I escaped from the dungeon?"

"How?"

"I'm Morgaine's true heir. Tell my aunt that when you see her."

Lori had no intention of finding out how Rianna would react to his claim.

"Caersiddi is mine by right. I know every secret hidden in its stones. My mother wasn't as gullible as my aunt thinks. She could see what was coming and made sure I knew the escape route from the dungeon. One of my ancestors had the foresight to think it might be needed. My aunt isn't the first usurping traitor in Annwyn's history. My mother's biggest mistake was in assuming she would be questioned before being killed."

While talking, Gilwyn transferred the scrolls to a small sack. Once the pigeonholes were empty he tightened the drawstring. "Unfortunately for my mother, my brilliant aunt wasn't clever enough to work out that 'kill first, ask questions after' only works when you're not bothered about getting answers. She must have been so upset when she realised she'd murdered the one person who could tell her how to decode these scrolls."

Did that mean Gilwyn did not know either? "What do you want them for?"

"I don't want to leave them with my aunt. Not that she'd have a clue what to do with them." Gilwyn glanced at the table. "Though I can see she's been trying. It must be giving her a headache, poor dear. No wonder she's left the tidying up to you and has gone to bed."

Lori decided not to enlighten him.

"My aunt is not just a usurper, she's a stupid one as well. My mother should have executed her, first chance she got. I won't make the same mistake. You can tell my aunt that as well."

Another message Lori would not be passing on.

Gilwyn picked up a small cloth bag from another shelf and closed the cabinet. He continued edging around the room.

Lori wanted to keep the table between them, but dared not get too close to Gaius, just in case Gilwyn could control thralls well enough to have him attack her. The iron torc clearly unnerved Gilwyn, but the only way to use it as a weapon was to take it off and throw it at him, which definitely fell into the category of last resort, and she was not there yet.

However, Gilwyn's goal was not her, but the door to the gallery. That was fine. Lori was more than happy for him to leave. But instead of going, he took a pinch of powder from the pouch and threw it at the door.

"I don't want you raising the alarm." Gilwyn spoke as if it was an explanation.

What had he done?

"And now, I'll be on my way. Good night." He gave an ironic bow and backed onto the balcony.

Gilwyn again opened the pouch, this time sprinkling powder from it over his own head. It sparkled in the starlight, like glitter. As Lori watched, his figure changed, becoming shorter, squatter, darker. His chest ballooned out. His legs shrunk. His arms flattened and twisted back flat along his sides. His face pulled out into a point, a beak.

A huge raven stood on the balcony.

Lori watched in amazement as the bird hopped onto the balustrade and opened its wings. The raven launched itself into the air. By the time she had scrambled onto the balcony, Gilwyn was gone, a black bird, lost in the night.

Rianna was not going to be pleased, and Lori did not want to be the one to give her the news. Back in the study, Gaius was still sprawled across the desk.

Lori put a hand on his shoulder and gave a gentle shake. "Gaius. Are you all right?"

He was not. His body flopped sideways off the stool and crashed lifeless to the floor—utterly lifeless. She did not need to search for a pulse to know he was dead, although she tried, and even put her ear to his chest, listening for a heartbeat.

What reason did Gilwyn have to murder him? She shook her head in disbelief. As if the fay needed a reason to kill. Gaius was dead, and Lori was certain the only thing that had saved her own life was the iron torc around her neck.

She should tell someone what had happened. Rianna would undoubtedly want to question her, which was unlikely to be a pleasant experience. Gilwyn's escape was hardly her fault, but Rianna was going to be furious.

However the door would not budge. After several fruitless tugs on the handle, Lori looked more closely. The join around the sides was gone. Gilwyn had transformed door and frame into a single piece of wood, in the same way that he had transformed himself into a giant raven.

It would take similar magic to change it back, and Lori had no other way out of the room. A hunt for the opening mechanism on the bookcase got her nowhere. There was nothing to use as a rope for reaching the other balconies, so it was irrelevant to wonder whether she would have risked it. She had a good head for heights, but the sea was an awfully long way down.

She was stuck in the study with Gaius's body until someone rescued her. How long before anyone came? Hammering on the door was pointless. Nobody would be walking around at that time of night. She should wait until the morning before bruising her hands, or until someone emerged on another balcony and she could call to them.

She positioned Gaius flat on his back and arranged his limbs with dignity, folding his hands on his chest. His eyes stared blankly at the ceiling. She would not have thought it possible, but they were even more empty than in life. Getting his eyelids to close was not as easy as TV shows made it seem. Why had Gilwyn murdered him? But maybe it was a kindness. What would Gaius have wished for, back when he was able to make his own decisions?

She had to get home to Earth, and Gilwyn had unintentionally done her a favour, as long as she survived the interview with Rianna. Nothing remained for her to decode, except the one dropped scroll, missed by Gilwyn and forgotten by her, until now.

Lori reached under the table. Why not get rid of it? Throw it out the window and say Gilwyn had taken it with all the rest. But supposing it landed on another balcony? Burning it was more certain, and the lanterns would provide her with a flame.

Lori unrolled the scroll. The first king of Annwyn had thought its contents so important they needed to be kept secret. *Dammit. I want to know.*

If Rianna kept her word and sent her home tomorrow with her weight in gold, she would be able to decode the scroll at her leisure. And if Rianna tried to keep her in Annwyn, the information in the scroll might be the only thing that could help her. She needed to hide the scroll, and she knew just where.

Lori stripped off her ancient jeans. The stitching on the waistband inner seam had pulled loose at one spot. The parchment was as thin and light as tracing paper, and when rolled lengthwise, was small enough to feed in through the hole in the seam. Lori massaged the wad of parchment around to the back, where the faint bulge was hidden by her belt. She pulled the jeans on again.

With luck, the scroll could stay there until she was back home in England. She just had to remember to take it out before she put the jeans into the wash.

"Did he say how he escaped from the dungeon?" Rianna's high, tinkling voice was a screech.

Midmorning sunlight fell through the large stained glass window. Reversing Gilwyn's magical sealing of the door had not been quick.

"No. Not really, Your Majesty."

"Not really? What do you mean?"

"He was talking just to hear his own voice. He didn't make an effort to explain anything, and he didn't ask me any questions. He made it clear he didn't think I was worth speaking to."

"What did he say? Did he name anyone? Another traitor who helped him?"

"The only person he mentioned was his mother. He said she'd told him about the secret passage."

"Why didn't you try to stop him?"

"I was taken by surprise. I didn't know where he'd come from, or why. He'd just murdered Gaius, and I didn't know what else he was capable of."

Rianna looked as if she was also ready to commit murder. She launched herself from her throne and paced the room, then rounded on an attendant. "Summon Captain Tamsin. My nephew may run, but he will not get far."

"Yes, my queen." The flunkey scuttled away.

Rianna returned to Lori. "And he stole all the scrolls?"

"Yes, Your Majesty." The urge to adjust the set of her jeans almost overwhelmed her, but fidgeting would make her look nervous and guilty.

"Did he say he knew how to decode them?"

"No, Your Majesty. In fact, he said his mother was the only one who could."

The answer took the faintest edge off Rianna's anger. "Which is something. You may go."

Lori did not hang around, in case the queen changed her mind.

Lori waited with her shoulder against a tree trunk and her eyes fixed on the gateway to the inner bailey. All night, she had been locked in a room with a corpse. Did that justify the inane way she had cheered herself up with happy thoughts of going home? It was not going to happen. Maybe Queen Bitch was too wound up over Gilwyn's escape to worry about anyone else right now, but it would not last.

It was a dead certainty that the Silver Ravens were going after Gilwyn, and Tamsin would not have any time for escort duties until he was recaptured. How long this would take was anyone's guess. The same went for how long it would take Rianna to calm down enough to think about other things. But when that time came, Lori wanted to be far away. Rianna no longer had a reason to leave her brains in functioning mode.

Tamsin appeared in the gateway. Lori moved to intercept her.

"Can I talk to you?"

"If you don't mind doing it while we walk. I have messages to pass on."

"That's all right." She fell into step beside Tamsin. "Is Queen Rianna sending you after her nephew?"

"Yes."

"When are you leaving?"

"Straight after lunch. Are you..." Tamsin looked apologetic. "I'm sorry. I know I said I'd take you home. But it'll have to wait. We can't have Gilwyn running around, causing havoc."

"I realise that." Lori took a deep breath. "Can I come with you?"

"What?"

"You said you needed a sniper. If I've got to hang around in Annwyn, I might as well see more of the world."

"It isn't a game."

"I know. But I'm serious. There's nothing more for me to do in Caersiddi, since Gilwyn stole all the scrolls."

"Join the Iron Ravens. It's less risky and their entrance qualifications are easier. All it takes is being human and getting to Annwyn. You pass."

But it would not get her out of Caersiddi. "I've done the army training course. I want to see if I can put it into effect." The argument sounded decidedly weak, even to her own ears. What would Mum say? "There's a whole world here, full of amazing things I'd never thought I'd see outside of a game. I don't want to end up at home, regretting not taking advantage when I had the chance."

Tamsin came to a stop. "You really are serious."

"Yes." She met Tamsin's eyes. "What are your requirements for a sniper?"

"Hit three, head-sized targets at half a mile."

Ouch. Once the range went over six hundred yards, her accuracy dropped rapidly. This would be more than eight hundred. Lori looked up. Visibility was perfect, there was hardly a breath of wind, and she could forget any thought of the Coriolis Effect. She was never going to have a better chance.

"Do you have the Leupold scope for the M24?" Another scope might make little difference, but that was the one she was familiar with.

"Yes."

"I can take a couple of practise shots to set the range?"

"Of course. Though if ever you find yourself gunning for a dragon, it might not be so obliging."

"Okay. When do I give it a go?"

"You're sure?"

"Yes."

Tamsin was clearly torn between surprise and amusement. "All right. I need to pass on the message to the others. But then I'll meet you at the armoury in the outer bailey. We've got the distance marked out on the beach. There isn't room in the castle. I'll be spotter."

Could she do it? Lori clenched her hands into fists. She did not want to question whether they were shaking. She had to match her best ever shooting. Dwelling on thoughts that her life and sanity might depend on the outcome would not help.

❖

The crack of her final shot echoed back from the castle walls. Lori flipped the safety and got to her knees, while brushing sand from her shirt. She kept her eyes in the direction of the distant targets, not daring to look Tamsin's way. "Well?"

"You did all right."

"I did?"

"Don't sound surprised. It gives the wrong impression. Come on, let's look up close."

She matched her stride to Tamsin's as they crossed the hard packed sand. This was the first time she had been outside the castle walls since her arrival. The chance to stretch her legs was good. She had spent too much time cooped up in a small room—not that long periods indoors normally bothered her. A strange thought, but what she had said before was not a total fabrication. If she made it home safe and had missed out on seeing more of Annwyn, she really would kick herself. Mum and Dad would be so proud of her.

"I'll have to clear it with Queen Rianna, of course," Tamsin said.

Of course. "Do you think she'll approve?"

"She wants Gilwyn taken alive. You're the best person to put a silver bullet through his knee, if he tries to run." Tamsin grinned. "I think she'll be happy for you to join us."

"Aren't silver bullets for werewolves?"

"They're for anything here you don't want to kill outright. Any wound from a normal bullet is fatal to Annwyn natives, both fay and boggarts."

"Lead as well? It's not just iron?"

"All base metals are harmful to them. Copper won't kill fay, or bronze so long as there's not too much tin in it, but it can give them a nasty case of hives. Lead isn't as poisonous as iron, but has unpredictable effect. A steel tipped bullet though…" Tamsin shook her head. "One scratch and it's over."

"Are there really werewolves here?"

"Were-everything. I told you about transmutation."

"Oh, yes." How could she forget watching Gilwyn turn himself into a giant raven?

They reached the targets. Her first shot had clipped the edge, but was a hit nonetheless. The other two were central.

"You did well."

"Thanks."

Tamsin placed a hand on Lori's shoulder and turned her so their eyes met. Lori felt a flutter in her stomach, but Tamsin's expression was stern. "So, you've proved you can do it. I want you to stop and think very carefully. Take a minute—take two. Annwyn is dangerous. Anything can happen, and probably will. There's no guarantee of safety. Are you absolutely sure about this?"

As if anything could be more dangerous than staying in Caersiddi. Still, she made a show of thinking. "Yes. I'm sure."

"Then you can come along and see how you do. Afterwards, when we get back…if we get back, you'll be free to say it's not for you and you want to return to Earth."

"Perfect."

Tamsin started towards the castle gates. "I'll send a message to Rianna. Then we need to eat lunch, pack, and leave. You've got two hours."

"No problem." She did not have much to pack.

Lori put a hand on the horse's flank. It was solid—surprisingly so given its phantom-like appearance, although it felt more like clay than flesh.

"What are they?"

"Flying horses," Hippo answered. "Have you ridden before?"

"Not ones that levitate."

"These aren't so different. Easier in some ways. Less risk of being thrown off when you go over a jump."

"Right. But no getting straight back in the saddle if you are."

"Nope."

The harness jingled as the horse moved. Silver bells, of course. Fortunately, no one was asking her to wear them on her fingers and toes. Lori put her foot in the stirrup and swung her leg over the horse's rump. The saddle had no modifications for flight, such as a seat belt. She urged the horse into a slow walk. The animal moved in a normal way, but something felt off. Or was she was overanalysing?

"What do you think of Cirrus?" BH brought her own horse alongside.

"That's her name?"

"Yes."

She patted Cirrus's neck. "I'm sure we'll get along fine."

"She likes you. That's a good sign." BH gave a broad smile.

"You can tell?"

"It's part of my job." BH urged her horse on. "Catch you later."

"Right."

The news Lori would join in the pursuit of Gilwyn had been greeted with varying degrees of surprise. Only Finn displayed outright disapproval, although Shorty had rolled his eyes. BH had been unexpectedly supportive, given their limited previous contact. Maybe she was hoping for a chance to hone her matchmaking skills. She had volunteered to show Lori where the kit was stored, and helped pick out a warm fur lined flying jacket, along with a set of the black leather uniform, complete with knife, pistol, and Silver Raven belt buckle.

Lori's old jeans, along with the scroll in the waistband, were stored in the chest in her room. She had toyed with hanging on to the scroll, but would not be able to work on the decoding while away. It should be safe, unless a boggart decided to do her laundry while she was gone.

"I should have asked if you've ridden before." Tamsin joined her.

"My parents took me trekking when I was a child." Crossing the Himalayas by mule as a ten-year-old had been particularly memorable. "I haven't done much since university, but I'm sure it will come back to me."

Tamsin manoeuvred closer. "This is your last chance to back out. Are you sure you're sure?"

"Yes."

"Right then." Tamsin raised her voice. "Time to move out." The Silver Ravens followed her through the gates in single file.

She had escaped. Relief washed through Lori in a wave. Until their return, the only things she had to worry about were dragons and other assorted monsters. Catching Gilwyn was another issue, but Tamsin must have some sort of plan. Though, now that Lori gave it thought, how were they going to find him? Where would they start? Regardless of BH's skill as a tracker, Gilwyn had flown away. Even a real bloodhound would have no trail to follow.

Once clear of the castle walls, Tamsin stood in her stirrups. "First stop, Mud Town. We'll see what Segann can tell us." She urged her horse into a canter.

Lori was in the middle of the line, between Widget and BH. How did you do the flying bit? It was too late now to ask. She could only hope Cirrus knew what to do. In front, Tamsin began to rise up, and then Finn in second place.

Suddenly, the vibration of hoof beats stopped and the ground dropped away. Cirrus still moved her legs in a canter, but the action felt as if it was purely for show. Their speed increased, far beyond the limits of an earthbound horse. Wind rushed in Lori's face. The flying jacket was welcome. Goggles would have been a good idea as well.

The last time she had flown was just two years before, on a holiday to Corfu. But the memories that now flooded back were from her childhood, sitting between Mum and Dad, listening to them make excited plans for the things they would see and do.

Far below, the coastline stretched from horizon to horizon, mile upon mile of bays and headlands. The castle of Caersiddi stuck out into the sea on its rocky promontory, looking even more like a child's toy than before. The miniature landscape of forests, rivers, hills, and valleys was just like the view through an airplane window. Something she had seen on dozens of flights, between watching films on the seatback screen. But she was not in a plane. There was no TV screen, no window, no comforting shell of the fuselage around her, no seat belt. It was exhilarating and terrifying in equal measure—and fun.

The last thing Lori had expected. Fun.

Chapter Thirteen

For a long time, they flew over wilderness, without any sign of habitation. From up high, the differences between a flat world and a round one were slight, yet unsettling, giving the bizarre sensation she was looking at a reflection in a fairground mirror, without anything actually being distorted. The mountains retreated, but did not drop over the horizon.

After four hours, the wilderness gave way to fields in a patchwork of crops and pastures speckled with grazing herds. Dirt roads linked isolated farmhouses. The sea drew close again, now dotted with small boats. Then, far ahead, trails of smoke rose above a dark smudge.

The smudge hardened into a sprawl of buildings as the Silver Ravens started their descent. They landed a short way outside town, on the largest of the roads leading in.

Widget dropped back beside Lori. He made a show of breathing in a deep lungful and then exhaling. "Doesn't that smell bring it all back?"

"It might, if I'd ever been here before."

"Your first visit to Mud Town. Ohhhh, you're in for a treat, pet."

"Mud Town? That can't be the real name."

"The locals have a pretty name for it, but who can be buggered with that, I ask you?"

BH was close enough to join in. "It depends on whether we want King Segann to help us." She smiled at Lori. "He prefers calling his town Trethbuder."

"He's king here? I thought Queen Rianna ruled all Annwyn."

"She does. King Segann is—"

Widget cut BH off. "He's a jumped up little arsewipe, but he calls the shots around here, and we're wanting his help. So yes…" He shrugged. "I guess it's King Segann and Trethbuder while we're here."

"And his title is King of the Bukka," BH finished.

"Who are the Bukka?"

"Boggarts with sticks up their arses."

Lori was unsurprised to see the farm workers in the surrounding fields were all boggarts. In Caersiddi, the hard, dirty work was left to them, and she would scarcely expect fay to be tending sheep. But, on entering the town, she saw nothing but boggarts, including some who, if not wealthy, were clearly a few steps above the bottom rung of society.

The outskirts were a shanty town of wretched hovels, well deserving the name Mud Town. Farther on, the buildings became more substantial as they rode along streets of houses, two or three stories high, with half-timbered frontages and slate tile roofs. However the effect could never be described as charming or quaint, and the smell got worse.

The streets and alleyways were filled with boggarts, who flattened themselves against the walls to make way for the mounted humans. They acted in a manner showing neither curiosity nor hostility, but Lori did not feel welcome.

The buildings were crammed together, as if elbowing each other aside for room. They overhung the street, blocking out light. The state of repair was mixed, with some relying more on hope than mortar to remain standing. A few windows were glazed, but most had only wooden shutters. Deep ruts scored the unpaved roads.

Mud Town was a dump—or Trethbuder as Lori reminded herself. Then she made the mistake of looking too closely at the coating of muck on the ground. Actually, Mud Town counted as a polite euphemism. She fixed her eyes on the road ahead.

The boggarts were dressed in everything from filthy rags to well-made garments in the style of the fay. Some even carried a scarf or gloves made from the same shimmering material. Craftsmen worked in their shops. Porters pulled carts piled high with merchandise. Homeowners hung out of windows shouting to those below. There were even children, dashing around underfoot. They screeched at each other, sounding more like angry cats than anything else.

Widget rode beside her. He grimaced at their surroundings. "If you do want to say something tactless, like you think Mud Town is a complete shithole, you can always switch to English. The boggarts won't understand a word you're saying." He was taking his own advice.

One boggart, wearing a thick leather jerkin and helmet, had the appearance of a guard or policeman. He swung a heavy wooden club in time with his steps as he lumbered along the street. The other boggarts kept out of his way and scuttled past with their heads down.

Or was it a he? "How do you tell males from females?" Lori decided to stick with English.

"Take their clothes off, if you're feeling brave."

BH laughed. "Or you could look for rings. Females pierce their ears, males their noses. It works most of the time."

Shorty was a few yards in front. He twisted round. "And if they're too poor to afford a ring, nobody gives a fuck what they are."

Lori looked at the boggart they had just passed. The guard had two gold rings in either ear. A she. Best leave it at that.

The street opened onto a small square. The increase in daylight was a relief. The air was also able to circulate, reducing the oppressive clamminess, though doing little about the smell. The building directly ahead was the grandest yet seen, three stories high and fully glazed.

Tamsin was clearly heading for it, but any hopes it might be the king's palace faded. The lack of guards, the door propped open, and the sign outside created the nasty suspicion it was an inn. So much for wishing they could conclude their meeting with the king quickly and be on their way. Spending a night in Mud Town was not on Lori's bucket list.

An archway at the side of the inn led to the stable yard at the rear. Tamsin jumped down and tossed her horse's reins to a boggart.

Finn did likewise, with a muttered, "And don't eat it." Lori could not tell if he was joking.

Getting out of the saddle was a relief. Her legs were stiff and she was yet to warm up. A walk to get her blood circulating would have been nice, although maybe not in the current surroundings, and certainly not alone.

A bobbing, simpering, bowing boggart with a ring in his nose greeted them at the entrance. "Come in, madam. Come in, sir. You would like food, yes? And something to drink? We have good wine, good beer. You would find this pleasing, yes?"

"Yes. And rooms for tonight," Tamsin replied. "I also want a message taken to King Segann. We wish to speak with him, as soon as is convenient."

"Yes, yes, I will see to it all, madam. You will have everything you want."

The boggart scrambled away after another couple of head bobs. He was still abjectly fawning, but his diction and vocabulary was noticeably more advanced than anything heard from boggarts in Caersiddi. Did only idiots go to work there, or did boggarts deliberately act dumb around the fay?

Either way, Lori was unsure about the food. Did she want to eat anything in this inn? Admittedly, the common room, when they entered it, was not quite as bad as she feared, although it would have struggled to rate one star on a customer review website. The windows were too dirty to see through. The tables and benches had been crudely hammered together. Damp patches marked the walls and mould grew in the cracks between the flagstones. The ceiling was so low, Shorty was forced to stoop.

He dropped onto a bench. "Who wants to put a bet on how long before we get to see his fucking highness?"

"Maybe tomorrow, if we're lucky." Hippo as ever, sounded cheerfully unworried.

"Or the day after." Finn did not.

Lori slipped onto the end of the bench, then shunted along when Tamsin indicted she wanted to sit beside her. The resulting flutter in her stomach was irritating, as were the amused looks exchanged between the other Silver Ravens. She tried to ignore both. Her leg tingled where it was pressed against Tamsin's. The sensible thing was to move away, but she was not going to.

"What did you think of the journey?" Tamsin asked.

"Not as scary as the thought of eating here. Are you sure it's safe?"

"It's the same as you had in Caersiddi. All the food comes from around here."

And was prepared by boggarts. It had not killed her yet. "King Segann, is he a boggart?"

"Yes. But don't call him that when you're speaking Hyannish. Stick with King of the Bukka. We want to keep on his good side."

"I dread to think what his dungeon is like, if this tavern's anything to go by."

Tamsin laughed. "No risk of ending up there. He won't dare annoy Queen Rianna, which is what would happen if he locked us up. But he could give us the runaround, and we don't want to waste time."

"He's a client king under her?"

"Nothing so formal. Queen Rianna lets the boggarts sort themselves out, so long as they send their tithes on time. Segann put himself on the Mud Throne by killing anyone else who wanted the title. He's done a decent enough job though, and kept things running smoothly."

Fay lived in luxury, on the backs of boggart workers, and did not even have the hassle of organising them. Easy to see why Rianna was happy with the arrangement. "The tithes they send, is it just food, or does it count the workers in Caersiddi?"

"Everything, including manufactured goods from Wydlow. That's the other main town Segann controls. It's where you find the mines and heavy industry, so it isn't as pretty as here."

"I don't think I want to see it."

"Nope. You don't." Tamsin smiled. "I guess Mud Town must be a bit of a shock, after England in the twenty-first century. I did warn you."

"It's not so much worse than some places I saw as a child. Though back then I was too young to worry about germs."

"Where were you?"

"All over. My parents are eternal globetrotters."

"Jet-setters?"

"No. New Age backpackers who never grew up. They write travel books and articles for *National Geographic*, and now they have their own environmentalist blog with several million followers."

"So that's why you were keen to see more of Annwyn. It's in your blood."

"No. I gave up travelling in my teens. My parents wanted me to sit exams, so I stayed with my grandmother for most of secondary school. After that I went to university, then got into computing, and…" Old, awkward emotions bubbled up in her chest. "I'd had enough of life on the move. I like knowing where I'll be sleeping tonight."

"How about your brothers and sisters?"

"There aren't any. To be honest, I think I was an accident. Babies don't fit the lifestyle."

Rootless trees don't bear fruit. Grandma's voice echoed again in her ears. Dad had been her precious baby boy, and she would never forgive Mum for helping him cut the apron strings.

"Hey. Are you all right?"

Her face must have given too much away. "Yes. I'm fine. Secondary school wasn't a good time in my life."

"You must have resented your parents leaving you behind."

"It wasn't that." Or was it? Had that been the start? "The other kids picked on me. They thought I was odd. I knew all about living in a yurt in Outer Mongolia, but I didn't know the names of pop stars, TV shows, or actors. Then I made the mistake of letting them know I was gay."

"Ah. That." Tamsin looked unusually reticent. Her eyes fixed on the tabletop. "BH did mention that you'd said something."

I bet she did.

"And that you'd split up with your previous girlfriend."

Yes. She'd have mentioned that as well.

"But you're not looking for anyone at the moment." Tamsin raised her eyes, challenging, questioning.

"No, I'm not." Time to slide along the bench, although Lori's leg complained of being lost and abandoned, now that it was no longer pressed against Tamsin.

If Tamsin's leg was similarly upset, its owner showed no sign. Tamsin's normal easy smile returned. "I'm sorry you had a tough time. But for what it's worth, where I grew up, things would have turned out far worse if I'd been caught with a female lover. I might even have had a hot date with a pile of wood and a stake."

So now they were both on the same page. "I didn't think the laws applied to women."

"Maybe not. But it was the sort of thing that got you the attention of the Witchfinder General." Tamsin shrugged. "Any excuse would do."

The door opened and three boggarts arrived, carrying trays of food. As Tamsin said, it looked identical to the meals at Caersiddi. The interruption was a good chance to change subject.

"What help are you hoping for from King Segann?"

"Boggarts have their own way with magic, though nowhere near the level of the fay. They're strongest with illusion, and some can manage transformation as well."

"So this is the last place in Annwyn to take your torc off."

"Right. With illusion, boggarts have something they call the weave. It's a shared illusion they all take part in. Who knows how it works, but the king is the one in the middle of the weave."

"Can the king use this weave to tell us where Gilwyn is?"

"Not directly. Fay are immune to boggart magic."

"But you still think the king can help us in some way?"

"Yes. Gilwyn won't be roughing it, in a tent. He has supporters, fellow traitors. They'll have set him up in a hideout, and he won't be alone. Boggarts will be there, and they'll be making their own input to the weave. Segann has followers who can spot them by shifts in the weave."

"Surely Gilwyn will be aware they can do this."

"Fay refuse to believe boggarts can do anything they can't, and since they can't access the weave they assume it doesn't exist, especially since it has no effect on them. Even Queen Rianna can be a little too quick to discount boggarts' abilities."

It was hardly news the fay held every other species in contempt. More surprising was that Tamsin would send a hint of criticism the queen's way.

"So Gilwyn won't see the weave as a risk."

"He won't give it a second thought. Count on it. Anyway, no matter what's at stake, no fay is ever going to empty his own chamber pot."

❖

"Check." Widget was happy. "You don't know how long I've been waiting for someone who can give me a decent game."

Lori feared he was in for a disappointment. Widget refused to believe a computer programmer was not also a chess whiz, and had pulled out a small travel set as soon as the food was cleared away. The other Silver Ravens were playing cards on another table, except for Hippo, who had adopted the role of audience, and was switching back and forth between games.

Lori moved a pawn to block. "Do you really think it will be tomorrow before King Segann agrees to see us?"

"Definitely. He'll make us wait at least a day, out of pure bloody-mindedness, just to show he can."

"Nothing like Queen Rianna." Lori kept her tone neutral.

"Nothing what-so-fucking-ever, as Shorty would say." Widget picked up his queen from the board and gave it a pantomime kiss. "She's amazing, and I love her to bits."

Hippo chipped in, "And she's a damn sight prettier than him."

"My arse is prettier than him."

Lori just smiled and nodded. Why could the Silver Ravens not see the same conniving bitch she did? On the other side of the room, Tamsin had just won another hand. Judging by the comments, this was not unusual. Tamsin's expression was calm and controlled, a classic poker face. She was clearly reading the other players better than they were reading her. Yet she was being completely outplayed by Rianna. How?

Lori's confusion must have shown on her face.

"Is the chess making your brain hurt, pet?" Widget returned his queen to the board and moved his bishop.

"It's a long time since I last played. I—"

The door opened and a boggart entered. He was wearing a leather jacket and helmet, like the guard seen earlier. He stamped to a halt and glared around the room, without the faintest trace of subservience.

Tamsin laid her cards face down on the table. "You have a message from King Segann?"

"Yes. His Majesty, Segann, King of the Bukka, will see you. You must come at once."

If Tamsin was surprised, she gave no sign. "Wonderful. Finn, you'll come with me, and—"

Lori cautiously raised her hand. "I'd like to meet the king as well, if that would be okay."

"Sure. And three's enough."

Lori sidled off the bench.

"Running away, are you?" Widget sounded more amused than upset. He switched to English. "Ready to be bowled over by the Mud King's charm?"

"Something like that." She gestured at the chessboard. "Hippo can take over for me."

"Don't be silly. He can't tell a rook from a prawn."

Hippo frowned. "Don't you mean pawn?"

"In your case, no."

Hippo laughed good-naturedly and flicked a chess piece at Widget.

Lori smiled. If she stayed in Annwyn, could she make friends and fit in, maybe even win over Finn? Not that it was going to happen with Rianna in the picture.

Outside in the square, evening was drawing on, but the streets of Mud Town were as chaotic as before, especially so when viewed from ground level, rather than horseback. Lori felt vulnerable, although the crowds still parted meekly to let them through. Was it the sight of three humans or their escort, marching in the lead, swinging his club?

"Why did you want to come?" Tamsin asked in English.

"Curiosity."

"You know what that did for the cat, don't you?"

"As I said, this is my chance to see Annwyn. I want to make the most of it." Dammit—it was the truth. Thoughts of Mum and Dad were becoming stronger. So why fight it?

"I hope you don't come to regret leaving Caersiddi."

Like that's going to happen.

"This is…" Tamsin was frowning.

"You think something's up?"

"Yes. Segann agreeing to meet us this quickly means he wants something. On past form, that isn't a good sign."

"As the queen's representative, don't you have the upper hand? Can't you say no if he's unreasonable?"

"Annwyn politics. I can't afford to piss him off. Like I told you, fay don't acknowledge boggart magic. As soon as I tell him why I'm here, he'll know I'm acting on my own. He can deny having any way to find where Gilwyn is, and there'll be nothing I can do about it. I need his cooperation."

They crossed over a river. The other side was cleaner, calmer, and clearly wealthier. This was where rich boggarts lived, although it still would not count as a prime location on Earth. The ground rose to a headland, overlooking the sea. At the top was a jumble of buildings. This had to be their destination.

When they finally reached it, if King Segann's palace was not exactly what Lori expected, neither did it surprise her. The surrounding wall and gaggle of guards at the gate gave it the look of a fortified compound rather than a royal residence.

The gate was solid wooden timbers, stout enough to withstand a siege and wide enough for a carriage to drive through. At the guard's shout, the sounds of a bar being lifted came from the other side. The gate opened sufficiently for the party to enter one at a time, and then it was slammed shut. King Segann was clearly worried about unwelcome visitors.

An interlinked sprawl of poorly maintained buildings took up most of the compound. The strips of lawn were more weeds than grass. The overall effect fell somewhere between rundown fort and a prison. More guards gathered by the entrance to the main building. One placed herself squarely in the middle of the doorway and folded her arms.

"Leave your weapons here. All of them."

Tamsin and Finn had their handguns and knives ready to turn over before being told.

The surly guard turned to Lori. "You too."

She fumbled with the catch on her holster. The pistol was part of the standard kit. Up until then, the unfamiliar weight on her hip had been off-putting. Now she felt anxious without it. Maybe she should have stayed behind.

They were escorted into a room with the look of a medieval banqueting hall, minus any of the quaint, decorative touches. The tables and benches running the length on either side could each have sat forty boggarts. Fading daylight was supplemented by lanterns giving off a pungent smoke that did nothing to mask other odours. Unwashed bodies and stagnant water were two Lori recognised. She tried not to think about the rest.

King Segann sat behind the high table on the dais at the end of the hall. He appeared older than most other boggarts, and fatter. The nose ring would have helped her determine his sex, had she not already known. A cape of shimmering fay cloth was draped over his shoulders, and a golden circlet held down lank wisps of hair on his round head.

Guards lined the walls. Another clump of attendants huddled in a dark corner behind the king. They were further concealed by long robes and hoods that cast deep shadows. Their faces were hidden except for where lantern light glinted on eyes and teeth, making the group look like deranged monks from a horror movie.

King Segann's gaze was shrewd and calculating, neither hostile nor welcoming. It fixed on Tamsin as she stopped before the table and gave the smallest of bows.

"Captain. It's good to welcome you here again." His voice was a raw, dry whisper that carried the length of the hall.

"The honour is mine. Thank you for graciously agreeing to see us so soon after our arrival in Trethbuder."

"Always, I am happy to see you. But what brings the Silver Ravens here this time?"

"A small matter—embarrassingly so. I almost feel guilty at wasting your time, but I have a favour to ask."

"Think of me as a friend. Ask."

"Her Majesty, Queen Rianna, has lost something."

"Something valuable?"

"Very. Her nephew. He's run away from Caersiddi. A juvenile prank, no more. Her Majesty is anxious no harm should come to him. I hoped one of your subjects might have news of his whereabouts."

"Who is this nephew?"

"Gilwyn, son of the queen's late sister."

"Ah yes, him. I'd heard he was at another of Queen Rianna's castles—Caerbonec wasn't it?"

"He was, but he recently joined her at Caersiddi, until last night, when he ran away."

"Families can be so much trouble."

Tamsin nodded in reply.

What the two were not saying was clearly every bit as important as what they were. Before then, Lori had viewed boggarts with sympathy. The humans treated them almost as badly as fay did. However, she had assumed the small creatures lacked intelligence. Yet, the king was going toe to toe with Tamsin in the verbal fencing. Either he was exceptional, or boggarts were definitely playing dumb in Caersiddi.

Thoughtfully, King Segann picked at one of his long canines, while his eyes never left Tamsin. He beckoned one of the robed figures forward. The pair conferred briefly in whispers, before the king turned back to Tamsin.

"It's a strange thing, but I've recently lost one of my kin as well."

"How odd."

"Isn't it? A cousin of mine has gone missing. Nysian is his name. He was working for me, looking after the mines at Wydlow. Ten days ago, he vanished."

"You've no idea where he might be?"

"None at all." King Segann shook his head sadly. "Nysian was always rash. I expect he's just gone exploring and not told anyone. He might even be on his way to visit me here. I'd be very keen to see him. We've not spoken for a while."

"We'll be happy to look into this matter for you."

"You would? Thank you. I know it's foolish to worry. I'm sure he'll turn up, safe and sound. But I'm thinking how awful if he's been hurt. Accidents can happen to any of us."

"Exactly. I'll discuss this with the rest of my squad, and we'll start looking for him first thing tomorrow."

"Good. While you do this, I'll see what I can find out about this missing nephew." King Segann nodded. "Hopefully, we'll talk again soon, with a happy outcome for us both."

Tamsin gave another small bow. "Hopefully."

Nothing more was said until they were outside the king's compound and on their way back to the inn. Finn added a globule of spit to the refuse covering the street. "Another bloody ghost hunt."

Chapter Fourteen

The Silver Ravens gathered around Tamsin.

"What's the score, Captain?" Shorty asked in English.

"Segann has family problems."

"Someone he wants rid of?"

"He doesn't know for sure. His cousin Nysian is supposed to be overseeing the Wydlow mines, but has gone AWOL. Most likely scenario, he's been murdered."

"Or assassinated," Finn added.

"Aren't they the same thing?" Lori asked.

"From Nysian's point of view, maybe," Tamsin said. "But murder is either random or personal. Assassination is political, so it's more worrying to Segann, since he could be next in line. And of course, the other likely option is that Nysian is going to make his own bid for power. That's what Segann meant when he said his cousin might be on the way to visit him." She frowned. "So what can anyone remember about Nysian?"

"Snivelling little runt," Finn said. "He didn't kick off when Segann claimed the throne. Not like his sister did. Instead he supported Segann's bid and got command of Wydlow afterwards, partly reward, partly to keep him out of the way."

"Right. So why might he start trouble now, when he didn't before? Because that's the way Segann is thinking. But I don't know why."

"Segann's a sharp bugger," Widget said. "He's had his arse on the Mud Throne for over three years now. You don't do that without growing eyes in the back of your head."

Tamsin looked Lori's way. "I don't suppose you picked up on anything at the meeting?"

"No. I was struggling to keep up with all the stuff going on between the lines. Most of it didn't make much sense to me. Like, I assume there's a reason he can't tap into that shared boggart consciousness you talked about and find his cousin without our help."

"It's because the weave doesn't work that way, from what we understand. Not that any human will ever fully get to grips with it. The hooded group standing behind Segann are called the Derwyddon. They watch the weave for him, and when they all work together they can influence the flow of the weave, to help keep Segann in power."

"They make him Master of the Dreamtime," BH said.

Tamsin grinned. "Which is a poetic way of looking at it. As boggarts go, all Segann's family are powerful magicians, but some are stronger than others. Nysian's sister bumped off their mother to get a chance at the throne but couldn't stand up to Segann. Since Nysian caved in, it implies he's weaker than his sister. But he'll still have enough power to hide from the Derwyddon. For Segann, finding his cousin is like looking for an invisible needle in a world-sized haystack. Once he's found his cousin, he'll overpower him. Until then, Nysian is—"

"A prick in waiting." Shorty raised a laugh.

"That's if he hasn't been murdered. Whichever it is, we need to cover both bases. If another boggart overthrows Segann, there's no guarantee they'll help us find Gilwyn. We'll split into two teams. Finn, take Hippo and BH and see what you can find out at the mines. Your team needs to leave at first light tomorrow."

"Right, Captain."

"Widget will set up base here in the inn. Shorty, Lori, and me will hunt for Nysian in Mud Town. Which means, Lori," Tamsin looked at her, "you've got the job of eyeball."

"Tough luck," BH said with feeling. "Normally it's me."

"Eyeball?"

"For the ghost hunt." Hippo also looked sympathetic.

The role of eyeball clearly came with a downside. "What do I have to do?"

"Remember saying Mud Town was the last place to remove your torc?" Tamsin asked.

"Yes."

"This is the exception to the rule."

"I have to take my torc off?" Already, Lori was not liking the idea.

"Afraid so."

"And why is that a good idea?"

"If Nysian is here he'll be using illusion to hide from Segann's guards. However, iron torcs block illusions. So we'll have no idea what the boggarts are seeing, and they'll have no idea what we're not seeing."

Widget had been digging around in a large rucksack. He held up two metal hoops, smaller than the torc. "You need to wear these amulets."

"They're iron?"

"Yup."

"They work like a torc?"

"Not quite."

"How, not quite?"

"They're lighter and farther from your head. They'll give you some protection, but you'll still be seeing the illusions. Except..." Widget laid the amulets on the table, and then held up a small jar. "You'll put this paste on one eye. It's an iron compound. Between it and the amulets, that eye will be able to see things as they really are. But the other eye won't. It's the mismatch where you'll be looking for clues."

Lori did not feel any happier. "Don't take this the wrong way, but why me? Wouldn't it be better if whoever's playing eyeball is more familiar with things?"

Tamsin looked apologetic. "It's not just visual illusions we need to worry about. Illusion affects all your senses. The amulets won't protect you against sound and touch."

Or pain. "I, um..."

"That's why it needs to be the weakest member of the team physically. Me and Shorty will be with you at all time, ready to snap the torc back on at the first sign of trouble."

What option did she have? *I asked to come along. I was warned.* Lori nodded and raised her hand to her neck. "Okay."

Finn grabbed her wrist, moving with the speed of a snake striking. "First put on the amulets. Then take off the torc."

He acted if he was talking to an idiot. But maybe she was, to have let herself get caught up in this. "Right." She reached for the amulets.

Widget came around the table, holding the open jar. "Can you close either eye? Otherwise I've got an eyepatch."

"Yes."

"Good-oh."

He smeared a liberal coating around Lori's right eye, gently dabbing more on the lid. The ointment was bright green, and undoubtedly looked ridiculous, although, in the circumstances, her appearance did not register on Lori's list of concerns.

Widget replaced the lid on the jar. "How's that?"

Lori opened her right eye, then cautiously removed her torc. "Whoa."

"Are you all right?" Tamsin asked.

"I think I'm going to be sick."

BH laughed. "Welcome to the club."

Lori closed both eyes. She felt movement on the bench beside her.

"Give it a few moments," Tamsin said.

"Right." Lori took a deep breath. "The stink has gone."

"I can put some ointment on your nose, if you'd like, pet," Widget offered.

"No, thanks. This is fine." She was not giving up the one benefit.

Lori experimented with opening one eye at a time. The tavern, seen through her right eye, was the same filthy shambles as before. Through her left eye, the scene changed—cleaner, brighter, the colours richer, the walls and ceiling unstained and whole. The table and benches were still made of heavy beams, but now the effect was sturdy rather than crude. The wood was sanded smooth and showed the grain in the oak.

Opening both eyes together was when the trouble started. Her stomach rebelled. She braced her hands on the table to steady herself. The illusion also changed the feel of the wood, making it flat, without cracks or warping.

"I understand why the boggarts are happy to live with the illusions. But part of me wants to stick with my right eye. I feel I can trust it. Together though..." She opened both eyes. A wave of nausea washed through her. "I feel seasick."

"Take it steady. You've got the rest of this evening to get used to it. We'll start searching the town in the morning." Tamsin put a hand under her elbow. "Close your eyes and come with me."

Lori let herself be steered from the common room and up a flight of stairs. A door closed. Sounds softened.

"Here, you can lie down."

Lori's legs touched the side of a wooden frame. A soft mattress lay on top. She sat down on the cot and started loosening the heavy belt around her waist. At a touch on her right foot, she cautiously peeked through her right eye. Tamsin knelt before her, untying the shoelaces.

Once belt and boots were gone, Lori swivelled around and lay flat. Now she could risk opening both eyes.

She was in a small room, lit by soft candlelight. The walls were either painted panels or plain, rough cut timbers. The ceiling was too dim to show much difference between eyes. Despite the bedding feeling crisp and clean, this was most likely illusion, but she did not dare check with her right eye. She would sleep better not knowing.

Tamsin sat on the side of another cot, a few feet away. "How do you feel?"

"I've been better."

"Tomorrow morning, we'll just walk around town. You'll find it easier if you only have one eye open at a time, but you need to keep switching between them."

"What am I looking for?"

"Something odd."

"That's not very helpful."

"Sorry. Mostly, what you'll see when you switch eyes is that the world looks a lot nicer with the illusions. But if Nysian's in town, he'll be trying to stay hidden. Any illusions he casts won't be simply putting a pretty cover over crap."

"He might make himself invisible to other boggarts."

"Exactly. And that's about it." Tamsin leaned forward, resting her arms on her knees. "Would you like me to stay or go?"

"Stay." Lori spoke without thinking.

"All right. Anything you'd like to talk about?"

You. This time Lori was able to keep the thought to herself.

The attractively painted panels that were not there surrounded the row of three pristine, soiled bunks. The filthy, polished floorboards gleamed in the pathetically cheerful candlelight. Her stomach did the worst sort of cartwheel. Tamsin was the one thing in the room that was unchanged.

"You know about me splitting up with my last girlfriend. How about you?" There. She had said it.

"You really want to know?" Tamsin sounded amused.

"It's only fair, since BH spilled the beans about me."

"BH didn't say much."

"Is there anything you'd like to know?"

"Is there anything you'd like to say?"

"Not really. It wasn't the world's most exciting relationship." With someone who very definitely was not the world's most exciting woman.

"You were together a while?"

"Four years."

"Why did you stay that long?"

"I thought it was what I wanted."

"And what do you think you want now?" Lori was not sure she could answer that question, even to her own satisfaction. "We were supposed to be talking about you."

"If you want."

"I saw you one night, on a balcony at the rear of the keep."

"You did?"

"Yes. I'd finished work for the day and was standing outside, admiring the sunset. You were on a lower balcony with Queen Rianna."

"We meet to discuss things from time to time."

"It seemed like a very…informal meeting."

Tamsin gave a bark of laughter. "So that's it. You want to know if we're lovers?"

"You can tell me to mind my own business."

"But you'd like to know?" Tamsin's smile broadened. "We were, once upon a time. But it's been over for years. The queen needs heirs, and enough of them to cover accidents and things. She has commitments, responsibilities, a realm to govern. She can't be seen to have favourites, especially not human ones. We both knew that from the start. It was fun while it lasted, and has left me with nothing but good memories, and a lot of affection for her. Does that answer your questions?"

"I was just being nosy."

"That's all right." Tamsin stood. "But if it's okay with you, I'll go down and check how the others are doing. You should try to sleep. The effect of the ointment won't be so raw once your body has adjusted to it."

Lori lay staring at the shadows on the ceiling. She had some answers, but did Tamsin's attachment to the queen make any more sense? The woman Tamsin described bore no resemblance to the royal bitch in Caersiddi.

❖

"Ready to move on?"

Lori took another deep breath before answering Tamsin's question. "Yes. I think so."

The body lay in an untidy heap at the end of an alley. Green blood pooled under the smashed skull and soaked into the boggart's ragged clothes. It was the third murder victim they had found that morning.

"Are you sure this has nothing to do with the hunt we're on?"

Shorty gave a humourless laugh. "Yeah. This is just boggarts being fucking boggarts."

"And we don't need to tell anyone?"

"If the guards checked every killing in Mud Town, they wouldn't have time to take a crap."

"What will happen to the body?"

"Probably get eaten by something."

"Rats?"

"Maybe."

Lori did not ask what the other options might be.

They left the alley and continued along the street. Tamsin and Shorty matched pace with her on either side. Finding murdered boggarts was the last thing Lori needed. The disconnect between her eyes was making her nauseous. Just as well she could not smell the rubbish covering the ground. She stopped, hand pressed to her mouth, hit by an urge to gag.

The moment passed. "Sorry. I don't mean to be a wimp."

Tamsin put a supportive hand on her arm. "You're doing well."

"Am I?"

Shorty was first to answer. "Better than me. I always puke my guts out when I'm eyeball."

"I might yet do that."

"Just let me know first so I can jump out of the way," Shorty said.

"Will do." Even in her current state, she was becoming more at ease with the Silver Ravens. Finn was the only person showing little sign of thawing towards her.

The road ended on the fishing quay, where the arm of a sea wall cradled a small harbour. Piles of nets and lobster pots were dotted along the dockside. King Segann's compound overlooked the scene, from its hilltop roost.

Lori stared at the horizon, waiting for her nausea to abate. Sea and sky were two things unchanged by illusion. Shorty stood at the water's edge, breathing deeply. Fresh air must be very welcome, since he and Tamsin had no other respite from the stench.

Tamsin stayed at her side. "If you want, we can go back to the inn and take a break."

"I don't need wrapping in cotton wool. We need to find Gilwyn, and I asked to come along."

"I wouldn't have agreed if I thought you'd hold us back. You're not. You're coping well with playing eyeball, and you're quick on the uptake. You've got more to offer the Silver Ravens than just sniper skills." Her tone was supportive rather than flirtatious.

"Thanks." Lori kept her eyes out to sea. Even if Tamsin's words were open to interpretation, in her current state, romance was the last thing she was ready for. Puking on a first date was never a good look.

With her left eye, a few small, brightly painted, fishing vessels were bobbing in the water. With her right eye they looked like death traps. "Are those boats seaworthy?"

"Not especially."

"What happens if they sink? Do the sailors have the illusion of not drowning? Would that save them?"

"No."

"Does nobody care?"

"Apart from them?"

"Somebody must miss them."

"They're boggarts." Tamsin shrugged.

"That means their lives are worthless?"

"Don't try applying human morals to them—it doesn't work. They don't think like us. When we get back to Caersiddi, sit down with one and try explaining the concept of theft or murder. They just don't get it. They're incapable of valuing any life other than their own. Boggart lives are short and cheap. They spawn and die like rabbits. How old do you think King Segann is?"

"Fifty-five, sixty, something like that."

"No. Mid twenties. He'll be doing well if he lives another three years, even if he doesn't get bumped off."

Lori gestured at the boats. "Isn't a king supposed to protect his subjects?"

"Don't be silly. Even human kings on Earth never bothered much about their subjects. Segann keeps order and makes sure things are ticking over smoothly. He'd prefer his people are happy, because there's less risk of them causing trouble. But he's not like Queen Rianna. His only concern is keeping his own arse on the Mud Throne as long as possible."

So, completely different then?

It was a reminder that Tamsin belonged to Rianna, heart and soul. Even if the existence of zombie slaves was hidden from her, Tamsin had no qualms about supporting a queen who had overthrown and murdered her own sister. She was indifferent to the pitiful status of boggarts, unconcerned by the total absence of justice and democracy, and happy to take part in kidnapping innocent computer programmers.

Lori clenched her jaw, hit by the thought that she too was working for the queen. Admittedly, her sanity was at stake, and Gilwyn was just as bad as his aunt. But had he been a kind, innocent soul, would she still have helped hunt him down? How hypocritical was she in criticising other people's ethics?

Tamsin gave a sweep of her hand, taking in the entire dockside. "Between reality and illusion, is there anything out of place here?"

"Nothing leaps out at me."

"How about the boggarts?"

"They're the same. Maybe a bit cleaner. The guards are bigger, more muscles, longer teeth."

"More intimidating."

"Yes."

"Segann wants them taken seriously."

She studied the harbour for another minute. "Nope. Nothing."

"All right. Let's go."

An hour later, they reached the frenetic maelstrom of the main market. Images of a termite mound came to mind as Lori studied the scene. Her nausea had subsided, but the effort of comparing reality to illusion was taking its toll, and the riot of noise and activity would have been daunting, even without the need to reconcile two versions.

"Is it all right if I sit for a bit?"

Without waiting for an answer, she plonked herself on a low wall at the shady side of the market square. The day had heated up and sweat trickled down her back.

Shorty sat beside her. "It's about lunchtime, wouldn't you say, Captain?"

Tamsin nodded.

"Are we going to eat here?"

"No. We should check in with Widget. Finn should have reached Wydlow a couple of hours ago."

"How will he report back?" Lori asked.

"Battery powered, shortwave radio—when it works. Annwyn plays havoc with the signal. The connection will pop in and out at random. That's why Widget has to permanently monitor things. We don't want to miss messages."

Depending on which eye Lori favoured, the rows of stalls looked like either a holiday fair or a mouldering junk yard. The chaotic flow of boggarts was unchanged though, whichever version she considered. Except...

She closed one eye and then the other.

"Have you spotted something?" Tamsin had noticed her actions.

"Someone."

"Who?"

"By a stall, five back on the left. There's a boggart I can see with my right eye, but not with my left. That means he's using illusion to hide from other boggarts, doesn't it? He's thin and...oh." The scrawny boggart had calmly slipped a bunch of carrots off the stall and put them in a sack. "He's stealing food."

"Indeed he is. I think we should have a word with him." Tamsin pointed to a narrow passage leading away from the market. "Shorty, take the bolt hole."

"Right, Captain."

"Lori. Stay here. If he runs towards you, shout and move to your left. We want to herd him into Shorty's arms."

"Okay."

Tamsin and Shorty faded into the crowds, crouching down to boggart height. Meanwhile, the thief was headed to another stall, festooned with strings of either plump or greasy sausages, depending on which eye Lori used. Regardless, the sausages were not served to humans in Caersiddi, which was probably a bad sign.

The thief was ducking and weaving around the shoppers. They could not see him, which left him at risk of being trampled. Given the surging crowds this took his total attention. He negotiated the gap between a stack of crates and an overladen porter.

"Hey, you! Thief! Stop." Tamsin's voice rang out. Her head appeared above the surrounding melee.

The boggart did not wait to see if he was the thief in question. He fled in the opposite direction, straight towards Lori.

"Stop right there. I can see you." She sidestepped to the left.

The thief changed direction, and charged headlong down the passage.

Tamsin cleared her way through the boggarts. She beckoned as she jogged past. "Come on."

Even before entering the narrow passage, Lori heard the hysterical screeching, echoing off the walls. The thief was face down on the ground, pinned in place, with Shorty's knee in his back.

"So. What have we got here?" Tamsin asked.

"I don't know, Captain." Shorty hauled the thief up by the scruff of his neck. The boggart's feet did not touch the ground. "What does it look like to you?"

"I'm sorry. I'm sorry. Please, sir, please." The boggart was crying. Tears dripped off his bulbous nose.

"What next, Captain? Do we hand him over to Segann's guards?"

The boggart's sobs changed to a squeal. "No, no, no. Pleeeeeeeeeease."

Tamsin pulled a length of cord from a pocket. "First we'll go back to the inn and check in with the others. Then we'll see what this thief has to say for himself." She tied his hands behind his back as she continued talking. "Who knows, he might even have something interesting he'd like to share with us."

Chapter Fifteen

Widget adjusted the dial with the air of a bank robber trying to crack a safe. "There. Got it." He looked up. "We're through."

Tamsin leaned over the mike. "Finn, are you there?"

The speaker whistled and popped, and then his voice broke in. "Here, Captain."

"Anything to report?"

"Nysian's deputy confirms what we were told. One day he was here and the next he wasn't."

"No talk of strangers in the area?"

"None, but—" A lengthy burst of crackling drowned out Finn's voice. "—can track down."

"Finn. We missed most of that. Can you repeat."

"No strangers. But there are rumours of odd things going on in an outlying village, and there was also a mass killing there at—" Pop, pop, pop, pop. "—he went missing. They might be connected. It has the boggarts spooked."

"Sounds interesting."

"We're about to head over and see what the truth is. Hopefully, BH can make sense of it."

"Good. Let us know what you find out."

"How's—" Screech. "—hunt going?"

"Lori found us a sneak thief. We're about to ask him a few questions."

The boggart in the corner of the room whimpered.

"We'll check in when we get back." Finn's voice faded in and out. "Right. We're—"

A rising howl made Tamsin lean away from the speaker.

Widget shook his head. "Gone."

Lori was finishing her lunch while listening. She put down her knife and pushed the empty plate away. "Does that count as significant? The bodies turning up?"

"Probably not. Boggarts have a tendency to kill each other over nothing—as you've seen. It's probably a family squabble got out of hand."

Widget gave a snort. "Like that isn't what we're dealing with now."

"True. But when royal families get out of hand it's all a bit stickier." Tamsin turned to the boggart in the corner. "The question is, can our thief tell us anything useful?"

Shorty grabbed the boggart's ragged shirt and hauled him into the middle of the room. "I'm not holding my breath, Captain."

"Me neither. But you never know."

The boggart made a pitiful sight, curled in a tight ball, as if hoping he could make himself so small he would disappear. "I'm sorry. Please. I'm sorry. I'll be good. Please."

Tamsin was unmoved. "I don't care whether you're sorry. To be honest, I don't even care about you stealing. It's not my problem. I'm just wondering if there's anything you can say to make us think twice about handing you over to the guards."

The boggart wailed pathetically.

"No. I don't want to hear you singing. And stop acting stupid. I want you to talk to me." Tamsin grabbed a fistful of lank hair and tugged his head up, so she could stare into his face. "You're not the one I'm after. You're too young. But you've got the strength at illusion to hide from other boggarts. I want to know if you've spotted anything new in town. Things other boggarts can't see."

"I'm nobody, madam. I can't do nothing. I'm just hungry."

"And if I hand you over to the guards, by the time they've finished with you, you'll never be hungry again. Stop snivelling. Talk to me. Tell me something that will make me want to give you another chance."

The boggart gulped and tried to wriggle away, but then went so limp Tamsin might have been holding a sodden, understuffed toy. "A few days back, someone new came to town. Someone powerful. I felt them in the weave near my home. They're so strong, I was scared, so I moved away." The boggart's face crumbled. "Please, madam. I'm sorry. I won't go back to the market. I'll leave the traders alone. I promise."

"I don't give a toss about the market traders. Tell me about this powerful magician."

"Three, four days ago, that was the first time I felt it. Someone slipped into the weave. I couldn't match the power and I was scared the magician would see me if I slipped in my own weave, but I was hungry. So I left my home and came to the market."

"If this is true, why haven't the Derwyddon spotted the change in the weave as well?"

"I don't know."

"Guess."

"It's just an easy shift, slipping in soft. Fading it a little, like I try to do. This magician is so strong, they could tear the weave up, but they don't. Just a little blend and then softening the edges."

"Damn." Tamsin released her grip. The boggart flopped in a heap on the floor.

"Did that make sense to you?" Lori asked.

"Unfortunately, yes."

"Do you want me to see if I can raise Finn again, Captain?" Widget asked.

"No. He may already have left to check out the bodies." Tamsin prodded the boggart with the toe of her boot. "And we ought to check that what this little arsewipe has told us is true before we change plans."

"It's true. It's true, madam. I promise." The words were muffled by the boggart's own knees.

"The area you used to live in. Where is it?"

"I was between Northwold Bridge and the Goose Market."

"And that's where the strong magician is?"

"Maybe not the same street, but somewhere close."

"How close?"

"I don't know. Very close. I was frightened when I felt the weave shift."

Tamsin yanked the boggart back to a sitting position. "How close?"

"Maybe the Goose Market. Maybe the next street over. Please. That's all I know."

Tamsin released the boggart again. "So that's where we go next. Scout out the area between Goose Market and the bridge."

"Do you think it's Nysian?" Lori asked.

"No. He doesn't have the power or the skill to hide from the Derwyddon this close to the centre. More likely whoever murdered him and has come to Mud Town looking for more victims. Or maybe our thief is making it all up."

"No, no, no. it's true. Please, madam." The boggart was crying again.

"What do you want to do with him?" Shorty asked.

"Widget can keep an eye on him while we check it out. If the information is good, we let him go. If not, we turn him over to the guards."

❖

No geese were on sale in the Goose Market.

"Are there ever?" Lori asked.

"Once or twice a month, maybe." Shorty sounded indifferent.

Lori stood in the middle of the open square and looked around using her right eye. The houses were as decrepit as the rest of Mud Town. But why put time, money, and effort into doing a proper job, when you could get the same effect by illusion? Likewise the pockmarked, rubbish strewn gravel which, to her left eye, was level slabs of clean paving.

However, the district was less crowded than other parts of town, making it a good out of the way spot for someone wanting to lie low. Most of the noise came from a group of children, playing a game using a dead rat in place of a ball. The only others present were a trickle of porters trundling through on their way to and from the bridge, and a huddled group of older boggarts, gossiping. They sent suspicious scowls in the direction of the three humans.

The rat landed with a splat, a few inches from Shorty's boot. "Watch where you're throwing that fucking thing."

One of the children edged close enough to snatch up the rat, and then fled out of arm's range.

"Bloody spawn."

"It's a shame they don't have a real ball to play with," Lori said.

"They're happier with the rat. You can't eat a ball when you've finished playing with it."

Whether or not he was joking, he clearly had no sympathy for the young boggarts. Surely they deserved a better childhood, for however long it lasted. If King Segann was only in his mid twenties, they must grow up fast.

"How old do you think they are?"

"Maybe a year and a half."

"How long before they're fully grown?"

Shorty shrugged. "Three years or so."

"From now?"

"From birth."

"How old before they become parents?"

"Too fucking young. The females start popping them out..." He shrugged. "Who knows? Not something I want to think about. They screw like rabbits in heat. Just as well fathers don't count for anything. None of them have a clue who their pa was."

"Really?"

"Yes."

"So who'll succeed King Segann?"

"Whoever's left standing when the fighting stops."

"Doesn't he have a chosen heir?"

"That'd be a quick way to get himself bumped off. The heir wouldn't hang around, leaving it to old age. When Segann's ready to kick the bucket, if he wants to pick someone, it'll be one of his sisters' spawn. He can sit by the bed and watch her pop them out. It's his only hope of being sure he's looking at blood kin."

Tamsin played no part in the conversation. She stood, fists on hips, watching the flow of boggarts through the square. "That's the road where the thief used to live. We need to check the area."

"Okay." Lori was about to follow Tamsin, but stopped. "Maybe we don't need to go anywhere. From this angle it's..." She caught her lip in her teeth.

"What do you see?"

"That door over there." She pointed.

"The one with the small brat sitting on the step?"

"Yes."

"What about it?"

"It's completely boarded up when I look with my left eye. With my right, it's sort of hazy." She rubbed her eyes and looked again.

"Seems normal to me," Shorty said.

"Which means somebody with a lot of power wants to keep other boggarts out." Tamsin adjusted the set of her pistol on her hip. "Which in turn means I'm very keen to see what's inside. Come on, let's check it out."

The gang of children split left and right as the Silver Ravens approached. Only the child on the doorstep remained, frozen in place. Neither nose nor ears were yet pierced, but Lori felt sure the boggart was a girl. After a morning walking around Mud Town, the clues were easier to spot.

The girl's eyes stretched wide, and she pressed herself against the door, clearly frightened by the approaching humans. But no—it was not them. Something else had the girl transfixed. Lori turned to look back, just as screams erupted behind her.

A huge multicolour demon stood in the square, complete with fangs, claws, and burning eyes. Its head was red, its body was blue, its legs were yellow, and its feet were green. It stood twelve feet tall, brandishing a long pole in one hand and a burning whip in the other. Shimmering globs of saliva dripped from its open mouth.

The demon's gaze riveted on the humans. Lori was about to shout a warning, even as she realised it was only visible with her left eye—an illusion, but it felt so real. Despite her better sense, panic swept over her, utter, blind, raw panic. And she was not the only one. Every boggart in the square could see the demon, and was victim to the avalanche of fear. Shrieks rang out.

"Lori, what is it?" Tamsin shouted in her ear.

"It's...it's..."

The words would not come out. Fear clawed at her, senseless, primeval. The demon was coming for them, step by step. It roared at the sky, flinging back its head. Another step. It swung the pole, which passed though Tamsin, but struck Lori's elbow in an explosion of agony. She screamed and dropped to her knees. Her arm was broken, cut to the bone. Her hand dangled useless.

Suddenly, pain and demon were gone, and a cold weight lay around her neck. Tamsin had replaced the iron torc. Lori rubbed her hand, feeling the life in her fingers. The memory of terror retreated. The absurd monster had been so very real.

"What is it?" Tamsin asked again.

"An illusion. A demon was attacking us. But..." Lori sucked in a lungful of air. "I'm all right. It's gone."

For her, but not for the boggarts. Most still ran screaming in panic, others lay petrified, curled on the ground. Two club wielding guards cowered at the opposite side of the square with their backs pressed against a wall. The child on the step had finally fled into the arms of a female boggart—mother, aunt, or older sister. The girl was dragged away down a side street, still staring back at the humans, wide-eyed.

Tamsin shouted over the tumult. "It's a distraction. Someone doesn't want us to go through the door."

"I…" Lori's legs lacked the strength to stand, and an aftershock kicked her stomach. She pressed her hand to her mouth.

Tamsin put a hand on her shoulder. "We're going in. Will you be all right on your own?"

"Yes. I'm fine. I just need a few moments."

"Okay. Join us when you're ready."

A kick from Shorty splintered the wooden frame and burst the door open. Tamsin followed him inside. The door swung back, although hanging noticeably less straight than before.

Slowly, the pounding of Lori's heart eased. The sounds in the square also softened and faded. She looked up. A few boggarts remained in view, but now they stood motionless, dazed and confused. The illusion had ceased, and the torc around her throat was no longer necessary. She could take it off. More illusions might need picking apart. But no, maybe later—not right now.

Cautiously, Lori levered herself to her feet. Her legs were still shaking, but could support her weight. After another long deep breath, she pushed open the door. On the other side was a narrow room, scarcely wider than a corridor. Shutters on the window at the far end were flung back. The watery light revealed a space empty apart from broken crates and other strewn debris. There were no other exits.

Tamsin knelt to one side, sifting through a pile of junk. She looked up. "How do you feel?"

"Better." On a closer look, Lori spotted blankets and a half loaf of bread amid the rubbish. "Somebody was living here?"

"Was." Tamsin emphasised the word.

"Where's Shorty?"

"Checking outside." Tamsin jerked her thumb at the window. "But I doubt there's much to see. I'm hunting for clues. But we aren't going to get much better than what happened. Someone wanted to slow us down and get a head start." She rose and came to Lori's side. "It wasn't just a visual illusion, was it?"

"No. I mean, there was sound as well. But more than that, the feeling of terror. I knew it was an illusion, but it took over. It…" She swallowed. "I don't know how to sum it up."

"No need. " Tamsin put her hands on Lori's shoulders, turning her so they were facing each other. "I'm sorry. I heard you scream. It was…I wish I could have…" Her voice was soft and huskier than normal. Her eyes fixed on Lori's face.

"It's all right. I wasn't really hurt. I just thought I was."

Tamsin shook her head in denial. "No. You shouldn't be here, dealing with this. I shouldn't have let you come with us. I'm sorry."

"I was the one who asked."

"And I'm the one who should have said no."

How to explain that an imaginary broken arm was nothing compared to what might have happened back in Caersiddi? There was no point talking. Tamsin would not believe a word of it. Suddenly, the pain, the terror, the nausea, the absolutely stupidity of it all was too much—more than she could take. *Don't say anything.*

Lori moved forward, sliding her arms around Tamsin's waist. Her head nestled into the hollow of Tamsin's neck. All doubts were washed away, leaving a moment of desperately needed peace. Tamsin's arms wrapped around her, holding her gently. The only sound was the thudding of their hearts and the whisper of breath between their lips.

They stood, unmoving, until Lori heard the scuff of footsteps outside. She broke away as Shorty clambered in through the window.

"Bastard did a fucking runner."

"Yes." Tamsin's voice regained its normal firmness. "And I don't think there's much more to learn here. Whoever was behind the illusion is powerful—amazingly so for a boggart. You could tell from how the others reacted. Boggarts understand illusion, but this had them going crazy. Normally, it takes a fay to have an effect like that."

"Could one of them be here?" Lori managed to keep her tone even.

"No fucking chance."

"Shorty's right. No fay would ever set foot in Mud Town, let alone live in a room like this. But it's definitely not Nysian either. He doesn't have the ability to pull this off. So…" Tamsin kicked a soiled blanket aside. "My guess is that bumping off Nysian was a trial run. Now the killer's come to get their arse on the Mud Throne." She headed to the door. "And we need the rest of the Silver Ravens back here, as quick as the horses can make it."

❖

Finn's voice battled with an onslaught of hisses, whistles, and clicks. "There were seven dead. None could have been him. The only one about the right age was female. The males were all too young. They died—" A salvo of crackling swallowed his voice.

"Finn. We lost you there. Can you repeat that last bit," Tamsin shouted into the mike.

"They died the same day Nysian went missing."

"That's too much for coincidence. What did you learn about them?"

"Just gossip."

The radio went silent for a moment and then BH came on. "Maybe just gossip. I heard one of the dead females used to work in Wydlow. She was Nysian's housekeeper fo—" High pitched whistling drowned out the next words. "—nant, when she ca—" More whistling. "—ck home."

"So she might have picked up personal information about Nysian? Something worth killing her for?"

Finn came back on. "She might."

An idea struck Lori. She leaned over the table and pulled the mike towards her. "BH, did you say she was pregnant when she returned from Wydlow?"

"Yes."

"Do they know who the father was?"

On the other side of the table, Tamsin shook her head. "Doesn't matter. Boggarts don't care about fatherhood."

"I know. Shorty told me. But it doesn't matter what boggarts think. The genes get the casting vote."

"And?"

"Magic runs in families. Just because Nysian's weak, it doesn't mean his children will be." Lori shouted into the mike, "The baby was a girl?"

"Yes."

"And she wasn't among the dead?"

"No. How did—" An eruption of hissing.

Tamsin reclaimed the mike. "Finn. There's no time now. We need you back here."

Nothing but static.

"Finn. Did you hear that?"

"Yes, Captain. We're on the—" His voice was lost in a piercing squeal that shot up through the octaves.

Widget adjusted the dials on the radio. "I don't know if I can get him back."

"It's okay. We've said all we need to." Tamsin patted his shoulder, then turned to Lori. "You weren't guessing when you asked about the girl, were you?"

"No."

"So what? You've seen something that makes you think Nysian's daughter killed the rest of her family?"

"No. She's too young."

"Boggarts grow up quickly."

Lori held her hand out to indicate the child's height. "She was this tall."

"That'd be a quick developer. Boggarts don't normally start bumping off their relatives until they're at least a year old. Where did you see her?"

"Sitting outside the house. She was staring at the demon. At the time, I thought she was frozen with terror, but…" Lori probed the memory. "It didn't feel right. I think she was the one creating the illusion."

"That would be amazing for one so young."

"Yes and no. The rainbow colours, the huge fangs, the big stick—it was a kiddie's demon. It's what you'd expect from a four-year-old with a packet of crayons."

"Don't overestimate boggarts. Even adults can be infantile."

"Not like that. I've spent all day picking apart their illusions. I know what sort of images they come up with, and this demon was childish like nothing else I've seen so far."

Tamsin nodded. "I'll take your word on it. You've been doing a good job as eyeball."

"Thanks." Lori felt her face colouring.

"I guess if the child's that young, she'd be a soft target for Nysian to trick into doing what he wants."

"Or bully." Lori rested her chin in the cup of her hand. "The mother was working for Nysian. He got her pregnant so she had to go back to her family."

"That's the human in you talking. Annwyn is different. There's no issues about females of any species having sex with whoever they want. But—" Tamsin held up her hand when Lori tried to interrupt. "It still works. She'd go back to her family for them to witness the birth."

Shorty cut in. "Like I said, the way they fuck around, the only thing any of them can be sure of is who their ma was."

"Or they watch their brothers and sisters get born, or their aunts give birth to their cousins. Boggarts take the witnessing of births seriously. A pregnant boggart would go home to her family and stay until the child could look after itself. Except this one was powerful enough to upend things." Tamsin's forehead knotted in thought. "As for how news got back to Nysian? Who knows? Maybe the mother was hoping to sell her. But when Nysian found out, it gave him ideas. He snatched his spawn, killed the mother and anyone else who could report him, then brought the youngster to Mud Town and settled in, waiting for a chance to…" Tamsin blew out her cheeks. "Kill Segann."

"Makes sense." Widget nodded.

"Would Nysian be able to make himself king?" Lori asked

Tamsin shrugged. "He might have a chance with Segann out of the way."

"What about when the girl grows up?"

"She won't live long enough. He'll get rid of her as soon as he's got his arse on the throne." Tamsin drew a deep breath. "So, the next question is, what'll he do now that he knows we're looking for him? The Derwyddon will have noticed the fuss in Goose Market today as well—nothing subtle about that."

"Why was he waiting before?" Lori asked. "The thief said he's been in town for days."

"Reconnaissance. Waiting for the right opportunity," Widget suggested.

Tamsin bounced to her feet. "Something like that, no doubt. But he can't afford to wait any longer. He'll make his move today. And we can't afford to wait around for Finn and the others. We have to get to Segann before Nysian does."

CHAPTER SIXTEEN

"Come back tomorrow." The guard spat out the words.

"We have to see King Segann right away."

"No. Nobody gets in without permission. There was trouble today in town, and we have orders."

"That's what we're here about. Take a message to King Segann. Tell him the captain of the Silver Ravens has an urgent message."

"I don't take orders from you."

Tamsin sighed. In one fluid move, she snapped open the catch on her holster, drew her pistol, and pointed it at the guard's head. "If I shoot you, do you think your replacement will be more reasonable?"

The guard's manner flipped from surly to shocked, but he did not back off. "You're surrounded."

"And you're an easy target."

With matching clicks, Shorty and Widget also drew their guns. Lori copied their action, although her hand was shaking so much she would be no use should the shooting start. They were hopelessly outnumbered. Was iron really so deadly to Annwyn life forms?

"I have orders from King Segann. He's having a feast and does not want anyone to come in without him saying so first."

"If I don't get to talk to him, this feast will be his last. Now open the gate, or we will demonstrate something called gelignite."

Tamsin put her free hand on the guard's chest and pushed. The boggart stumbled away, barely keeping his balance. He scowled at his fellows, who shifted their feet anxiously, but then the group of guards stepped back, allowing them past.

The scene in the great hall was livelier than the last time Lori had been there. The long tables were filled with boggarts, eating, drinking, and squabbling. Servants went up and down the lines, filling tankards while dodging groping hands. A drummer and two pipers were making a noise that might count as music. King Segann was in the middle of the top table, with a selection of better dressed boggarts on either side. A mound of sacks, boxes, and baskets was piled on the ground before the dais, either gifts or tribute.

The disturbance as the Silver Ravens barged past the guard on the door made him look up. He pushed aside the servant who was filling his tankard. Silence flowed over the hall.

"Why are you here?" The last of the drumbeats punctuated the king's words.

Tamsin marched to the centre of the hall "Because you're in danger."

"Here? Now? Could this not have waited until tomorrow?"

"I don't think Nysian intends for you to see another morning."

"He hasn't the power to strike me here, in my own hall."

"You've gathered everyone he wants to impress. So yes, this would be a very good time and place."

"Nysian is too weak."

"No doubt. But if I read things right, the young female he sired isn't. And I think they're both in this hall, right now."

"That would mean—" Segann broke off and clamped his hands on either side of his head. However his posture did not suggest either fear or confusion, rather that he was channelling his abilities. A magical contest was taking place.

Lori sidled closer to Widget. "Do you know what Nysian looks like?"

"Absolutely no frigging idea."

"Does Tamsin or Shorty?"

"I doubt it."

Which was the problem. The torc wearing humans could only see the true appearance, but could not recognise Nysian. The boggarts knew what he looked like, but would see only illusion.

The amulets were back in the inn, but there had not been time to wash off the green ointment. Lori pulled the torc from her throat and pressed it into Widget's hands. "Hang on to this."

Dual images were again superimposed. As expected, in her left eye, the barren hall was cheerfully decorated. The plank walls were oak panels. King Segann was taller and younger. His features were more finely drawn. His skin held a trace of blue, giving an almost fay-like sheen. Everyone was better dressed, but otherwise unchanged.

"Hey. Be careful." Widget was alarmed

Lori shook her head. "He's not here. Nobody is disguising themselves with illusion."

"Even so, you shouldn't do that."

Tamsin turned around. "Transmutation. That's what he's been up to."

"Right. On it." Widget shrugged his pack off his shoulder and rummaged inside.

Tamsin took the torc and thrust it back at Lori. "Get this—"

The hall exploded in flame. Lori's skin blistered. Her hair was on fire. She sucked in a breath to scream, but the scalding air burned her throat and lungs. Her hands blackened, seared by the inferno.

And then it stopped as if a switch had been thrown. The torc was back around her throat. However, the boggarts were still in the grip of the illusion. Around the hall, they writhed and screeched in agony—all except two.

King Segann was clearly struggling, but his shouts were of anger and effort, not pain. And although he might withstand the illusion for himself, he could do nothing to break its hold on his followers.

The other unaffected boggart was the serving maid, standing behind the king's chair. Now Lori recognised her, the relative in the square who had dragged the girl away. "That one. There."

The servant dropped the wine flagon and tugged on Segann's shoulder, shoving him back in his chair. Her other hand lifted high, grasping a dagger, ready to bring it down in Segann's heart. Her whole attention was given to her victim, ignoring all other activity in the hall.

Shorty charged forward. He hurdled the high table and slammed into the serving maid, knocking her away from the king. Tamsin was a half step behind. She wrenched the dagger from the would-be assassin's hand and held it up to inspect.

"Silver? That's handy. Won't need to use my own." Tamsin's words were barely audible over the uproar.

Shorty slammed the captive onto the table, smashing her face against the wood, without heed for the goblets and platters of food.

Tamsin grabbed a flailing wrist, pulled it down, and then drove the dagger through the boggart's hand, pinning it to the table. The boggart howled in pain, struggling ineffectually, but immediately a change began to flow over her. In the space of a few seconds, the boggart was older, heavier, and male.

However, the scene did not calm. The hall was a mass of thrashing bodies. Howls, sobs, and screeches came from every corner. Boggarts flailed around, engulfed in their phantom inferno.

"The girl. She has to be here somewhere." Tamsin shouted to be heard.

"How about there?" Lori pointed to the largest of the baskets heaped in front of the king's table.

Before she could move, a hand grabbed her ankle. A boggart lay on the floor, clinging to her like a drowning man. Lori did not have time to be gentle. She kicked her leg free. More boggarts blocked her path, crawling, contorting, staggering around roaring and slapping themselves, to put out the nonexistent flames. She ducked around those she could and shoved aside the others, at one point narrowly avoiding a backhand to the face

She reached the mound of tribute and pulled the basket lid off. The girl from the Goose Market was curled in a ball at the bottom, crying.

Lori dragged her out. "Stop it. Stop hurting everyone."

The girl struggled at first, but then went limp. The screams and shrieks began to abate, replaced by gasps and moans. As the hall calmed, the girl's sobs grew louder.

"No. You mustn't. No. He said he'll kill my ma." Tears flowed down the girl's face.

Behind them, Widget muttered, "Too late for that, pet. He already has."

"Do you hear that?" King Segann spoke to the girl sitting beside him. "He murdered your poor ma and all your ma's folk and tricked you into doing bad things."

The girl nodded. A fresh tear rolled down her face, but the sobs had stopped. Apart from Segann, Nysian, and the girl, only a few guards and the Silver Ravens remained in the hall.

Segann turned back to the bound prisoner. "Nysian, you've been very naughty, don't you think?"

The girl nodded, but Nysian did not react. He was probably still dazed from the beating he had received. Despite offering no further resistance after he was freed from the table, it had not stopped the guards from dealing out retribution. The burning had been an illusion, but the pain had been real. And although, technically, the girl had cast the illusion, Segann's guards had not let a mere technicality get in their way. Nysian's clothes were smeared with green blood.

More droplets splattered the floor around where he knelt.

"What should I do with you? I've tried being nice."

Nysian remained silent.

Segann turned to the child. "What do you think I should do with him?"

She wiped the last tear away and a sullen smile touched her face. "Eat him."

"There's a good idea. Especially since he's spoiled this feast. But we'll have to cook him first…slowly." Segann gestured to his guards. "Take my cousin somewhere safe. I don't want him to have any more accidents before I can deal with him. And take my young friend as well. Find a nurse to look after her. We need to get to know each other better."

Only the Silver Ravens were left. King Segann settled back in his chair and smiled. "That was a surprise, wasn't it—Nysian showing up like that? If I'd known he was in town I'd have invited him. Still, Nysian never did wait to be asked. And he brought a surprise guest. One who'll need careful handling, I'm thinking."

Was that a threat to the girl? Lori was getting tired of the verbal sparring. "What will you do with her?"

Segann turned his head slowly in her direction. "Why do you ask?"

"Because she's a child, and innocent. She's lost her mother, been taken from her home, been intimidated, lied to. And now she's all alone. I'm worried about what might happen to her next."

"You care about Bukka spawn?"

"Yes. And I'd call her a child, not spawn."

Segann gave a yelp of laughter. "There's something I never thought to hear from a human." He fixed Lori with a hard stare. "You say you're worried. Don't be. She's no concern of yours."

"I get to pick what I worry about."

"Do you?" He laughed again. "Well, there's two ways things can go. With power like hers, in six years, she'll either be dead or Queen of the Bukka. As for which? I don't know."

"I didn't think she counted as part of your family."

"Not at the moment, but to be honest, my sisters' offspring have been a disappointment. Half don't have the magic to rule, and the other half don't have the brains. This girl, she's got the magic—oh, yes indeed—but does she have the brains? That's the question, and it'll take time to answer. I admit, I'd rather pass things on to blood kin. But there's no point giving the throne to someone who isn't able to keep themself there. So, to answer your question, I'm going to see how things go. If we get along, I might adopt her. And if we don't...well, I told you the two ways it could turn out."

Segann turned back to Tamsin. "Anyway, Captain, you and I agreed to keep an eye out for missing people. You've done a great job with Nysian. I'm afraid I can't be quite so helpful with Queen Rianna's nephew. But I've heard someone's moved back into Castle Farraon. You could try checking it out."

"Thank you. We'll call by and see what's going on."

"If I hear any more, maybe we can come to an agreement."

"Do you think you're likely to hear more?"

The king shrugged. "Who knows?"

"Who indeed?" Tamsin gave a polite nod of her head. "We'll take our leave."

Now that Lori had the iron torc on, the common room at the inn had reverted to being a squalid dump, and they would have to stay there one more night. Finn, BH, and Hippo had only recently arrived back, and their horses needed a rest. If it were not for memory of the illusory inferno, Lori might have asked Widget for the amulets. The damp stain on the wall that looked like an upside-down map of Australia had limited amusement value. She sat in a corner, half listening to the conversation. Tamsin had nearly finished updating the others.

"Castle Farraon?" Finn looked scornful. "We should have guessed."

"It was high on the list of possibilities, I agree."

"Do you think we can believe Segann?" The king had not impressed Lori with his sincerity.

"Oh yes. He'll play fair with us because he never knows when he might need our help with other problems."

BH leaned back, resting her shoulders on the wall behind her. "Sounds like it was tight on the timing. We might have been dealing with King Nysian."

Tamsin nodded. "And I don't think he'd be as reasonable as Segann. We're lucky Nysian didn't have any shapeshifter dust."

"What's that?" Lori asked.

"It speeds up transformation. Otherwise fay need hours, if not days, to fix a new form. Few boggarts can master transformation, and even if they can, takes them far longer."

"Oh, right. That would be the powder Gilwyn sprinkled over himself to turn into a raven, when he escaped from Caersiddi. The change was instantaneous."

"Sounds like it. But it explains what Nysian was doing, hanging around in Mud Town. No matter how good his daughter is, she was going to need time to transform him into a new shape that could get past the guards. I'm guessing his plan was to kill Segann, then nick himself with the silver dagger, so he reverted, and try to pass it off as illusion and all his own magic."

"Would it have worked?"

"It might."

"Why did he want his daughter there?"

"As backup in case something went wrong with his plan—such as us turning up. I'd guess he'd also want her on hand to dispose of quickly once Segann was dead."

"He ballsed up all round," Shorty said.

"In a nutshell, yes." Tamsin stretched her arms so her shoulders cracked. "But I think that's all we need to cover, for now. So, I'm going to finish my beer, then have another, followed by a good night's sleep. We're done in Mud Town, but there's no need to rush away. We'll leave late morning and take it easy, to time our arrival at Farraon for dusk tomorrow night." She matched her words by draining her tankard.

The briefing broke up, and Shorty went in search of more beer. BH waved a pack of cards in the air. "Who wants to play?"

"Count me in, when Shorty gets back." Tamsin stood, looking uncharacteristically hesitant, but then she joined Lori in the corner. "How are you doing?"

A matching awkwardness blossomed in Lori's chest. "Fine."

"You were chancing it, pushing Segann with questions about Nysian's daughter."

"I was worried about the girl."

"It's all right. I think you amused him. But you should be careful. When in doubt follow my lead, or one of the other Silver Ravens."

I wasn't in doubt. Maybe she should have been, but she was old enough to make her own mistakes, and deal with the consequences. She did not need a babysitter. "I was tired of all the games."

"Games here can be deadly. You don't know enough about the way Annwyn works." Tamsin met Lori's eyes and her voice dropped. "I wouldn't want anything to happen to you."

The irritation faded into warm fuzzy feelings. "I wouldn't want anything to happen to me either."

"Today in the Goose Fair, and afterwards..."

Lori's pulse quickened. Before she could work out what to say, Tamsin continued. "The army training course you went on?" Her tone made it something close to a question, and her gaze was now fixed on the floor between her feet.

"Yes?" Where was this change in tack going?

"It covered chains of command, army structure, military protocol?"

"Bits, but there wasn't time for much more than an outline of daily life for a grunt."

"When Queen Morgaine recruited the first human fighters and called them her Raven Warriors, it was way back in Earth history, before 1000 BC. The force she put together was based more on a Hittite war band than anything else. Over the years, both the Silver and Iron Ravens have been updated where it seems useful, but at its core, our structure falls well short of Cromwell's New Model Army. There's no need for anything else in Annwyn."

Lori confusion was growing. "I can see that."

"To any soldier in a modern Earth army, we'd seem appallingly slipshod and amateurish." Tamsin raised her eyes briefly. "And in that category, I'd include letting you come with us. There's no way anything like it would be allowed on Earth. And as I said, I was wrong to agree."

She's going to send me back to Caersiddi. Lori's blood turned to ice.

"Though, I'd add that modern Earth armies never have to deal with dragons or magic." Tamsin's attempt to lighten the tone did not deflect from her serious expression. She scratched the back of her neck, then suddenly raised her eyes again to met Lori's. "All of which is a long way round to say that, at the moment, we're officer and subordinate, and there are rules covering inappropriate behaviour—important rules that even the Silver Ravens follow. But I think, once we get back to Caersiddi, there are things you and I need to talk about. Agreed?"

"Yes. Agreed." But what had she just agreed to?

The door opened as Shorty returned, carefully carrying two full pitchers. Seeing him, BH shuffled the pack with a dramatic flourish. "Okay. Who's in?"

"Me." Finn settled down on the bench beside BH. They were joined by Hippo and Shorty. However, Widget had his travel chess out and was casting hopeful looks in Lori's direction.

"I'm coming." Tamsin stood and patted Lori's shoulder. "Go on. Give Widget a real game."

Lori had one last question. "The bit about eating Nysian, that was a joke wasn't it? Segann was just playing along with the child?"

Tamsin did not say anything, but did not need to. Her wry pout was the only answer necessary.

CHAPTER SEVENTEEN

Cirrus's hoof clipped the top of a tall fir, sending a shower of snow cascading down through the branches. A few wayward flakes swirled in the draft caused by the riders and stuck to Lori's cheeks. She brushed the snow away. The fur lined gloves and jacket were doing a reasonable job of keeping her hands and body warm, but her exposed face stung in the raw air. The temperature was dropping as dusk thickened.

They had been passing over densely packed forest for mile upon mile. However, it was finally coming to an end, where the trees ran into the flanks of a mountain chain. The jagged peaks stretched away on either side, in an unbroken line, until swallowed by the fading light. For the last quarter hour they had flown low, brushing the upper branches, so as not to be conspicuous to lookouts. Castle Farraon must be close at hand.

A small break in the trees appeared in the wintry forest ahead, where banks of snow surrounded a frozen pond. To Lori's relief, the Silver Ravens were making for the opening. It was not just the cold. After hours in the saddle, she was stiff, tired, and hungry.

Cirrus skidded to a halt beside the other horses, sending up a cloud of powdery snow. Firs overhung the glade, hiding the lower mountain slopes, but peaks towered above the treetops, stark against the last wisps of sunset. Was it the edge of the world? If they flew over the barrier of rock and ice, would they arrive on the other side of Annwyn?

Lori took a moment to gather herself. She swung her leg over Cirrus's rump and slipped her foot free of the stirrup. Her feet hit the ground, and her knees buckled. She was more tired than she had realised.

She held on to the saddle for support while stamping her legs to get the circulation going.

"Are you all right?" Tamsin was at her shoulder.

"Yes, fine." She pushed away from Cirrus's side.

"We'll get camp sorted quickly."

"Right."

Tamsin moved on.

Lori took another moment to make sure both legs were working before unbuckling the saddle and pulling her pack from Cirrus's back. Did the horse need rubbing down? Food? A coat? The Silver Ravens had let their horses loose, without even a hobble to stop them from wandering. Presumably, whoever had created the flying horses went the extra mile and made them low maintenance as well.

At the far end of the clearing, several of the Silver Ravens were erecting a round, yurt-like tent. Lori went to help. Even before the shelter was finished, the amount of equipment on show was cause for surprise. Where had it come from, given the absence of a packhorse? Confusion changed to bewilderment when she entered the yurt and saw BH fitting a flue to a small cast iron stove.

"How did that get here?"

"It was in Widget's bag o' tricks."

"What's that?"

BH pointed to where Widget knelt at one side of the tent, feeling inside the large rucksack he always carried.

He grinned at Lori. "This. A magic bag." He produced a succession of thick blankets. "Can put a house in there, you know. Never gets full. Never weighs anything. Food stays fresh in it, though you can't put in anything that's alive if you want it to stay that way."

"Right." She watched him pull out kindling and sawn logs. "How do you find things in there?"

"Practice." Pots and pans appeared. "And for my pièce de résistance." He flourished a box of tea bags in the air.

Lori's heart leapt at the sight. "Why didn't you get them out before?"

"Because the bloody boggarts eat them. The little buggers are all tannin addicts."

Lori mentally ran through all the other things she had been missing. "I don't suppose you have something in there to charge a laptop."

"Of course. I've got a couple of solar powered units and more back at Caersiddi. Why, do you need one?"

"Not now. But I could have done with it while I was working on the decoding."

"You should have said something, pet."

Too late now. Another idea struck. "Does it work if you take it to Earth?" She could have done with it in Adam's spare room.

"To tell the truth, I've never tried. But if it stopped working, and everything exploded out, it'd get terribly messy."

❖

With food cooking atop the stove, the yurt was a huge step up on the Mud Town inn. Lori sat with a blanket draped over her shoulders and her hands wrapped blissfully around a mug of tea. Outside, the wind whistled over the trees. Then a long, drawn-out howl came from the distance. Wolves, werewolves, or something else? Whatever its source, the call did not bother the Silver Ravens.

Tamsin dropped down beside her. "I thought I'd fill you in on the background and some hints about what to expect tomorrow."

Lori battled to act relaxed, ignoring her body's reaction. "Sure."

"History-wise, Castle Farraon was built about eighty years ago by Havgan, who was a distant cousin of King Arawan."

"Is that eighty years Earth or Annwyn time?"

"Annwyn. It'd have been something BC on Earth. Havgan wanted to carve off a piece of the world as his own kingdom and was shaping up to make a fight of it. Castle Farraon was built to withstand a siege but was never put to the test. Back then, a man called Powel was captain of the Silver Ravens. Powel wasn't about to do anything as stupid as launch a head-on attack. Instead, he waited and caught Havgan by surprise when he was out hunting."

"So King Arawan kept all Annwyn and got a new castle as a bonus."

"Except it was a castle he had no use for, nor his heirs. I don't think Queen Rianna has set foot in it. Our problem is that Havgan created Castle Farraon as his stronghold, and we've got bugger all idea what it's like inside, especially since the one person who did take an interest was Bronwen, during the short period she was in charge. I believe she was preparing Castle Farraon as her final refuge. However, Queen Rianna was smart enough to follow Powel's example, so it never came to an all-out fight."

Just a knife in the back. "Gilwyn came here with his mother?"

"Yes. In truth, it's such an obvious place for him to hole up I'd been in two minds about coming straight here and not bothering with Segann. Except it was too obvious. I thought he'd try to be a little less predictable."

"He was double-bluffing you."

"He's a slippery bastard, but I doubt he'd thought it through that far."

Lori put down her empty mug. "Based on my conversation with him, you could be right. He definitely thought humans weren't as clever as he was. He'd assume outsmarting us would be easy."

"Exactly. With any luck, Gilwyn won't expect us to track him down this quickly. He hasn't had much time to prepare, but even so, we need to stay sharp. Take nothing for granted. If in doubt, check. If not in doubt, check anyway. I…" Tamsin stared at her clasped hands. "I shouldn't have agreed to let you join us. Now I'm half tempted to leave you here in the yurt tomorrow, while we tackle Gilwyn."

"No. I want to come along." She certainly did not fancy being on her own with whatever it was that had howled.

"It could turn nasty."

"I understand."

Tamsin's lips twisted into a wry smile. "But that risks spoiling my cunning plan."

"What cunning plan?"

"When I let you try the sniper test, in part it was because I thought you'd fail, which would spare me having to say a flat no to you. But in part I thought if you saw more of Annwyn, you might want to stay here. You're—" She broke off again, and brushed imaginary dust from her legs. "Be careful tomorrow. I still want to have that talk with you."

Farraon had been built where a wide chasm split the side of a mountain. The outer battlements sealed the breach, running from the cliff face on one side to the other. BH drew a sketch on the ground, highlighting the main points. "This is the only area where there's any activity. The rest of the castle is deserted. Gilwyn's not alone, but there aren't many with him, maybe three or four fay and a few dozen boggarts. They're trying to keep out of sight, but…" She smiled. "They aren't doing a good enough job."

"Any sign of humans?" Tamsin asked.

"No."

"Great." Was her response due to an ethical dislike of fighting other humans, or the absence of Earth weapons? "Any sentries?"

"Just one. There's always a fay standing watch on top of the gatehouse. But there's a clean shot from here"—BH pointed to her sketch—"without being seen."

"How far?"

"About a hundred yards, give or take a few."

"Okay."

Everyone glanced Lori's way. They were expecting her to shoot someone, and it was not a video game. The realisation hit like a kick to the gut. She took a gulp of tea. It burned her throat but did not thaw the ice in her chest. Most of what followed passed in a haze. Fortunately, there was not much to it.

Tamsin stood. "Right. Do we all know what we're doing?"

She might have missed a few details, but Lori nodded. She knew exactly what she was about to do—she was going to kill someone. Anything else was a minor detail. She should have thought things through before asking to come along as a sniper, although her options had been limited.

The Silver Ravens began assembling and checking their kit. Lori blindly copied their actions until Tamsin knelt beside her, holding another rifle.

"You'll need to take this. It's a high-powered airgun. We don't want to let the entire mountainside know we're here. The range is limited, but it's fine for what BH described. Accuracy isn't an issue. It's got steel tipped pellets. A scratch is all it'll take. Widget can carry your other rifle in his bag o' tricks, in case you need it later."

"Right." The gun was cold, hard, and heavy in her hands.

The rising sun was behind them when they set off from the clearing. A light breeze stirred the tops of the branches, sending flurries of snow down on their heads. It whispered around Lori's ears. The only other sounds were snow crunching under their feet and the raucous shriek of a hunting bird. Cold air pinched her cheeks and the weight of the rifle dug into her shoulder.

Under the trees was quieter still. The blanket of snow was replaced by fallen pine needles, deadening all noise. The Silver Ravens moved silently, weapons at the ready. Lori tagged along towards the rear, moving when she was beckoned and standing where she was pointed. A sense of awkwardness grew. She should not be there. She did not have the training. Nor, now that the moment came, did she have the desire. She was a programmer, not a soldier.

The Silver Ravens moved on, taking up positions, shifting from tree to tree. Their actions were precise and coordinated. They had done this before, many times. Emotions rattled through Lori, too quick and unfamiliar to name, except for one—anxiety. She did not want to fail.

They reached a patch of heavier firs, where low hanging branches swept close to the ground. At Tamsin's signal, Shorty, Hippo, and Widget broke away, heading in the direction of the castle. The rest got down on their stomachs and wiggled forward, inching under the covering of evergreen boughs.

BH and Finn stopped, but Tamsin beckoned Lori on a few more feet, until just a thin green curtain separated them from a rutted track through the forest. A fallen tree provided additional cover. Tamsin and Lori shuffled forward slowly, until they could peek over the top.

No traffic was on the road, or had been for days. The pristine coating of snow was broken only by the prints of birds, deer, and other wildlife. The track curved gently up to the castle gates. The distance matched BH's estimate—an easy shot, even with an airgun. Tamsin trained a pair of binoculars on the battlements, while Lori shrugged the rifle off her shoulder.

The sentry atop the gatehouse was visible through the veil of pine needles, without needing scope or binoculars. Lori adjusted the sights, wishing she could take a practice shot to get the range, but the light breeze was at her back. Unless an unlucky gust caught the pellet, the weather would not be an issue. The sentry was standing upright and unmoving, as if to attention. He could not have made an easier target of himself if he tried.

Lori rested the rifle barrel on the trunk, so the tip of the muzzle just parted the pine needles, and squinted into the scope. The head of the sentry filled her sight. The only movement was the ends of his silver hair, stirring in the breeze. His features were utterly impassive. His eyes were locked on the track to the gates, ignoring the rest of the castle. Were it not for puffs of steam as he breathed, he might have been a dummy. Had he blanked out through boredom? What was he thinking about?

A tremor started in Lori's hands. Her stomach tightened. The fay was living, breathing, carrying hopes for his future and memories of his past, and she was going to wipe it all out. It was not a game. Lori closed her eyes, willing her hands and heartbeat to still. She was going to do this.

The scene had not changed when she opened her eyes again. The safety catch released with the faintest click. The crosshairs lined up with the fay's head. She slid her finger onto the trigger. All she needed to do was squeeze gently and it would be done. But her hand had seized and her finger turned to stone. The muscles in her palm sent darts shooting up her wrist. And now her shoulder was locked. She had to stop and massage life back into her arm.

Someone tapped Lori's elbow, soft but insistent, demanding her attention. Finn had shuffled into position beside her. Slowly, he lifted the rifle from her unresisting hands and set it against his own shoulder. He pressed his cheek against the stock, taking aim.

Lori let her forehead sink onto the trunk and scrunched her eyes closed, wanting to shut out everything. She could not watch. The rifle chuffed, a sound no louder than the sigh as Finn let out his breath.

"Good shot," Tamsin's voice was one degree above a whisper.

The fay man was dead. The world would go on without him. Seconds trickled by—seconds that had been taken from him.

"Any reaction?" Finn asked.

"I'm not seeing it." Tamsin had the binoculars to her eyes. "You and BH take up position on the other side of the road, in case Hippo needs cover."

"Yes, Captain."

As Finn shuffled back under the trees, his expression was one of grim satisfaction. He did not spare a glance for Lori. What was he most pleased about, his successful shot, or that his low opinion of her had been proved right?

"I..." Lori did not know what to say.

"You couldn't pull the trigger."

"No. My hand...it..."

"That's all right. Better to find out when your life isn't dependent on it."

She had failed. Lori stared at her empty hands. She had failed.

"If you want to do something useful, take these binoculars. Now that the sentry is gone, Hippo will be climbing over the wall. We don't want him to be caught out."

"Right." That was something she could do.

Her pulse still pounded. The wannabe soldier course did not count as true military training, she knew that, but she had not thought she would fall so short. The beta testers had said *Rank and File* was too realistic. In truth, it had not come close to reality—no game could.

The trees ran right up to the castle walls. They had clearly grown up after the stronghold was abandoned. The first sight of activity was when Hippo, Shorty, and Widget emerged near the gatehouse. After a moment to sort himself out, Hippo started to climb. Rather than the line and grapple beloved by movies, he looked to be using standard rock-climbing harness, rope, and spring-loaded cams. It would be slower, less dramatic, but undoubtedly safer.

Lori turned her attention back to the walls. But there was nothing. No shouts. No friends rushing to the sentry's side. He was dead and nobody knew. The empty spot where he had stood kept hooking the binoculars, dragging on her thoughts. He was lying there, unnoticed and unmourned. Yet surely someone would cry for him when the news got out. Somebody would care he was dead.

Hippo reached the parapet and disappeared over the top of the wall.

Tamsin tapped her shoulder. "Come on. Time to take the fight to them."

Lori could not move. "I'm sorry."

"Don't be. Killing shouldn't be easy."

"My hand just…"

"Now's not the time for talk. Either come with us or stay here. Your choice." Tamsin rolled over the trunk and through the curtain of pine needles.

Lori clasped her hands over her head. Part of her pleaded to stay beneath the trees, hiding from everyone. But another, even more childlike part, was desperate and frightened, and did not want to be left alone. She forced herself to follow Tamsin onto the track. Finn and BH emerged from the trees on the other side. Lori could not meet anyone's eyes. She did not belong with them and now everyone knew it.

By the time they reached the castle, the wicket gate was open. Hippo stood there grinning while Widget returned the climbing equipment to his rucksack. The Silver Ravens slipped through the narrow entrance and assembled under the archway, with a first view of the castle's interior.

A tight maze of stairs, alleyways, and buildings was carved from the living rock of the mountain, until the buildings blended with the sheer cliffs on either side. These had been shaped and tunnelled into, triggering Lori's childhood memories of Petra, except the stone was granite rather than red sandstone. Drifts of snow spilled from unused doorways. The blank eyes of empty windows were festooned with lashes of icicles.

A door at the side of the gatehouse was open. The sentry had not closed it when he climbed the stairs for the last time, back when he had been alive and expecting to come down again. Now there was only a body up above, waiting to feed the crows. Lori could not push the image of the fay sentry from her mind, his frozen, blank expression and empty eyes, just like Gaius's...

Exactly like Gaius's.

The fay sentry had been enthralled. Suddenly, Lori was quite certain of it. Which meant—

Tamsin was a few steps ahead, rifle at the ready, about to lead the way forward.

Lori scuttled to her side. "I need to go up and see the sentry's body."

"No point. Just forget about him."

"It's not a guilt trip. Something's wrong. His eyes. I..." She drew a breath. "It's what you said. 'If in doubt, check. If not in doubt, check anyway.' We need to check."

Without waiting for a reply, Lori headed through the doorway. An open stairway ran up the inside wall. Like everything else in the castle, it was carved from solid granite, without ornamentation or handrail. When she glanced back, Tamsin, Hippo, and Finn were following. The others remained at the bottom.

She stepped out onto the platform over the gateway. The body lay in a heap on the snow. Lori knelt, grabbed the fay's shoulder, and rolled him onto his back. Violet eyes stared upwards, set in a pale blue face. Green blood trickled from a small pit on his cheek. The pellet had broken the skin, but would normally count as just a minor wound.

The others arrived on the roof. Finn looked condescending. Hippo looked embarrassed. Tamsin was harder to sum up.

Lori pulled the knife from the sheath on her belt. "This is silver, isn't it?"

"Yes."

Ignoring any qualms, Lori grasped a limp blue hand. When she sliced the palm, the dead flesh parted but did not bleed.

"What do you—" Hippo stopped.

Already, the figure was changing, shrinking in height while growing stockier. Skin darkened from light blue to dull green. The face widened, teeth lengthened, hair withered. Within seconds, a boggart lay dead before them.

"Shit." Finn spat the word out.

"Not a sentry. An alarm bell. Gilwyn even has a bag of shapeshifter dust to speed things up." Tamsin stood over the body. "He knew we'd come, and now he knows we're here."

"Will he have been keeping a watch on the sentry?" Lori asked.

"Count on it." Tamsin drew in a breath. "We need to change plans."

Hippo headed for the stairs. "I'll let the others know."

"What are you thinking?" Finn asked.

Tamsin was silent for a while. "My betting is that he's going to flee, rather than make a stand, though I don't doubt he'll leave a few surprises behind to slow us down. Take Shorty, Hippo, and BH. Go back to the camp and get airborne. Me, Widget, and Lori will make as much fuss as possible—make him think we're all on his tail. We'll see if we can't flush him out."

"Right, Captain." Before leaving the roof, Finn met Lori's eyes and gave just the faintest nod of approval, then he was gone.

Lori got to her feet, still looking at the dead boggart. "Poor sod."

His death had not gone unnoticed after all, but Gilwyn and his friends had not cared. The life lost was merely an alarm bell to help them save their own skins. Maybe boggarts were not sweet, innocent, babes in the wood, but they ought to matter more.

"What made you suspicious?"

"His eyes. They were just like…" Lori stopped. There was no point naming Gaius. Tamsin would not believe he existed. "They were soulless. You could tell there was no one home."

"You should give us lessons sometime. That's a good trick."

Lori shrugged. "Thanks."

Tamsin placed a hand on Lori's shoulder. "You couldn't kill him. That's because you're not evil. None of us found it easy at first. If you want to stay in Annwyn, I can teach you how to kill, but I can't teach you how to be a better person. And to be honest, I like you the way you are."

"Is this where I say I like you too?"

"You might as well do it now, because I'm leading you into a trap. We'll be playing the role of bait in a high stakes game. By the time we get out…if we get out, you might not think so kindly of me."

Chapter Eighteen

If the open air section of the castle was a maze, inside the mountain it became a warren. Halls and stairways interlinked dozens of rooms, hollowed out, one on top of the other, like an apartment block designed by Escher. Most of the castle had been deserted for decades, home only to birds and wild animals. However, people had passed through recently. Multiple sets of footprints disturbed the layer of dust, feathers, and droppings.

Widget scuffed the trail with his foot. "Don't think we'll be needing BH."

"She'd be more use here than me."

What role was she supposed to play? Widget had returned the normal rifle to her, but why? She was not going to shoot anyone, although admittedly, holding the weapon made her feel safer. She tightened her grip on the stock. Of more use were the sets of ear defenders he had also handed out. One pair was currently around her neck, on top of the torc. If shooting started underground, they would go deaf without them.

"Don't fret, pet. If Gilwyn makes a bolt for it, BH will track him down. She can follow a fart through a blizzard. All we need to do is make a lot of noise." He spoke in a whisper.

Even so, Tamsin frowned at them, holding a finger to her lips. Clearly, it was not yet time to be noisy.

They crept on, around the edge of another large hall. The walls were flat and featureless, devoid of decoration, not even flakes of old paint. The castle was purely military, with no concession to comfort. The windows were narrow arrow slits along one wall, letting in light and an arctic breeze.

An archway at the corner gave access to a staircase spiralling down into the rock. Tamsin flatted herself against the wall and peered around the corner. Widget slipped over to the other side and Lori tried to keep out of the way. Then she heard it, voices echoing up from below. She forced her hands to loosen their grip on the rifle. Her fingers were aching.

Tamsin crept down, a step at a time. Widget urged Lori into the middle position. She would have preferred being at the rear, until she saw him looking back, rifle at the ready. Of course, they did not want to get caught in an ambush from behind. Maybe she was better where she was. The daylight above faded, while a flickering yellow glow blossomed below.

At the bottom of the staircase, Tamsin used a periscope to check the next room. She made a series of hand signals that obviously meant something to Widget. He nodded and lifted the defenders over his ears, before flipping the catch on his rifle to fully automatic. Lori took the hint with the ear defenders, but she assumed she would play no part the shooting. However, Tamsin tapped her gun and pointed back up the stairs. *All we need to do is make noise.* That much was easy.

Three. Two. One. Tamsin gave the countdown on her fingers. In unison, she and Widget leapt through the doorway, guns blazing. Lori stayed where she was, firing up the stairway at nothing.

Making noise was not an issue. Lori could scarcely pick out the screams and shrieks over the gunfire. Even with the defenders, her eardrums were ready to implode. The sound was so loud it made her insides shake. Flakes of stone pelted her. She turned her face away.

The shooting in the room stopped. Lori let her finger relax. Her hands were shaking. Her heart pounded loud in the silence, even with the ringing in her ears. She took a step back and looked over her shoulder. Loose rock chippings dropped from her hair.

In the light of burning torches, a barricade of barrels and broken crates bisected the room. Tamsin and Widget stood on the other side with a prisoner face down at their feet. Three other boggart bodies lay amid splatters of green blood. Everyone else had fled, leaving a collection of wooden spears, bows, and silver tipped arrows behind. Lori pulled off her ear defenders and scrambled over the barricade.

Tamsin tapped the gibbering boggart with her boot. "Stop that and answer some questions."

"No, no, no. I didn't mean it. I didn't want to fight you. Lord Gilwyn forced us." The words were muffled between the ground and the arms wrapped over the boggart's head.

"I'm sure he did, because you didn't stand a chance. He wasn't here risking his own skin. So answer my question and you can go."

"I had no choice. None of us. We are—"

Tamsin grabbed a fistful of shirt, hauling the boggart around to face her. "Two questions. Where's Gilwyn? And how many fay does he have with him?"

The boggart, a female, gulped. "Three friends. Lady Gowyna, Lord Elphen, and another one. Haven't heard his name. He came the day before yesterday. I don't know anything else."

"Gowyna and Elphen. Now, there's a surprise." The names were clearly known to Widget.

Tamsin kept her eyes on the boggart's face. "Right. The other question. Where's Gilwyn?"

"In his room, maybe. Maybe he's gone. He has a secret way out. A passage."

"Gilwyn does love his secret passages. Do you know where it goes?"

The boggart looked as if she was trying to nod and shake her head at the same time. "The other side of the mountain, I think. There's a stable with flying horses. I take food to them sometimes, but we go over the top of the mountain. Maybe the passage goes there."

"Where is this passage?"

The boggart held out a shaking hand. "Along there. Down the steps. You will see the way. Lord Gilwyn has nice rooms."

Tamsin released her grip on the boggart's shirt. "All right. You can go."

The boggart did not hang around. She dived over the barricade and fled, head ducked, as if still fearing attack.

"Gilwyn is all set to do a runner," Widget said.

"That's what it sounds like. We just need to keep him too busy looking back to see what's in front of him."

The pathetic bodies of the dead boggarts claimed Lori's attention, and her conscience. Gilwyn sacrificed their lives to buy himself time, but Tamsin and Widget were the ones who had pulled the trigger. Had their deaths been necessary?

"We were aiming high. They got in the way of ricochets." Tamsin must have noticed her expression. "We didn't shoot them on purpose. Apart from anything else, it works better for us if they're running around creating havoc." As she spoke, Tamsin removed the magazine from her rifle. "Okay. Reload and move on."

❖

The underground section of the castle where Gilwyn had set up base was lit by torches set in wall sconces. The flames wobbled and twisted in drafts. Shadows leapt across the walls, beneath smoke blackened ceilings. The boggarts they encountered put up even less of a fight than the first group. Mostly, they ran squealing or tried to hide. The occasional volley of shots that Tamsin and Widget let off were purely so Gilwyn would know they were coming.

Identifying his private quarters was easy. They were the only rooms where the floors had been swept clean. Food and other supplies lay scattered, speaking of a hurried flight. The table and chairs were the first furniture yet seen in the castle. In the adjoining darkened room a bed was piled with blankets and furs. One wall even had a hanging tapestry, although of dubious quality and subject matter. Lori would still not have described the room as nice, but if Mud Town was anything to go by, boggarts did not have high standards.

Tamsin looked around. "The passage starts here."

"How can you tell?" Lori asked.

"Two things. Firstly, Gilwyn wouldn't risk being cut off from his escape route if he was asleep when we got here. And secondly..." She pointed at the empty wall sconces. "Four torches are missing. Gilwyn has taken his friends with him."

"You recognised their names?"

Tamsin nodded. "Their parents were supporters of Bronwen. Queen Rianna gave them a second chance. They abused her trust."

Or maybe it was less about trust and more that if Rianna killed everyone she had reason to doubt, she would be the only fay left alive in Annwyn.

"How do we find the entrance?"

"Easy." Widget pulled aside the tapestry, revealing a wooden door. "As secrets go, it's not up there in the top rank, you know."

"Is it locked?"

"I imagine so." He pulled on the handle. "But luckily I have a universal key."

"You do?"

"Yes. It's called gelignite."

Lori and Tamsin retreated down the corridor. No one else was in sight. The boggarts had all fled.

Widget joined them, grinning broadly. "I'd recommend putting your ear defenders back on."

The blast, when it came, shook the ground, bringing rolling clouds of dust so thick Lori could not see past her knees. She covered her mouth and nose, trying not to breathe it in, but could still taste the strangely sweet rock. The gust blew out most of the torches in the hall. Between the darkness and the dust, it was impossible to see a thing.

"Do you think Gilwyn will have heard that?" Widget sounded happy. "Should have given him a bit of a move on, don't you think?"

Something was pressed into Lori's hand—a high-powered flashlight.

Tamsin's shape emerged from the dust. "Let's see if it worked."

"How can you doubt me, Captain?"

Widget had nothing to worry about. The door hung off its hinges. Scorch marks streaked the walls on either side. Splintered wood and scraps of smouldering tapestry were scattered around the bedroom.

Lori's flashlight probed into the tunnel as far as a curving bend. Swirls of dust glittered in eddies. The cave was not natural. Walls and floor were chiselled smooth. The air smelt dank and the ground was littered with chips of rock, probably a result of Widget's explosion.

"How far ahead do you think he is?" Lori asked.

"Some way, I'd guess," Tamsin said. "He'd have started running even before his decoy sentry was flat on the ground. It doesn't matter. We don't have to catch him, just make him think all the Silver Ravens are here."

With Tamsin in the lead, they advanced cautiously, keeping to the sides of the tunnel. Their footsteps echoed back from a long way off. The only other sounds were their breath and the occasional drip of water.

After a couple of minutes, they reached a junction. "Which way?" Lori asked.

"Just let me check. Here, hold this." Widget passed over his flashlight. He pulled a pair of large goggles over his eyes. "Right. Turn the flashlights off."

The darkness was absolute, but Lori could hear him moving.

"Righty-oh. You can turn it back on, pet." Widget stood a few steps along the right-hand fork. "They went this way." He grinned at Lori. "It's why burning torches are a bad idea. They leave a hot trace on the roof, see. These goggles are infrared."

Tamsin slipped her ear defenders on and raised her rifle. "Before we go, we might as well let him know we're still here." She waited until Lori and Widget were equally protected before letting off a salvo.

Over the course of the next hour, Widget had to use the infrared goggles thirty or more times. The route branched, twisted, and looped back, alternately climbing and descending stairways. The caves were literally a 3D maze, and without the goggles as guide, they would have been hopelessly lost. Fortunately, they did not have to deal with any other traps. The designer evidently felt navigating the maze was sufficiently hazardous in itself. The remains of skeletons they passed suggested the designer was right.

They climbed another stairway, the longest yet. The suggestion of a draught touched Lori's face. She took a few experimental sniffs. The air was definitely getting fresher, and a tinge of daylight dusted the walls ahead. They were nearly through.

Around the next corner, the wall on the right-hand side of the passage fell away. They had emerged on a narrow ledge at the side of a huge natural cleft, piercing the mountain like a sword-thrust from the heavens. Fifty feet above, daylight spilled in through a rent in the rocks. Below, the crack sliced deep into the roots of the mountain. The breeze carried the scent of wet earth and pine trees.

After the journey underground, the natural daylight was bright enough to make Lori's eyes water. "Do you think we're nearly out?"

Tamsin nodded. "Which means this is where it gets dangerous. Keep alert." She took the lead, back against the wall, sidestepping along the ledge.

Lori leaned forward and peered into the depths. A glimmer far below could have been water, although the slope of the wall opposite, undercutting where they stood, made it certain you would hit the other side first if you fell.

"Be careful." Tamsin spoke in obvious alarm.

"I was just looking."

"And I don't want you just falling."

Had the ledge been chalk marks on a pavement, nobody would have given walking along it a second thought. However, Lori did not want to be provocative. She copied Tamsin's cautious progress.

The side of the cleft curved slightly. Only once they rounded the midpoint could they see where the path crossed to the other side of the chasm on a stone bridge, before disappearing into another tunnel. The twenty-foot span was clearly not natural.

"What do you think of it, Captain?"

"I don't know. I can't see a booby trap, but I don't like it. Get a rope out. We'll cross one at a time." Tamsin pursed her lips. "Will you be all right with it, Lori?"

"Oh, I'll be fine." The bridge was at least a foot wide. "As long as it doesn't explode when I'm in the middle."

Tamsin gave her a sideways look and then laughed. "You've got a head for heights."

"I get it from my dad."

The bridge did not explode, and the platform on the far side was wide enough for them to stand comfortably three abreast. Unlike the twisting maze, the way ahead ran arrow straight for a hundred yards or more, before ending in the unmistakable glare of daylight. However, the walls on either side had been cut away in sections, turning the tunnel into a series of three interconnected rectangular rooms.

They advanced slowly, rifles at the ready, until they reached the entrance to the final, largest room. This accounted for half the total tunnel length, and was also by far the widest part. The vaulted ceiling was three stories high at its peak. Tempting sunlight flooded in from the far end. Nobody was in sight.

"Gilwyn and friends didn't hang around for us then," Widget said.

"Nope. Hopefully, Finn's making them feel welcome."

"I could try raising him on the radio, but I wouldn't hold out much hope of getting a signal in here."

"We can wait."

The stone floor of the room was scored in a grid, imitating the look of large square tiles. A row of arches lined the walls, twelve on either side, but these were purely decorative features, shallow recesses carved into the rock, no more than a couple of feet deep. The carving was the first trace of ornamentation seen in Castle Farraon. The hall was completely empty, yet it clearly had a purpose.

Lori debated with herself whether to say anything. "I've worked with RPGs."

"Rocket propelled grenades?" Tamsin looked surprised.

"No. Role-playing games. And I know this isn't a game, but this setup is screaming *Boss Fight* at me."

"Is that the same thing as smelling a trap that stinks to high heaven?"

"Yes." Lori and Widget spoke together.

"Then I'm right with you. Have you looked up?"

Suspended over their heads were the silver teeth of a portcullis, and on the ground where they were standing was a matching set of mortise holes.

"Do we need to go out this way?" Lori asked. "As you said, Finn should have Gilwyn prisoner by now."

"Chancy. The heat from the torches is fading. I can't guarantee there'll be enough to find our way back. Unless you can remember the route?" Widget finished hopefully.

"No," Lori said.

"Ah. Well, how many skeletons did we see on the way here?"

"I didn't keep count."

"Nine." Tamsin took a half step into the hall. "We have to go on. But I think we can guess how this will play. Is there anything in your bag o' tricks for the portcullis?"

"A heavy duty, portable car jack?"

"That should do. And there's no need for us all to go at the same time. I'll cross first."

This was the point in movies where everyone demanded the right to play the hero. Lori drew a breath, ready to speak. She did not get the chance.

"No. You stay here with Widget. And be ready for anything."

Tamsin waited until the car jack was in place before advancing slowly into the hall, step by step, watching her footing. The risk had to be that one of the tiles would set off a trap, yet they all looked identical. Nothing else moved in the hall. She reached the halfway point.

Lori's heart was pounding. Her hands were clammy, making the stock of her rifle feel slick. She glanced up at the silver teeth, a couple of feet in front of where she and Widget were standing.

Tamsin took another step.

With an ear-piercing screech of metal on metal, the portcullis dropped. At the other end of the hall, a matching grate also fell.

"Quick, help me with the jack." Widget began pumping the handle. Lori knelt, adjusting the position of the base so the rising column was squarely under a silver bar. With a groan, the portcullis began to rise slowly. Running footsteps made her look up.

Tamsin had raced back, not waiting to see what might happen next. In the hall behind her, the walls under the arches were disintegrating, flowing away as if turned to sand. Something had to be inside, something dangerous, but what? Suddenly, a blast of fire erupted, turning a wall to molten globules. Despite being half the room away, Lori felt warm air on her face.

The angle into the entrance of the nearest archway allowed Lori to look deep inside. At the back, curled around itself in a ball of fire-red scales, was a lizard, the size of a carthorse. It tumbled clumsily from the alcove, as if newly born, emerging from an egg. Farther down the hall, another twisted it neck and stared straight at her. Two yellow eyes blinked. Its mouth opened and a tongue of fire spewed across the room.

"Shit. Dragons." Widget redoubled his efforts on the jack.

"I thought they'd be bigger."

"Take it from me. These are big enough."

Especially when there were twenty-four of them. The teeth of the portcullis were six inches clear of the floor. Other dragons emerged from the alcoves. The first out were becoming more alert as they roused from their dormant state. One reared on its hind legs. It buffeted the air with its wings and roared.

The gap was now eight inches. Tamsin lay down, ready to roll under the instant there was room, but the dragons had seen her. Half the reptilian heads were turned in Tamsin's direction, and the dragons preferred humans barbequed, of that Lori had no doubt. Another roar. Another gout of fire. A dragon leapt into the air, bounding towards them.

The jack had done enough. Tamsin squirmed through, heedless of her torn shirt. Lori grabbed her hand, yanking her to her feet, and all three raced back up the passage. Where the next room widened out would provide a stone bulwark against the dragon's breath. They got through. Lori and Tamsin dived one way, Widget the other. A river of flame roared past. Even out of the direct line, the wave of heat stung her face and hands.

"Are we safe here?" Lori wanted the reassurance.

"No. Once they're fully revived, dragon fire can melt silver. They'll be through in a few minutes." Tamsin spoke between gasps. "The good news is, like everything in Annwyn, they can't handle iron. The bad news is, their scales are too tough for ordinary bullets."

"What do we do?"

Tamsin raised her voice. "Have you found them yet?"

"Yup. Coming over." Widget skidded a new magazine across the floor to them.

Tamsin swapped it over on her rifle and then grinned at Lori. "Armour piecing shells." She sidled closer to the corner. "You ready, Widget?"

"Yes, Captain."

Another torrent of fire filled the tunnel between rooms. As it died away, Tamsin leaned around the edge and let loose with a burst of fully automatic fire, then ducked back before the next inferno arrived. On the other side of the passage, Widget mirrored her actions. Screeches and bellowing reverberated, loud enough to make the stone walls shake. But after the sixth barrage of bullets sent into the hall, the noise started to lessen. Tamsin continued until there was silence.

She leaned her head back against the wall behind her, breathing heavily. Sweat and soot marked the long line of her throat. Then her lips twitched. "That was fun."

"Do you think we've got them all, Captain?" Widget called out.

"Wouldn't like to count on it."

"Should we check?"

"Yes."

They cautiously made their way back. The bodies of dead dragons were piled high in the hall. Twice, Tamsin fired at signs of movement, but no more flames came. By the time they reached the portcullis, all was quiet. The silver had melted in spots, and globules dripped into the jack, rendering it unusable. The spikes of the portcullis had dropped back in the mortises.

"Okay. What do you have in your bag o' tricks to get through this?" Tamsin asked.

Widget looked worried. "That's just it, Captain. I'm not sure. Gelignite won't shift it without bringing down the roof. The blowtorch will take ages to get us through, and I doubt I've got enough gas for the other side. The angle grinder is what we want, but it's in for repair at the moment."

"You're saying we can't get through this way, and we'll be lost if we go back?"

"I'm sure I'll think of something." Widget knelt, staring at his rucksack.

"We could climb out," Lori said.

"Up the fissure back there?" Tamsin looked surprised. "Did you look at it? The sides are sheer."

"They're not that bad, but anyway, hasn't the bag o' tricks got the climbing equipment in it?"

"That's Hippo's speciality. Unless you know how to use the stuff."

Lori shrugged. "It's been a while. But I used to go rock climbing with my dad."

They had spent the weekend of her fourteenth birthday going up and down Cathedral Ledge. Mum could never see the fun in it, so they used to tease her with stories of sheer drops and overhangs. Lori felt a lump form in her chest. The next few times her dad had asked her to go rock climbing with him, she had made stupid excuses. She had never gone with him again, and after a while he stopped asking.

"Do you think you can get us out that way?" Tamsin's voice jerked her back to the present.

"We could have a look."

In fact, Lori had no trouble identifying a potential route out, and the slope was in their favour. Maybe not child's play, but nothing a moderately fit, agile person could not handle.

Lori smiled. "It'll be easy. Just follow me and take it one step at a time."

Chapter Nineteen

Widget's face appeared over the top of the lip. Lori kept tension on the line, while Tamsin lent a hand to pull him up.

The climb had been harder than Lori expected. Coaching two novices had been an extra challenge, as was the state of her muscles. She needed to get back in shape, and going to the gym was no substitute for real activity. When she returned to Earth she would contact Dad and see if they could fit in a weekend's climbing. That was, if she returned to Earth. Lori slapped her thigh in annoyance at herself. There was no if about it. She had to stay positive.

While Widget packed away the equipment, Lori took the chance to look around. They stood on a patch of barren, scree covered mountainside. Fortunately, there was not much in the way of wind, but the air had an arctic bite. Despite the cold, a wall looking like heat-haze cut across the hillside a short way off. Specks of light glittered in the depths, shifting in random patterns. Through the distortion, Lori could see other snow clad peaks, yet they seemed strangely unreal.

"Is this the end of the world?"

Tamsin smiled. "You could call it that. Luckily, we don't have to go through. But it totally screws up radio reception, so we can't contact the others to come get us. We're going to have to walk back."

How long would getting to the yurt take? She had sweated while climbing, but now a chill was setting in. A night in the open would not be fun, though Widget was undoubtedly carrying emergency equipment to save them from freezing to death. She glanced at her wristwatch. The display said 13:07, a result that needed adjustment for the longer Annwyn days. She had been there just under two weeks, so...

Lori sighed and looked at the sun. As a means of telling the time, it was just as accurate, except she had no idea which side of the equator they were on.

"It's nearly midday, pet." Widget had guessed what she was trying to do.

"Thanks. I didn't know whether we were north or south."

"We're nearly dead bang in the middle."

Admittedly, they were partway up a mountain, but there had not been any great change in elevation on the journey from Mud Town. "Why is it so cold? Shouldn't it be more tropical?"

"Annwyn is colder around the edges, and warmer in the middle."

"How does that work?"

"It just does." Widget stood and shrugged on the magic backpack. "Which way now?"

Tamsin pointed to a line of trees at the bottom of the slope. "Over there's a building. I'm guessing it's where the passage comes out."

The top of a slate roof peeked through the firs. It turned out to belong to a small stable block, now empty. The nearby tunnel entrance was still closed off by its silver portcullis. Lori peered in cautiously. The mound of red scales at the far end was just visible in the gloom, but there was no sign of life, dragonish or otherwise.

"There was me hoping Gilwyn would have left us a horse or two." Widget sniffed, in mock distress. "Selfish bastard."

"But at least we know which way to go." Tamsin set off along a narrow track through the woods. "According to our boggart friend, this should lead back to Farraon."

The still air under the trees felt warmer, but as the sun dropped, so did the temperature. The underground passage was clearly a short cut, even with the tortuous route through the maze. It felt as if the forest went on forever, but finally, they emerged at the top of a cliff. Castle Farraon was laid out beneath them, in the light of the sinking sun.

The zigzag route of a staircase was cut into the cliff face, each bend reinforced by a short tower. The entrance at the top was guarded by another gatehouse, the twin of the one below. The track ran up to the closed gates.

Widget rattled the inset wicket. "Locked and barred, it feels like. So, pet, you've got two choices. Either you climb over like Hippo did, or I take this out with gelignite. Which is it?"

"Gelignite." Lori's fingers and toes were frozen, and the last thing she felt like doing was scrabbling around for handholds.

"Actually, we've got a third option." Tamsin was facing in the opposite direction.

A black shape circled high in the sky. With the fading light, Lori could make out no details, beyond that it was too big and the wrong shape to be a bird. "Are you're sure it's not a dragon?"

"Yes." Tamsin placed two fingers in her mouth and gave a piercing whistle

Immediately, the shape changed direction. A minute later and the flying horse landed with Hippo on its back.

"Hey. What kept you?"

"We took the scenic route. Dead pretty, you know." Widget matched the bantering tone.

"Do you want to carry on walking, or shall I get your horses?"

"The horses, I think. We don't want to be late for supper. Don't you agree, Captain?"

Tamsin nodded. "Did you get Gilwyn?"

The smile on Hippo's face broadened. "Sure. And I can tell you, he is not a happy bunny."

Lori ducked through the doorway of the yurt, followed by Tamsin.

Shorty waved a bottle at them in welcome. "You've decided to join us?"

"If we'd have known you were breaking out the wine, we'd have got a move on." Widget settled down by the others, relaxing around the stove, and grabbed the bottle from Shorty's hand.

The Silver Ravens were clearly in high spirits. The same could not be said of their prisoner. Gilwyn sat propped against the side of the yurt, hands and feet bound. His expression was sullen and bitter. If he grieved for his companions, it was yet to make a dent in his anger. On the way back, Hippo had given an account of Gilwyn's capture, including the deaths of two fay, and the escape of the other, who had fled before his horse could be shot from under him.

Tamsin crouched by Gilwyn's side and exchanged a few words, spoken too softly to be overheard, then stood and ruffled his hair, as if he were a mischievous schoolboy. Gilwyn looked suitably furious.

Tamsin turned her back on him. "Well done, everyone. I think this is just about mission over. It's too late to leave tonight, so we can take it easy, except Finn will sort out a rota to keep watch on Mr. Grumpy here. Don't drink so much you can't stay awake when it's your turn. We leave after breakfast tomorrow morning."

Happy cheers greeted her announcement. Even Finn had a smile on his face. Only Gilwyn looked as if he was about to be sick. Lori watched him glare at the Silver Ravens in turn, finishing with herself. Did he remember her from Rianna's study?

Once he was handed over in Caersiddi, Gilwyn's life expectancy would not much exceed that of his fallen friends, but memory of Gaius quashed any feelings of pity for him. Except Rianna had insisted he be taken alive. She had some use for him, and it was unlikely to be pleasant. How much did he know about the queen's plans? What would he have to say? And could she trust a word of it?

Lori had to know more, and there was one other source of information. She knelt beside BH. "Did Gilwyn have anything with him when he was captured?"

"Just what was in his saddle bags."

"Were there any scrolls?"

"I don't know. Shorty checked there were no weapons, but that was it."

"Where are the bags?"

"Over there." BH gestured with a half-empty bottle, and then offered it to her. "Would you like some?"

"Thanks, but no." She wanted a clear head.

All the scrolls from the cabinet were there, including Morgaine's spell. Lori settled down in the light of a lantern and flipped open her notepad.

"What are you doing?" Tamsin sat down well inside her personal space, and Lori did not mind in the slightest.

"Decoding."

"Now?"

"The queen wants them done quickly." Lori smiled, trying to look innocent. Tamsin was not to know this was a scroll she was not supposed to decode.

"I'm sure Her Majesty would let you off for one night. Especially after your contribution today."

"What contribution? I couldn't pull the trigger."

"You aren't the first person that's happened to. But without you, we'd all have chased Gilwyn into the castle, while he was escaping out the back door. What made you suspicious?"

"As I said, the eyes. They were dead. Empty. Just like..."

"Just like?"

"Somebody you don't believe exists."

"Who?"

What was the point of saying anything? "A zombie. Like in the movies. You don't believe in zombies, do you?"

Tamsin frowned, clearly unconvinced by the switch in tack. Their faces were scant inches apart. If the mission was over, were they still officer and subordinate? Tamsin's lips were tempting. It would be so easy to lean forward and kiss her. Far easier than persuading her that Rianna was an evil bitch who could not be trusted.

Lori dropped her eyes. If she did not want to be quite as forward as kissing she could take hold of Tamsin's hand. Instead she asked, "What did Rianna do to win your heart so completely?"

"We aren't lovers any more. I told you that."

"But she still owns you, body and soul, doesn't she." It was a statement, not a question.

Tamsin sighed and shifted back. "She saved my life. Her sister, Bronwen, had a grudge against me. I can't think why she gave a toss about a lowly human, but she did. Maybe it was because Rianna made no secret about caring for me. The sisters didn't get along. Put it down to Bronwen being a bitch. After she became queen, Bronwen used me to get at Rianna. She was going to have me executed—" Tamsin broke off, shaking her head. "No, not executed—she wanted me put down, like a rabid dog. That was why Rianna started her rebellion. She did it to save my life. She killed her own sister for my sake. My life is hers, literally. I'd be dead without her. And she still cares for me. Except, things are difficult, now that she's queen. She has politics, and stuff like that to deal with. Which is why we've had to become..." Tamsin tried to speak three times before continuing. The words were manifestly painful. "The last time we made love was the night before her coronation. I...I've never talked of it before. It's not easy."

Lori mulled the story over. It went a long way to excuse why Tamsin was so blindly devoted, but did nothing to explain why the other Silver Ravens were equally besotted. Pieces of the jigsaw puzzle were missing—like the sky, the fiddly middle section, and the picture on the lid of the box. Rianna was playing games and keeping secrets. But what could she be accused of, with total certainty? Even in Gaius's case, the full story was unknown. Maybe he deserved what had been done to him.

Tamsin touched her shoulder, reclaiming her attention. "You don't need to worry about Rianna and me. It's over. We've moved on. And even before, she was never possessive. It's not the fay way."

It would be so easy to give in to the lure of Tamsin's soft, husky voice. But something was awry. Something was off kilter, and it jangled every nerve in Lori's body.

Tomorrow they would fly back to Caersiddi, where Gilwyn and the scrolls would be handed over. Then, if she was lucky, Rianna would be too occupied with her evil plans to worry about an insignificant human. Tamsin could take her home, before Rianna thought to give different orders. Once safely back on Earth, she need never again worry about the fate of Annwyn, or wicked fay queens, or sexy captains of fairyland elite forces.

As if. She might not need to worry, but it was absolutely certain that she would. What chance was there of finding answers in the scrolls? Because she had just one night left to root them out.

"I think we're due a conversation in Caersiddi." Lori picked up her notebook. "But for now, I need to get on with this."

Tamsin looked surprised, and then resigned. "I did say that, didn't I? And you're right." She pushed herself to her feet. "Good luck with the decoding." She took a step, then stopped and looked back. "And I'm looking forward to our conversation."

Lori watched her join the other Silver Ravens around the stove. A sudden onslaught of images rushed over her—Tamsin's slow grin as she joked about killing dragons, leading her squad through an abandoned castle, leaping over the table in the hall of the Mud King, shooting slua apparitions. Suddenly, it was all so obvious. Lori knew what had gone wrong with all her previous relationships.

She had never really wanted safe at all.

Lori put down the pen and stretched her arms so that they cracked. As expected, the scroll provided more questions than answers. But now she had an idea as to what the right questions were. The yurt was peaceful. Everyone else was asleep apart from Hippo, who was taking his turn to guard the prisoner. Gilwyn had not moved and was still sitting upright, although his eyes were closed.

Hippo looked up as she wandered over. "Hey there."

"Hey, you, too. I'll keep watch if you want. I can't sleep." Which was true enough. Her mind was far too busy running in circles.

"Are you sure?"

"Yes."

"Well, keep an eye on him. He's a crafty bugger."

"Takes after the rest of his family."

"Yup—apart from Queen Rianna, of course."

"Of course."

In the amber light of the stove, she watched Hippo pull a blanket around his shoulders and lie down. The only sounds were the occasional crackle of firewood and Shorty's snores. Minutes trickled by slowly. Was she really going to do this? She pulled the knife from its sheath on her belt and studied the blade in the dim light. Silver. She didn't want to kill anyone by accident—not even Gilwyn.

Tamsin was a blanket covered hump nearby. Lori scrunched her eyes closed, torn six different ways. Beyond a doubt, this was one of the silliest things she had ever considered doing in her life, but either she or Tamsin was severely deluded, and she had to know which of them it was.

She tapped Gilwyn with her foot. His eyes opened immediately. Had he been asleep?

"What is it?" His whisper was so soft it was mainly breath.

"I want to ask you some questions."

"Anything interesting?"

"That'll depend on your answers."

Somebody rolled over, mumbling in their sleep. Lori waited until all was quiet, then returned to Gilwyn. His eyes widened when he saw the dagger in her hands, but his expression was mostly one of bored contempt, shifting into derision when she attempted to cut the cords around his ankles. Of course, it was not rope—fay could untie that using magic—but electrical cable with steel wire inside. She put the dagger back in its sheath and undid the knots binding his legs. His hands were staying tied.

They edged their way to the door flap. Once outside, she guided him just far enough so they could talk freely, but close enough that a shout would rouse the sleepers in the yurt. Starlight sparkled on the snow. The horses were dim shapes under the trees, browsing on fallen pine cones.

Where to start?

Gilwyn beat her to it. "If you're hoping to find out whether it's true what they say about the prowess of fay lovers, you'll have to untie my hands first, if you want the best experience."

"After what you did to Gaius, no chance."

"Who?"

"You don't know, do you? And you don't care. Gaius was the man you murdered, the night we met in Rianna's study. Why did you do it?" That would do as a first question.

"It was a mistake. I admit it. I didn't want to leave any witnesses. Unfortunately, I'd stopped his heart before I realised you had one of those ugly things around your neck. You know you'd be so much more attractive without it?"

"I'd be dead."

"Yes. But what a beautiful corpse."

Lori dangled her knife between her fingertips so it swung like a pendulum. "This is silver, you know, not iron. It won't stop me getting answers from you if I decide I want a pair of pointy ear souvenirs."

"Threats. I like it." Gilwyn's smile glinted in the starlight. "So what are your questions? And can you make it quick? It's cold out here."

"You're Morgaine's true heir. Your mother named you. That's the way it works for fay, isn't it? Monarchs can choose their successor from anyone in Morgaine's bloodline."

"Yes. My poor, foolish mother could have chosen me or her sister before she died. For some reason she picked me."

"You don't sound concerned over your mother's death. Or should I say, murder?"

"Oh, it was murder for sure. And my mother and I didn't always get along well. Though it won't stop me from avenging her if I get the chance."

Lori held up Morgaine's scroll. "This spell. It requires the true heir's blood." No surprise that Rianna had lied. "That's why the Silver Ravens have been ordered to bring you back alive."

For the first time, Gilwyn appeared startled. "Why do you say that?"

"I've read the scroll."

"How?"

"That's why I'm in Annwyn. Rianna had me kidnapped to decode it for her."

"You!"

Lori laughed at the astonishment on his face. "Yes, me. A lesser mortal. Mind you, it took me six whole days to do it."

"If you tell my aunt she'll be able—"

"Too late. She already has a full transcript. Or I assume she has, otherwise it'd make no sense to put the original back in the cabinet."

Gilwyn's eyes narrowed in anger. "Do you know what you've done?"

"To use a cliché from Earth, I was hoping you'd tell me."

"Why do you think I'd give you the satisfaction?"

"Because when we finish talking, I plan on taking you back to the yurt and tying you up again. This is your chance to give me a reason to do something different."

"What do you hope I can tell you?"

"To be honest, I don't know, and I won't until you say it. Parts of the picture are missing. Maybe, if you fill in the gaps, I'll see a way forward. Or, to look at it another way, nothing you say is going to make your situation any worse."

Gilwyn glared at her sullenly, but his arrogance was slipping. "How much do you know?"

"I know what's written in the scroll and I know some things Rianna has said. However, I also know that I can't trust a word out of her mouth."

"Something we agree on."

"Beyond that, I've got guesswork. So come on. Tell me the whole story."

"Where do you want me to start?"

"The beginning would be nice."

"We don't have time."

"Try the condensed version."

"Once upon a time…" He clenched his teeth, clearly regretting the need to speak.

"It's not original, but please, don't stop there."

"Once, we fay could freely visit your dull little world, and liven up your sad lives."

"Kind of you. I'm sure it was appreciated."

"Then your ancestors started playing around with base metals, spoiling everything."

"So inconsiderate."

He ignored Lori's taunts. "My forebears were too complacent. Bronze was an unpleasant nuisance, but little more than that. Fay overlords on Earth made half-hearted attempts to stop your tinkering, but there were too many humans, and too few of us. As soon as one bronze smelter was destroyed, another got built. Things turned awkward, yet still most fay did not see our danger. Then you started making weapons from iron, and we had to stop visiting. It was no longer safe."

"What a shame." Despite getting answers, Lori did not feel any warmer towards him.

"Many still didn't see how dangerous the situation could become. Your science and engineering was such a weak talent, compared to magic, few took it seriously. However, one person who did take it seriously was Govannon, leader of the Council of Elders. He foresaw your use of metals becoming ever more lethal. Your iron would be our doom. With the help of others in the Council, Govannon found a way to break all contact between the worlds."

"But Morgaine's spell does the opposite, it holds them together." That much the scroll had taught her.

"Only in part. She was the youngest and bravest of the Council. She risked her life visiting your miserable little world to see what she could learn." Gilwyn sneered. "What she learned was that if she offered humans gold they'd happily do anything she asked."

"Sad to say, I don't think we've changed much." Lori had to concede him the truth in that. "I can see Morgaine didn't want the worlds separating because she needed human mercenaries to set herself up as High Queen of Annwyn. Where does her spell come into the story?"

"She didn't want other fay getting their own armies. She modified the world-splitting spell so only a few points of contact remained, which she could control. Once, there were hundreds of places where the unwary could pass from your world to ours. Now just Dorstanley remains."

"Then why does Rianna need the spell now?"

"Govannon wanted to break the link between the worlds completely. Morgaine modified his spell so it merely loosened the bonds, but it has to be renewed from time to time, otherwise the worlds will drift apart, and the bond will be broken forever."

"No more Raven Warriors."

"No. Humans cannot breed in Annwyn."

"The experiment has been tried?"

"Many times." He leered at her. "Would you like me to demonstrate?"

She did not rise to the bait. "The spell requires the true heir's blood. Doesn't that get in the way of founding a dynasty?"

"A few drops will suffice. Though I doubt my beloved aunt will be so frugal with mine. She always goes for the dramatic."

"Couldn't she kill you and make herself the true heir? Or would murdering you invalidate her claim to the throne?"

"If that were the case, half my ancestors would have been disqualified. But no, I'm the rightful King of Annwyn, and I get to name my heir. And, in case you haven't noticed, my aunt's name never passes my lips."

"How does that work? Supposing somebody doesn't get a chance to name an heir?"

"There's magic involved, but as long as you're careful, things sort themselves out. And I'm very careful."

"You've named an heir?"

"Of course. And it isn't my aunt."

Which was understandable. Lori stared at the yurt, imagining the sleepers inside. Everything Gilwyn said made sense, and none of it explained why Tamsin could not see Rianna for what she was.

"What prompted Rianna to overthrow your mother? Was it just to make herself queen?" Would he support Tamsin's story?

"I'm sure she's happy with the current state of affairs, but what pushed her to usurp the throne was my mother foolishly confiding that she was going to let Morgaine's spell lapse and let the worlds separate forever. My poor mother wanted to re-establish the Council of Elders and thought if she offered my aunt a seat on it, she could talk her round. She was altogether too fond of talking. My aunt wheedled out as much information as she could, then murdered her."

"Why did your mother want the spell to lapse?"

"She thought Annwyn would be better off without any of you humans here. When our two worlds first made contact, your ancestors were illiterate, wretched creatures, grubbing in the dirt. We fay were as you see us now. Since then, twelve thousand years have passed in your world, four hundred in Annwyn. In that time, your world has advanced, and ours has not. If anything, we've gone backwards. With each generation our birth rate falls, our lives grow dull and bland, knowledge and wisdom are lost. My feebleminded aunt is testament to that. We need to restore the council and put an end to the decline. I admit, I'd like to be High King of All Annwyn, but I want it to be a world worth ruling. My aunt just wants to sit on a pretty throne."

"If we deposed Rianna and put you in her place, you'd follow your mother's plan and let the worlds separate?" Much as she disliked the idea, it was a way forward.

"Yes."

"And you'd let all the humans return to Earth, including those who're enthralled?"

"Yes. Your presence in Annwyn has not been to our ultimate benefit."

Did she believe him? Not that it mattered. She did not have a hope in hell of persuading Tamsin and the others. "Do you know why the Silver Ravens are so devoted to Rianna? How has she tricked them?"

"I imagine she tinkered around inside their heads and changed their memories."

"They've got iron torcs on."

"They didn't always. All the Silver Ravens were once my aunt's thralls. And knowing the way she treats anyone misfortunate enough to end up in her power, I'm certain she had to get very creative with their memories before she dared let them wear a torc."

"Their memories stay changed?" But of course they did, she realised, even before Gilwyn answered. She herself had kept the ability to understand Hyannish.

"Yes. It's transmutation, not illusion."

"Silver will take the fake memories away?"

Gilwyn laughed. "How far do you think you'd get if I told you to run inside and stab them all with your knife? But no—entertaining as the idea is. Transmutation of the mind is hard to reverse. You start with a false memory, but soon it's replaced by memories of the false memory, and removing the initial falsehood has little effect. Whatever my aunt put in their heads has been there for years."

Which gave some hope he was currently speaking the truth, since it was exactly what Tamsin had said. "You said it's hard to reverse. Does that mean it's not impossible?"

"Anything's possible."

"How?"

There are various ways. Unfortunately, you don't have access to any of them."

"None?"

"The Waters of Clarity are your best option. But the well is five hours away from here on flying horses."

"There's a well, with water that will restore the Silver Ravens' memories?" Lori wanted to be clear about it.

"Yes."

"Do they have to drink it or wash in it?"

"Drink it. Just one mouthful will suffice."

Lori stared at Gilwyn. Beyond a shadow of a doubt, some of what he had told her was a lie, but as things stood, she trusted him a fraction more than she trusted Rianna—though this was a very low bar. His story made sense, it explained much, and it left her with two options. Either she took him back into the yurt and let him be handed over to Rianna, or she took the risk and tried to get the Silver Ravens to drink the Waters of Clarity.

Like there was a choice. If she returned safely to Earth, she would never be able to live with herself, knowing she had left Tamsin beguiled and cheated. Everyone deserved the truth.

If Gilwyn drew a map, would she be able to find the well, fill a bottle, and slip some of it into Tamsin's tankard? However, regardless of feasibility, she did not have time. Once they returned to Caersiddi, she had to leave Annwyn immediately, or risk never being able to leave at all. So, if she could not get the water to Tamsin, she needed to get Tamsin to the well.

Lori groaned and rubbed a hand over her face. "Right. Here's what we'll do. I'm going back in the yurt, getting flying gear for us both, and leaving a note for Tamsin. Then you're taking me to this well. If you try anything silly on the way, I'm going to shoot you." She stared directly into his eyes. "But you're not going to do anything silly, are you? Because you've got the brains to know that going along with me is your best hope. There's no point running away, because the Silver Ravens will hunt you down again. But if we can get them on your side, you just might have a chance."

"Does that mean you're going to untie my hands?"

"No."

"How will I stay on the horse?"

"Grip with your knees." She patted his cheek. "I'm sure you'll do fine."

Chapter Twenty

The well stood in the middle of a sunlit forest clearing. A pair of crows had taken to the air when Lori and Gilwyn landed, shortly after dawn, but now only songbirds fluttered through the branches of oak, birch, and ash trees. The horses grazed on a swathe of grass dotted with scented wildflowers. Shy deer peeked between the leaves of hazel bushes. The air was warm and fresh, with only the lightest of breezes. In short, the spot was the prototype for enchanted glades everywhere.

Lori sat with her back against a trunk. After a night without sleep, keeping her eyes open was a battle, but she did not trust Gilwyn anything like enough to risk giving in to tiredness, although he clearly had no similar doubts. He lay curled on his side in the dappled shade, with his bound hands under his head as a pillow.

Another yawn made Lori's jaw crack. Focusing with both eyes at the same time was a strain. If she did not do something, she was going to doze off. More than ever before, the absence of coffee in Annwyn was a serious failing. In an attempt to wake up, she levered herself to her feet and marched the length of the clearing and back, in time with the repeated chant of, "Latte, espresso, cappuccino, flat white." It did not work. She was still seeing double.

The well was surrounded by a stone wall about two feet high and covered by a little thatched roof. A wooden slat bucket balanced on the wall, attached by a rope to the winch. All it needed was for Snow White to sit under the thatch and sing to a pair of bluebirds. Lori resisted the urge to pick up the bucket to see if "Made in Fairyland" was printed on the bottom.

She returned to where Gilwyn was lying and kicked his ankle. If she had to stay awake, he could too.

He rolled onto his back. "What is it?"

Lori sat down under the tree. "Talk about something."

"What?"

"Anything. Your family. Do you have brothers and sisters?"

"No."

"Aunts and uncles, other than Rianna?"

"No."

"Cousins?"

"My aunt has a daughter who she keeps locked up."

"In a dungeon?"

"Not that extreme, but she's a long way from anywhere she can cause trouble. Apart from her, I have a couple of second cousins, and a great-uncle who's still alive."

"You don't have big family get-togethers then?"

"No." Gilwyn pouted at her. "Are you really interested in this?"

"No. Except it sounds like the royal line is at risk of dying out."

"As I said, our birth rate is falling."

"And humans don't reproduce here at all."

"No. The only species that procreates at will are boggarts, and they spawn like flies."

"How closely related are fay and boggarts? Could you interbreed with them?"

"Oh, please!"

Lori laughed at the outrage on his face. "Come on. You have to be related somehow. You're both vulnerable to iron, and you both work the same sorts of magic."

"Boggart magic!" His tone was incredulous. "I assure you, there's no similarity between fay magic and boggart trickery."

"It was their trickery that helped us find out where you were."

"If you'd like to take your torc off, I can demonstrate the difference."

"No, thanks. I'll pass." Mention of the torc sparked new questions. "You said you killed Gaius before you realised I was wearing a torc. Why didn't you ensnare both of us at the same time?"

"I thought I had."

"You mean you only discovered you couldn't control me when I didn't die?"

Gilwyn sighed. "You wouldn't understand."

"Try me."

"You've no knowledge of what magic feels like. I don't have words that will make sense to you."

"Try an analogy."

He thought for a moment. "Enthralling a human is like grasping a glass rod. You feel it more than see it, and can only be certain of the length by experiment. A human mind shielded by iron is like grasping sand. You feel it in your hand, but when you try to poke something, you realise it has no length, and when you open your hand, it's empty." He pursed his lips. "And that is a very poor analogy."

"It'll do for now."

"Anything else?"

What could they talk about? There were things she wanted to know, if only for the sake of curiosity. "You said your mother was the only one who could read the scrolls. Does that mean you can't?"

"Not at the moment, but if you worked it out, how difficult can it be?"

Lori smiled at the disdain he put into the word "you." *Knock yourself out, sunshine.* "But you know what the spell does, and that your blood is needed." How much was he making up? Lori was sure some of what he said was unreliable.

"As I told you before, my mother was too fond of talking. She shared some details with me, and unfortunately, with my aunt as well. Any more questions?"

"Yes." Lori closed her eyes, trying work out how to raise the subject. Had Tamsin really been Rianna's lover? Was any truth mixed in with the false memories? What had been the true state of the relationship between them? The image of Tamsin and Rianna on the balcony came so easily to her mind's eye.

Lori jerked awake. She had drifted off. Her hand instinctively went to the silver dagger on her belt, but it was still there and Gilwyn had not moved.

He smiled without any trace of good will. "Was I boring you?"

"No. It was all quite scintillating."

"Is there anything else you want to know?"

"I'm thinking."

"While you think, how about if I take a turn at picking a question. What are you going to do when the Silver Ravens get here?"

There was movement in the undergrowth. Lori turned her head as Tamsin stepped into the open. The others appeared in a ring around the clearing. All had their pistols drawn and pointing in her direction.

Tamsin wore the mask of a poker player. "What a coincidence. That's just what I was going to ask."

❖

"I thought you were smarter than to fall for his lies."

And I wanted to believe something similar about you. Lori bit back the words. Further inflaming the situation was unwise. She looked up at the circle of faces surrounding her. None showed any sign of being swayed. So far, Tamsin was playing from the script that had her as the naive dupe of the queen's treacherous nephew—a dupe who had acted with a level of stupidity bordering on the insane, but primarily well intentioned. However, the more she argued her case, the more Tamsin and the Silver Ravens shifted towards hostility.

Lori's wrists were bound, but she had not been gagged, unlike Gilwyn. The rag tied across his mouth split his face in the parody of a smile that did nothing to counteract the contempt in his eyes. How much further could she push things before she was silenced in a similar fashion?

"I'm sure he is lying, in part. But in part he's telling the truth. I know it."

"I don't doubt Gilwyn mixed in just enough truth to make his story plausible," Tamsin said.

"Then what do you think his plan is? Why would he make it up?"

"I wouldn't want to try thinking myself into his warped little head. He's evil. Take it from me."

"You don't believe it's possible your memories have been altered?"

"Which fay had the chance to do that? When? How? It couldn't have been done without the queen knowing, and she'd never have allowed it."

And that was the awkward bit. If she accused Rianna, she would lose any hope of winning Tamsin over. However, the story of an unknown fay changing unspecified memories during some indeterminate period in the past was not convincing anyone.

"The well over there. You agree it contains the Waters of Clarity?"

"Yes."

"And the water is harmless, apart from undoing the effects of mind altering magic?"

"Yes."

"Then why won't you drink it? What harm will it do?"

"Because Queen Rianna has given us orders not to."

"Why?"

"She has her reasons, and whatever they are, I'm not going to question them, and nor are you." Tamsin hauled Lori to her feet and turned away. "We're heading back to Caersiddi. We've wasted more than enough time here."

A last throw of the dice. What did she have to lose? Someone would report that she had spoken to Gilwyn and believed what he said. Any chance she would be allowed to return to Earth had surely gone. Rianna could, of course, simply scrub her memories, and neutralise any issues that way. Except, this would require pardoning the attempt at turning the Silver Ravens, and a forgiving nature was not something Lori associated with the queen. Lori's only hope lay, ironically, with Rianna herself, who had shown every sign of being unimaginative, lazy, and careless. Would she have gone to the trouble of creating six different stories?

Lori raised her voice. "Think about it. The only effect of the Waters of Clarity is to undo any tinkering that's gone on inside your head. If Queen Rianna has forbidden you to drink from the well, the only possible reason is that she's changed your memories and doesn't want you to know the truth."

Tamsin spun round. "You dare accuse her!" She shouted into Lori's face from scant inches away. "That's what the bastard told you, isn't it? Of course he did. And you believed the filthy lies." For a moment, Lori thought she was about to get her face slapped. Instead, Tamsin stepped back, pointing a finger at her. "Not another word." She marched away, towards the horses.

Lori waited until Tamsin was just far enough away to be unable to stop her speaking. "I know what you think she means to you. The pair of you, making love for the very last time, the night before her coronation, but—"

Tamsin was on her in an instant. She grabbed the front of Lori shirt, half hoisting her into the air. "How dare you! I spoke to you, trusted you, and—" She choked off, speechless with rage.

However, Lori already knew her guess was right. All the confirmation she needed lay in the bewilderment on the faces around her. And she was not the only one to spot their reactions. Despite the gag in his mouth, Gilwyn's shoulders were shaking with laughter.

Hippo was first to speak. "No. No, you can't have. Because…"

"The night before the coronation." Finn shook his head. "Rianna was with me."

Tamsin released her grip on Lori and faced the others. "No, she wasn't."

"You all have the same memory, and I'll bet you've all felt compelled not to share it with anyone." Lori spoke with renewed confidence. "She's manipulated you."

"Shut up. You don't know what you're talking about." Tamsin's anger had lost its edge, but she was a long way from being calm and rational.

"Neither do you. You can't rely on your memory. Go on, try something else. Pick another memory that makes you adore her. Like her overthrowing Bronwen to save you from execution. See who else is convinced exactly the same thing happened to them."

"It's him." Widget pointed at Gilwyn. "He's done something. Played some trick." But his voice lacked certainty.

Lori met Tamsin's eyes. "You'll have to drink from the well, otherwise you'll be forever wondering."

"I won't break Her Majesty's trust in me."

"What trust? She doesn't trust you to follow her without tampering with your head."

"What are we going to do, Captain?" Hippo asked.

Tamsin stared into the distance, breathing deeply, like a diver about to submerge. Her expression struggled through pain, despair, denial, and dread. "I'm going to drink the Waters of Clarity. And if anything goes wrong, you're going to take as many pieces out of the prisoner as you can, and still have a live body to hand over to the queen."

The group gathered around the well. Tamsin dropped the bucket in, letting the winch spin freely. Far more rope was let out than Lori had expected, but finally a splash rippled up from below. The Waters of Clarity ran deep underground, a phrase sounding decidedly metaphorical.

Would this work? Rianna had shared the same memories among all the Silver Ravens—it required less work and less imagination—but had she started with the genuine experiences of one person? After all, that would require the least imagination of all. If she had, was it purely Lori's own feelings that saw Tamsin as the most likely source? The one who had genuinely been the queen's favourite? What arguments could be used to get a second Silver Raven to drink if Tamsin declared her memories were unchanged?

The handle rattled as Tamsin winched it up. Slowly, the bucket appeared from the depths. From her experiences in Annwyn, Lori had expected the water to appear either boringly normal, or multicoloured and sparkly. To her surprise, it turned out to look and smell like syrupy orange cough medicine.

A ladle dangled by a silver chain from the roof support. Tamsin took a scoop and raised it to her lips. Her eyes met Lori's. The denial was gone. The despair and dread had softened to resignation, but the pain had grown.

She knows. In the time it had taken to draw the water, Tamsin had made her calculations, and reached a conclusion. Her gaze shifted to the sky, with the look of a condemned prisoner, saying farewell to the world she had known. She took a sip.

Immediately, Tamsin's face contorted in shock. She dropped the ladle and fell to her knees. Gasps of pain alternated with almost inaudible whimpers. Her hands clasped over her head, pulling herself down into a tight ball.

"What have you done?" Widget shouted at Gilwyn, shoving him so hard he stumbled and fell. Shorty drew back his leg, about to lay his boot into Gilwyn's side.

"Hold on." BH put a hand on Shorty's arm. "Give it a moment."

Tamsin was still gasping, fighting a battle to suck enough air into her lungs, but her hands had dropped and were now braced on the ground. She raised her head. Although her eyes were closed, her face was strangely calm. She swallowed, visibly clenching her jaw.

"Captain? Are you all right?" Finn asked.

Tamsin nodded slowly. Her breathing eased. Finally, she opened her eyes. "I'll kill her." Her voice was soft and serious. "I swear, on my mother's grave, I'll rip her fucking heart out."

After the initial outpouring of shock and rage, the mood in the glade changed to an eerie calm. Finn and BH vanished into the forest, marching off in opposite directions. Hippo lay on his back in the middle of the grass, staring at the sky, and Widget was intent on a handheld game console from his bag o' tricks, blind to everything else. Even Shorty, who was demolishing trees to burn off his fury, did so with a face set like stone.

Lori's hands were untied, although Gilwyn was still bound and gagged. Even without being able to speak, his enjoyment of the Silver Ravens' distress was too blatant to mistake. Nobody was yet ready to hear what he might have to say, but they must talk with him before too much longer. If nothing else, he knew how to find Caersiddi's secret passages.

In fact, as Lori was well aware, they had to do something soon. The sort of memories that had just been dumped on the Silver Ravens must be ripping them apart. They all needed and deserved trauma counselling, but quite apart from the absence of trained psychotherapists in Annwyn, there was not time. The day was progressing, well past midmorning, and they had to get back to Caersiddi to face Rianna. It was a bitch of a thing to ask, but Lori had to get them moving.

Tamsin had walked a short way into the woods and sat behind a hawthorn bush, partially shielded from view. She had not moved in an hour, and showed no reaction when Lori approached. Her eyes were glazed—the eyes of a woman staring into hell.

Lori knelt by her side. "How are you doing?"

At first it seemed Tamsin would not respond, but then her face twisted into a tight grimace. "Badly."

"I'm sorry."

"It's not your fault."

"You were happy, before I talked you into drinking from the well."

"I know. That's the worst part. She…" Tamsin took several deep breaths. "I'm going to kill her."

"That's understandable. I can only imagine what you've been through."

"No, you can't." A flare of anger cut through Tamsin's voice.

"I'm sorry. I didn't mean…" What did she mean? "I know you're in pain. I'm sorry for the part I've played in it."

"No. It's not you. Not you at all." Tamsin reached over and grasped Lori's hand, squeezing it. "I was sixteen when I stumbled into Annwyn. Guards at the portal brought me to Caersiddi. At first, there was talk of me joining the Iron Ravens, but Rianna saw me and claimed me as her thrall. And that's when it all turned to shit." Tamsin's expression started to crumble. Suddenly, tears rolled down her face and her shoulders shook in a sob.

Without stopping to think, Lori wrapped her in a hug. "I don't know what to say."

"Does it still count as rape if you're too far outside your own head to say no?"

"Yes."

"After a couple of years, she got bored with me. Others took my place in her bed, but it didn't get any better." Tamsin slid her arm around Lori's waist. Her cheek rested on Lori's shoulder. "There are scars on my back. Before I drank the Waters, I remember them as the result of a flogging on the orders of King Orfran. It wasn't him. Now, I remember her laughing."

I want to kill her too.

"There can't have been any reason for it. I was a thrall. All I could do was what she told me to."

I really want to kill her. "I wish it was different. Rianna gave me the chills from the moment I met her. She just didn't match up with the woman you talked about. I knew one of us was completely wrong about her. Now I'm wishing it was me. I'm sorry."

"Never apologise for being right. Because I've been so wrong, for so long. And I've believed so many lies. How could I have been that stupid? I know she'd messed up my memories, but I should have tied more clues together. There were so many ridiculous contradictions in my head, but I never tried to square them. I should have known that things weren't adding up."

"She'd scrambled your mind. Put in blocks to stop you asking questions."

Tamsin shook her head. "Even so, I can think of a dozen times Finn, or Hippo, or BH would say something, and I'd be confused. But I could never bring myself to say anything. The memories stayed locked in my head, until last night, with you. For the first time, I was able to talk, and I was able to talk, because it was you."

"Rianna only needed to stop you from comparing notes with the other Silver Ravens."

"No. It's more than that." Tamsin pulled back and looked into Lori's eyes. The tears had dried, and she was calmer, more resolute. "You've got your own way of getting inside my head. I wanted to talk to you. I wanted to trust you."

"And I threw it back in your face. I'm sorry, but I had to make you drink from the well."

"It needed to be done. Thank you. I'm grateful, truly." Tamsin leaned forward and placed the softest, gentlest kiss on Lori's mouth, their lips brushing.

Lori felt the breath catch in her throat. The shock rippled through her, but before she could respond, Tamsin pulled away and stood up.

"And we haven't got time to hang around. We must make plans and get back to Caersiddi."

"Do you have a plan?"

"A vague outline of one. We take Gilwyn back as a prisoner. Wait until everything is quiet. And then we'll…" Tamsin stopped and looked down at her hands. "I could almost overlook the rape, the beatings, the humiliations, all of that. The state I was in, as a thrall, I wasn't fully aware of most of it. But afterwards she made me think I loved her. That I'll never forgive."

"You're going to keep me tied up?" Gilwyn sounded disgusted.

"Yes. Otherwise nobody will mistake you for a prisoner. Deal with it." Tamsin looked around. "Are we all good?" Good was maybe a little too optimistic, but a desire for revenge had brought out the steel core in the Silver Ravens. "Right. We leave in ten minutes."

While the others attended to their horses, Tamsin took Lori aside. "Are you sure there was nobody here when you arrived?"

"Yes. We startled a few deer when we landed, and a couple of crows took off, but that was it."

"Right. Next question. Do you have any idea how many human thralls Rianna has?"

"No. I've seen three, including Gaius, who's gone now. But I suspect there's more."

"Probably. I'm sorry I didn't believe you before."

"We can blame Rianna. But Gaius was how I recognised the transformed boggart in Castle Farraon. I can't forget his eyes."

"So that's the trick." Tamsin pursed her lips. "I don't want to fight thralls. But it would be typical of Rianna to sacrifice them."

"Maybe Gilwyn can wrest control from her. Though I'd hate to rely on him."

"Me too. I know a slippery bastard when I see one, but he was right about Rianna screwing with our memories, and for now, we're on the same side. We're both out for revenge."

"I'm not sure how attached he was to his mother."

"Oh, it'll be mere pride when it comes to her. The revenge is more to do with his own treatment by Rianna. The sad thing is, now that my memories are back, Bronwen was the only fay I'd put any faith in. Though I'm still not sure I'd have trusted her enough to lend her my favourite shirt." Tamsin forced a smile. The pain was still in her eyes. "This spell Rianna wants to cast. Is there any special date for it?"

"When it's one of the quarterdays on Earth."

"Okay, I'll have Widget run the sums, but I think the next is five or six days from now. So we've got no need to rush into things. There's time to get you back to Earth before the fun kicks off."

"No. I'm staying."

"I'd be happier with you safely out of it."

"Not gonna happen. If I wanted to run away, I should have left Gilwyn alone, and not tried to restore your memories. I chose to be a player in this game, and I'm not backing out."

"You're sure?"

"Yes."

"Really sure?"

"Yes."

Tamsin sighed. "I wish you'd change your mind, but it does simplify the planning." She patted Lori's arm. "I need a quick word with Finn before we leave."

Whatever Tamsin's plans were, Lori's main hope was that she could snatch a couple of hours' sleep first. At the moment she was good for absolutely nothing. She raised a hand to cover another yawn. How was she going to stay on Cirrus's back? Fortunately, the Waters of Clarity lay almost directly on the route between Farraon and Caersiddi, and the remaining part of the journey was short.

Lines of ice ran in prickling waves over her scalp. Her eyes were burning and her head felt stretched. Lori pouted ruefully. At university she could pull all-nighters and still get to lectures the next day.

Dammit. I guess I'm getting older.

CHAPTER TWENTY-ONE

By the time the Silver Ravens reached Caersiddi, Lori was sleepwalking through treacle. Despite all that had happened, and what might lie ahead, she could not get beyond thoughts of her bed, and the chance to lie down and close her eyes. She spared one glance for the others, manhandling Gilwyn up the interlinked stairways of the middle bailey, on their way to give a repeat performance of handing him over to Rianna, and then she literally crawled up the stairs to her room. Her boots were the only thing to go before she collapsed on her bed, fully clothed, and let herself sink into the warm, dark arms of slumber.

Daylight still flooded the room when Lori awoke, but the shafts came almost horizontally. Sunset was at hand. Her head was thick and her mouth felt as if she had been chewing old socks. She slid off the bed and tottered across to the window. Activity in the middle bailey appeared the same as normal. Had she missed anything while she slept?

The first, obvious, answer to this question was of course, dinner. As she watched, a small group of Iron Ravens barged their way out of the mess hall, jostling each other in light-hearted rivalry. Maybe, if she hurried, she could get something to eat. A proper wash and a change of clothes were also high priorities, but they could wait. She shoved her feet into her boots and hurried downstairs.

The mess hall was not deserted. Apart from serving boggarts and a few stragglers, the Silver Ravens were all at their table in the corner. Lori was greeted with smiles as she joined then. Even Finn gave her a nod of acknowledgment.

"Is any food left?"

"After Hippo's been at it? Get serious." Widget grinned at her.

Tamsin snapped her fingers to get the attention of the nearest boggart. "We'll have another trencher with meat and potage."

The boggart jiggled his head earnestly and scurried off.

BH pushed an empty wineglass and a bottle in Lori's direction. "A gift from Her Majesty, in recognition of a job well done."

Lori sniffed the open top. "Brandy?"

"Something like that."

A drink with lower alcohol content would have gone better with the meal, but the usual weak beer was not on the table. She took a sip. The taste was closer to Greek than French brandy, with a fruity fullness.

"What do you think of it?" Hippo asked.

"It's all right."

"Good, we've got four bottles to get through."

"We could save some till tomorrow."

"Where's the fun in that?"

Everyone cheered. Lori laughed, for the first time fully a part of the group, included as the jokes and banter flowed around the table. Everyone looked as if they were having a good time, happy and animated. Yet, only a few hours before, they had gone through an emotional trauma on a scale hard to imagine. They had to be tearing up inside, but the Silver Ravens would do whatever it took to get the job done—including acting as if nothing was up.

"You don't want to be our sniper then?" Widget asked. "Typical. Just when I thought I'd found another chess player."

"No. The instructors on the training course called me Annie Oakley, but I'm like her, best sticking with shooting at targets for fun."

"Annie Oakley?" Tamsin said. "You know, I met her once, when I was in the USA, sorting out Earth investments. Except it was before she got famous and she was still called Annie Mosey."

Shorty laughed. "Mousie? I can see why she picked a stage name."

"Maybe we should start—" BH broke off at a commotion by the door.

A boisterous group of Iron Ravens surged in, carrying fiddles, flutes, and drums.

"Hey. Party time." Hippo gave a whoop.

"Oh no. He's going to start dancing." Widget feigned despair.

"Better than him singing," Finn muttered, but this time Lori caught the undertone of dry humour.

Tamsin reached under the table and pulled up another bottle of spirits. "Time to open the next one, courtesy of Her Majesty."

Her Majesty—not Queen Rianna. The only blip in the act. Nobody was voluntarily saying her name. Lori pushed the remains of her bread bowl away. "Did the queen say anything else?"

"She wants to see us tomorrow and congratulate everyone personally, after we've had a rest."

"And a bath?"

"Wouldn't be a bad idea."

But washing away the grime would have to wait until morning. The alcohol was hitting, harder and quicker than Lori expected. Already she had to be well over the limit. Maybe it was due to her disrupted sleep pattern. Either way, it was time to slow down, or even stop drinking altogether.

Meanwhile, the musicians had finished tuning their instruments. Darkness had fallen outside, and only candlelight lit the hall. The door opened as more Iron Ravens streamed in. News was spreading. The fresh arrivals helped their comrades move tables to clear a dance floor. Before long, the music had started and the mess hall was full of drunken soldiers gyrating around. A few could dance, but most floundered around, out of time with the rhythm. The tune was closer to Irish folk than anything else, but overlain with other influences.

Since arriving in Caersiddi, Lori had heard sounds from previous parties in the mess hall, but had always been too tired to join in. With hindsight, staying in her room had been a mistake. Maybe the brandy had gone to her head, but it was all too much fun. Between the music, the leather, the lighting, and the male-female ratio, the effect was somewhere between a barn dance and a BDSM gay disco during a power cut. Despite her previous resolution, she poured herself another glass.

Tamsin slid onto the bench beside her. "How are you doing?"

"I see how Hippo got his name."

"It didn't take much imagination." Tamsin leaned in close to be heard over the noise. "I knocked on your door this afternoon, but you didn't answer. Where were you?"

"Dead to the world." Lori shifted around, so that she was pressed against Tamsin's body. "What did you want to say?"

"I was going to try again to talk you into going back to Earth." Tamsin's breath tickled her ear.

"No chance. I'm here till the end."

"I'd feel happier knowing you were safe."

"Like I said, it's not gonna happen. Anyway, would you have had time to escort me?"

"I'd have commandeered a squad of Iron Ravens."

"Can—"

"Hey, Tazer, are you going to join us?" Shorty shouted from the dance area.

"Later."

Tazer, not Captain—they were definitely off duty, not that officer and subordinate roles counted any more. "Do you prefer Tamsin or Tazer?"

"You can call me whatever you want, as long as it's not Thomasina."

"I think I like Tamsin better."

"Fine by me."

The dancing stopped to allow the musicians to take a drink. However, one player continued with a haunting tune on the pipe. Around the room, singers picked up the ballad, and then dancers took to the floor, couples moving in slow unison. Lori was acutely aware of Tamsin's body pressed against hers.

"Would you…"

"I don't suppose…"

They both spoke at the same time. Tamsin started laughing. "Oh, come on."

"Weren't we suppose to have a conversation first?"

"It can wait." Tamsin grabbed her hand and tugged her off the bench.

Her body moulded against Tamsin's. Whistles and catcalls from the other Silver Ravens faded into the background. Lori's head nestled into the hollow of Tamsin's shoulder. Her hands pressed against Tamsin's back, following the movement of leather encased muscles. She could feel the beat of Tamsin's pulse against her cheek. The strength of Tamsin's arms around her was good.

She sank into the body magic, letting Tamsin and the music guide her. The start of a relationship, the heady, giddy, heart-stopping, soul-burning first steps, when lust turned from imagination into reality. That was where they were. The build-up had gone so slowly, or seemed as if it had. Lori could not be bothered to count the days since they first met.

The ballad finished. A moment of peace. They stayed locked together and then stepped apart. Tamsin caught hold of Lori's hand. "Thank you."

"Thank you, too."

The drummers began pounding out a beat, and chaos erupted back on the dance floor. Lori was a little surprised to see that Shorty and Hippo had also been sharing a slow dance. They separated and launched into energetic action, while Tamsin towed her back to the table, worming a way through the heaving crowd. The rest of the Silver Ravens greeted them with cheers and the flourish of a third bottle of brandy.

BH was about to refill her glass. Lori placed a hand over the top. "I've had enough."

"You sure?"

A nod. She knew her limits when it came to spirits. What she really wanted was something thirst-quenching, water, or even beer. She looked around, but the boggart servants had left.

Tamsin stood behind her, with both hands on her shoulders. Lori closed her eyes and leaned back, feeling ridiculously happy and secure. Beyond ridiculous, if she were to take the slightest account of their current situation. But then her head started to accelerate backwards and a wobble flipped in her stomach, and not in a good way. She had drunk far too much.

She pulled Tamsin's head down to mouth level. "I need to go."

"Now?"

"Yes."

She followed Tamsin around the edge of the mess hall and out into the peace of the middle bailey. The night air was cool on her face. Other couples were also in the starlit garden, but there was no difficulty finding a space to themselves. Tamsin leaned against a tree and pulled her into an embrace. Lori was a good three inches the shorter, forcing her to look up. Tamsin's eyes reflected the light of unearthly stars.

Their lips met, but unlike the kiss that morning, this was not quick, or soft. Raw desire burned through Lori, overriding any thought beyond right here, right now. Their mouths moved, hard and passionate. She sucked hungrily on Tamsin's lower lip. The first touch of their tongues was like an electric shock, a jolt that ran though the core of her body. She ached, needing to be touched, needing release.

Lori broke away, breathing harshly. "We should go to my room, or yours."

For the space of a dozen body-shaking gasps Tamsin made no reply. "No. I don't think so."

The words were like being doused with cold water. "Then what?"

"We kiss and say good night."

"That's it?"

"Call me an old-fashioned girl. After all, I was born in the seventeenth century."

There was more. There had to be. Tamsin was not saying something. Was it a rejection, or part of a plan to deal with Rianna? Then nausea bubbled up in Lori's stomach. Maybe backing off would be for the best. If she had not drunk so much brandy, she could have argued, but throwing up really was not a good look on a first date. How much had she drunk?

After another kiss that all but melted her socks, Lori returned to her room, alone.

❖

Despite her extended afternoon nap, Lori was asleep the moment her head hit the pillow, dropping her into a deep, dark pit of unconsciousness. Although, this time she managed to remove her outer layer of clothing first.

She awoke while it was still dark, with the beginnings of a hangover spearing her temples. The room spun. She switched on the flashlight she had taken to keeping by the bed and lay still, concentrating on breathing. Her stomach was fragile and her mouth had turned to sandpaper. She could only hope Tamsin's plans would not require any effort from herself until after midday, because she was going to be absolutely no use before then. How much had she drunk?

Lori rolled off the bed, battling with the floorboards which heaved under her feet like waves. A pitcher stood by the basin on the table. Before now, she had used the water only for washing. Was it safe to drink? She was dithering between risking it, or going in search of a better source when the crunch of footsteps sounded on the path outside. Multiple people were approaching the Silver Ravens' quarters. The steps did not have the rhythm of a military march, yet nobody was talking. An alarm stirred in Lori's gut.

By the time she opened the window shutters, the group had entered the building and were out of sight. The footsteps now sounded on the stairs. They passed her door, and continued along the corridor. Whoever the people were, she was not their immediate concern. Should she investigate? Something was up, and in the circumstances, that something was almost certainly bad news.

But first, she needed a drink, in the hope it would ease her head and calm her stomach. Water from the pitcher would have to do. Whatever was coming, she should face it in the best shape possible—which was a joke. She could barely stand. Was it just alcohol to blame, or had the brandy been drugged?

Mid-gulp, she heard muffled shouts. An alarm? A warning? Her standard issue pistol was in her footlocker, in accordance with rules forbidding Earth weapons in the middle bailey for everyone not on active sentry duty. Trying to be as quiet as possible, she opened the lid and fumbled with the holster.

Having the gun in her hand was reassuring, but before she went to investigate, she ought to put on more clothes. She was trying unsuccessfully to slip her foot into her trouser leg when the footsteps returned. Too late to worry about getting dressed. She held the gun securely, one hand bracing the other, the muzzle pointed midway between her feet and the slowly opening door.

Four strangers stood in the corridor, torcless humans with blank faces and dead eyes. Rianna knew about the Waters of Clarity. Whatever plans Tamsin had were out of time and luck.

Lori raised her gun, fighting to control her shaking hands. "What is it? What do you want?"

She might as well have brandished a bunch of flowers. The thralls marched in like automatons, showing no reaction to the pistol, even after she flicked off the safety catch.

"Stay back."

They ignored her.

Her finger was on the trigger, but the memory of Gaius's dead face swam before her eyes. Paralysis gripped her hand and her finger refused to move. But even had she shot the first thrall, there was not time to get them all. They surrounded her, grabbing her arms and forcing them behind her back. Cold metal touched her wrists, accompanied by the click of handcuffs.

BH, Hippo, and Widget were already in the bailey when she was dragged out to join them. All looked dazed, and were standing as if they needed the support of their thrall captors to remain upright. Widget's head lolled to one side. If anything, their condition was worse than her own, since she had drunk the least brandy.

Shorty was also dragged out. "Fuck you, bastards."

He was struggling, but his movements were clumsy and uncoordinated. His legs splayed left and right, doing little to support his weight. In Mud Town, Shorty had downed large quantities of beer without showing anything close to the same level of intoxication. It confirmed her guess about the brandy being drugged. Rianna had hedged her bets.

Without a word said by their captors, they were dragged to the audience hall in the keep. Tamsin was already there, handcuffed and kneeling. Blood oozed from a cut on her forehead, and a graze marked her cheek. They joined her in a line before the empty throne.

Finn was also present. Alone of the Silver Ravens, his hands were free, and he was on his feet. He stood to the side, arms folded, watching with a disinterested air.

"Finn? What's going on?" Hippo shouted.

"That'll be Captain Finn to you. And I'd have thought it was obvious."

"Captain?" BH sounded shocked. "Finn. You've sold us out? Why?"

"I'm not going to lose everything in a fool's game."

"After what she did to you?"

"Maybe I'm not so much of a wimp as you lot." Finn shrugged. "Nothing happened that I couldn't handle. Anyway…" He pointed at Lori. "It's her fault. If she hadn't stirred things up, none of us would be any the wiser. Revenge isn't worth missing out on a golden retirement. I'm not giving up my future for the sake of a past I can't change. It's as simple as that."

"If I get out of this, I'm going to rip your fucking guts out and ram them up your arse." Shorty spoke through gritted teeth."

"That's a big if. I don't—" Finn broke off.

Rianna arrived, complete with entourage. She settled calmly on her throne and cast her eyes along the row. The silence dragged out, but at last she smiled. "What a pretty bunch of traitors. Did you think I wouldn't find out?"

"You wouldn't have without a fucking rat," Shorty shouted. A thrall cuffed him on the back of the head, sending him crashing face first on the ground. He struggled back to his knees.

"Be quiet. You'll now remember I have ways to make you regret any show of insolence."

Lori glanced left and right. The Silver Ravens were angry, defiant, and not one was showing a trace of fear. She pushed her shoulders back and her chin up.

"Finn knows where his duty lies. So, now I have a new captain for my Silver Ravens and six more house thralls."

"You'll come to regret this. Both of you." Tamsin spoke for the first time, calmly and clearly.

"You think so?" Rianna leaned forward, her eyes glinting. "Remove their torcs."

Cold fingers slipped under the metal band around Lori's neck. The ornate ends scratched her neck as the torc was yanked away, and then fog rolled into her head.

The audience hall softened. The fear went away. The surprise went away. The world was a distant painting she drifted through. Nothing was worth fighting over. Yet, somewhere she was screaming. Somewhere, she was buried alive in a coffin of fog. She was confused, and she did not like being confused. Somewhere there was panic, and pain, and a lost voice sobbing and pleading to be set free. It made no sense.

"Follow the others to the pen and wait there."

That was easy. Maybe, if she did as she was told, the confusion would go away. She did not want to hear the lost voice. The pen would be quieter, she was sure of it. She would go to the pen and wait for the confusion to go. It was all very easy.

If only the screaming would stop.

Scrubbing the floor did not stop the screaming, but it made it less annoying. Lori thought possibly the voice was inside her, but that would be puzzling, and puzzles were not worth the bother. What was the point in wondering why the voice was screaming? What was the point in wondering about anything, when it was so easy to dip the brush in water and scrub the floor instead? Maybe her hands were wet, cold, and raw, her knees ached, and her stomach was empty, but it did not matter. The floor was easy to deal with.

"Empty the bucket in the drain and go back to the pen for tonight. Your food is there."

Confusion turned into a moment of distress. Scrubbing the floor protected her from the screaming in her head. But then she realised her mistake. She would be safer in the pen. That was where she was supposed to be. The voice would not trouble her there.

Lori did not feel hungry after she had eaten, which was good. She found a clear patch of ground and lay down to sleep. Everything would make sense tomorrow. She was sure of it.

❖

A hand on her shoulder. "Wake up. Follow me."

Did she need to wonder why the man spoke so quietly? It would be easier to hear him if he did not whisper. How awful it would be if he wanted her to do something and she did not hear what he said. Perhaps she could ask him to speak louder. But it would be better to wait to see if he raised his voice when they got to wherever he was taking her.

The fog shattered. The world crashed over her in a wave that made her head implode. Lori groaned and wrapped her arms over her skull in an attempt to shield it from reality. Memories seethed and ripped into her—clean floors and coffins of fog. The screaming voice tried to crawl up her throat. She slapped a hand over her mouth to hold it back.

Slowly, the tempest settled. A weight of cold metal lay around her neck. Someone had replaced her torc.

She raised her head and opened her eyes. She was in a wine cellar, lit by a single candle. Cobwebs hung from the low ceiling and racks of bottles lined the walls. A figure stood silhouetted in the candlelight, just out of arm's reach.

"How do you feel?" Finn's voice.

"What?"

"You can take a moment to gather yourself, but we don't have time to waste."

"Finn?"

"Yes?"

"What…why…" Which question needed an answer first?

He gave an impatient sigh. "Even though you didn't see anyone when you arrived at the well, there was a high risk Queen Arsehole had a watch set. I would have in her place. It might even have been the crows you saw. The captain thought me playing stooge was safest. Most likely I was only telling her frigging highness something she already knew. But if it came as a surprise, she'd have been in my debt. Either way, she'd end up trusting me more than she did before."

"You planned this with Tamsin?"

"Of course. I've allowed two days for things to calm down. But now we need to move." He picked up an iron torc from a pile on a shelf and placed it in her hand. "If you're ready, you need to find the others and bring them here, one at a time."

"Where is here? Where are we?"

"Underneath the keep. Gilwyn knew a secret tunnel from the middle bailey, which conveniently ended up by the thrall pen."

"You've talked to him?"

He shook his head. "The captain got the details when they spoke by the well."

Lori's legs were shaky. "Wouldn't it be better if you rescued the others, since you know where they are?"

"No. Because they might rearrange my face before I had a chance to explain. I reckoned I could handle a mousie."

"None of them knew?"

"Just me and the captain. Less acting required, and less risk if the bitch dug around in your heads."

"Won't she dig around in Tamsin's head?"

"The captain will be on a long leash." Finn's voice was rougher than normal. "It's no fun torturing a thrall. They don't react to pain."

"What?"

"Tazer really did have a special place in her affections." He gave a humourless laugh. "I'd thought it was me. Now I'm glad it wasn't. On past form, she won't have the captain deeply enthralled."

The full implication sunk in. "You mean, she'll…"

"Let's just say, I think the captain will be very pleased to see us."

"We need to rescue her, right now."

"Yup. So you need to stop talking and start moving."

Finn led the way down a corridor and pointed out the door to the thrall pen. There were no locks or guards. The thralls were not going to run away. Finn vanished into the shadows.

Inside, over three dozen humans lay on the cold stones. The air stank of stale sweat, mildew, and filth. She stepped over sleeping bodies. No one stirred, although some muttered in their sleep. Were they listening to their own insane voices, screaming about the fog?

The first Silver Raven she spotted was Shorty, a head taller than anyone else. She knelt by his side.

"Wake up and come with me."

CHAPTER TWENTY-TWO

The Silver Ravens formed a huddle in the wine cellar, listening to Finn. "First step, we have to free Gilwyn."

"Arrogant fay shithead. We can't fucking trust him."

"Yup, Shorty. I agree with you, one hundred percent, but for now he needs us. He knows the secret passages, and he's our best hope if Queen Arsehole has some magic tricks up her sleeve."

"Do you know where he's being held?" Widget asked.

"Good news and bad. He's in the dungeon, one level below us. But after his last escape, there are guards watching him round the clock."

"Which species?"

"Human. Iron Ravens. She wouldn't want Gilwyn talking to any of the fay. And he could take control of thralls or boggarts."

"I'd rather not fight other humans," BH said. From their expressions, the others agreed.

"We may not have to." Finn held up a flask. "The Waters of Clarity. I brought it back in my saddlebag. It'll only take a mouthful each."

"How do we get them to drink it?" Hippo asked.

BH had a second question. "Will their memories have been altered like ours?"

"I doubt there's a human in Annwyn who hasn't had their mind fucked with by the fay. They have to do something to ensure our loyalty. Otherwise they'd run the risk of ambitious captains making their own bid for the throne. As for the Iron Ravens here, the queen wouldn't let unsupervised humans in the keep without turning their brains inside out first. They might not have been through everything we have, but I'm betting, once their memories are restored, they won't have much love left for her. As for how we get them to drink, I'm open to ideas."

"Stick a gun in their face?" Shorty suggested.

"They're armed and might raise the alarm."

"Why not simply order them to? They ought to recognise you," Widget said.

"I'm not their commanding officer, and it's not a normal order. If I wander in and say, 'Here, lads, have a drink on me,' they'll know something's up, unless they're plain stupid."

With each second, Lori's nerves unravelled a bit more. Tamsin was not in the thrall pen, and the implications were bad. They had to rescue her as quickly as possible. "Did you bring Widget's bag o' tricks?"

"Yes," Finn said.

"The iron amulets. If I wore them, would I be safe from enthrallment?"

"Not if one of the fay targets you directly," Widget answered. "But otherwise, you could get away with it."

"What are you thinking?" Finn asked.

"If I wore the amulets and took the torc off, I could pass as a thrall, bringing them a drink. I'm dressed for the part." The slave rags barely covered more than the underwear she had been captured in. However the sleeves went to her elbows, and would cover the amulets. "In this part of the keep, they'll be used to seeing human thralls around."

"It's the middle of the night," Finn pointed out.

"I'll be there on the orders of Queen Rianna, for her loyal troops to toast the news that has just arrived, of the birth of Her Majesty's first grandchild."

"Is her daughter pregnant?"

Lori smiled. "If you don't know, they won't."

Lori tapped on the door, concentrating on the rhythm. Not timid, not demanding, more as if she was hitting her knuckles against the wood without understanding why.

The door opened. "What is it?"

She stared straight ahead, working on keeping a passive mask. "The queen wishes you to celebrate the birth of her first grandchild. News has just arrived."

"What?"

"The queen wishes you to celebrate the birth of her first grandchild. News has just arrived."

"You said that. How are we to celebrate?"

"I have brought you a drink." The man should have been able to work it out for himself. In her free hand, she was carrying a tray with a bottle and twin glasses. Maybe he was plain stupid after all.

"Okay...um. Come in." He stepped back. The sight of a thrall, without a torc, clearly did not surprise him, although he did not seem at ease with her.

The dungeon was a similar size to the thrall pen, but, unlike the room on the level above, would have no natural lighting during the day. Gilwyn had been asleep on a bunk in the corner, but was now woken by the noise. He raised himself on an elbow, twisting awkwardly due to his bound wrists and feet. His expression was its normal condescending sneer.

Apart from the bed, the cell had a small table and a stool. Lori put the tray down and poured two shots, working at copying the deliberate way Gaius had moved, and how his eyes fixed unwavering on whatever lay directly before him. "The queen wishes you to celebrate the birth of her first grandchild."

"I heard." Another Iron Raven, a woman, picked up a glass and gave a cautions sniff.

"What is it?" the first guard asked.

"Rat's piss, going by the smell."

The man joined his companion and raised his glass. "Boy or girl?"

Lori said nothing. Gaius would not have taken the words as a question.

The man sighed. "Is the baby a boy or a girl?"

"It is a boy."

"Does he have a name yet?"

"I do not know."

"Right, then. A toast to his young lordship." The Iron Ravens tossed the drink back.

The woman stumbled away, hands pressed over her face. The man was rooted to the ground, while his shoulders shook with ragged gasps. Lori was able to catch both glasses before they hit the floor.

"Oh, well done." Gilwyn's tone dripped sarcasm. "I wondered how long you'd take."

Lori ignored him. She opened the door and beckoned to the Silver Ravens waiting a short way along the corridor outside.

Finn was first in. "There's another two Iron Ravens around here somewhere. They watch Gilwyn in shifts. They aren't allowed out of the keep, so they have to sleep close by. We should take care of them too."

"Why aren't they allowed to leave?"

"I guess Queen Arsehole is worried about what they might see and hear that she won't want passed on. They could have had their memory scrubbed when the job was over."

"Right." Lori picked up the tray. "I'll see to the others."

She found the sleeping guards on the third door she tried. Torchlight from the passage spilled into the narrow room, showing two bunks. She nudged the guards awake, and went through the same routine as before. This took a little longer, due to the darkness and the men being groggy from sleep, but the outcome was the same.

She stepped back into the passage and signalled to Hippo.

"Good job." He grinned at the stunned Iron Ravens. "We'd better give them a hand along. We don't want to hang around all night."

It took a combination of encouragement and firm shoves to get the guards moving. Back in the cell, Gilwyn was now freed from his bonds, but remained seated on the side of his bed, watching with his usual disdain. The first pair of Iron Ravens appeared to have got over their shock and were now willing participants. Widget knelt in the middle of the floor, laying out the small arsenal pulled from his bag o' tricks.

Finn looked up from inspecting the weapons. "Right. We're all here, and we've got plenty of firepower to share round. We'll split into two groups. Me, Widget, Shorty, and Hippo will head straight to the royal apartments. We'll have his highness with us"—he jerked a thumb over his shoulder at Gilwyn—"who knows the shortcuts. BH will lead the rest of you out through the tunnel that got me in here."

While Finn was talking, Widget handed out weapons. He pressed a rifle into Lori's hands. Her first, instinctive reaction was to reject both the gun and Finn's plan. She was not going to shoot anyone—taking revenge on Rianna could be left to the Silver Ravens—but she wanted to help rescue Tamsin. However, insisting on being part of Finn's group was idiotic. She would be ignored, and quite rightly so. The Silver Ravens knew what they were doing, and she did not.

Finn continued. "Co-opt a few more Iron Ravens if you get the chance, but don't worry if you can't." He looked at his watch. "You've got thirty minutes. That should see us all in position. I want a nice loud distraction at the keep entrance. Are we all clear?"

Everyone nodded, except for Gilwyn, who merely gave a bored sigh.

"Okay. Let's go."

❖

BH patted Lori's shoulder. "Don't worry, it's the same as before. You don't have to shoot anyone, just make a lot of noise."

Lori nodded and continued adjusting straps on the silver breastplate. The secret tunnel from the thrall pen had led to a storeroom full of equipment for the Iron Raven officers. The standard shirt and leather was an improvement on the slave rags, and the metal armour was reassuring, although heavy.

BH was doing likewise. She slid a crested helmet over her head and joined the man standing watch by the door. "Is it still clear out there?"

He gave her a thumbs up.

"Right. Follow me." BH slung a grenade launcher over her shoulder and led the way, gliding silently between trees and flower beds.

Lori tagged on at the end. The middle bailey gardens were silent except for the splash of fountains. The first pale hint of dawn silhouetted the castle walls, though the light was not yet strong enough to challenge the brilliant Annwyn stars. Their soft radiance touched the leaves and lawn with silver and turned the cascades to diamonds. Footprints stood out starkly black in the dewy grass.

They stopped with a view of the inner bailey gates. In the light of guttering torches, four armed sentries stood guard, two on either side. A fay official would be inside the gatehouse, although probably not overly vigilant. The fay had a low boredom threshold.

BH whispered, "Any ideas? We've got the Waters of Clarity, but these guards won't have seen thralls, so they'll not fall for toasting the queen's grandchild." She pressed the light on the watch Widget had given her. "And we have seven minutes."

Lori thought furiously. "Yes. I've got an idea. You need to take the Waters and say—"

BH pressed the flask into her hands. "There's no time to explain. You do it."

"Okay. In that case, you'd better stay out of sight. Just give me the bottle. And the rest of you, follow me. Act like you're on duty, and are pissed off about it."

Lori pushed the helmet down on her head, hoping to put her face in shadow, and marched forwards boldly. The footsteps of the Iron Ravens followed. The sentries on the gate looked surprised, but did not otherwise react. With luck, they would recognise their four comrades, which should ease any suspicions.

She stamped to a halt. "You're relieved of duty and may stand down." She gestured sharply for the others to take their place, then beckoned the real sentries aside.

"You've heard the Silver Ravens got into trouble?" Sharp nods, but the uncertain frowns confirmed that they had been told few other details. Rianna would not have wanted the truth broadcast. "They were in Mud Town and got exposed to Ganymede Fever. Surprising they didn't get worse in that shithole. Anyway, it's highly infectious, and potentially deadly. Luckily, we've got a cure, if it's taken soon enough." She held up the flask. "You need a swig of this. You'll feel strange at first, and you may have to lie down. But you'll be all right." She pressed the flask at the first man. "Well, go on. Don't just stand there. Drink and pass it on."

The first three did not react as severely as those in the keep had done. Presumably, their minds had not been upended to the same degree. However, they were still dazed. The final sentry had the bottle to his lips when a high fay voice called from the gateway.

"What's going—" A swish sliced through the air and the words cut off abruptly.

The sentry turned his head at the sound. Lori rammed her knuckles into his shoulder, jerking him back. "Hurry up. I haven't got all day. There's others to see."

He took a mouthful which rocked him back on his heels as if he had been punched. Lori retrieved the flask from his slack hands. It was nearly empty, but should not be needed again.

BH appeared from the darkness. "Quick. Get everyone inside."

A fay woman lay dead. Helped by one of Gilwyn's former guards, BH dragged the body back inside the gateway. The stunned sentries required shepherding, though they put up no resistance. Once everyone was through, two Iron Ravens turned a large wheel to lower the silver portcullis.

A small metal star was stuck in the dead fay's chest. BH wiped off the blood and slipped the star into a pouch on her belt. "Much handier than a boomerang." She looked again at her watch. "And we have a minute to spare."

"What's going on?" One of the sentries had recovered enough to ask questions.

"You should now remember how Rianna murdered our rightful queen, Bronwen. We're restoring Gilwyn, her son and heir, to the throne. The potion you drank reversed anything Rianna did to fuck around with your head." If nothing else, BH's explanation was technically correct. "Are you for or against us? You have thirty seconds to make up your mind."

"Dammit. She…" The man rubbed a hand over his face. "For. I guess."

"Great. Wait for my count."

"What are we doing?"

"Making a distraction for the main force."

"There's more of you?"

"Of course. They're with King Gilwyn and already inside the keep. Don't worry. You've picked the winning side."

"Right." His expression cleared and he pulled the machine gun from his shoulder. "I guess that means I won't get to off the bitch myself." He shook his head, as if trying to dislodge a bad memory.

BH glanced at her watch for a final time. "Okay. Three. Two. One."

A grenade exploded against the wall of a tower. Automatic rifle fire blasted away, left and right, at no obvious target. Lori slid her finger onto the trigger, feeling quite out of her depth. The thunder of a second grenade rent the air.

"Go. Go. Go." BH raced forward, followed by Iron Ravens spraying the air with bullets.

Shouts came from the middle bailey, audible between the rattle of gunfire. Lowering the portcullis had been a smart move. The fighting would be more straightforward without confused Iron Ravens getting involved. Lori raced up steps and into the keep, although the weight of the breastplate slowed her down and she was now some way behind the rest.

The bodies of two fay lay crumpled and oozing green blood on the floor of the lobby. A boggart burst from a doorway, but seeing her, squealed and ran away again. Explosions and automatic gunfire reverberated from a passage to Lori's right, but was moving farther away. Letting herself become isolated was a bad idea. The sensible thing was to follow the sounds of fighting

Lori took a step, and then stopped. The only thing she wanted was to find Tamsin. Who cared whether it was sensible? A fresh blast shook the ground. BH and the others did not need any help making noise, they were doing perfectly well on their own.

Rianna had always arrived in the audience chamber via a door at the rear, which must be where her private quarters lay. Lori was about to head up the main staircase but heard voices above. A group of sword wielding fay were gathering on the floor above. They were arguing among themselves and showing no sign of yet seeing her.

Maybe if she ran at them, they would flee, and maybe they would fight. But this was an unnecessary risk, since she knew how to go around them. Lori turned and jogged along the familiar route through the service section of the keep.

Grasping the rifle was comforting, even with no intention of firing it. As long as she was not seriously outnumbered, all she had to do was look threatening. However, the only people she saw were the boggart cook and helper, cowering under the table in the kitchen. Everyone else had either fled or gone to join the fight.

She reached the familiar gallery overlooking the audience chamber. The hall below was deserted and quiet, apart from the reverberation of distant gunfire. She leaned over the handrail, gasping to regain her breath. There had to be a way to get down to the main floor.

A crash made Lori jump. Instinctively, she pulled the rifle up to ward off a blow. However, the sound came from the twin balcony at the other side of the hall. A door had been flung open, then Rianna backed out, followed by Tamsin. Rianna slammed the door shut and ran to the far end, with Tamsin trying to keep up. The lurching, wooden movements left no doubt she was enthralled. Rianna looked back over her shoulder. Her expression was a mixture of fury and doubt.

Lori hastened along the gallery on her side of the hall, until she was directly opposite where Rianna was standing, clearly unaware of her presence. The rifle had never felt so light in Lori's hands. She lifted it to her shoulder and lined up the sights, but froze, paralyzed like before. Her trigger finger would not obey her.

The same door burst open again. Finn and Shorty leapt through, guns drawn. A few seconds later, Gilwyn stepped out behind them, and then Hippo. Widget was last to appear. Tamsin shuddered to a halt, before staggering on, slower than before. However, she was now within reach of Rianna. Finn and Shorty had their pistols raised, but were not firing. They could not. Rianna had Tamsin as a shield. But Lori had a clear shot, if only her finger would unfreeze.

"Gilwyn, can't you make her move out of the way?" Finn shouted.

"What do you think I'm trying to do!"

The fay were fighting for control of Tamsin, and Rianna was winning.

Another door opened midway along the gallery, and three half-naked humans stumbled out. They plodded towards Finn, arms outstretched in classic attack of the zombies mode. Riana's control of her thralls was clearly under attack. Gaius had never moved so woodenly.

Abruptly, one thrall stood erect, head held high. Her arms dropped by her side. She took two quick steps and dived head first over the handrail. She crashed to the ground far below, with a sickening crunch that gave no hope of survival. Gilwyn had won control.

"There was no fucking need to do that," Shorty shouted.

Gilwyn was unconcerned. "So say you."

Finn kicked the legs from beneath a second thrall. The man rolled helplessly on the ground, lacking the motor control to get back to his feet. The last remaining thrall lurched forward.

The slam of a door reverberated around the audience hall. Rianna had taken advantage of the distraction. She and Tamsin were gone.

Finn was first to reach the door. "It's locked."

"Here." Widget tossed a rope to Hippo, who launched himself over the railing, and abseiled to the floor of the hall. The instant his feet were on the ground he rushed to a door, directly under the locked one above and flung it open, revealing the start of a spiral staircase.

Of course. That was the way down. Lori pulled open the corresponding door on her side of the hall and stepped onto a midpoint landing. With Hippo at the foot of the stairs to the other balcony, Rianna would have to go up. Even if the only thing above them was the roof, maybe there were walkways to other escape routes.

Lori charged up the stairs two at a time, ignoring the burning in her legs and lungs. Daylight grew stronger with each circle. She skidded out onto the roof of a round tower. High overhead, a flock of seagulls wheeled against a pale turquoise sky, dotted with fading stars. Bands of purple and orange lined the horizon. Sunrise was moments away. Lori braced her free hand on the battlement, gasping for breath, and looked down through the nearest embrasure. On one side, all of Caersiddi was laid out below her. On the other was a sheer drop to the waves, crashing against the rocks, hundreds of feet below.

An identical tower was a stone's throw away. Together they formed twin horns sprouting from the crest of the keep, and separated by the sloping roof of the audience chamber. A bitter wave of despair and frustration washed over Lori. Not only was there no way to cross the gap, but the other tower was deserted. The staircase on the other side of the hall obviously had other exits.

Lori was about to retrace her steps when she heard a sound. At last, two figures appeared atop the other tower. Rianna had taken longer to climb the stairs. Either Tamsin had slowed her down, or she had stopped to block the stairs in some way. Yet this would surely be a pointless delaying tactic. Rianna was trapped with nowhere left to run.

Yet still she did not stop. Rianna hopped up onto the battlements. Was she going to jump? Tamsin was less graceful, levering herself first into an embrasure and then onto an adjacent merlon. Her actions were wooden, but clearly she was no longer torn in a magical competition between rival fay. In her right hand, Rianna held a small pouch, identical to the one Gilwyn had taken from the cabinet in the study—the shapeshifter dust he had used to transform himself into a giant raven.

Rianna was not trapped after all.

Lori shouldered her rifle and braced her elbows on the wall. She could not let Tamsin be taken away. Would killing be easier if Rianna turned into a bird first and no longer looked so human? Lori snapped off the safety and put her finger on the trigger.

More sounds echoed from the stairwell of the other tower, carried on the morning air. Finn's group had cleared any obstruction put in their way. But would they be in time to help Tamsin?

Rianna had also heard. She turned her head. "This isn't the end. You don't get my throne so easily, or so cheaply. Look for your captain on the rocks below."

Rianna was not taking Tamsin with her. Lori's blood turned to ice. Both Rianna and Tamsin took a half step, so they stood on the very edge. Rianna dipped her hand in the pouch and smiled sweetly at Tamsin, but her voice was still pitched loudly enough for those climbing the stairs to hear, teasing, taunting. "Good-bye, my traitorous pet. We won't—"

Time dropped to a crawl. Rianna's head was the size of a beach ball. Her profile was silhouetted against the dawn, as clear as a target on the range. The sights on the rifle lined themselves up. The tremors left Lori's hand and squeezing the trigger was as natural as breathing. The recoil jammed against Lori's shoulder. For a moment, Rianna was frozen in space, and then she folded, sagging backward, and dropped from view.

Tamsin jerked upright, her head snapping back, like a sleepwalker roused by a jug of cold water. She rubbed her face, clearing cobwebs from her mind, but was unsteady on her feet. Her left knee buckled. Immediately, she fought to right herself. Her arms shot out for balance. It was not enough. Like Rianna, Tamsin pitched over the edge of the battlements.

The air solidified in Lori's lungs. She was in a nightmare, where she had no voice to scream. The rifle slipped from her grasp and clattered to the ground at the same moment as Finn and Shorty scrambled onto the roof. They looked around in confusion, then raced to the spot where Tamsin had fallen.

Finn dived over the edge, at risk of falling himself if Shorty had not caught his leg. Hippo, Widget, and Gilwyn also arrived on the roof. The blood pounded in Lori's ears, blocking whatever Shorty said to them. Gilwyn shrugged and turned away, but Hippo and Widget rushed forward and grabbed Finn's other leg. Together they hauled Finn back onto the roof.

Lori worked out what was happening just as Tamsin's head and shoulders came into view. Lori dropped to her knees, then twisted round so she was sitting with her back against the parapet. Nausea rippled in her stomach and she was shaking so hard her teeth chattered.

Tamsin was safe. Rianna was dead. And she had killed her.

Lori held her head in her hands. The images came flooding in. The spray of blood against the morning sky. The fleeting expression of shock on Rianna's face. Her body, dropping lifeless from the tower. But Lori felt no regret, no guilt, no sorrow. She tried prodding her emotions. Would they come? Beating herself up over killing Rianna would be pointless and stupid, but pointless, stupid things happened all the time.

Yet, however she felt in the days ahead, Tamsin would be alive and safe. Lori drew another deep breath. Maybe there would be guilt, possibly even sorrow, but no regret.

Never that.

CHAPTER TWENTY-THREE

Someone was knocking on the door. Lori rolled onto her back and groaned. Judging by the angle of the beams squeezing through cracks in the shutters, it was late morning. After the night's events, she had been sure she would not sleep. However, she had been out cold. Her head felt correspondingly thick and her eyes were gritty.

The knocking came again.

"What is it?"

A boggart sidestepped into the room. "His Majesty, King Gilwyn, wants me to collect the scrolls, please, madam."

"The what?"

"The scrolls, please. King Gilwyn says you have scrolls that are his. He has sent me for them, madam."

"Now?" Could it not wait?

"Yes. Please. I'm sorry. King Gilwyn wants them." The boggart shuffled his feet nervously. "Please, madam."

What the hell? Gilwyn had just acquired a kingdom. Surely he had more important things to deal with. Was he worried she might be sitting there, decoding scrolls and learning all sorts of fay secrets? It was tempting to send the boggart away and make the arrogant sod come in person. Instead she swung her feet out of bed.

Boggarts had cleaned and tidied her room while she was enthralled, but her belongings were still there, including Gilwyn's saddlebag, draped over the back of the chair. The boggarts would not have emptied the room of their own accord, and Rianna had obviously been too intent on her plans to bother with other matters. Being detail minded was a requirement for any managerial post, royal ones included. But Rianna's past failings were hardly Lori's concern. She pointed out the bag.

The boggart opened the flap and started counting out the scrolls. "One. Two. Three—"

"Take the whole damned thing."

"I have to check, madam."

"That I'm not secretly hiding one away, and lying about it?"

"Please, madam. I have been told to." He squirmed.

"For fuck's sake." As if waking her up was not enough, Gilwyn was adding insult to injury.

"...nine, ten, eleven. Yes. Very good. They are all here. Thank you, madam. King Gilwyn will be pleased."

But I'm not.

Lori remained standing, chewing ideas over after the boggart had scurried away. He had been sent to collect eleven scrolls. Gilwyn knew nothing about the twelfth, oldest of all, in the seam of her jeans. In fairness, he had not actually been wrong about her hiding one away.

She lifted the lid of the footlocker. Her faded jeans lay on top, neatly folded. She felt the bulges of the folded scroll at the back of the waistband and her lucky pound coin in the front pocket. The wisest thing was to leave Mathanwy's scroll where it was until she got back to Earth, and she could decode it for fun. But Gilwyn's needless pestering had annoyed her. Why was he so bothered?

She went to the window and opened the shutters. The middle bailey was quieter than normal. Only Iron Ravens sentries were visible. Where was Tamsin? They had not yet had a chance to talk. Was it worth going to find her, or would she be sleeping?

Lori sat at the table and fed Mathanwy's scroll out through the seam. The parchment was in good condition for having been folded and hidden for so many days. If Gilwyn was to be believed, Morgaine most likely worked out how to decode it when she was part of the Council of Elders, looking for a way to separate the worlds. What did it say?

There was little chance of getting back to sleep, and she had nothing else to do. Lori pulled a notebook from her bag—the same bag she had taken to the meeting in the Halfway House a couple of lifetimes ago, and picked up a pen.

❖

Lori read through the transcript one final time then flipped the notepad closed. She turned her head to stare at the sky. The scroll's contents fell somewhere between ironic and terrifying, and she needed to share the information with Tamsin, the sooner the better.

An increase in noise caught her attention—footsteps, mixed with shouts and laughter. Something was going on outside. Lori stood for a better view. A stream of Iron Ravens were flowing through the garden, all heading towards the outer bailey. Their mood seemed puzzled but cheerful, as if they had received a pleasant surprise. Most carried bags. Tamsin, with Hippo and Widget, stood outside the mess hall, watching them pass.

Before joining them, Lori had to take care of the transcript. The contents were far too explosive to leave lying around. She ripped the pages from the notepad, and picked up the box of matches by the fireplace. There was a perverse pleasure in watching four hours' work go up in flames. However, there was no risk of forgetting the important bits. She refolded the original scroll and fed it back into the waistband. Then, on impulse, she stripped off the Silver Raven leathers and pulled on the jeans and a T-shirt. She was not letting the original scroll out of her possession again.

By the time she left the building, Tamsin had gone and the flow of Iron Ravens subsided to a few stragglers, dawdling along.

"You're not taking that old thing are you?"

"Why not?"

"I can see the holes from here."

"It's supposed to look like that."

"My arse it is."

Lori had no idea what the item in question was, but the soldiers were clearly not responding to an emergency. She followed them to the outer bailey, where dozens of Iron Ravens milled around a line of six wagons. The Silver Ravens were also present, keeping to the periphery, except for Hippo, making the rounds, shaking hands and slapping backs, and Finn who stood deep in conversation with a woman.

Tamsin was at the head of the wagons, in a huddle with the Iron Raven officers. When she saw Lori she raised a hand in acknowledgement. After a few more words, she shook the officers' hands and jogged over.

"What's going on?" Lori asked. "Are they leaving?"

"Yes. The Iron Ravens are heading back to Earth today. Gilwyn wants all humans out of Annwyn as soon as possible."

"Is this everyone?" Fewer than a hundred soldiers were present.

"The current strength stands at seventy-three. Enough to man the gates and intimidate other fay, but not so many as to get out of hand."

"How will Gilwyn intimidate other fay now?"

"I don't know. I didn't ask him."

"Why aren't the Silver Ravens going as well?"

"Gilwyn doesn't have enough gold for us, after what he's given this lot. He doubled what they were due, to silence any complaints. You can see how happy they are. But it means we have to wait a day or two, for another shipment from the mines." A faint edge in Tamsin's voice suggested she was not convinced by this. But questions could wait until there were not so many ears around.

The final items of baggage were loaded on the wagons, and the convoy set off, with a column of Iron Ravens marching on either side. They passed under the gatehouse and the sound of their footsteps faded.

"I need to talk to you. Somewhere we won't be overheard," Lori whispered to Tamsin.

"Will your room do?"

"If you think it's safe."

"It's as good as anywhere."

As soon as the door closed, Lori said, "You don't trust Gilwyn."

"I'm not stupid. He's sworn an oath all the Silver Ravens will be paid four times our weight in gold, as soon as he has the resources on hand. And I made sure he counted you in."

"You don't think he'll keep his word?"

"He will, but—" Tamsin gave a lopsided shrug. "Fay will lie themselves black and blue, but they take promises seriously. No fay will break a sworn oath. But they're tricky buggers. They stick to the literal words, not the spirit."

"Has Gilwyn said anything about the thralls?"

"No. He dodged the subject."

"So if he disbands the Silver Ravens before more gold arrives in Caersiddi, and turns us into thralls, he won't have broken his oath?"

"You've got it. We need to keep on our toes." Tamsin moved a step closer and lowered her voice. "So, what did you want to talk about?"

Lori's pulse quickened. The memory of them kissing caught her breath. However, there were more urgent matters. She backed away. "Gilwyn sent a boggart to reclaim the encrypted scrolls this morning."

Tamsin looked confused. "And?"

"There's one scroll he doesn't know about. He missed it the night he fled from here. I hid it so I wouldn't have to decode it for Rianna. I wanted to get back to Earth as quickly as possible. I might have played with it when I was home, just for fun. However, after being woken this morning, I was pissed off and curious. So I decoded it."

"It says something interesting?"

"Oh yes. It was written by Mathanwy, the first of the fay."

"He's not a myth?"

"No. He was real all right. He came from a world in another dimension. Mathanwy extracted essence from his universe and used it to form Annwyn. He then suspended his new creation in the aether between dimensions and anchored it to Earth."

"Is that supposed to make sense to me?"

"I don't know how else to explain it. But the important thing is that Annwyn's not stable. It came from somewhere else, and the only thing holding it in place is its bond with Earth. However, forces are trying to drag it back to where it came from, and they're growing stronger all the time. There's only so much the bond can take. Someday it's going to snap. Which is what Morgaine found out from Mathanwy's scroll. With hindsight, it's clear from her written comments that she was familiar with it. She most likely worked out how to decode his scroll while looking for a way to break the link with Earth."

"But I thought her spell does the opposite."

"She changed her mind. Initially, when humans first discovered how to smelt iron, the Council of Elders wanted to keep the new weapons out of Annwyn."

"I knew Morgaine was a member of the council, until she overthrew it." Tamsin frowned. "But if I'm understanding you, there was no need for the council to do anything. The bond will snap of its own accord."

"Yes. It will. In fact, without Morgaine's spell it would have broken long ago. However, that wasn't all she learned from Mathanwy's scroll." Lori drew a breath. "Mathanwy didn't just create Annwyn. He created the inhabitants. He formed fay from boggarts—or from something that was far more boggart than fay. He took what he saw as the best and worst parts of his people and split them to create two races. Obviously, he didn't see being a sadistic, arrogant, arsehole as a bad trait. However, when Annwyn bounces back to rejoin the original world, the fay will be mostly boggarts again, along with millions of others, in a place that hasn't been created with the sole aim of making them feel special."

"I can see fay getting upset about that."

"Exactly. Finding this out was undoubtedly what pushed Morgaine into strengthening the bond with Earth rather than breaking it. But in order to do it, the links had to be concentrated into fewer and fewer points, until now only Dorstanley is left. But things are reaching a stage where even her spell won't be enough. The forces pulling on Annwyn are growing exponentially. They double every month. It started minuscule, and for centuries it was insignificant, now it's ramping up to a crisis point."

"Is Gilwyn aware of this?"

"Bits. He knows a few details about Morgaine's spell, and that it has to be recast repeatedly to maintain the bond with Earth, but he made no mention of Annwyn returning to where it came from. Maybe he doesn't know that part, or maybe he wasn't being straight with me."

"Which wouldn't be out of character for him."

"True. Either way, I can't see him letting the spell lapse once he finds out what will happen. And as for his chances of finding out, I really can't say. He doesn't know anything about Mathanwy's scroll, but there are other encrypted scrolls that I haven't read. Who knows what's in them?"

"Does he know how to decrypt them?"

"If he doesn't now, he soon will. Rianna made notes while I was explaining things to her. Presumably those are somewhere in the royal apartment."

"Okay." Tamsin thought for a moment. "But from what you've said, even if he finds out, and decides to renew Morgaine's spell, it will only be a short-term fix. The bond will break in the end."

"Yes. It has to be close to snapping at the moment—which would explain why Rianna was desperate enough to allow a human to work on the scroll. She was running out of time before she turned into a boggart. But you're right, even if Gilwyn renews the spell, the forces pulling on Annwyn are increasing. He'll be forced to cast the spell more and more frequently, until he's doing it a dozen times a day, if he's able. And it still won't be enough."

"So what's the problem? Eventually, Earth will be free of the fay. Or does the bond breaking have serious consequences?"

"No. There'll be a bit of a bounce back effect, but barely noticeable, certainly not enough to hurt anyone. The problem for Earth is what happens before then. The bond is powered by energy taken from both worlds. As the forces pulling on Annwyn increase, it's will need to suck out more and more energy. The dimension Mathanwy came from is magical, mystical, spiritual—I don't know what the right word is. Basically, it's more mental and less physical than our world. Opposites attract, and all that. To balance things out, the bond draws on physicality from Annwyn and mentality from Earth. Does that make sense?"

"I think I get the gist."

"It means fay in Annwyn are being physically weakened. The falling birth rate is a symptom."

"How about boggarts?"

"Mathanwy didn't care about them enough to say much. But I think they're getting stronger due to being more in tune with their home dimension."

"Okay. You said we need to worry about the effect on Earth."

"We certainly do. Humans are suffering mental effects. Except, since there are only a few hundred fay and several billion humans to share the drain, the results aren't too apparent yet—a fraction of a percentage point shift, a few slightly more extreme acts of mass stupidity, some crazy election results. But it won't stay that way. Another month in Annwyn, two and a half years on Earth, and the effect will be twice as strong. A month more and it will have doubled again. If Gilwyn maintains the bond for another Annwyn year, the power drain will be two thousand times what it is at the moment. The only question is whether Gilwyn and the rest of the fay drop dead before everyone on Earth goes insane. I'd like to think he'll realize the futility of it all, but he won't give a damn about Earth, and he'll persuade himself that with a bit more time, he'll find another solution."

"Not to mention that he'd rather die than turn into a boggart." Tamsin pursed her lips "We have to get the scrolls off him before we leave, unless he pulls a stupid trick to force our hand, which I'm not ruling out. It'll be about two days until the gold gets here. We've got time to think, unless there's anything else you've found out?"

"No. That's it."

"In which case, it's my turn to say something to you. Thank you for saving my life. I admit, I'd been hoping to be the one to shoot her. I think we all were. But I'm not complaining. As long as you're not troubled by it."

"Oh, that. No. I'm not upset." A series of emotions blurred into the next. The strongest was still surprise. "I just pulled the trigger. I didn't have time to think."

"No regrets?"

"Of course not. But how are you? Finn said Rianna would want to hurt you, and…" Lori swallowed.

"Rianna thought she had plenty of time. She'd barely got going." Tamsin shrugged. "I've got worse memories of her. To be honest, it hadn't got close to as bad as I'd expected—though I'm sure it would've in time. I'll confess to being on edge during the party in the mess hall, knowing what was coming. It was a bit of a passion killer. I'm not really that old-fashioned."

Lori looked down at her hands to hide her grin. "I'm pleased to hear it."

"Then I'll also confess, if I'd kissed you one more time, I might have changed my mind. But I didn't want to risk Rianna's thralls finding us together."

"She'd have been jealous?"

"No. She didn't work that way. But she might have got ideas about a threesome."

"Uh." Which was an image in need of a bargepole.

Tamsin moved closer. "So is this our chance for that conversation?"

Lori looked up and met her eyes. "This is no time for talking."

Heart pounding, she moved out of the chair and into Tamsin's arms. Their kiss was as all-consuming as the first. Lori felt herself melting in the heat of her desire. Their lips moulded and shifted, working together in rising passion.

She was aflame. Tamsin's back was firm beneath her hands. The contrasting textures of crisp cotton shirt and leather waistcoat were sensual, but no substitute for bare skin. Lori was long past lying to herself. The only thing she wanted to do was to strip away that black leather. She twisted, trying to worm free of Tamsin's embrace. Initially, Tamsin still held her close, but then relaxed her grip.

The waistcoat would be first to go. Lori started on the tightly laced front. The knots put up a fight, but she was determined, giving the task her entire attention. Even so, she was aware of the growing amusement on Tamsin's face.

"Do you want me to untie it?"

"No. I'm doing it. Stand still."

The final knot would not loosen, but there was enough slack in the cord for Lori to pull the front wide open. Now Tamsin helped, flexing as Lori peeled the waistcoat over her head. The freed shirt lay loose against Tamsin's torso, hinting at the body beneath. Lori placed a hand in the middle of Tamsin's chest, feeling the warmth, the hardness of bone, and the soft swelling on either side.

Lori increased the pressure of her hand, guiding Tamsin in reverse across the room, until the back of Tamsin's knees hit the bed frame. Tamsin fell onto the quilt cover. Lori dropped to her knees. It was time for more leather to go—the left boot, then the right. Tamsin swivelled around and lay with her head resting on the pillow. She reached out, clearly inviting Lori to lie beside her. However, the invitation was ignored. Lori scrambled onto the bed and sat, straddling Tamsin's hips.

It took a firm tug to pull the white shirt free of Tamsin's waistband, Lori put both hands on the newly exposed skin. The contact released a fountain of desire, flowing up Lori's arms and engulfing her entire body. She could feel the slickness grow between her legs.

Tamsin's laugh was mainly breath. "Does it get to be my turn soon?"

"Maybe."

"There's no maybe about it." Without warning, Tamsin arched her back and flipped Lori onto the bed.

"You want to make a fight of it?"

"No. Just levelling the playing field."

Lori's stretchy T-shirt put up little resistance. The rest of her clothes followed, ending up scattered across the floor.

All rational thought was lost in the touch of skin on skin, bodies moulding together, warm and pliant, hard and soft. Lori was consumed by passion, by raw burning desire. She needed Tamsin's touch. She needed Tamsin's fingers inside her, Tamsin's tongue exploring her, Tamsin's body pressed hard against her. She needed Tamsin to take her to the summit and send her over the edge.

And she got it.

Lori's climax exploded, leaving her weak and gasping. When she recovered her breath, she opened her eyes to meet Tamsin's, staring at her from scant inches away.

"Was that okay?"

"Oh yes." Strength slowly returned to Lori's arms. She pulled Tamsin's head down into another long, searching kiss. Then, shifting around, Lori rolled Tamsin onto her back. "Now it's my turn."

Lori ran her fingers the length of Tamsin's side, exploring the softness of skin overlaying firm muscle. Tamsin groaned as her body tensed and arched, her eyes closed, her hands clenched, her breasts rose and fell with each ragged gasp.

The sight of Tamsin responding to her touch was enough to reignite the hot desire in Lori, but it could wait. First, she wanted to enjoy the sense of power and control, making Tamsin shake and groan, watching Tamsin hit the peak, again and again.

At last, Tamsin caught hold of her wrist. "Dammit, woman. Don't you take prisoners?"

"No quarter asked for or given."

"If that's how you want it."

Tamsin's arms wrapped around Lori's shoulders, again taking control. Laughter bubbled in Lori's throat, caught between the gasps.

A long while later, they were both sated, and lay together quietly, exchanging soft kisses. Lori traced the line of a thin scar along Tamsin's thigh.

"A werewolf. I didn't see it in the dark." Tamsin offered the information.

"Really?"

Tamsin nodded.

"I've never had a lover who fights werewolves. I think that's where I was going wrong before."

"That would have been a tough requirement, since there's no werewolves on Earth."

"It's not the werewolves themselves, it's the lack of spirit to tackle them. You were right, when we spoke, way back, I did resent my parents for leaving me behind. And then, what with Grandma criticising everything they did, and the other kids at school laughing at me, I just decided everything was Mum and Dad's fault and I wasn't going to be like them. Of course, computers are fun, but..." Lori grinned. "Virtual reality is an oxymoron. I need to take some risks, now and again."

"I could have told you that the day we met."

"As a general life principle?"

"No. You in particular. When you walked into the Halfway House, with your pen and notebook, asking for fruit juice and looking down your nose at us, I was expecting all sorts of trouble. I thought you'd be terrified. I imagined we'd have to carry you out to the wagon, and you'd be crying and whining all the way to Annwyn, or doing stupid things like trying to escape. Instead you just sat there, unfazed and totally pissed off at me." Tamsin stared into Lori's eyes. "Do you have any idea of the effect you and your snippety attitude had on me?"

"Really?"

"Yes. And it hasn't gotten any less. Let me show you."

Tamsin's hands began tracing new patterns over Lori's skin.

Chapter Twenty-four

The change struck Lori the moment she stepped through the door. The aroma of food was the same, but the mess hall was eerily deserted with just the Silver Ravens seated at their normal table in the corner. A huddle of boggarts dithered around the kitchen doorway, unsure what to do, now that dozens of people were no longer shouting conflicting demands at them.

Shorty looked up as Lori and Tamsin wove between the empty tables. "Hey, where've you been?"

"I can guess." Judging by her smile, BH was guessing correctly. Her eyes danced with amusement. "Had fun?"

Lori slid onto the bench beside Tamsin, hoping she was not turning red. "Yes, thank you."

Widget had also put two and two together. "And we know a song about that, don't we, boys and girls?"

"I think you know over a hundred." Hippo flicked a wet pea across the table at Widget. "Ignore him, Mousie. He's just jealous because he can't find the blow-up sheep in his bag o' tricks."

"So you're the one who took it!" Widget feigned surprise.

Lori joined in the laughter as she helped herself to vegetable soup from the pot in the middle of the table. She was well on the way to becoming one of them, if she wanted, not that they had a future in Annwyn. It appeared she had even acquired a nickname.

"Please, madam." A boggart stood at Tamsin's shoulder.

"Yes?"

"His Majesty, King Gilwyn, sent these for you. A reward for your help."

Tamsin accepted the rack of four bottles. Her expression was a polite poker face. "Please convey our thanks to His Majesty."

"Yes, madam. Thank you, yes." The boggart scuttled away.

"Just how stupid does he think we are?" Finn muttered under his breath.

"He might not know Rianna has already tried this trick," Tamsin said. "They may both have happened to read the story in the same book and decided to give it a go."

Gilwyn's lack of imagination was breathtaking. Lori held a bottle up to the light. The colour was right for brandy. "Chalk one up to the Dunning-Kruger effect."

"What's that?" Tamsin asked.

"Ill-informed people are unaware of what they don't know, which means they fail to account for others being way ahead of them. Gilwyn is too sure of himself to think he needs to put any effort into outsmarting us."

"It'll be fun, educating him." Tamsin waited until the room was clear of boggarts "Have we all had enough soup?" With no objections, she emptied the bottles into the pot.

A pair of boggarts appeared, carrying a large roast bird between them. Lori did not think it was either a turkey or a peacock, although the size was right. They placed the platter on the table and left again, taking away the soup pot, with its drugged contents.

Finn stood up, wielding a carving knife. "Shall I play mother?"

"You just want an excuse to put those false boobs on again."

Tamsin wrapped her arms around Lori and planted a slow kiss on her lips. She then gave a regretful smile. "Unfortunately, that's all for tonight. The others will be along in a minute."

"Okay."

Even so, Lori made the most of snuggling against Tamsin's body. The old roller coaster. The start of a relationship, when everything was exciting and intense, before mundane familiarity set in. Or would things be different with a woman who was more adept at fighting dragons than balancing columns of numbers? Time would tell.

The expected tap on the door came. Lori stepped away and tried to act cool and relaxed, while feeling anything but. This was the first time she had seen Tamsin's quarters. The room was no larger than hers, but Tamsin had spent her years in Annwyn upgrading her home comforts. Cushioned chairs faced the fireplace. A set of shelves held books and ornaments. The walls were hung with tapestries, paintings, and a rack that looked as though it was intended for tools of varying sizes and shapes, although it was currently empty.

"Is that supposed to have weapons on it?"

"Yup."

"Gilwyn had our rooms searched while we were at dinner?"

"That's what it looks like." Tamsin opened the door.

"Bastards have swiped my bag." Widget sounded disgusted as he stomped into the room.

BH followed. "And everything made of iron or steel, except my throwing stars." She patted the pouch on her belt.

"You know you're not supposed to carry them in the mess hall?" There was no rebuke in Tamsin's voice.

BH grinned. "Report me."

"Weren't they taken off you when Rianna had us enthralled? How did you manage to keep hold of them before?" Lori asked.

The grin widened. "That's my secret."

Finn, Shorty, and Hippo arrived, also minus weapons.

"It confirms Gilwyn is up to something," Finn said.

"Yes."

"And he isn't completely stupid."

"Nobody is. But some come closer than others." Tamsin's tone left little doubt where she ranked Gilwyn. "It cuts out the option of making a run for it. We don't want to be unarmed if any slua are hanging around the portal."

"Oh well, look on the bright side. We were right to pour the brandy away. Otherwise, just think of the waste. And we still have our knives." Hippo patted the sheath on his belt.

Tamsin moved to the window and peered through a crack in the shutters. "Silver blades will be useful. We want to take Gilwyn alive, so we can bargain our way out. If he's dead, we'll have a volatile situation, and there's no saying which of the fay will come out on top. It's also vital we pick up some scrolls, and he's the one who knows where they are."

"What's with the scrolls?" Finn asked.

"It's a long story, and we don't have time now. We need to move quickly, while he's waiting for the drug to take effect." Tamsin left the window. "The gates are guarded by boggarts armed with silver tipped spears. We can handle them, but not before they raise the alarm. Fortunately, thanks to Gilwyn, we know another way into the keep."

"Won't he have guards on the secret passage?" Widget asked.

"Probably. But he'll expect us to do the same thing he would in our shoes. If he could use firearms, and they were taken off him, he'd be desperate to get them back. He'll be looking to the armoury for the first sign the brandy trick hasn't worked. The last thing he'll be ready for is us attacking the keep, armed with silver daggers and a couple of broom handles."

The Silver Ravens slipped silently through the garden of the inner bailey, keeping to the darkest shadows. Once in the storeroom, Finn twisted a wall sconce first left than right. In the best traditions of kids' movies and TV shows, a trapdoor appeared, revealing the steps leading down.

The air underground smelt of mould and wet stone. The tunnel had been carved from the bedrock beneath the castle. The passage was so narrow they were forced to go in single file and Shorty had to duck. Dust, cobwebs, and soot decorated the walls and ceiling. Widget was at the front, with the one flashlight that had escaped the boggarts' notice. Lori was towards the rear, armed with a broom handle from the storeroom. Tamsin had been speaking quite literally about their weapon options.

As it turned out, Gilwyn had put a guard on the passage exit—a single boggart with a hand bell, who had fallen asleep at her post and was safely overpowered and tied up, even before Lori emerged from the tunnel.

"The thrall pen is full," BH whispered, peering through a crack in the door.

"Good," Tamsin said. "That means Gilwyn hasn't sent anyone to capture us yet. Hopefully, we can get a lot closer to him before the alarm is raised. There's another secret passage from the dungeon to the study above the audience hall."

"Do we know how to find it?" Lori asked.

Finn smiled. "Luckily, Gilwyn showed us when we were going after Rianna."

The lower levels of the keep were deserted, and they reached the dungeon without encountering anyone. Finn led them into the new passage which branched and squeezed its way between walls and up ladders. The castle was honeycombed. Without BH's sense of direction they would surely have become lost, but eventually, a section of wall swung open on the familiar study.

Lori tried the cabinet door. "Do you think Gilwyn would have put the scrolls back in here?" She threw the question over her shoulder.

"We'll ask him when we see him," Hippo replied.

"Why wait?" Widget spent a moment examining the lock, then placed the tip of his dagger in the narrow gap between the door and struck the end of the hilt with his fist. The door popped open. "Now that's what I call a really crap lock."

The scrolls were back in their pigeonholes.

"Leave them for now. We can't carry them." Tamsin stood at her shoulder. "But we know where they are if Gilwyn doesn't want to be helpful."

"Or has an accident," Finn added.

Meanwhile, BH had opened the study door a crack and peered out. "All clear."

Staying close to the back wall, they followed BH along the balcony and down the spiral staircase to the floor of the audience chamber. She signalled a stop by an open archway behind the throne—the entrance Rianna had always appeared through. Over BH's shoulder, Lori saw into the most opulent hallway yet. Thick tapestries lined the wall. Gold inlaid floor tiles sparkled around the edges of deep pile runners. Candlelight cast rainbow colours through crystal chandeliers. This could only be the royal apartment.

BH peeked around the corner, then indicated to the others, holding up a single finger. She slipped a throwing star from the pouch at her waist. A soft whoosh and then two thumps. "That'll teach him not to pay attention on guard duty." BH whispered the words.

Now Tamsin took the lead, creeping along the corridor to where a dead fay was crumpled outside a heavy wooden door. His silver halberd lay beside him on the carpet. Tamsin shoved the body aside with her foot and placed a hand on the door handle. From inside came the soft sound of a harp, then voices and a low groan.

After a moment to ensure everyone was ready, Tamsin wrenched the door open and barged in, with the Silver Ravens on her heels. Shouts, squeals, and yelps erupted in the room. Coming in at the back, Lori clipped someone's foot and half fell through the doorway.

The room was large, yet gave the sense of being cosy, due to the warm candlelight. The panelled walls were painted red, matching the thick rug on the floor. Settees were strewn with embroidered cushions. The air was heavy with the scent of perfume and alcohol. It was a room just begging to be called a boudoir. Windows on one side gave access to a balcony, the same one Lori had viewed from above, watching Rianna with Tamsin.

Gilwyn, shirtless, was on his feet, backing away. Another fay man was struggling to rise, his efforts hampered by the naked human woman straddling his lap. When he succeeded in pushing her off, there was no surprise to see his clothes unbuttoned and untied, from neck to codpiece. Six more blank faced human thralls, in varying states of undress, were frozen like statues. The only one who was fully clothed was the harpist, sitting by the fireplace. Three boggarts made a comical tableaux by a small round table in a corner. One had been midway through pouring a drink and was now too taken aback to stop. Red wine spilled over the brim of the glass and trickled to the floor.

"I'm sorry. Are we interrupting something?" Tamsin's voice was innocently cheery.

"I—" Gilwyn choked off. He snapped his fingers.

Something moved in a dark corner of the room—something large. Three hellhounds shook their heads, roused from sleep. Fire-rimmed eyes fixed on their targets. In an instant, the dogs were on their feet and bounding across the room, surging in a living wave of fur, muscle, and teeth.

Tamsin, Finn, Shorty, and Hippo met the onslaught, armed only with a dagger apiece. The long blades definitely counted as combat knives, but they were hopelessly outmatched against the monstrous hellhounds.

The first dog leapt for Tamsin's throat. She ducked and twisted aside, cracking her left elbow into the side of its head. Her right hand, holding the knife, lashed out, slicing down the animal's ribs. Neither action deflected the hellhound. Its weight carried it on, slamming into Tamsin, and knocking her to the ground. The cut could be no more than a light wound.

For a heart-stopping moment, the beast stood over her, teeth bared, but then the hellhound began to convulse, twitching, yowling. It fell to the side, curling into a heap—a shrinking heap. In the space of two seconds, the dog was the size of a rat. It hissed, spat, and ran under a settee, gone so quickly Lori could not say for sure what the animal was, but the silver had done its work. Had Tamsin known the hellhounds were the result of transformation magic?

The other two beasts met a similar fate, but the fight was not over. A second wave was coming—blank faced thralls, slow, lumbering, silent, and yet, in a strange way, no less frightening than the dogs. They were so poorly coordinated, they presented a limited challenge, but like the zombies in movies, they refused to stay down. Tamsin and Finn struggled to restrain the largest man. They clearly did not want to harm the innocent victims of fay magic, but might have no choice.

Meanwhile the two fay had retreated to the far wall, and the boggarts were all trying to huddle under the table, despite the lack of space. BH had another throwing star in her hand, although in the hectic activity, she was unlikely to get a clean shot, even had she wanted to kill Gilwyn.

Lori fended off the harpist, using her broomstick. Having swapped the leathers for her old jeans, she did not have a silver knife, or any other weapon, except...

She shouted over the chaos, "It's just iron that's automatically fatal to the fay, isn't it?"

"And steel," Widget shouted back.

"What about a nickel-brass alloy?"

"Should make them as sick as a dog, I'd guess. But—"

A hand landed on Lori's shoulder. More thralls had arrived in the corridor behind them, forcing their way in. Gilwyn had called up reinforcements.

Lori wrenched herself free, ducked under the harpist's outstretched arms, and rolled over the top of a settee, losing her broomstick on the way. She looked back at the doorway. Despite the thralls' lack of coordination, their sheer weight of numbers evened the battle. In order to win, the Silver Ravens might be forced to start killing.

The whoosh of another door opening bought a waft of cleaner air and the sound of the sea. Gilwyn had fled to the balcony. Lori raced after him. The second fay man had been about to follow Gilwyn, but seeing her, he scooted back, and ended up cowering with the boggarts.

Lori skidded onto the balcony. Gilwyn was at the far end, with a small pouch in his hand. His eyes glinted in the light of the hanging lanterns.

Lori gave him her best, taunting smile. "Not going so soon, are you?"

Gilwyn glared at her, his lip curling. "I will. But not before I make you pay." He drew a silver dagger from a sheath on his belt and took a step forward.

Lori slipped her forefinger into the small front pocket of her jeans and dug out the hard round shape of her lucky pound coin. Gilwyn moved in, halving the distance between them, his knife held out. Another step, and then another. He was so close she could not miss, especially given the target his bare chest presented. She flung the coin at him with as much force as she could manage.

Gilwyn jerked as he was struck on the shoulder. He took one more step, but then his left knee buckled slightly. He grabbed at the balustrade for support.

The uproar from the room quietened, until there were just groans and the whimper of boggarts, and then the beat of footsteps.

Tamsin swung around the open doorway. "Are you all—"

She stopped at the sight of Gilwyn, bent double over the handrail, throwing up into the sea below.

"What did you do to him?"

"Hit him with my lucky pound coin." Lori looked at the tiled floor. "And I'll be bummed if I've lost it." How would she go shopping at the supermarket?

Grey, rolling fog filled the portal between the standing stones—clearly the work of magic. But after being chased by dragons, riding a flying horse, and spending days as an enthralled slave, a bit of misplaced fog was hardly anything to wonder at. Lori twisted around and looked back at the distant castle by the sea. These were her last minutes in Annwyn.

Hippo pulled on the reins, bringing the gold laden wagon to a halt a few feet from the wall of fog. Lori jumped down. Before she left, there was one more thing she wanted to know.

The ex-thralls formed a straggling line behind the wagon, with the Silver Ravens playing the role of sheepdog. Even though they were now wearing iron torcs, many had been enthralled for so long they might never be fully restored to their own minds. However, Tamsin had made sure there was enough gold to see them well cared for.

Gilwyn had trotted behind the wagon the whole way from Caersiddi. He had no choice, his hands were tied to the tailboard. The swollen cut from the coin was still red and angry, just visible at the neck of his shirt, although he had finally stopped throwing up.

Lori stood before him. "Why? Why did you double-cross us?"

Gilwyn clamped his lips in a tight line and turned his face away.

"You could have paid us off. Why didn't you? The gold isn't an issue. It's as common as sand here."

Tamsin came over to release him. "Do you want my guess? It's because we laughed at him. And he couldn't bear knowing he'd needed our help. He wanted to put us in our place. He wanted revenge for us ever acting like we were his equals." She finished untying the cord and patted his shoulder. "There you go. Now run back home like a good lad."

Gilwyn reacted with fury, his hands balled into fists. "You dare to—"

"Don't even think about acting like an idiot. We don't have any further use for you, so there's no reason why we shouldn't put a bullet through your head." Tamsin turned her back on him and walked off.

Gilwyn's mouth twisted in a snarl. There was not a trace of remorse on his face, only hurt pride and anger. He was not one iota better than Rianna.

Lori called after Tamsin. "We just let him go? How about justice for Gaius and the others?"

"It's not the same as putting his head in a noose, but if it makes you feel any better, imagine him turning into a boggart." Tamsin had reached the front of the wagon.

Lori turned back to Gilwyn. "Did you hear that? You're going to become a boggart."

"If you're trying to insult me, at least be sensible."

"I am. There was one scroll you missed. I kept it hidden. It was written by Mathanwy himself, describing how he created Annwyn. But he didn't just form the land, he formed the fay as well. He created you out of boggarts. When the bond with Earth breaks, you'll revert to being boggarts again. And there's nothing you can do about it, because I've got all the scrolls with me in the wagon."

"You believe that nonsense? My mother made the story up." Despite his words, Gilwyn's eyes showed a hint of doubt.

"Your mother knew?"

"It was just a ridiculous story. Mother was playing some sort of trick on my aunt."

Lori was hit by a sudden insight. "That was it. Your mother told Rianna what would happen when the bond with Earth broke, and Rianna was not willing to let it happen. That's why she usurped the throne."

"Mother made a misjudgement. I don't know what she thought making up the story would achieve, but that's what she did. None of it is true." Gilwyn's voice rose as the doubt turned into something much closer to panic.

"Your mother was telling the truth. She'd read all about it in Mathanwy's scroll. If we had the time, I'd let you decode it for yourself." Lori laughed. "Don't worry. I think slime coloured skin and weeds for hair will suit you." She followed Tamsin's example, turning away and leaving Gilwyn to stew in his helpless rage.

A weight slammed into Lori from behind, knocking her to the ground. Her face was squashed into the grass.

"You lie."

A knee pressed hard in her back. Hands were at her neck, scratching her skin as fingers dug under the iron band.

"I will not let—"

The torc was ripped from her throat. The wall of fog built up, threatening to flow in and overwhelm her. A fist clenched around her heart. And then, in an instant, fog and fist vanished. Gilwyn's body crashed to the ground beside her.

More people arrived. Lori was surrounded by feet. Her heart stuttered, and then resumed beating. Someone stretched out a hand, helping her up.

Finn twisted the torc from Gilwyn's lifeless fingers and passed it back to her. "Here, put this on."

On Gilwyn's palm was a graze from grasping the iron torc too tightly—the faintest scratch. All it took to kill a fay.

Then Tamsin was there, putting an arm around her. "Are you all right?"

"Yes. Yes, I'm fine." Lori drew a deep breath. Now that it was over, she could piece together what had just happened. "Gilwyn...I pushed him too far."

"Nobody is going to cry over him." Tamsin gave her a light squeeze. "It's not your fault. Don't worry. It was his action, not yours."

"I, um..." If Gaius was avenged, Lori did not feel any better about it.

She looked back at Caersiddi. Some other fay would take the throne, and lie, murder, and cheat. But soon, the bond would break. They would be gone forever, and not before time. The fay had given Earth some good stories, but the price was far too high.

Tamsin pointed at the wagon. "Do you want to get back on?"

"No. I'll walk for a while." It would help her think.

"Okay." Tamsin drew her pistol and raised her voice. "Right, onward. And keep an eye out for slua."

EPILOGUE

The sun dipped into the Pacific Ocean. Strands of orange and pink clouds lined the horizon. Lori put her phone on the side table and took another sip of martini. She was still coming to terms with a home overlooking a Californian beach. According to Tamsin, the view was better from her house on the Amalfi Coast, but going there would have to wait until the paperwork was concluded.

The patio doors opened. Lori twisted her head. "How's it going?"

Tamsin joined her on the deck. "Fine. I was just clearing up a couple hundred emails. And sending off the forms to let the IRS know that High Hopes Mine has struck another mother lode." She flopped onto the sun lounger next to Lori's. "Life was so much simpler back in the seventeenth century."

"As well as being generally shorter and lacking in plumbing."

"There was that." Tamsin took a swig of beer from the bottle she was carrying. "Who was on the phone?"

"Mum. She's threatening to visit. She's been reading stuff about communicating with sharks and wants to give it a go. Hopefully, Dad will talk her out of it, before they get here."

What would her parents make of Tamsin? Lori suspected they would view her far more positively than any previous girlfriend. Adam had definitely been impressed when they stopped by his house on their way between Dorstanley and Heathrow. "Hang on to this one," had been his parting advice to her.

Lori swirled her martini. "How about you? Anything interesting in the emails?"

"Hippo and Shorty are buying an island off the coast of Thailand. BH called in on them a week ago, but nobody's sure where she is now. Widget wants you to know he's made it to the Lost Outpost and is going crazy looking for the Orb of Ephestia. I assume that means something to you."

"Yes. He's stuck playing *Firelord Rebirth*. I could tell him where the orb is, but he'll have more fun finding it himself. Anything else?"

"Finn's invited us to his wedding."

"He's getting married?"

"Wouldn't have invited us if he wasn't." Tamsin grinned. "Alicia. I don't think you met her. She was one of the Iron Ravens."

"Right." Lori had not given much thought to the social life in Caersiddi, but obviously, normal human interactions would have gone on, whenever the Silver Ravens had time off from playing heroes. She watched the fading sunset for a while. "Do you miss Annwyn?"

Tamsin wrinkled her nose. "A bit."

"Do you think you'll get bored here?" Even as she spoke, Lori was hit by an unexpected rush of excitement. After all, there was a whole world to see—mountains, forests, deserts and icecaps, ancient ruins and modern cities.

Tamsin also seemed unconcerned. "I doubt it." Her smile broadened. "Did your mum have any information as to what sharks like talking about?"

About the Author

Jane Fletcher is a GCLS award-winning writer and has also been short-listed for the Gaylactic Spectrum and Lambda Literary Awards. She is a recipient of the Alice B. Reader Appreciation Awards Medal.

Her work includes two ongoing sets of fantasy/romance novels: the Celaeno Series—*The Walls of Westernfort, Rangers at Roadsend, The Temple at Landfall, Dynasty of Rogues,* and *Shadow of the Knife*; and the Lyremouth Chronicles—*The Exile and The Sorcerer, The Traitor and The Chalice, The Empress and The Acolyte,* and *The High Priest and the Idol*. She has also written three stand-alone novels, *Wolfsbane Winter, The Shewstone,* and *Isle of Broken Years*.

Her love of fantasy began at the age of seven when she encountered Greek mythology. This was compounded by a childhood spent clambering over every example of ancient masonry she could find (medieval castles, megalithic monuments, Roman villas). Her resolute ambition was to become an archaeologist when she grew up, so it was something of a surprise when she became a software engineer instead.

Born in Greenwich, London, she now lives with her wife in southwest England, where she is surrounded by enough historic sites to keep her happy.

Website: http://www.janefletcher.co.uk/

Books Available from Bold Strokes Books

Death Overdue by David S. Pederson. Did Heath turn to murder in an alcohol induced haze to solve the problem of his blackmailer, or was it someone else who brought about a death overdue? (978-1-63555-711-4)

Entangled by Melissa Brayden. Becca Crawford is the perfect person to head up the Jade Hotel, if only the captivating owner of the local vineyard would get on board with her plan and stop badmouthing the hotel to everyone in town. (978-1-63555-709-1)

First Do No Harm by Emily Smith. Pierce and Cassidy are about to discover that when it comes to love, sometimes you have to risk it all to have it all. (978-1-63555-699-5)

Kiss Me Every Day by Dena Blake. For Wynn Jamison, wishing for a do-over with Carly Evans was a long shot, actually getting one was a game changer. (978-1-63555-551-6)

Olivia by Genevieve McCluer. In this lesbian Shakespeare adaption with vampires, Olivia is a centuries old vampire who must fight a strange figure from her past if she wants a chance at happiness. (978-1-63555-701-5)

One Woman's Treasure by Jean Copeland. Daphne's search for discarded antiques and treasures leads to an embarrassing misunderstanding, and ultimately, the opportunity for the romance of a lifetime with Nina. (978-1-63555-652-0)

Silver Ravens by Jane Fletcher. Lori has lost her girlfriend, her home, and her job. Things don't improve when she's kidnapped and taken to fairyland. (978-1-63555-631-5)

Still Not Over You by Jenny Frame, Carsen Taite, Ali Vali. Old flames die hard in these tales of a second chance at love with the ex you're still not over. Stories by award winning authors Jenny Frame, Carsen Taite, and Ali Vali. (978-1-63555-516-5)

Storm Lines by Jessica L. Webb. Devon is a psychologist who likes rules. Marley is a cop who doesn't. They don't always agree, but both fight to protect a girl immersed in a street drug ring. (978-1-63555-626-1)

The Politics of Love by Jen Jensen. Is it possible to love across the political divide in a hostile world? Conservative Shelley Whitmore and liberal Rand Thomas are about to find out. (978-1-63555-693-3)

All the Paths to You by Morgan Lee Miller. High school sweethearts Quinn Hughes and Kennedy Reed reconnect five years after they break up and realize that their chemistry is all but over. (978-1-63555-662-9)

Arrested Pleasures by Nanisi Barrett D'Arnuck. When charged with a crime she didn't commit Katherine Lowe faces the question: Which is harder, going to prison or falling in love? (978-1-63555-684-1)

Bonded Love by Renee Roman. Carpenter Blaze Carter suffers an injury that shatters her dreams, and ER nurse Trinity Greene hopes to show her that sometimes hope is worth fighting for. (978-1-63555-530-1)

Convergence by Jane C. Esther. With life as they know it on the line, can Aerin McLeary and Olivia Ando's love survive an otherworldly threat to humankind? (978-1-63555-488-5)

Coyote Blues by Karen F. Williams. Riley Dawson, psychotherapist and shape-shifter, has her world turned upside down when Fiona Bell, her one true love, returns. (978-1-63555-558-5)

Drawn by Carsen Taite. Will the clues lead Detective Claire Hanlon to the killer terrorizing Dallas, or will she merely lose her heart to person of interest, urban artist Riley Flynn? (978-1-63555-644-5)

Every Summer Day by Lee Patton. Meant to celebrate every summer day, Luke's journal instead chronicles a love affair as fast-moving and possibly as fatal as his brother's brain tumor. (978-1-63555-706-0)

Lucky by Kris Bryant. Was Serena Evans's luck really about winning the lottery, or is she about to get even luckier in love? (978-1-63555-510-3)

The Last Days of Autumn by Donna K. Ford. Autumn and Caroline question the fairness of life, the cruelty of loss, and what it means to love as they navigate the complicated minefield of relationships, grief, and life-altering illness. (978-1-63555-672-8)

Three Alarm Response by Erin Dutton. In the midst of tragedy, can these first responders find love and healing? Three stories of courage, bravery, and passion. (978-1-63555-592-9)

Veterinary Partner by Nancy Wheelton. Callie and Lauren are determined to keep their hearts safe but find that taking a chance on love is the safest option of all. (978-1-63555-666-7)

Everyday People by Louis Barr. When film star Diana Danning hires private eye Clint Steele to find her son, Clint turns to his former West Point barracks mate, and ex-buddy with benefits, Mars Hauser to lend his cyber espionage and digital black ops skills to the case. (978-1-63555-698-8)

Forging a Desire Line by Mary P. Burns. When Charley's ex-wife, Tricia, is diagnosed with inoperable cancer, the private duty nurse Tricia hires turns out to be the handsome and aloof Joanna, who ignites something inside Charley she isn't ready to face. (978-1-63555-665-0)

Love on the Night Shift by Radclyffe. Between ruling the night shift in the ER at the Rivers and raising her teenage daughter, Blaise Richilieu has all the drama she needs in her life, until a dashing young attending appears on the scene and relentlessly pursues her. (978-1-63555-668-1)

Olivia's Awakening by Ronica Black. When the daring and dangerously gorgeous Eve Monroe is hired to get Olivia Savage into shape, a fierce passion ignites, causing both to question everything they've ever known about love. (978-1-63555-613-1)

The Duchess and the Dreamer by Jenny Frame. Clementine Fitzroy has lost her faith and love of life. Can dreamer Evan Fox make her believe in life and dream again? (978-1-63555-601-8)

The Road Home by Erin Zak. Hollywood actress Gwendolyn Carter is about to discover that losing someone you love sometimes means gaining someone to fall for. (978-1-63555-633-9)

Waiting for You by Elle Spencer. When passionate past-life lovers meet again in the present day, one remembers it vividly and the other isn't so sure. (978-1-63555-635-3)

While My Heart Beats by Erin McKenzie. Can a love born amidst the horrors of the Great War survive? (978-1-63555-589-9)

Face the Music by Ali Vali. Sweet music is the last thing that happens when Nashville music producer Mason Liner, and daughter of country royalty Victoria Roddy are thrown together in an effort to save country star Sophie Roddy's career. (978-1-63555-532-5)

Flavor of the Month by Georgia Beers. What happens when baker Charlie and chef Emma realize their differing paths have led them right back to each other? (978-1-63555-616-2)

Mending Fences by Angie Williams. Rancher Bobbie Del Rey and veterinarian Grace Hammond are about to discover if heartbreaks of the past can ever truly be mended. (978-1-63555-708-4)

Silk and Leather: Lesbian Erotica with an Edge edited by Victoria Villasenor. This collection of stories by award winning authors offers fantasies as soft as silk and tough as leather. The only question is: How far will you go to make your deepest desires come true? (978-1-63555-587-5)

The Last Place You Look by Aurora Rey. Dumped by her wife and looking for anything but love, Julia Pierce retreats to her hometown, only to rediscover high school friend Taylor Winslow, who's secretly crushed on her for years. (978-1-63555-574-5)

The Mortician's Daughter by Nan Higgins. A singer on the verge of stardom discovers she must give up her dreams to live a life in service to ghosts. (978-1-63555-594-3)

The Real Thing by Laney Webber. When passion flares between actress Virginia Green and masseuse Allison McDonald, can they be sure it's the real thing? (978-1-63555-478-6)

What the Heart Remembers Most by M. Ullrich. For college sweethearts Jax Levine and Gretchen Mills, could an accident be the second chance neither knew they wanted? (978-1-63555-401-4)

White Horse Point by Andrews & Austin. Mystery writer Taylor James finds herself falling for the mysterious woman on White Horse Point who lives alone, protecting a secret she can't share about a murderer who walks among them. (978-1-63555-695-7)

Femme Tales by Anne Shade. Six women find themselves in their own real-life fairy tales when true love finds them in the most unexpected ways. (978-1-63555-657-5)

Jellicle Girl by Stevie Mikayne. One dark summer night, Beth and Jackie go out to the canoe dock. Two years later, Beth is still carrying the weight of what happened to Jackie. (978-1-63555-691-9)

Le Berceau by Julius Eks. If only Ben could tear his heart in two, then he wouldn't have to choose between the love of his life and the most beautiful boy he has ever seen. (978-1-63555-688-9)

My Date with a Wendigo by Genevieve McCluer. Elizabeth Rosseau finds her long lost love and the secret community of fiends she's now a part of. (978-1-63555-679-7)

On the Run by Charlotte Greene. Even when they're cute blondes, it's stupid to pick up hitchhikers, especially when they've just broken out of prison, but doing so is about to change Gwen's life forever. (978-1-63555-682-7)

Perfect Timing by Dena Blake. The choice between love and family has never been so difficult, and Lynn's and Maggie's different visions of the future may end their romance before it's begun. (978-1-63555-466-3)

The Mail Order Bride by R Kent. When a mail order bride is thrust on Austin, he must choose between the bride he never wanted or the dream he lives for. (978-1-63555-678-0)

Through Love's Eyes by C.A. Popovich. When fate reunites Brittany Yardin and Amy Jansons, can they move beyond the pain of their past to find love? (978-1-63555-629-2)

To the Moon and Back by Melissa Brayden. Film actress Carly Daniel thinks that stage work is boring and unexciting, but when she accepts a lead role in a new play, stage manager Lauren Prescott tests both her heart and her ability to share the limelight. (978-1-63555-618-6)

Tokyo Love by Diana Jean. When Kathleen Schmitt is given the opportunity to be on the cutting edge of AI technology, she never thought a failed robotic love companion would bring her closer to her neighbor, Yuriko Velucci, and finding love in unexpected places. (978-1-63555-681-0)